The Dog Walker's Diary

The Dog Walker's Diary

KATHRYN DONAHUE

North Star
—EDITIONS—
Mendota Heights, Minnesota

First Edition
First Printing, 2017

Book design by Jake Nordby
Cover design by Madeline Berger
Cover images by f8grapher/iStock; DeirdreRusk/iStock; logoboom/Shutterstock

Library of Congress Cataloging-in-Publication Data (Pending)
978-1-63583-902-9

North Star Editions, Inc.
2297 Waters Drive
Mendota Heights, MN 55120
www.northstareditions.com

Printed in the United States of America

To Mike, who loves me

I
The Apology

10/20/15
Dog Diary
Tuesday, 4:00 a.m.

Dear Ms. Doherty,

I am mortified.

The fidgeting, the inappropriate laughter, the lurch that knocked you headfirst into the beveled glass door—good God! I'm wincing even now. Once free of me, did you stumble to your Jeep, fingers exploring the new lump on your brow, lips raining Gaelic curses on my head?

I hope not the last.

My behavior last night to the contrary, I do not have a brain tumor, schizophrenia, or Tourette's—though you could bunch them together into an ailment turducken, serve it with a side of Asperger's and a woodsy Merlot, and it would still be less awkward to explain than the truth.

I've been searching for a skillful mix of words to somehow make myself sound charming and quirky, but I see there's no sweetening the pot so I will have to say it plain:

I acted like a total nut job for no other reason than the color of your hair.

(Again: *Mortified.*)

For making you wait on the stoop, for all my social

blunders, and especially for the new lump between your eyes that doubtless has its own heartbeat by now, you deserve not just an apology but an explanation. Here's the best I can offer:

When I was sixteen I had something between a fantasy and a dream that involved mythological characters, sorcery, the Inquisition, and redheaded girls. It wasn't the first time teenage testosterone led me down a lurid path, but it was the only time I found myself a helpless bystander, unable to steer, brake, or turn away. It was during this semi-delirious state that I became the lone witness to an epic and clandestine ceremony.

One that no mortal male was meant to see.

Moments later, my sister banged on my door to remind me it was time to drive her to soccer. As we crossed the first intersection our car was violently T-boned on the driver's side. My sister was okay, but I suffered cracked ribs, a broken nose, and a concussion. As I stumbled to the curb and collapsed, the driver of the other car rushed over. "I don't know what happened!" he cried. "I was slamming on the brake, I swear it!"

He turned away to call for an ambulance, and a little girl with red hair jumped out the open door of his car and headed my way. She was no more than four years old, yet I'd never seen a more solemn face or felt eyes as intense upon me. She stopped at my feet and pointed at my face. "You," she said, her voice so full of portent that I felt the blood halt in my veins, "need to be more careful."

She walked back to the car. She turned, lifted her arm, and pointed at me again.

It was a warning. Meekly, I nodded. We understood each other, she and I. What I'd seen in that fantasy-dream, what I knew about redheads, had to remain a secret.

Logic would have it that the little girl couldn't possibly know that I was the uninvited and unwelcome witness to the clandestine ceremony of her red-headed ancestors. Logically she could not have caused her father's brakes to fail. And all that good logic would have won out long before my nose and ribs had healed, except for the last, critical element to my story.

By the next morning I had been cursed with a new malady. One that no one could see.

One that plagues me to this day.

Ms. Doherty, I know the fantasy-dream was just a figment of my imagination. I do. But the sixteen-year-old version of me could not ignore the timing of that Technicolor Figment to my accident, the creepy kid, and my unfortunate new malady. By the next morning red hair, supernatural powers and punishment had congealed together and cured like a resin marble in my brain. On the slightest chance that my accident and malady were indeed the result of irking the mystic world, it became vitally important that I never do it again.

Avoiding mythological characters and members of the Inquisition in twenty-first century L.A. is a cinch. Redheaded women, however, still freely walk the earth. When I see one I skirt around her as I would an open sewer grate.

It's not that inconvenient. Your kind is relatively rare and easy to spot. Sometimes I have to wait for a different bank teller, or change tables at a restaurant. I've excused myself from a few dinner parties. I don't go on blind dates. I ... Well, you get the picture. I've been at it so long it's as mindless as the way I tie my shoes. And until you appeared at my door, I was batting a thousand.

Ms. Doherty, I beg you, please, do not be insulted. Mine is hardly the kind of prejudice where I think myself superior in any way. Instead, I hope you see it for what it is—a respect-ful homage to the ancestral powers I can't quite believe you don't possess.

(As I said: *A nut job.*)

On the odd chance you haven't already dropped this diary from your hands and leapt on the first plane back to Ireland, let me apologize again and say that I still want you to walk my dogs. But for the sake of my blood pressure and the health of your forehead, let us agree to never be in the same room again.

Thanks for taking me on as a client. My guilt about leaving Sparks and Eddie alone all day has already been reduced to zero.

Daniel

P.S. I forgot to tell you about Eddie's little quirk. Always take an extra bag as he doesn't "go" all at once. Why twice? That's what I'd like to know! He's been doing it since day one.

II
Croi

That night, while making a beeline through my kitchen for a beer to wash the day out of my throat, a glance at the open dog diary stopped me so fast I almost came out of my socks. The dog walker had drawn a portrait of Eddie, my yellow lab, with a thick lion's mane—and there I was standing next to him, wearing riding breeches, a top hat, and holding a ring of fire above my head.

What the...?

I flicked on the overhead light. Her rendition of us was spot-on, yet whimsical. Somehow, she captured an expression of supreme confidence on my face when all she'd really seen was a tall, jittery man who blinked like a bad liar.

I turned the drawing over and found neat, cursive handwriting that filled the next four pages.

Sweet Jesus! What could have gone so wrong on a simple dog walk to warrant this much of an explanation? I called for Eddie and Sparks, ran my hands over their bodies, felt between every paw pad, and looked in their mouths. Both were fine.

I slumped into a kitchen chair. For twenty years, I'd been spooked by the hypothetical magic of the hybrid DNA of the American redhead, and last night I'd handed over my house key to one who came directly from Ireland—the full-strength, banshee-screeching mothership of druids and sprites.

With a prickle at the back of my neck, I began to read.

10/20/15
Dog Diary
Tuesday, 2:30 p.m.

Dear Mr. Ashe,

All went well this first day.

I had planned to say no more, but after reading your post script I looked at Eddie and asked him, "Handsome dog, why is it you always do an encore?"

He studied me for several moments, then his eyes became moist and far away. "It all started back in my circus days," he said.

"Eddie," I whispered as I knelt in front of him, "how is it you were in a circus?"

"I was once a lion," he said. "Stolen from the heat and the love of my family to spend many days on a steamship, then many more traveling over land in a carriage pulled by horses. Finally I found my new home with The Great Todor. Perhaps you have heard of him?" I shook my head.

"He was the most renowned lion tamer in Europe. Of course, he wasn't famous when I met him. It was our unique collaboration that would make him so."

Eddie was staring at the wall as if scenes from this past life were animated on its painted surface. For just an instant— and surely it was a trick of the light—his eyes flashed a wild savannah yellow.

"I was known then as Croi," he said. "When I arrived at the circus I was just a cub and missed my mother so much that I refused to eat. I was only hours from death when a tall boy stepped into my cage. He crawled right up to me and spoke in soothing tones but—being a lion and not a beloved dog—all I heard was the same gibberish all humans spoke. He inched even closer, and that's when I saw his right hand had only three fingers. The thumb and the little finger were normal, but between them was one thick, unbendable mass of flesh. When he was right next to me, he put that hand on my throat and said, 'We're in this together, lion. I hope you save me and I save you.'"

"'I understood every word! *Who are you? How is it that I can understand you?*'

'I have no idea,' he said, 'but I hear you plainly as well!'

'*Take that strange paw of yours off me and say something else.*' Todor did, and it was gibberish again. He sensed that immediately and rested his hand on my head.

'What about now?' he asked.

'*Yes. There is something about your paw that links us.*'"

"That was our beginning. Once I had a friend I could talk to, I thrived, and Todor became the only lion tamer in history to never use a whip or a prod. Everyone flocked to see the man who could take requests from the audience, relay them to a lion, and watch it perform feats never seen in the history of the circus. Kings summoned us to their courts. Lords and ladies watched in nervous awe as I put my paws in the laps of queens and was hugged and kissed by princesses. I did anything Todor asked because I trusted him never to allow any harm to come to me."

"What a special man!" I said. "Do you know his history?"

Eddie nodded. "Of course. On the nights that Todor could not sleep, he would come to my cage to rest his hand on me and we would speak of everything. The story of his childhood was an unhappy one. He had tried to make friends, but when adults saw his defect they pulled their own perfectly formed children away. He was not yet five when a drought gripped the land and the simple people of his village began to blame Todor and his cursed hand. His mother feared for his life. One morning, so early that the sun had yet to gnaw the edges off the dark, she pulled him from his little bed to walk him many miles to the monastery. She kissed him three times and then pushed him through the door. The monks took him in and gave him an education, but their love was given to God, with little left over for Todor.

"His nights were restless. He woke to every footfall in the dark, believing his mother had returned to take him home. As he got older, a girl appeared in his dreams. She was as unique as he was, and they found happiness in a special place where no one turned away from their unconventional appearances.

"When Todor woke from these dreams he knew for certain that it was her love alone that would fill the hole in his heart.

"Todor grew tall. He had clear blue eyes, thick black hair, and light brown skin. When he smiled even the ill-tempered cook smiled back. When Todor was just fifteen he heard Brother Aiden tell the other monks that a circus had come to town. The boy had never heard of such a thing, and the good Brother explained it was a caravan full of trained animals and dancing girls, outcasts, freaks, and gypsies—all of them intent on taking your money.

"Todor's heart leapt with joy. Certainly the circus was the place in his dream! That night, while the monks were at vespers, he rolled up his few belongings and tucked them under his arm. He wrote a note thanking the brothers for all their care and slipped out the front door.

"As Todor approached the big tent, he saw the Ringmaster step through the flap. He ran up to him and said, 'I have come to join the circus.'

"When the Ringmaster scoffed and told the boy to run

home to his parents, Todor lifted his hand and held it in the air. The older man was quiet for several moments then said, 'Follow me.'

"Todor soon found himself face to face with Petar, the gruff owner of the circus. Petar scowled at the tall teenager and his unique hand and barked, 'No. It's not enough to draw a crowd. Go home.'

"Todor stood his ground. 'I have lived with the monks for many years,' he said, 'I am strong and learned. Surely I can be of help to you in some way.'

"The Ringmaster cleared his throat and said, 'Petar, we talked just last night about Yakef the lion tamer being too old and ill to continue on much longer. With training this boy could take his place one day.'

"Petar tented his fingers and looked Todor up and down. 'Women will like the looks of you, that's certain, but do you have it in you to tame a lion?'

"Todor knew his moment was at hand, but why did it have to involve the most fearsome creature there was? He could run back to the monastery where he would be safe, or he could leap into the dazzling world of the circus and find the girl in his dream.

"'I should like to try,' he said.

'Tell you what, there's a new cub just arrived that isn't eating. If you can keep him alive you can stay. If he dies, you're out.' He turned to the Ringmaster. 'Go ahead. Take the boy to Yakef and tell him he has an apprentice.'"

"And that was the night my dear friend Todor found his new home."

Eddie paused. Then, in a voice so low I had to strain to hear him, he said, "It was on one of his sleepless nights that Todor revealed to me the secret in his heart. I have kept that secret to this day. But now that you have ...." He stopped and swung his muzzle to look at me.

"Sorry. I was rambling. Your original question was about my customary practice. Calling such a base physical act 'an encore' wasn't just tactful, it was astute—and for that you deserve an answer. As Croi I performed every afternoon, and again every evening. For twenty-six years I had to twice jump through the fire ring, twice leap over barrels, twice hug my friend Todor, and twice take my bows. Everything in twos."

He shrugged. "Old habits die hard."

Annie

P.S. Mr. Ashe, in Corsica when the locals pass a red-head on the street, they spit and turn around. I believe this time-honored tradition eliminates both the threat of being pointed at by sinister toddlers and developing invisible medical conditions.

P.P.S. If my ancestors caused your malady, then perhaps I can help. But first I would need to know what ails you.

———————

Wait.

Did she just say she could cure me?

I stood up so fast the chair toppled.

I walked around my kitchen breathing like a woman in labor, going over in my mind how I'd gotten myself into this predicament.

I'd come home an hour late last night, after dusk, and as I approached my front door the sensor light clicked on illuminating a trifold flier stuck in my door jamb. As soon as I touched it I knew from the quality of the paper it wasn't just another take-out menu, and curious, I waved it open.

"Professional Dog Walker" was written on the top, and

on the bottom was a line drawing of a dachshund so long the artist bent the tail up to ninety degrees to get it all on the page.

It happens that my dachshund, Sparks, also has a ninety-degree crook at the end of her tail. But if the similarity even registered in my mind, it was forgotten a moment later when I stepped inside my house and into a pool of urine.

Eddie.

It was happening more and more. My best friend in the whole world was getting too old to hold it in all day, and I wondered how long he had waited by the door to be let out, and how much pain did he suffer before he simply had to break the rules?

I looked up. Eddie was sitting in the corner, his tail slowly thumping, too embarrassed to greet me. I slipped off my shoe and went over to hug him.

"Forgive me," I said, kissing his head. "This will never happen to you again. You are the best boy in the world, and I'm going to get you your very own dog walker."

I let the dogs out back, spread the flier open, and made the call.

"Annie here," a lilting Irish voice said, instantly piquing my interest. After a few minutes of delightful conversation, I was insisting she come right over to get a key and start the next day. Not half an hour later she rang my bell.

One look through the beveled glass of my front door at that head of red curls, and I was twitching like an electric eel had curled around my brain stem. But it wasn't just her hair color that scared the bejesus out of me. Annie Doherty looked very much like the grown-up version of the kid who had pointed at me after the accident.

I stood silent and gaping until she raised her eyebrows and pointed to the knob like *Hey, are you going to let me in?* I feigned trouble with the latch, lifted my right hand to show her it was handicapped by a bandage, then pushed open the door, and jumped aside as she stepped over the threshold.

Eddie greeted her like a long-lost friend. I watched her cup her hands around his muzzle, I saw her lips move; but whether she said, "I'm Annie Doherty," or "I'm here to turn you into a toad," I had no clue, for whatever sound she made bounced off my shield of panic.

I led her to the kitchen. Along the way I managed to choke on my own spit and cough like there was a bone in my throat. With hand motions I convinced her I was fine, and she knelt on the kitchen floor to get acquainted with Sparks. I clutched the counter for a silent pep talk.

In twenty breaths she'll be gone, and I'll never have to see her again. Nineteen breaths. Only nineteen. Eighteen. I can do this, I'm okay ....

Sparks had rolled on to her back, and when I heard the dog walker say, "Yer not ashamed at all a' your fine round belly are y'now?" breath number sixteen froze in my lungs.

That accent ... no makeup ... her clothes and hair, good lord! The woman could be plunked down in the middle of Sherwood Forest, *as is*, and no one passing by in a skull cap or a suit of armor would think her out of place.

My internal monologue did nothing to ease my effort not to twitch like a TASER victim.

What if she lifts her arm? I thought. *What if she points at me? What if she says, "You need to be more careful!"*

There was no time to waste. I had to get her out of my house, and the only way I could think to do that was to give her what she came for. I cleared my throat and held out the key, the tape around my index, middle, and ring fingers creating an awkward pincer grip.

"Here you go."

She stood right up and reached for it, but at the approach of her hand my palm jerked and the key popped up like a heated kernel of corn. At the height of its arc she grabbed it from the air with a *Ha!*

"Sorry. It's my injury," I said, hoping she would think I had a burn and couldn't bear being touched. And then, for no reason I can fathom, I said, "When my nosy neighbor sees you letting yourself in, she's going to think I have a new girlfriend."

Before I could exhale breath nine, the dog walker's face turned scarlet, and I reared back about a foot.

No one blushes in L.A. No one is shy or embarrassed or humble or modest. It's as though there's an emotional trash can at the city limit where you shuck all the sweeter sentiments. But blush she did! Was it possible she had developed an instant crush on me, the twitchy babbler? Normally I'm grateful for any tug of attraction, and fortunately for me there are some who like gangly men with an ethnic look they can't quite put their finger on. But the women I lusted after had polish. They were players. Like Victoria Millman, the stunning blonde who just made partner at the law firm down the hall from my office at Floodgate Media. Now *there* was a woman as firmly at home in the twenty-first century as Ms. Doherty would be stirring a pot of venison stew for Friar Tuck and the boys.

I gestured for the dog walker to proceed to the front door, but instead she reached into her tote bag and pulled out a white, three-ring binder full of paper. On the front was a label that read "Dog Diary." She held it out, her cheeks still burning like the surface of Mars, and said, "Use this t' write me any instructions, and I'll write back everythin' y' need t' know 'bout the dogs."

I held my hands up like she had pulled out a gun. I planned to squirm out of this ill-conceived agreement with a brief text message in a few hours, and didn't want to take anything from her she'd have to come back to get.

"Thanks, but that won't be necessary."

"All the same," she said and placed it on the counter.

She walked ahead of me to the door, then stopped as if she'd thought of something else to say. I was down to breath three and desperate. "I'll get that," I said and reached around her shoulder to untwist the lock. When our heads were only inches apart, closer than I have ever been to any redhead, she looked up at me.

Her eyes were beautiful, a green like a marriage of the forest to the ocean, but in the iris of her right eye, from three to six on a clock face, there was a pie wedge of the deepest brown.

Too shocked to check my forward motion, my chest knocked solidly into her and she staggered. I grabbed her shoulders—but was so off balance myself that it became more of a push than a save and ... God help me ... I *shoved* her into the beveled glass.

Thunk from her head. *Jaysusgod!* from her lips.

I let go, stammered apologies, and swiped blindly for the door handle, missing it three times.

Once she left, I lurched to the sofa and collapsed.

Now I took a picture of the drawing and texted it to my sister Leandra, then called her, sputtering about the story the dog walker left me until she said, "Stop! Take a deep breath and just read it all to me—what you wrote her and what she wrote back."

When I finished, I said, "Take a good look at that drawing."

"I'm looking at it on my tablet. You *are* Todor."

"Yes, but spread it open so you can see his right hand."

"Hang on. Okay, it's deformed, like in the story."

"Which is what *my* hand looks like right now. I was shooting hoops with a couple of stunt guys, dislocated my middle finger, and the urgent care doc taped it to the index and ring fingers. So I have a normal thumb and pinky, and between them a fused-together lump. Just like Todor."

Leandra clucked her tongue. "She also referenced your dream, but put a positive spin on it. And what do you make of the coincidence that Todor had a crusty boss named 'Petar' and you have one named 'Peter?'"

My heart jumped an inch forward in my chest. "Christ, I didn't even pick up on that."

"And the plot really thickens when you consider that you and Todor are both love-impaired insomniacs."

I heard the smirk in her voice. "Look," I said, "I know you think I'm a mental case about redheads ..."

"That's because you *are*. You had some stupid dream twenty years ago that you should have ignored, but you picked it open like a poison ivy blister and now it covers your whole body."

"It was more than that."

I heard her long intake of breath. "Please no, not that phantom redheaded kid again."

"She was real."

"I was standing right next to you until the ambulance came. If a spooky preschooler had walked over and pointed at you, I would have seen her."

I rubbed my forehead. "Don't you understand how that's even *worse*? If I'm the only one who saw her, that means ..." I stopped, unwilling to say the obvious.

"What? That she wasn't human? That she emerged from

the netherworld of your dream to warn you to keep your mouth shut about what you saw? For Pete's sake, you had a serious concussion. You just nodded off and that kid stepped out of your scrambled brain."

This was old territory. I wasn't going to argue.

"And you know something, Daniel? Your clever Irish dog walker wrote that story to mess with you. She read your phobic note and thought, 'Crazy American thinks redheads are capable of sorcery? Okay, I'll throw him a little fireball!' And just in case you were too dim to figure that out, she went ahead and used that bit about Corsica to hammer it home."

"You didn't see her," I said, still ruffled but calming down. "She's a human elf!"

"Oh God, you are off the deep end."

I righted the chair and sat down. "Let me paint you a picture. Even for a redhead she had this extraordinary glow, as if her skin was lit from her bones—as if she just emerged from an underground warren of magical creatures. She's probably twenty-eight, twenty-nine, but still has apple cheeks. No more than five foot two or three. And her outfit? Scuffed ankle boots, an oversized shirt and long baggy shorts—like she was ready to step onstage as an orphan in *Oliver!* or the newsboy in *Citizen Kane*."

"Golly, how weird. A dog walker wearing an appropriate outfit for walking dogs. Call in a SWAT team."

"Okay," I blew the air out of my lungs. "Consider everything I told you about her appearance, then top it all off with this Rumpelstiltskin smile on her face. Like we weren't strangers. Like we had once been in cahoots, and she was there to lure me back into a life of crime."

"Hmm. Let's back up. Just how charming were you on the phone when you called her to come over?"

"Not charming. But, you know, when I heard that accent ..."

"Ah, you flirted with her."

"Well," I closed my eyes to retrieve that conversation. "Maybe on the outer verge of flirting. We talked about the dogs for a bit, and when I told her she sounded like a screenwriter from Dublin who was famous around town for coming to meetings 'unencumbered,' she asked what that meant, and I said, 'Well, I call her 'Erin go Bra-less.' She laughed, in the middle of which she snorted, which made *me* laugh, and that's when I said, 'Hey, you're hired!' She showed up twenty minutes later to meet the dogs and pick up a key."

"So she was still smirking from the hilarious phone call, and when she turned out to have red hair, you shoved her head into the door. Good move. Well, before I pass judgment on her magical elf-ness, I'd need to see her for myself."

"I *want* you to see her. I want you to come over here tomorrow about one o'clock and get my key back. Tell her I died or moved to Istanbul. Anything. I don't care."

"Ha. Forget it. If I could fire anyone I'd start with my own useless cleaning lady. Look, I'm late meeting friends for dinner, but promise me you'll keep the dog walker. I like her. And just maybe, if you can get used to having a redhead in your house when you're not there, you'll graduate to being able to stand next to one at a crosswalk."

"Thanks, Dr. Phil."

I cobbled together a sandwich of old cheese and new pepperoni, watched the Lakers beat the Clippers, and got into bed to read until my eyes drooped. I turned off the light thinking *I'll fire her in the morning.*

It was all just too close for comfort—the three fingers, the Peter/Petar thing, Todor and I both loveless, both insomniacs. That's four coincidences, which for my money is four too many.

My text would be simple. *Sorry, changed my mind. Please drop the key in my mailbox tomorrow.*

I turned on my side and pulled the covers up.

Of course, I had to concede that if this Annie person had looked me up on Google—a smart move for a woman before she entered a strange man's house—she would have landed on the Floodgate Media webpage. It's right there that someone named "Peter" owns the company. So in fairness I could eliminate that as a coincidence.

As for the three fingers on Todor ... that didn't exactly belong in the coincidence column either, as my bandaged hand was her inspiration to take him down a couple of digits.

I bunched my pillow into submission and tried to clear my mind. It worked until I realized that Todor wasn't actually incapable of falling in love like I was. He just longed for the one girl he was meant to love.

Still, that left the insomnia thing, and that on its own merit was unnerving enough to ditch the dog walker.

I tried to clear my mind again.

Moments later I groaned, threw off the covers, headed to the kitchen and opened the dog diary. There it was on the first page, time-stamped in my own hand: "Tuesday, 4 A.M."

Normal sleepers aren't writing notes to their dog walkers in the dead of night.

I was ready to concede that Leandra was right, but then my eye landed on the tri-folded flier the dog walker had stuck in my door jamb.

Ah ha! *This* was no figment. Here was physical proof that Annie Doherty had dipped at least her pinky into the dark arts.

As it was too late to call my sister, I took a photo of the advertisement and shot it to her in an email.

Leandra,

Hey, forgot to tell you about this drawing on the dog walker's ad. Magnify it so you can appreciate the crook at the end of the dachshund's tail. Remind you of anyone?

I rest my case!

Daniel

I finally got in a few hours of sleep. At four a.m. I got out of bed, put on shorts and running shoes, and took a three-mile jog with the dogs. After my shower I made coffee and sat down to the dog diary. I re-read my letter to Annie and her response, and in the light of day I saw what Leandra saw: The story of Todor was wholly, completely, without a doubt, a well-deserved joke at my expense.

Still, there was no shaking off her second postscript. Absurd or not, if my insomnia was in any way connected to The Figment, it followed that a redhead from Ireland might just have the undiluted mojo to cure me.

Maybe the dog walker's offer to help with my condition was part of the joke. Maybe it was for real. Either way, the fact that she even held out that carrot of hope meant that redheads *liked* appearing magical.

No wonder the Puritans and Inquisition guys spent decades lighting fires under them.

III
Sparks

10/21/15
Dog Diary
Wednesday, 6:30 a.m.

Hi,

Annie, I don't know how things are in Ireland, but here in L.A. the service providers who come to our lowly abodes let us know at the door what an imposition it is to take them away from their movie role auditions, then, after minimal exertion, they hand us outrageous bills and stand there scowling while we make out the check. So the time and effort you put into the dog diary has left me thinking: While the physical distance you have traveled is understood, between your artistry and imaginative story, I suspect that Eddie isn't the only one to have vaulted through previous lives. Were you a spirit reader for Longshanks? A bard in Henry's court? Or is something else afoot here? Look, do me a favor. Open my utility room door, wrap your fingers around the handle of my broom, and tell me if the first thought that pops into your head is:

A) A useful cleaning tool, or

B) A sweet, sweet ride.

Confess, and I promise not to tell.

I do want to thank you for explaining the double-duty thing.

Have a good walk, and please make sure Sparks doesn't do her business on Mr. Bartowski's front yard—number twenty-two on the corner. Even though it only happened once and I immediately cleaned it up, he called to complain. In fact, try to avoid that property if you can as there is something about it that makes her blood boil. A couple of days ago she stopped right in front and yelped up a storm. I was dragging her away when Mr. Bartowski walked out his front door, shook his fist, and yelled, "Shut that bitch up!"

Were I a juvenile delinquent, that obnoxious jackass would get a flaming bag of dog poop on his porch.

Daniel

On my drive to work I wondered if the witch reference might offend her. I intended it to mock my own phobia, but would she get that? What if modern redheads still carried a grudge for the centuries of persecution of their female ancestors? For all I knew there was an international "Redheads for Revenge" organization, and Annie was a past president.

My last traffic jam of the morning was by the Andes Hotel. As I breathed in fumes and waited, I drummed my steering wheel and looked around. On my right was a stoplight guy cleaning windshields with bloody spit and newspapers; on my left, two clowns sat cross-legged on top of a Land Rover feeding each other with comically long forks; and in front of the hotel there were six white-haired Shriners careening in tiny cars, the tassels on their flowerpot hats snapping in the wind. Just another L.A. scene to make me feel like the last character in *Invasion of the Body Snatchers* to avoid alien takeover. But how could I claim to be the most normal person in town when a pie-eyed woman from Ireland thought of *me* as weird?

At least Annie wasn't menacing. And compared to what surrounded my car at that intersection, she didn't even register on the Wacko-Meter.

Then again ....

Clowns, Shriners and Bloody Spit Guy could normal-up and walk among us without drawing attention. They are at least on the trajectory of what the human race will look like in another thousand years.

Not redheads.

That blue-white skin of theirs isn't getting one iota thicker or darker than it was in the days when clerics tied them to stakes, and I don't mean to imply that was a good idea or even to belabor the point. Fact is, I'm no stranger myself to the reality of looking different. But I haven't suffered. And for that I have to thank Leandra. Our Caucasian, Asian, and African DNA mixed to perfection in that girl, and I grew up slipping in through the doors that flew open as she approached. But what turned heads was her beauty, not our skin color. In the swelter of Phoenix, where we grew up, tawny bodies were the norm. Redheads, on the other hand, were so rare that I'm willing to swear there was only one in our high school and one day she disappeared. Rumor had it her family moved to Vermont as a mercy gesture to get her out of the sun.

Okay, so the point, and now I *have* belabored it, is that ever since my paranormal sex fantasy—and the scary kid who (might have) caused my accident—I have recognized the thread of other world-ness in every redhead out there and steered clear.

When I finally got to my desk at Floodgate Media, I woke up my computer and prepared to spend a fat hour in the sorry business of being sorry.

"While your writing is very strong..."

"After careful consideration of your screenplay, I regret..."
"Needs are subjective and a different agent might..."

Having been a screenplay agent for the last seventeen years, I can dash off a rejection like you'd pull off a Band-Aid. But the tape that bound my fingers left my typing impaired. My left hand had done all the work the day before and was now in serious revolt, so I turned my right wrist sideways, intending for the free little finger to peck out the letters. Unfortunately, the mummified trio always hit the keyboard first.

W777e 798r wr7t7ng 8s very str99ng...

After several more number-dense sentences I gave up and headed to NBC Universal to nudge two optioned pilots.

As I stepped into the mouth of that thirty-six story behemoth, I thought about John Travolta. In *Staying Alive* he was an aspiring dancer who raced from one booking agent to another, pitched himself Jersey-style, and got nowhere. It wasn't until he went backstage to flirt with a major star—an Important Person—that he got his break. By the end of the movie he was in a leather loin cloth, leaping like a gazelle as the lead performer on the Broadway stage.

How I envied him.

Pushing talent in the twenty-first century, at least from my end, involved pinning down appointments with exactly the right development team gatekeeper, making my pitch sound like no other, convincing writers to make revisions that felt like amputations, more phone calls and team meetings and rewrites, then on to the next tier of stakeholders—all interspersed with me showing up in person to fan the flames. And the clock was ticking. A script, like a puppy in the window, needs to snag a home while it still looks fresh and full of promise.

Ah, but how I longed for the Travolta deal. Get an Important

Person to own your project, and all those other steps fell away like magic.

After forty minutes of cooling my heels in a gray pleather chair, a minor NBC mogul came out of his office. The news was bad. "Internal turmoil, Daniel. We're rethinking our fall lineup, and neither of your projects aligns with our darker, edgier vision."

I shook his outstretched hand, whooshed out the door, and barely resisted kicking the cars in parking lot C. I'd been teetering on the unholy edge of losing my job for a month. Without a green light on either of those pilots there'd be nothing to stop my fall.

I headed back to Floodgate. My boss, the legendary grump Peter Flood, billed our agency as multimedia, though in truth we stuck to television and film treatments. The few times each year I tried to pitch a novel, Peter gave me all of five seconds before growling, "Does it read like a goddamn movie or not?"

Such are his priorities.

A message waiting on my work phone gave me one last shot at redemption. A New York agent wanted our two-time-Oscar-winning screenwriter to adapt her client's bestseller. When I called to let her know he loved the book (*Nope*, he'd actually said. *Never heard of it and don't want to.*) and was anxious to start (*Seriously Daniel, fuck off.*) she said, "Sorry, but my guy just changed his mind and said he's going to write the screenplay himself. He doesn't want, and I quote, 'any L.A. crap' landing on his book."

I hung up. There was nothing for it but to head home to my dogs. I was turning off my computer when Peter stepped in.

"Nice hand," he said.

"Basketball."

He shrugged and dropped a teleplay on my desk. I looked

down at the cover sheet and groaned. I had hand-delivered this thing to the Hallmark Network on Friday.

"No. Not more revisions."

"Yup. Something about the ending." He headed out the door and said over his shoulder, "She's all yours, old man."

Old man. Christ, that's all I needed to hear. One month earlier Peter had declared there was going to be a "Floodgate revitalization" and immediately fired two agents in their mid-forties who were doing at least as well as I was. That made me the oldest one left. And while you wouldn't think age to be an issue when you work as far behind the camera as we did, here in L.A. everyone pretends their placental scars haven't healed up yet.

Good night, Chet. Don't go bald!
Good night, David. Don't go gray!

I made a few edits to the Hallmark project and sent it on with many an apology. As I made my way to the elevator, my fantasy dream girl, Victoria Millman, stepped in first and held the door for me. We descended eight floors together. Not only did I not say a word, I was almost too defeated to imagine her naked.

On the ride home I consoled myself that at least Eddie was getting walked during the day. And Sparks, of course, though if she had been the one leaving puddles on the floor it would have been a different fix. Sophie, my last girlfriend, had foisted Sparks on me, and even after six months of giving up half my bed to that fat sausage, the dog still had no great love for me. Worse, she invited ridicule. A tall man walking behind a wiener dog has built-in amusement value to begin with, but Sparks' one-of-a-kind tail added a cherry to that sundae. I never learned if it was a birth defect or an accident that crooked the end of her tail skyward, but when she walked, which she did with a stupendous amount of self-importance, she held her tail straight out behind her, looking to the world as if she came with her own exclamation point.

I am this long!

Then there was her bark. Once started it fed on itself, and she was as loud and recoiling as a machine gun. If she had been the one piddling on the floor, I would have hunted Sophie down, handed her the leash, and said *all yours.*

I got home after five. I was still worried that I might have irked Annie with my witch reference, so I headed straight to the dog diary. It was open again, this time to a drawing of Sparks standing on the deck of a ship. She was wearing a naval officer's jacket and had a bandage over the crook of her tail. And there I was again, this time drawn as a sailor with a peg leg and a neckerchief, standing behind Sparks.

I turned the drawing over to find five pages filled with Annie's script. In the top right corner of each was a tiny, bubbling cauldron. I took it as a hopeful sign that she liked being teased.

10/21/15
Dog Diary
Wednesday, 2:30 p.m.

"*You are lucky* not to be beautiful," Sparks said as we walked through the gate of the dog park. "It is a burden, I assure you. How I would love to walk this world unnoticed the way you do. Fortunately, it is different in Ornadia. There I am celebrated for my accomplishments and not for my looks."

"Ornadia?"

"Shh!"

Sparks trotted over to an isolated tree and I followed. Once satisfied no one could overhear us, she said, "Every nap I take transports me to the sea world of Ornadia. There I am known as Cap'n Sparks, buccaneer extraordinaire!"

I clucked my tongue. "Sounds a wee far-fetched."

"You believe Eddie was a lion, but you doubt that I lead a dual life?"

"Sorry, Sparks. I've heard of past lives. But you are talking about some kind of alternate sea world, and where on Earth could that possibly be?"

"Earth!" she snorted. "Surely you have heard of 'The Owl and the Pussycat'? Captain Hook? *The Pirates of Penzance*? They are luminaries in alternate sea worlds, but I am just as worthy of fame as they are. All I need is someone to write my biography." She tipped her head and pointed her muzzle at me. "Yesterday you spent a good deal of time scribbling Eddie's story."

"Ah, I see. Sparks girl, I'd be happy to write down whatever you tell me."

"Excellent. I've had so many adventures, where do I begin? Ah, I know! Since we were just talking about great beauty, I will start with the story of Nin. Yes, yes, very appropriate, especially since the day I saved her from the black-hearted Bartowski was also the day I became captain of the *Minerva*."

"Bartowski? Daniel's neighbor?"

"Shh! Yes. But in Ornadia he is the pirate Black Bart. His only purpose in this world is to take revenge on me. If he can murder me here, he can return to Ornadia as captain of my ship."

This sounded like a worthy tale indeed. I sat on the grass and took out my notebook.

Nin

by

Cap'n Sparks

I went to sea as a puppy first mate. My natural gifts led to a quick promotion to lieutenant, and by then I had already heard much of Black Bart—a notorious pirate who burned and sank the vessels he plundered, but not before he sent the crews of those unfortunate ships off the plank and into the iron jaws of the sharks below. Our ship, The Minerva, made its way in trade that was ... mostly legal. Our Captain Petros had a kind heart and provided safe passage to many a desperate refugee, though he was rarely paid for his trouble.

One coral-sky morning we had just delivered a sultan to port—a disagreeable man who had paid us an extravagant sum to escape his enemies—and no sooner had he stepped ashore than The Minerva pulled away with his seven clever wives still on board. These ladies had slipped away from the sultan our first night at sea to show me, the only other female on the ship, the fearsome bruises he had left on their bodies. "Can you help us escape, Lieutenant? Is there a small boat we can steal away in?"

I told them Captain Petros was a good man who would help. We knocked on his door, and found him playing chess with Ensign Blend, my good friend. When I told the men what I had seen, Blend jumped up. Fortunately his peg leg was not firmly under him, which gave Captain Petros the chance to grab hold of his arm before the tall sailor could storm out to find the sultan and thrash him.

"Dear ladies, bear with me a moment," the captain said as he stood and opened his safe. He took out a heavy leather bag and set it on the table. "In this satchel is all of your husband's

gold. A goodly amount, is it not? And look," he said, pulling out a bar and holding it in the palm of his right hand, then picking up the granite queen from his chessboard with his left, raising and lowering them side by side like a balancing scale. "The weight of this stone chess piece is equal to one of these gold bars. What a coincidence!"

The captain turned to me, "Lieutenant, didn't I ask you to throw out this old chess set? Please take care of it while Blend and I make our nightly walk around the deck. Then you may escort the ladies back to their rooms."

We all understood the Captain's intent, and once the men left we set quickly to work. In minutes all the gold bars were slipped discreetly into bodices, the captain's chess pieces were off the board, and the sultan's satchel was back in the safe as heavy as it was before.

The next morning we were rounding a newly formed island when, from out of a hidden inlet, appeared The Blasphemy, Black Bart's ship. The villain himself stood at the bow. Our Captain Petros feared the worst for his crew and the sultan's wives, but the wind blew well, and I learned through my nose and my bones that Black Bart had a secret Achilles' heel. It wasn't a fear of fire or storms or a witch with red hair—he could tolerate all that and more. What he couldn't bear was a particular sound. A malformation of his inner ear had left him with such an acute sensitivity to high-pitched, pealing tones that he had gone to sea for no other reason than to get away from church bells and street musicians and the laughter of children.

I knew at once it was a pitch that was well within the repertoire of the female dachshund.

In moments The Blasphemy was upon us. Black Bart's crew scrambled over the railing of The Minerva, and in seconds they surrounded Captain Petros and slit his throat!

I jumped against Ensign Blend's wooden leg and cried, "You are the tallest and strongest. Pick me up and throw me to their deck. I can save us!"

The next moment I was sailing through the air. I hit Black Bart in the chest, knocking him over, and I howled in his face. He writhed in agony. He threw me off and ran to his cabin with me in pursuit. He reached into an alcove and pulled out a small treasure chest. I howled again, and, in a desperate attempt to silence me, he stomped on my tail. I chased him back to the deck and bit into his ankle. When he turned to kick me off, the lid of the treasure chest bumped open to reveal three large, perfect emeralds. As he groped at the lid to keep the gems from spilling out, I let go of his ankle to bark him up onto the gangplank, and from there I forced him to jump.

Black Bart nearly drowned but he wouldn't give up that treasure. He kept hold of the chest of priceless stones as he sputtered and kicked his way to the island. His men, seeing their captain in the water, jumped in as well and followed him.

I was about to summon Blend to help me return to my ship when I heard a woman say, "Good dog, your tail is surely broken."

I turned. She was lovely, dressed in sailor pants and a white billowy shirt. There was something incandescent about her. Magical. "I will bind your tail, brave one," she said as she tore off her sleeve and knelt to tend to my wound. I asked her why she was aboard a pirate ship. "I am Nin," she said. "Black Bart captured me two years ago and has held me captive ever since. I have been the most miserable creature alive. If only I could find my fur I could return to the sea." And with that she wept silent tears.

Now I understood. I'd heard stories of these extraordinary and sensual creatures from old sailors.

"So you are a selkie," I said.

"I am. I left the sea with my seal friends. We took off our fur to sun in human form, and I fell asleep. Suddenly I was caught in a net! My friends surrounded the ship and cried piteously to Black Bart to set me free, but the villain just laughed and hauled me onto the deck. He held my fur over his head and said, 'Do you see this? Well, you will never see it again!' Then he locked me in his cabin. Oh good lieutenant, without my fur I cannot return to my home!" and with that she began to sob in earnest.

"Then we shall find it!"

"It is no use," she said, her lashes heavy with tears, "I have looked everywhere."

"Dear Nin," I said. "Dry your eyes and behold: I am not just the lieutenant of a ship, I am a long-snouted dog!" I sniffed the air this way and that. "Yes, yes. I smell your fur already!"

I raced down to the hold of the ship. "It is in here. Quick, open this door."

We entered a room that was full of barrels of rum. I sniffed and snuffled until I found a cask that was not only nailed shut, but sealed with tar. "Nin, your fur is inside this barrel, but it will take someone stronger than you to open it, and while I am gifted in many ways, I am useless with hand tools."

Just then we heard footsteps on the stairs. Nin's eyes grew wide. "Oh lieutenant, it is Black Bart. He will never let me go!" And with that she swooned to the floor. I planted myself squarely to howl the rogue into the sea, but it was Blend who stepped in the room.

"Lieutenant Sparks, I am here to help you return to The Minerva."

"Blend, you have come at just the right moment. Help me open this cask. That lady on the floor is a selkie who has suffered much at the hands of Black Bart. He has sealed her fur *in here, and she is most desperate to return to the sea in her natural form."*

Blend found a hammer and a chisel and made quick work of opening the cask and pulling out the pelt, but when he turned to look at Nin, he stood as still as a man can stand.

"Blend," I said to break the spell, "do not fear the selkie. Her magic will not harm you. Please revive her so she can be on her way."

Still he didn't move. I trotted over and licked Nin's cheek until her eyelids fluttered. She sat up and smiled, but when she saw the officer, she blushed. Blend is a most handsome sailor, you see, and this made Nin shy.

"Dear selkie," I said, gesturing Blend forward, "here is your fur."

She let out a cry and held out her hands. Blend took a step toward her, but placed his foot on the tail of her hide, lost his balance, and tumbled on top of the poor girl.

He apologized and helped Nin to her feet. "Dear sir, worry not," she said, scooping up her pelt into her arms. "You have released my fur and I have never been happier than I am right now."

Their eyes held until I said, "To the deck, then!"

The three of us walked to the bow of The Blasphemy. *We saw Black Bart standing on the island, glaring at us.*

Nin took a deep breath and stepped up onto the rail. She peeled off her human clothes and stood there to let Black Bart see what was no longer his. She turned to Blend and me and said, "I will never forget you who have saved me." Then she stepped into her fur and dove in the sea.

Blend scooped me up and we looked down at the beautiful seal. She barked at me, I barked at her, and she was gone.

I directed the crew to plunder the spoils from The Blasphemy, *and we burned the vessel in sight of Black Bart and his pirates.*

That night, the crew of The Minerva *met to decide who amongst us would be the new captain. I was the highest ranking, but many balked at having a female dog in charge. One sailor said, "No offense, lieutenant, but Ensign Blend should be captain. If you was in charge people could say, 'Yer captain is a bitch!' It just don't sound good."*

"To hell with how it sounds!" Blend roared. "It was her seventh sense that saved us and brought us the riches of The Blasphemy. *It was her nose that discovered the whereabouts of Nin's fur so the gentle selkie could return to the sea. With Lieutenant Sparks at the helm, we will know the intentions of our enemies, we will know their weaknesses, and we will know if our friends are still our friends. That will make us invulnerable!"*

Another sailor said, "Yer point is well taken Blend, but we will be the only ship at sea with a dog fer a captain!"

Blend smiled. "Being different is a strength. Look at me."

"'Tis true Ensign, ya're different, being the tallest and smartest, and yer curious eyes see clear and true. If ya say Sparks should be captain, than I think we must agree."

And so it came to be.

The End

Black Bart moved to this world in hopes of getting even with Sparks. To provoke her, he buried that chest of perfect emeralds under the grass in front of his house. She tried to show you where it was, Daniel, but you scooped up her marker.

Why not take her back there tonight? Under the cover of darkness you could easily dig up the chest, remove the emeralds, and let Sparks refill it with the kind of deposit that the villain deserves.

(And wait … are those matches in your pocket?)

Annie

P.S. "Longshanks" and "Henry" were English kings, by the way. Were I a spirit reader, I'd have picked the Irish court of handsome King Tairrdelbach Ua Conchobair!

P.P.S. I remain most curious about this "epic and clandestine" ceremony of redheads you witnessed, and from which you suffer still. One eye blinded? Narcolepsy? Posterior warts? My offer stands. If you tell me what my ancestors did, I will try to help.

P.P.P.S. By the way, your broom, like America, looks young and disobedient.

———————

Here's the thing: when I read a book or edit a script, I look at plot, character, conflict, and denouement. What I don't get to see is the writer's sparking moment of inspiration. But in the dog diary it wasn't just in front of me; it *was* me.

And hold on. Was it my imagination, or did the second postscript come with a dose of leather-corset raciness? Certainly the selkie creature out-sexed the mermaids I grew up with by about a thousand percent. Interesting stuff from a woman who had blushed pimento red in my kitchen.

I was intrigued. And a little turned on.

My phone dinged with a text from Leandra, inviting me for dinner the next night.

Excellent. I will bring the dog diary with me.

IV
A Book Proposal

In the insomnia world, wisdom has it that if you can't fall asleep in one location, try another. That night, on my pilgrimage to the living room, I glanced in the kitchen and saw the drawing of Cap'n Sparks under the dim light of the stove hood.

I settled on the sofa.

No stranger to being helplessly conscious at 4:00 a.m. as thoughts and ideas roll through my head, I am also able to convince myself that there is no reason to get up to write the good ones down. Who could forget such brilliance?

The answer of course, is *me.*

But while I waited for the coolness of the sofa to warm up, I saw in my mind's eye that drawing of Cap'n Sparks as the glossy cover of a children's book and sat right up. There was a pen and an envelope on my coffee table. I reached for them and wrote: *children's book with animated film potential— dachshund hero lives both here and in a parallel sea world, hilarity of dual storylines, Sparks taking critical information from one world to solve conflicts in the other. We watch her get into a breathtaking battle at sea only to have her disappear off the deck of* The Minerva *because her human forced her to wake up for a walk. Audience riveted with worry. Would Sparks get back in time to save the day? Hurry Sparks, hurry! Oh no, her human stops to chat with the neighbors, and now he's buying a paper. Sparks desperately tries to fall asleep right there on the sidewalk, but human keeps yanking her leash. Aaagh! Kids would eat this up.*

Hell, I would eat this up.

I went back to the kitchen and turned on my laptop. Annie had been intruding into my thoughts long enough. Since she had twice teased me with an offer to repair the damage her ancestors did, I decided to call her bluff.

10/22/15
Dog Diary
Thursday, 4:30 a.m.

Hi Annie,

Past lives and alternate sea worlds? If there is any spare magic up your sleeve could you throw it my way? My boss is in a housecleaning mood, and it is almost certain that I will be out of a job very soon (like this time next week) unless I land a spectacular script.

Incentive to help me? You'd be out of a job as well!

Thank you for introducing me to the lore of the selkies. I spent an hour reading up on their legends, and by the time I turned off my computer I both hated and understood the men who captured them. What a temptation. Ensnare a wild, gorgeous creature—it doesn't matter that you love her, that you marry her, that she bears your children and you have many happy years together. The moment she finds her fur, that girl *bolts*.

That'd keep you on your toes.

Speaking of stories and legends and fairy tales, did I mention that I work for Peter Flood of Floodgate Media? We're an agency that handles screenplays and manuscripts. With your wonderful drawings and dog stories you're a natural for writing and illustrating books for children, and this Cap'n Sparks thing is perfect for such an endeavor. She could have as many adventures as you can dream up, all highlighted with your fantastical drawings of her swashbuckling around her water world. I think anyone who ever loved a dachshund would buy a copy for the children in their lives. Imagine the sales in Germany alone! My advice is to get writing and get drawing. By the way, I am honored to find myself in another story. "Ensign Blend." What a very clever name for me.

Annie, I have decided to take you up on your promise to cure me of the curse your ancestors inflicted. So once you turn this page you will read the details of the fateful hallucination that torched my brain at the impressionable age of sixteen.

As to the consequences I suffer, I'm sorry to say it isn't butt warts. It's insomnia. And up until that dream fantasy/car accident/redheaded child-pointer, I slept as soundly as any teenage boy. But from that night to this, I have not slept five hours in a row.

My official diagnosis is primary insomnia. It's called "primary" because it's not secondary to any physical problem; and with no discernible cause, there is no cure. Of course there is Benadryl and Nyquil but they both make me dry and stupid. There are the classes of pharmaceuticals that are not only effective for sleep, but for implanting brand new ideas in your head like: "Wouldn't it be a rush to drive this car off that cliff?"

Not for me.

I've tried valerian, melatonin, chamomile, lavender oil, tart cherry juice, exercise, beer, a full stomach, an empty stomach, and yogic breathing until I produced a little cyclone over my pillow. Soft mattress, hard, ocean sounds, utter silence, sleeping naked, old man pajamas, fat pillow, no pillow. One ex-girlfriend even gave me a video of cartoon sheep jumping a fence. Nothing works.

By being a witness to The Event I apparently vexed the participants—and they are a vengeful lot.

So tonight I have typed up, punched holes, and inserted *my* fantastical story. Once you finish reading I think you will agree that I have met your condition.

So pay up Annie. Restore me to sleep!

Daniel

P.S. By the way Ms. Doherty, America *is* young and disobedient, which is how we got free.

The Figment

aka

Bog Girls

(Visualized by Daniel Ashe at age 16)

Lunching with the nymphs used to be all sex and lobsters until Zeus started crying into his beer. For a millennium now Miss Nancy Pants has been whining about the Christians taking over while his own mystical clout slips away. Merlin is sick of it. He's about to tell the god to can it when he gets an idea.

"I'm thinking out loud here," the wizard says, scratching under his hat with the business end of his wand, "but why do we let them get away with it? Remember the very pleasant method we came up with to give the Amazons the strength they asked for? We could transfer our mystical powers the same way to a dozen worthy human breeders. Then those holier-than-thou Christians would have to contend with our magic forever!"

Zeus blinks.

He stands up.

He runs a hand through his gorgeous curls.

Finally—and for the first time since the Goths sacked Rome—the God of Thunder smiles.

"You are brilliant!" he cries and shakes Merlin by his bony shoulders, rattling the wizard's three remaining teeth. "When the Christians see our magic bubble to the surface in ordinary humans, that walking-on-water trick they're so fond of won't seem like such a big deal."

He releases Merlin and stomps around Mount Olympus, causing the nymphs to tumble and bounce. "One god, indeed. How long will the Christians keep that fantasy alive when one of their own can reset bones and make soufflé? Ha! Then they will rue the day they gave up on us to become lion chow!"

Merlin pops his shoulders back into place as Zeus gestures to the earth below. "Friend, I shall leave it to you to find worthy beneficiaries."

The wizard sweeps his gaze around the corners of the world, but not a single human appears to have the je ne sais quoi *for enchantment. He is about to give up when his eye catches a glint of red.*

He squints.

In a distant depression—a swamp really—he sees women with hair the color of burning embers. Merlin directs his wand to the distant mire. "To them! We give our powers to that small band of bog women!"

Zeus crouches behind Merlin, narrows his eyes, and then slaps the rickety wizard on the back, sending him airborne. "By Thor's hammer," he cries. "You have found humans that already look like they dipped their heads in a pot of magic!"

Merlin staggers back to his feet, they shake on it, and assign

Echo–the wiliest nymph—to the task of luring the redheads up the mountain.

Echo flits down to the bog and starts out with the hook. "Good humans, good humans, great news! The god and the wizard up that mountain want to give you bits of their power. You and all your daughters will still be mortal, will still live among mortals, but you will have pockets of unusual and magical gifts. Ladies, this is an opportunity not to be missed, not to be missed!"

Meggie, the tallest bog woman, steps up and says, "What's the catch? What do the old buggers get out of it?"

Echo shrugs. "They're men. What do you think they want, want, want?"

The redheads cry "Eeeww" and start to turn away, but Echo ups the ante. "Look, if you come with me now, we nymphs will show you a few of our tricks and the whole thing will be over before the sun sets. And while your bog is, ahem lovely, it does smell a lot like Diana's feet after she's been hunting all day. Think on it. With your new abilities, you could move to a land surface that doesn't ooze between your toes your toes."

Meggie scowls at her sodden ankles. Tapping her finger to her lips, she looks up at the mountain. "What would it be like then, takin' on those old boys?"

Echo can't suppress a smile. "Zeus is like any mama's boy who thinks he's a god, so don't expect any foreplay. But the wizard is phenomenal. He turns himself into Adonis and works it for all he's worth. Will you be sore for a few days? No doubt, no doubt. But once it's over you will have abilities that will bedevil ordinary men!"

Meggie peels a clump of muck off her instep and tosses it with conviction. "Then I'm in!"

The others agree.

They tramp up the mountain, lose their clothes, and a bawdy

transfer ceremony takes place that will keep all the participants smirking for decades.

Pleasantly relieved of their powers, Merlin and Zeus retire.

The redheads, disheveled and bowlegged, are halfway down the mountain when their skin becomes translucent, their tempers fierce.

The next morning the learned men of the world woke up holding on to a very worrisome ... shrinkage. Clearly, there were females about who had squirmed from under thumb! Fortunately, the culprits, with their flamboyant hair, their glowing skin, and their flagrant ability to identify bark that cures headaches, were easy to spot. So the scholars got down to business, and over the next ten centuries came up with endless excuses to drown and hang and burn the extraordinary girls out of existence.

Even so, they never got back so much as half an inch for their efforts.

Eventually science usurped blind fear, and the surviving redheads could draw back their scarves and walk out in the sun.

Big mistake.

Was it seventy generations under wraps that made their skin so vulnerable, or was it the price they paid for their powers? Either way, the girls quickly ducked under parasols and hats until SPF 50 became available.

Ah, but does the twenty-first century redhead even know about her magic? Generations of vigilant mothers would have had to squash all talents in that direction in order to keep their girls from ending up on the pyre. ('Lizzy, stop stirring the pot from the other side of the room or there will be no dinner for you!') So it would follow that while today's redhead knows she's lucky at cards, that she can bake a cake without eggs, and can talk herself out of a speeding ticket—she doesn't know why.

But I do.

V
Saved!

That morning I slogged through twenty-two lackluster writing samples, finding a luminous phrase here and there, but nothing to stir the soul. Where was my dream client? Where was the writer who would drop a script in my lap that would make the movie lions stand up and roar me into their golden sanctuaries?

My last three deals at work had fallen through, and, my fault or not (and I'm going with not) I still had the stink of failure on me. The marmalade dressing on that turd sandwich was Peter acting uncharacteristically interested in every half-developed, dystopian nightmare script recommended by Cameron—a despicable zygote with a Chinese symbol tattooed directly over his Adam's apple—and then when it was my turn to pitch, Peter would compress his lips in *pre*-disapproval.

There were four days until my annual review. Four days to sign on The Dream Client or find myself out on the street, competing with all the smarter-than-Cameron zygotes from Bard and Brown. I run into these wunderkinds at every L.A. party. We nod. We chat. We half-pretend we aren't all keeping one eye latched on the Important Person in the room as we finesse a diminishing orbit to get face time, straining all the while to interpret every twitch or smile or frown. *Does Annette look bored? Is Martin in a receptive mood? Rob's laugh–real or fake?*

I believe it is only the fabric covering their backsides that stop us from taking their rectal temperatures.

But much as I long for an Important Person to hear my pitch, grab my arm, and scribble a non-compete on a cocktail napkin, so far that hasn't happened. At best, they hear my most promising storyline and slip me the contact information of their elite acquisition team. Excited, I make an appointment, arrive on time, only to find a gaggle of other agents in the waiting room. When it's my turn to pitch, I lay my hands on the table, pause, and draw them into the opening scene of the brilliant script I've culled out of the hundreds that land in my inbox every month. If they lean back and break eye contact, I know one of them is about to say they have something just like it on spec, or under contract, or in production. But if they tip their heads and yell out names of famous actors for the characters, paperwork to option the script will soon appear on the table.

And in Hollywood, enthusiasm is *never* tempered.

"Best I've heard in years," they say while pumping my hand. "Oscar bait!" and "No one in this room is going to digest another meal until we get this ball rolling!"

Always I feel a current course though my body. Happily I drum the steering wheel on a detour back to Floodgate that takes me by a beautiful white stone building in West Hollywood that would be the perfect location for The Daniel Ashe Literary Agency.

Oh, optimism. Such a lovely bubble.

As a rule, the days will tick by without a name director or hot Golden Globe actor latching onto the project. A week. Then another and another, and …

That script is toast.

After two months, any follow-up call I make is met with tragic concern for my well-being.

Oh Daniel, give up on that dud!

Around ten thirty that morning I considered changing my profile on the company website. If I appeared younger, hipper, would that attract the kind of so-called "vibrant" authors that Cameron the Zygote was getting? Maybe I could leave out the dates I graduated, the years I've put in, and ditch my clean-cut photo for something more artsy. In Cameron's picture he is peeking through open fingers, his nails painted black, his wrists parted to expose the Chinese character on his Adam's apple.

Vomitus weasel.

I went back to my email. While I'd been musing, a new submission arrived in my inbox, this one for a novel. Strike one. In seventeen years Peter had never backed a single book proposal. I was half a second from clicking it away when I saw the author was from a rough part of South Central L.A.. Curious to see the kind of street grit might await me, I scrolled down to page one.

The Blue Season

by

Oliver Nikitin

Until Gautier brought his machine to Venice, there were only six reliable ways to kill a man.

I looked out the window and let the world beat on without me. Then I read it again.

While certified by the women of California as being incapable of love, I can and do fall head-over-heels for a great first sentence. In this one, Mr. Nikitin had me on a Venetian dock at the dawn of the industrial revolution, watching a man in a vested suit supervise the transfer of a mysterious wooden crate from a bobbing boat. This Gautier made me nervous. I had to learn who he was and (God help us all) how his diabolical machine snuffed out human life.

I almost hated to read on. It's hard enough to come up with a gripping first sentence, but sustaining the tension is a feat seldom mastered, and I braced myself for disappointment.

But by the end of the first page I was biting my lip. By the third page my tongue was so dry it stuck to the roof of my mouth. What was happening in the story, the way it was happening, yanked me in so deep I was powerless to stop reading. I finished the one-chapter sample, sat back in my chair, and closed my eyes.

This is it!

The writing was something new—theatrical and menacing, like the musical background in a Hitchcock film. Oliver Nikitin didn't live by the rules of ordinary writers. Clearly he didn't have to.

I needed a hard copy. I walked circles around my office as I waited for the printer to pop out pages, pausing each rotation to check the stack. What was taking so long?

I took a deep breath, and the influx of oxygen roared my pilot light of hope into a fireball. If I had this wild, bucking stallion of a property under contract in when I sat down with Peter in three days for my review, I was not only keeping my job, I'd be the platinum player at Floodgate. No need to empty my office. No signing up for unemployment. No putting my house on the market. What I *would* do is make a ton of money for the company, shake Peter's hand goodbye, and take Oliver

Nikitin and all the other brilliant writers that honed in on me to my new offices in the white stone building.

The printer stopped. I grabbed the pages, walked the stack to Peter's office and placed them on his desk. He raised one eyebrow. "Whatcha got here? *The Blue Season.* A goddamn novel?"

"Read. I do not want to talk until you read this."

Peter scowled and put on his glasses. He yanked the pull on his antique desk lamp and picked up the first page. I sat to the side and watched.

He betrayed nothing: no nodding, no vocalizations, just a steady reader turning one page over after another while I quietly panted. Peter read scripts. Period. What if he couldn't see the value in front of him? Would I quit and take it to another agency?

When he turned the last page he took off his glasses, knocked both sets of knuckles on the desk, and said, "Call him. Get this guy in here and sign him before somebody else does."

I jogged back to my office. After I punched in the author's phone number a young voice said, "Yeah?"

"Hello. May I speak to Oliver Nikitin?"

"What the hell do you want?

"I'm Daniel Ashe. You sent me the first chapter of your book, and I like it very much."

I waited several seconds for a reply then pressed on. "I see you're a local, and I hope you're available to bring in the rest of your manuscript sometime today or tomorrow. Would that be possible?"

He hesitated so long I thought we'd been disconnected. Finally, and in an odd stage whisper, he said, "I'll bring it to you at ten o'clock tomorrow morning."

He hung up before I could respond.

I was relieved, yes, but worried. Why didn't he sound excited? Had he sent his sample to other agencies and mine was not the first to call? And what was with that fake whisper voice?

Whatever. I had to be ready to battle if necessary. My career was on the line here. My life. My future as consort to the gorgeous Victoria Millman.

I left work early to stop back at the urgent care center for my follow up appointment. My imprisoned fingers were released and I was declared back to normal. As I drove home I worried. I'd been sleeping even less than usual, and now I had a make-it-or-break-it meeting in the morning with the writer who could save my career. I'd never get to sleep. Unless ...

Maybe Annie had left me another story full of lore and legend that would divert me with Google searches until my eyes drooped and my brain shut down. That would be a very good thing.

When I entered the kitchen I noticed there was a sticky note on the laptop.

I used this to check on a money transfer from my bank. Hope you don't mind. Annie.

The dog diary was open as usual, this time to a drawing of a curvaceous belly dancer. She was standing sideways, fists at her waist, while her *third* arm reached out to beckon me closer.

10/22/15
Dog Diary
Thursday, 2:00 p.m.

Dear Daniel,

At the same circus of Croi and Todor was a belly dancer with three arms named Allura.

At the age of twenty-three, Allura posed for a scandalous painting that would find its way into the private chambers of the wealthiest men in Europe, but no one—neither Habsburg, Romanov nor Bonaparte—could buy the painting at any price. The agreement was always the same: for a weighty bag of gold, the painting could be borrowed for one year and one year only. There was no reneging on the deal; in part because you would make a powerful foe of the next in line for his year with Allura, in part because the tall man who appeared at midnight to reclaim the painting had a lion by his side.

Today Allura is Elsa, reborn as a three-legged boxer. When Elsa saw us at the dog park, she loped over to greet Eddie with much love. When I voiced amazement that such a reunion was taking place, Eddie explained that our lives fold in and around each other like dough in a Mixmaster, so meeting again is inevitable.

While Elsa's human was texting on his phone, she sat down next to us and began her tale:

Elsa's Story

The leg I am missing was a small extra arm back then, attached just behind my right shoulder. A third arm might seem a peculiar gift for a Croatian farm girl, but I learned to use it to tell whatever story I wanted men to believe, and men were my only audience. Ladies were barred from my performances under the ruse that seeing my deformity would upset their sensitive natures. An obvious ploy—and one that worked brilliantly to quicken the hands of men to pull out those extra levs, forints, zlotys, or rubles needed to get inside my tent. Everyone guessed, quite correctly, that a woman who danced only for men would show a good deal more flesh.

I cared for none in the crowd. Enticing men was just my job, and I was good at it. My real happiness came from my friendship with the good-humored Todor. I would linger by Croi's cage every morning and speak lovingly to the gentle lion, knowing that soon his tall trainer would appear. I made up fairy tales for Todor and he teased me about my "magical" arm. We laughed together like innocent children.

The circus employed heralds who would infiltrate towns ahead of us to spread the news of our imminent arrival. Women and children were told that Croi the Lion would walk among them, just as he did in the palaces of kings. To the men they whispered that the beautiful Allura would use her third arm to point to the lucky one she favored most. He was to follow her behind a thick red velvet curtain where, for a price, he could satisfy himself that her arm was real—along with all her other charms!

Where men are, competition reigns. My every performance was at once an entertainment and a contest. I would work the crowd: tantalize this one and that, start to summon a blue-eyed man, then quickly divert to a brown-eyed one. Most men held gold and silver coins in the air, but often I chose a man who showed no money, surmising him to be the one to pay most generously to meet me behind that red curtain; and I ended my dance with my third arm and my kohl-rimmed eyes aimed directly at him.

One night there was a darkly handsome man in the audience who stared in a way that made me feel as if his hands and lips were already upon me. I should have turned away. I should have beckoned someone older, more affluent, to follow me to the velvet curtain. But I felt a longing at the core of my body that I could not refuse.

His name was Emil. When I led him behind the curtain he took my face in his hands. Before he kissed me, before his fingers moved through my hair and under my costume with an expertise that made me weak, he said, "You are to be my wife."

Foolish girl that I was, I married him.

Emil was an artist. In me he believed he had finally found his muse. He would take off my clothes and begin to make love to me, but at the height of my need he would stop and pose me and step behind his canvas to capture me while I tried to use my womanly flesh to lure him back.

There were days when he was too angry or sad to feel inspired, and he demanded I dance for him to renew his desire. If I couldn't arouse him he would shout, "Dance again!" If I fell to the floor in exhaustion, if I begged "no more," Emil would pull me up and slap me. My struggle, my cries, inflamed him, and he would push me back on the bed and use that energy to make my portrait more lascivious, more erotic.

One day I packed my bag and told Emil I was leaving him. He gripped my neck until I couldn't breathe, and with his face pressed into my ear, he called me a stupid child who didn't understand that he was the one in pain. Then he threw open my satchel, took my traveling papers, and put them in his pocket. "You are going nowhere," he said.

I felt my heart clench. Without those papers I had no hope of escape.

That was the first time I wished my husband dead. It would not be the last. I imagined it often. I prayed for it!

Then came the morning that Emil announced he had completed his masterpiece. He pulled me into the studio and stood me in front of it.

One look and I staggered back.

There was never a painting like it. Emil hadn't put a woman on that canvas as much as eroticism itself. He had captured the moment before carnal release.

"You must change my face," I cried. "And paint out my third arm!"

He laughed and kissed me. "There are already dukes and princes bidding against each other for your portrait. We will soon be rich! Stay here my wife, and pack your bags," he said. "I am going to town to make arrangements. Once it sells I will take you wherever you want to go."

Here was my chance at last. "I want to see my friends at the circus," I said.

Emil's face darkened. He gripped my arm and hissed between his teeth, "Enough about the circus. They are freaks, all of them." He threw me on the bed and said, "I will make you forget about the circus once and for all."

I resisted, but Emil pressed his thumbs into my throat and forced me. When he was done I whispered, "I curse you. I hope you die."

He cinched his belt and left.

I watched from the window as he crossed the street. Through blinding tears I searched for my traveling papers, hoping just this once he had left them behind. All I found was my marriage certificate. I burned it in the sink, my confidence as fragile as the wisp of smoke that rose from the paper. Then I sat down and wrote: "You have finished your masterpiece and no longer need me. Goodbye."

I threw my harem outfits and finger bells in my satchel, and decided I would dress myself as a boy. Boys went unnoticed and rarely got stopped for papers. As a boy I might even be able to slip by the border guards.

I stuffed my hair in a cap and unrolled the length of muslin I used to press down my extra arm when I went out it public. It would serve to flatten my breasts as well. I threw a pair of Emil's trousers on the bed, but I needed a belt or length of rope to keep them from falling off my body. I was on my hands and knees, feeling in the dark corners of the wardrobe, when I heard footsteps outside the door.

I held my breath. If Emil saw my note he would be enraged. My eyes darted around the room and fell on an empty wine bottle. If he came at me I could knock him out and pull my traveling papers out of his pocket. I grasped the neck of the bottle and leaned against the wall.

There was a knock on the door. A stranger's voice shouted, "Madame! I am Constable Tomavich. Open up."

I rolled the bottle under the bed, pulled the cap off my head, and clipped on one of the capes I wore to hide my third arm. My hand trembled as it reached for the handle.

The constable stepped in and coughed into his fist.

"Madam, I am sorry to inform you that a runaway horse and wagon have killed your husband. You must come with me to claim the body and sign the papers."

At the morgue I lowered my head and said, "May I have a moment alone with my husband?" As soon as the constable walked away, I slipped my fingers in Emil's pocket and eased out my travel papers.

That night I tied up the painting in brown paper and string and fled with it back to the circus.

Back to Todor.

Now I am flesh again, but this time, as you can see, the universe tried to balance out its previous mistake by sending me back short an appendage.

Obviously, there are still some kinks to be worked out in this rebirth business.

Annie

P.S. I believe "Bog Girls" to be the greatest piece of literature since *Ulysses*. Thank you. For your trouble, I have been given clearance by the World Confederation of Redheads to assure you that your insomnia has nothing to do with us. (In her shameless way, our president went so far as to make a few saucy comments about your looks. The only one I can share is: "We certainly have no desire to keep the likes of *that* one miserable.")

So, Mr. Ashe, skirt around us no longer!

"I brought this for you," I said and showed Leandra the dog diary.

"Oh excellent. Go out to the patio. I'll bring you a beer."

I walked through my sister's open floor plan. While she had a lot of prints, scrolls and pottery from her nine years living in Japan, there was no doubt the centerpiece of her collection was an antique silk kimono of brilliant colors. It was under glass on the wall in her dining area. Because the elaborate sleeves were held up on either side, every time I saw it I imagined the original owner in the same pose, lifting her graceful arms so her servant might attach the wide, embroidered belt.

The sun had yet to set as we took our seats outside, and Leandra said, "I'm going to read this while I still have the light."

I drank my beer as she turned the pages. When she finished she looked up at the ribbons of clouds that were turning pink from the setting sun and said, "Annie has a crush on you."

"Oh please. You said yourself she was just messing with me."

"It's a fine line between messing with someone and flirting with them. Look, at first Todor was just this great kid who could talk to a lion. Now, as you reveal yourself in your letters, and 'Bog Girls' is hilarious by the way, the more she turns your characters into romantic heroes. And the postscript makes it clear she thinks you're hot. Annie has stars in her eyes for you."

"Okay, Miss Marple."

"Let me ask you, do you want Blend to find Nin, and Todor and Allura to hook up?"

"Of course."

"Okay, then," she said and smiled as if she had just proved her point. "If Annie doesn't have feelings for you, why else is she writing you into these stories? Why is she even leaving you stories to begin with?"

"She's Irish. And a redhead. All magic, all the time. She has to let it out some way."

"None so blind as those who refuse to see."

"Oh, brother."

Leandra shrugged. "I give up. But I'm invested in the budding romances of your characters, so read me the episodes as they come in. I want to know if you had a kickass love relationship in at least *one* of your previous lives."

That night I fell right off only to wake at three thirty. On my back I worried I wouldn't be able to snag Oliver Nikitin. On my side I imagined how my career would soar when I did. Neither position was getting get me back to sleep, so I padded into the kitchen for a cup of coffee. Eddie followed me in. As I moved the dog diary out of the spill area, I said, "So, Eddie, Blend has a peg leg, Todor has three fingers, Nin turns into a seal, and Allura has an extra arm." I poured water into the coffeemaker. "Weird, right?"

I turned on my laptop and a box appeared asking if I wanted to end the last session or restore it. Curious to see what Annie had been looking at, I clicked *restore* and up popped the login page for Bank Vontel in Zurich.

Huh? My dog walker had a Swiss bank account?

10/23/15
Dog Diary
Friday, long before the dawn

Hi Annie,

Hmm, a belly dancer who uses her birth defect to entice men to pay for sexual favors? Okay, let's not make a children's book out of *that* story.

Well Ms. Doherty, it's time to stop pretending that you don't have magical powers. I asked for a spell to save my career, and a few hours later a brilliant novel appeared in my inbox that could do just that. What I need now is for the author to sign a contract with me. So the question is: Did your first incantation cover everything, or do I need another to make sure he picks up that pen?

(Insight: All these years of dodging magical redheads and never once did it occur to me that there might be an upside to befriending one.)

One more request: In your next note please describe the supernatural frequency that vibrates your imagination, because if I were to see a three-legged boxer I would flinch and turn away, not imagine that dog as beautiful dancer with an extra arm.

You clearly have a better heart than mine.

I'll leave my laptop on the table. Please feel free to use it for your stories. I certainly don't want you to make plot choices based on how tired your writing hand gets. The printer is in the dining room. Notice the three-ring hole-punch device next to this journal.

One more thing: Please thank The World Confederation of Redheads for their support. Just reading that they have no quarter with me has made the air taste sweeter.

Daniel

VI
Clear!

When ten o'clock came and went with no Oliver Nikitin, my imagination took a header into a dark well. Without even knowing what he looked like, I could picture him sitting with another agent, pen in hand and contract on the table. It was after eleven when he finally sauntered in, and by then my nerves were strung so tight I nearly tripped as I made my way to shake his hand. It wasn't comforting to see how young he was, or to hear him still using that fake whisper-voice.

Oliver handed over the complete manuscript. We sat in the conference room and he drank coffee and breathed audibly while I pored over his book.

Start to finish, it was brilliant.

Taking place in Kiev, Venice, and Paris from 1864 to 1871, there was murder and mayhem, dark sexual encounters, political links to the Civil War, and just enough pauses in the action to give the reader a chance to catch a breath before being swallowed whole again by the intrigue.

It was also full of technical distractions. Odd punctuation, confusing page breaks and paragraphing—all easy enough to clean up—and once we did, the story would be even more compelling. I quickly estimated that if I worked nights, and the two of us met each morning to go over my edits, we could have this jewel polished to perfection in a couple of weeks. Then Peter and I would send *The Blue Season* to the powerhouse publishers and smile like Cheshire cats as we waited for a bidding war to start. This book had the charisma to hit the bestseller list, and hit it fast. Its cinematic potential was nothing short of dazzling.

With as level a voice as I could manage, I told Oliver we were the perfect agency for his book. "Not only will we find the right publisher, our script writers and contacts in the film industry are second to none. All you need do now is sign this contract."

I slid it in front of him. Without reading a word, he picked up the pen and wrote his name.

Relief lifted me out of my chair.

"I think you will be very happy with us. Give me a few days to make my notes, and then you and I can meet back in this room to go over my edits. In about two weeks we'll be finished and it will be ready to go."

Oliver put the pen between his teeth and whispered around the plastic, "Why does the book need editing?"

The portent of his question held me captive for a moment. I looked down at the first page, and pointed out that with just a paragraph break, the reader would know who was talking.

He shrugged, "I think it's perfect just the way it is."

I smiled weakly. Clearly the dream manuscript didn't come with the dream *client*.

After he left I sat with *The Blue Season* in front of me and closed my eyes. Under my hands were five pounds of paper covered in twelve point Arial font. In the physical sense it was only pulp and ink, yet it showed up at the eleventh hour to save my job; and God willing, it would propel The Daniel Ashe Literary Agency into life.

How had I lucked out?

There was of course ... the Annie theory.

I smiled to myself. I looked forward to teasing her about how well her spell had worked.

Annie. No crotchety boss or deadlines or weird young authors in *her* life. Her imagination was crisp because she was free. She and Oliver were the true artists while I was just a minion in the business world. Sure, I got to use my editing skills, but twenty years ago I sat in a cellar and banged out page after page of my own screenplay, loving every grueling moment of being immersed and creating from my soul. When it was done I sent it to twenty-one agents and got back form rejection letters from everyone but Peter. His note said that what my writing needed was the equivalent of someone shouting "Clear!" while using paddles to shock it into life. His brutal honesty changed everything. A few days later I peeled myself off my futon, drove to L.A., and appeared at his office. "I love a good story," I told him, "and if I can't write one myself, then at least I want to help those who can." He hired me as an intern, and I became a full-fledged agent ten months later—a record that held until Peter elevated Cameron the Zygote after only twelve weeks.

It was a great job. Every morning I sat down with a coffee, waited for my computer to boot up, and wondered what would appear on my screen. An original idea? A brilliant comedy? A heart-pounding murder mystery? It was a game of roulette, and I was an addict.

Better still was making a sale, and better than that was calling the writer. That's when I got to hear the sound of pure joy. All those months and years of typing the white of the letters right off the keys, spending countless hours alone, ignoring accepted standards of diet and exercise and personal hygiene while perfecting the craft—and it had paid off! A labor of love or desperation had made it, and I was the one that got to tell them.

Still, in some of my sleepless hours, I imagined a day when it would be me: so inspired by a fresh idea or an incandescent character that the words would flow from my heart onto my computer screen in an effortless stream.

But there is no such thing as effortless writing—unless, apparently, you were an enchanted redhead from Ireland. Still, I clung to the daydream of being a writer the way an old bachelor perpetually plans to court the woman he adores. He never makes a move in her direction for fear she couldn't love him back.

Okay, so I wasn't an artist, but I was the agent for *The Blue Season*. One bestseller begets another and another. Talented authors would soon hone in on me, and once I had the right client base, I would kick-start The Daniel Ashe Literary Agency to life in that chic, white stone building in West Hollywood.

I grabbed my copy of *The Blue Season*, headed down the hall, and found myself once again stepping on the elevator with the stunning Victoria Millman. Just holding that manuscript infused me with confidence. I smiled and said, "Well, hello. Word has it that you just made partner. Congratulations."

Her eyes traveled slowly from my feet to my face. "I was hoping you'd speak to me one day," she said, "and finally you have."

"I must have been waiting until the perfect afternoon."

"Ah. Perhaps we should get together sometime to discuss ..." she leaned her head back and gave me a heart-breaking view of her long throat, "perfection. Say over a drink around five on Monday?"

"I'll meet you in the lobby."

And with that my fantasy woman swept out of the elevator.

———

10/26/15
Dog Diary
Monday, 4:00 a.m.

Dear Annie,

I am bursting to tell you that your second incantation worked as well as the first. I have landed the client who will save my career. I am not sure of the protocol for repaying Irish enchantments—do I leave you a loaf of soda bread? A case of Guinness? Maybe it would suffice to tell you that if we were in the same room again, I might not fidget, stutter, or knock you semi-senseless into a thick pane of glass.

Daniel

———————

At the stroke of five on Monday evening, Victoria stepped off the elevator in a fitted, cream-colored suit, looking blonde to the bone. We walked across the street to *Tam,* an ultra-modern bar of hard cold surfaces and young ninja staff in black jumpsuits, their iPads at the ready. A mirrored wall allowed the beautiful people of L.A. to bask in their glory, and I had to admit that when I saw how Victoria and I looked together, I thought *Damn!*

We chatted about the characters in our building until our drinks arrived. Then, circling the rim of her glass with an expertly polished nail, she said, "I've wondered quite a bit about you, Daniel."

My name on her lips was pure foreplay.

"Well, I'm here to answer any questions."

Her clear blue eyes bored into mine. She said, "You've never married."

It wasn't a question.

"That's true. I'm more of a sequential girlfriend kind of guy."

"And why is that?"

"Not the marrying type apparently, and sooner or later that becomes obvious."

"Well Daniel, in the spirit of full disclosure, you should know that I ran into an old girlfriend of yours at a party a few weeks ago. Sophie Pearson. We struck up a conversation about you, and I found what she said to be most intriguing."

"Uh oh. I doubt she was singing my praises."

"According to Sophie, you are a lovely man who is incapable of falling in love. She says she met two other old girlfriends of yours, and they told her the same thing. They joked about starting a club in your honor."

"Yikes."

I figured our little date was going to be over before it started, but Victoria brushed the back of my hand with her fingers and said, "We have a lot in common. I don't fall in love, either. Though I have walked down the aisle twice."

"If you weren't in love, why did you make those trips?"

"Is being in love the best reason to get married?"

"Isn't it?"

She shook her head. "Absolutely not. People call it 'falling in love,' 'head over heels in love,' *crazy* in love.' It sounds like a mental disorder. What really counts between two people is a foundation of trust, respect, sexual compatibility and mutual goals. That's where I went wrong. Neither of my husbands had much ambition. The first was from old money and only wanted to sail his boat, and the second was too pretty. But I know for sure that being married is better than not being married. You should try it sometime."

For the next half hour Victoria put me through a flirty

but expertly crafted prospective husband interview. I didn't sugarcoat my resume, and could hear how lame it sounded in comparison to hers. Me: state college, masters in fine arts, literary agent. Her: UCLA, doctorate law degree, and a partner in her up-and-coming firm. It was only when I told her about *The Blue Season* and how I planned to use the clout of its certain success to start my own agency, that I saw a fresh spark in her eyes.

When we walked back to the street to go our separate ways, she turned to me and said, "Daniel, I'd really like to see you again."

I drove home bewildered by my own reaction. First date husband-hunters had always sent me packing, but her take on what made a successful marriage aligned so well with my own inability to fall in love, that I had to ask myself: *Hey, what if?* Victoria was smart, beautiful, and successful. We wouldn't pretend anything. No jealousy or guilt. I wouldn't feel I was letting her down or get that over-the-shoulder glare from a woman who was giving her love to a man who couldn't return it.

I'd never find another woman like her.

The sexual chemistry felt so cool and clean that I'd rank it a hundred percent; except, and I know this is a very weak reason, her forehead was preternaturally unscathed by Father Time, and her eyes didn't crinkle when she smiled. Besides *Casting Director!*, and *Most Divorced Person in the Room,* another game I mentally play at L.A. parties—where there are more paralyzed faces than you'd find in a VA stroke center—is *Botox/No Botox.*

And Ms. Millman had a syringeful.

Foreheads are the classic giveaway, and, because I'm convinced that sooner or later personal injury lawyers are going to paste ads on those smooth, flat surfaces, I've named these individuals Billboards.

It was the zero-eye-crinkle that dropped Victoria's sex appeal down a couple of points for me. I love to see those when a woman laughs. But it was far from a deal breaker.

When I got home I took a deep breath and stepped into the kitchen.

The dog diary was open to a drawing of the deck of a sailboat. There I was as Blend, sitting up on the floorboards, and kneeling next to me was Nin the selkie, her long hair strategically covering but not hiding the fact of her nakedness. Nin had one hand on my chest, and the other hand was palm up, holding three large orbs.

10/26/15
Dog Diary
Monday, 1:30 p.m.

Dear Daniel,

Sparks met me at the door and cried, "Nin has been found!"

"What grand news! When we get to the park you must tell me all about it."

And so she did.

The Return of Nin

by

Cap'n Sparks

Two months ago Ensign Blend left The Minerva *and bought a small skiff to sail the northern sea. One evening while he slept he felt water sprinkle on his arm. He opened his eyes and there was Nin, kneeling beside him. She touched his face and said, "I have been waiting for you."*

Blend sat up and grasped her hand.

"Did you dream of me?" she asked.

"I did."

"Did you hear my siren song?"

"Every day."

"Did you fear my magic and try to talk yourself out of loving me?"

Blend looked into her liquid eyes and admitted it. "Yes."

"That is good. You have wrestled with reason and left it behind, and that is what it takes to be in love with me."

"And you?"

"As long as you walk the earth I can love no other."

Blend leaned in but Nin put her fingers on his mouth. "You must not kiss me if you are afraid of thunder."

He took her hand away and pressed his lips to hers.

Her wild flesh! Human and divine, her breath was the perfume of life itself. He was soaring into the stars and tumbling into the sea. There was nothing to fear, everything to marvel. Ordinary life was over. And farewell to it. He wanted only to exist only where his body touched hers.

Nin pulled back and smiled. Breathless, Blend said, "But I have nothing to offer you."

"That is not true. But if you mean fortune, fear not, for that will change momentarily."

Nin's pelt was beside her and she put her hand in the fur and pulled out three giant pearls of incomparable beauty and perfection. "There is a man in Aroby named Patar who will give you a kingly sum for these. It will be enough to buy a beautiful ship where we will live together. You will teach me how to help you sail. We can visit ports. I will live as human when it suits me, and still swim the sea when I feel the need. What say you to this plan?"

Blend said, "Will you marry me?"

Nin leaned over and kissed him.

"I am yours."

Annie

———————

I texted a photo of the drawing to Leandra, and she called immediately. "You look really good with a peg leg, Ensign Blend. Now read me the story."

When I finished she said, "Whoa. That kiss! Read it again."

When I was done Leandra paused a moment. "Okay, I'm standing by my original theory that Annie has feelings for you, and now I'm convinced that she is both Nin and Allura."

"Then why isn't she putting her face on these characters?"

"That would be too obvious. Don't you see? To win the hand of the lady fair, you have to earn it."

"Or more likely she's not those characters."

"She is. And the romance is heating up. I'm going to be thinking about that thunder kiss for a while, believe you me."

That night I fell into the best sleep I'd had in two decades. The next morning I picked up the dog diary, snapped the rings open, and took out Annie's stories.

10/27/15
Dog Diary
Tuesday, 6:30 a.m.

Hi Annie,

As you can see, all the previous pages are missing. I am so careless in the kitchen that the probability of me soaking or melting this diary is off the grid. In order to preserve your stories I am taking the precaution of making a copy to keep at work.

This is to be my first day working with my new young client. My initial impression of him was, and I'll use the proper Latin, "e pluribus dickhead."

So this idea came to me.

Annie, whether you own it or not, any wish you make is apparently the universe's command. So please, close your eyes and imagine me at a table going over a manuscript with a young man, and make him agreeable to everything I suggest. If it works, and he goes along with my edits, we will talk about getting you a *serious* raise in pay.

For the next few weeks I will be feverishly editing his book. That means I'll be coming home late more often than not. So I am more grateful than I can say that you are taking such good care of my dogs.

Daniel

VII
Oliver

Day one with Oliver quickly turned into an emotional blood-bath. "Not changing that!" he'd say and storm out of the conference room, returning ten minutes later reeking of nicotine. There was no flow, no agreements, and three hours into the torture I picked up half his manuscript and held it high. "Oliver, this isn't scripture. We can add a word or an occasional comma so the reader knows who's talking, and we will not be hit with a lightning bolt."

"My readers will understand me," he sneer-whispered, "even if *you* don't."

We glared at each other until I felt hate rising all the way up to my eyeballs. I took a deep breath. "Why don't we break and pick this up tomorrow."

He was almost out the door when I said, "Oliver, we can polish your book now and impress the hell out of the publishing houses, or send it on as is and have them tell us it's not ready."

He left without turning around.

I threw back my head and closed my eyes. What was the matter with me? I knew better than to lose my temper with a client. Authors can back out of contracts, and they do. That's the last thing I needed. I had to hang tight to this meteorite of a manuscript until it made its way to the publishing houses, to the real and virtual marketplace, and then, please God, to The

List. Once *The Blue Season* hit the top of *The New York Times* Bestseller list, not only would there be money and prestige up the yin yang, the sanctified doors of the Hollywood Lions would open wide to beckon me in.

So I resolved to keep my temper in check. Oliver was a brilliant writer with an immature personality, possibly some kind of savant. I had to learn to deal with him.

I was still licking my wounds when Victoria called.

"Are you busy?"

"No. But I'm reeling from a bad first day with my young genius."

"Well, come over to my office. I forgot to kiss you yesterday."

I broke the building's indoor speed-walking record until I crossed the threshold and into the rarefied air of the law offices of Anderson, Waisner, and Millman. The waiting room was all Nordic furniture, there were fresh flowers everywhere, and the receptionist hadn't a hair out of place. Victoria met me at the front desk. I followed her to her corner office, and took in the plaques and certificates on her walls while she leaned against the closed door.

"Very nice," I said. "Championship rowing team at UCLA and I see you were a Gamma Sigma Alpha girl. I take it your grade point average was 4.5?"

"Something like that."

"Way too smart for me. While NASA and the UN were calling you girls for advice, I was playing beer pong."

"It didn't stunt your growth any. Just how tall are you?"

"Oh, I bump my head a lot, but the NBA never called."

She gave me a crinkle-less smile and walked up to me. "Here's what I forgot," she said and tilted her head back. I put one arm around her waist and kissed her. Then we tried another.

She stepped back and said, "That was lovely, don't you think?"

I nodded. They were fine kisses, even if they didn't send me falling though the stars and into the depths of the sea.

Victoria said, "Would you like to have dinner at my place tomorrow?"

"You cook?"

"No, but I'm very good at ordering in. Seven?"

That night the diary was open to a drawing of a bonfire with the nude backsides of elderly people dancing around it.

10/27/15
Dog Diary
Tuesday, 2:00 p.m.

Dear Daniel,

Oh no, Samhain is here, and it's already 9:00 p.m. in Ireland! How will I be able to stop Grandma Rose and her sisters from doing the naked fire dance when I am seven thousand miles away?

No time for stories. I must get ahold of my childhood friend (now a monk) Brother Thumb Sucker (unfortunate story that) and tell him to find those redheaded grannies in the woods before they drop their robes. I do not want to see their ancient flesh prancing around on a YouTube video like last year!

Annie

———————

I turned to my laptop and searched "Samhain."

After an hour I went to bed, only to wake in the dark to

mull over the situation with Oliver. Why was the most important client of my career the most infuriating? Thank God I had
Annie's good-humored energy in my life. She came along just
in time to balance out that annoying kid for me.

As I wasn't sleeping anyway, I got out of bed to write her
a thank you.

10/28/15
Dog Diary
Wednesday: Dead of night
(When the heck are you going to cure my insomnia?)

Dear Annie,

My work days are wretched, yet even there, in the midst of
epic frustration, I smile knowing that when I get home there
will be a new story, and a new window into your imaginative
world.

I confess to doing some simple fact checking. Before reading this last note I'd never heard of Samhain.

Ye gads!

That's some Irish "holiday" you've got there. The cattle
raiding, the Dagda raping the Morrigan to amp up before
battling the Fomorians; High King Tigernmas bashing the
heads of newborn males against the stone idol of the god Crom
Cruach; birds turning into humans, goddesses birthing triplets
... jeez Annie, you know I'm already spooked about redheads,
so please reassure me that your grandmother and her sisters
are really more Sudoku fans than naked fire dancers.

Moving on.

The Allura story from last week got stuck firmly in my
mind. Of course I knew that rubles are used in Russia, but I'd

never heard of levs, forints, or zlotys. When Google confirmed they are indeed legal tender in Eastern Europe, I thought, *Okay, big deal, so I don't know jack about countries where women wear babushkas,* and off I went to bed.

I was on my side, about to drift off, when I heard myself think *Hmm. I wonder if Allura really existed?* and winced so hard I crinkled the pillowcase.

For you who slumber well, let me explain my mistake. To an insomniac, an unanswered question has the same effect on sleep as a double shot of espresso. Even though reason would have it that a child born with three arms in any previous century would have been hidden away, or even destroyed, still I got out of bed, turned on my laptop, and typed "woman with three arms."

A moment later two very different Alluras appeared on my screen.

Framed in gold, the first, *Woman with Three Arms* by Jean Auguste Dominique Ingres, lies nude; two arms circling her head, one at her side. She is thick and Spanish and the viewer knows her lover has just left, because her eyes, her lips and breasts entreat him to return.

The second, *Three* by Grace Merchant, hangs in the MOMA. This nude is young and slim, less seductress than trickster, for her third arm must be sought to be seen.

Which Allura is the one of your story?

I closed the laptop and headed back to bed with a question that even Google can't answer. Are all of these stories, the Eastern European settings, the past lives and alternate sea worlds in which we both play characters, the tales of love lost and gained, are they, God help me, pieces to a puzzle that you expect me to solve?

Just maybe, if I didn't have to laser all my attention on my new client, I might be able to figure out why Allura has three arms, Todor has three fingers, there are three perfect emeralds in Black Bart's treasure chest, and Nin presents Blend with three pearls. Then maybe, if my rival at work, Cameron the Zygote, wasn't trying to sabotage me, I could reason out why all your central characters have physical deformities.

Then again, maybe not.

Annie, just the thought that you might be leaving me clues to some kind of big reveal makes me insanely uncomfortable. I am not one to fly to New York to see *Three* up close, then jump the red eye to Paris, rent a Peugeot and race through the countryside to the Musée Ingres so I can study *Woman with Three Arms* to see which holds your next clue.

Christ, it would be exciting, but I am not Jason Bourne.

So I beg you: Forget, rescind, and obliterate what I said about never meeting me in the flesh again. There is a farmer's market at Third and Fairfax on Saturday. Please come at eleven o'clock. I will treat you to coffee and a scone, we will sit at an outdoor table, and you will tell me that I have an overactive imagination about your overactive imagination.

Daniel

P.S. Please bring a photograph of your grandmother. I promise I will try not to visualize her dancing around a bonfire in the altogether.

I hadn't yet backed out of my driveway before asking myself if that invitation was a smart move. What if Leandra was right and Annie had feelings for me? Had I been clear enough that my interest was only in finding the answers that would get me back to my less-than-ideal sleep habits?

Oliver showed up at ten, obnoxious as ever. Each time I

fantasized about slapping him into adulthood, I made an excuse to leave the conference room. I used these little reprieves to imagine myself walking around the farmer's market with Annie.

Me. Hanging with a redhead!

That night Annie's drawing was of the famous Hollywood sign tumbling over.

10/28/15
Dog Diary
Wednesday, 2:30 p.m.

Dear Daniel,

Once inside the park, Sparks and Eddie immediately ran to confer with the other dogs. Though their heads were low I overheard "… disaster … hide in the cellar … swallowed up whole!"

I called Sparks over and asked what was going on.

"The ground is telling us it is going to split open and send us to the next life."

I sank to the bench. How could I have forgotten about the San Andreas Fault?

Years ago when I learned in school that many of the richest and most famous Americans lived on a geological time bomb, I resolved right then to never, in my living life, set foot in California.

But there was a man here waiting for me. A promise made. I had to come for at least a day in order to complete a business transaction with him, and then, if all went well, I would get the blazes out of California before the earth under my feet cracked in two.

Ninety minutes after I landed I learned this man had recently died. He was supposed to take over the commercial aspect of my project, and without him I had to do it myself.

I would be stuck here for at least a month or two.

I found a furnished apartment, rented the Jeep, and set up an interim business as a dog walker, all the while keeping my eyes and ears alert for the public service announcements that would tell me how to conduct myself when the big one hit.

In Ireland, if we had such a certain disaster to worry on there would be rubber rafts by doorways, and priests on corners giving absolution so the doomed would always be ready for the watery grave. Was I the only one in Los Angeles whose feet were constantly checking for seismic activity? And was that *because* I was Irish? As a people we are said to have an abiding certainty that sooner or later life will knock you down. Maybe I needed to become more of a "When in Rome" traveler. Shrug off my natural inclinations. Relax and enjoy the sunshine. Smile like the natives.

So I put my mind to it, and how well it worked! Every day I was happier than the last.

Then Sparks reminded me.

Daniel, you are my only friend in L.A., and I don't think I could live with myself if I didn't warn you that all the riches that surround this golden town are here to blind us. There is a price for this beautiful weather, a piper to pay for the physical freedom and the vistas and the endless choices of restaurants and entertainment.

No one can fault you for not seeing it. You live here. Just look at how quick I let it slip. Three weeks ago I was terrified that the jolt of my landing airplane could trigger the fault, and a week later I was every bit as spellbound by the splendor I found here as they were in Pompeii.

My twin sister tells me I have "situational hypnosis." She reminds me that not so long ago I lived in a Russian town where gloom hung like lead in the clouds, and it made me sad and docile. Now I'm in a city that pulses with sunny American optimism, where no one believes their fate is set in stone at sixty much less at sixteen, and where, with a little luck, or talent, or hard work, anyone can make their dreams come true. I became so intoxicated by this enthusiasm as to forget about the earthquake and the watery grave.

So with my heart tight as a fist, I asked Sparks, "How soon before the big quake?"

"Hang on to that bench!" she said. Then, seeing the look on my face, she added, "No, no, I'm just having a bit a fun with you. The big shake isn't for at least half a dog year."

I felt the blood return to my head, the air to my lungs.

I'm not one for mathematics, but isn't half a dog year about six weeks away?

Annie

––––––––––––––

Dammit. Not a word about my invitation. I knew it was a bad idea asking Annie to meet me. Tension with Oliver I could handle, but being on tenterhooks with Annie felt like a burr between my lungs.

I showered and dressed and arrived at Victoria's house at the stroke of seven. She took my hand and led me through her well-appointed living room and into her bedroom. We undressed each other while we kissed. Her body was exceptionally hard, and I stopped to verify that, yes indeed, I was touching a female six pack. I unhooked her bra.

Implants.

Gamely I feigned appreciation, but Christ, they make me

nervous. I'm always imagining one will rupture under my hand, sending DuPont sludge into veins, heart, and brain. Still, for a first time together, it went very well. The word that springs to mind is "efficient."

She put on a long silk robe and reheated various Thai dishes while I dressed. When we sat down to eat, she asked how it was going with Oliver.

"Working with him is like driving nails into my temple."

"Daniel, hang in there. Think of the payoff. This time next year you could be opening up your own shop."

"Or I could be on trial for murdering him."

"Sometimes the best things that ever happens to us come from the worst people. Let's put all thoughts of him aside and eat."

Over dinner we told each other our How-I-ended-up-in-L.A. stories.

While I came hat-in-hand, looking for a job after failing to prove to anyone I was a writer, Victoria was being courted by top firms from all over the country before she even graduated from law school. After a stint in New York, she decided to leave both the snow and her first husband behind, and spent a month looking over her options before picking a law firm that was vibrant, well-established, and that would put her on partner track.

As we skimmed over the highlights of our romantic pasts, it was clear again that Victoria had a far more focused approach. While I had girlfriend after girlfriend, none of my relationships lasted more than three months. "Ninety days seems to be the limit that I'm given to fall in love. After that, it's hit the road, Jack."

Victoria had little patience for random dating. "If a man is a poor fit, I know it, like *that!*" she said, snapping her fingers. "It's not in my nature to waste time."

After dinner I brought the dishes to the kitchen while she scraped and put them in the dishwasher. The two of us moved around each other easily, like we had a long-established relationship, and we took any near passes as an opportunity to lightly kiss.

When it was time to leave, Victoria put her arms around me. "I think we're good together. Don't you?"

"We are. Perhaps you'd like to come to my dog-infested townhouse Saturday night to see how the other half lives."

"I'd love it!"

When I got home I walked Eddie and Sparks, then sat down to read Annie's story again. It reminded me of my first years in L.A. when I felt like I had stumbled into the epicenter of all that was golden in the world. Everywhere I went there were famous and talented and happy people. As a single man working for Floodgate Media, I got my share of invites to A-league soirées, and I went. I jockeyed for time with the up and coming. I slept with preposterously beautiful women. My every conversation was a calculation.

Two years in, maybe three, that golden glow had worn thin enough for me to see through. Behind almost every smiling face I sensed a desperate need to climb the next rung of the ladder, or a thirst for attention that could never be slacked.

So I had to give Annie credit. It took her far less time to detect what really lies behind the grand façades. What I didn't like was her timeline for leaving Los Angeles I would have to try to convince her that even though it was all sleight of hand, perhaps she, like me, could learn to enjoy the show.

I hit the sheets wondering why someone as smart and educated as Annie was walking my dogs, when I decided it wasn't a slip of the pen that had the dachshund on her flier end up with the same crook at the end of its tail as *my* dachshund. Annie had seen Sparks and drawn that tail to get my attention. Perhaps a reasonable ploy to get a new customer, or—and the more I masticated this cud the tastier it became—Annie Doherty had a screenplay up her sleeve.

L.A. is an expensive town. To make ends meet a real dog walker would have to race from beagle to collie to poodle, not spend hours at kitchen tables writing stories for her customers.

Had I been played? Had Annie used her generous imagination to find a way to get her work in front of an agent? Some writers will do anything to stand out. At a conference last year, a colleague told me about a woman who wrapped a pair of panties around her screenplay and sent it to his home. His wife was so furious she picked it up with oven mitts, walked it outside to their fire pit, lit a match, and tapped her foot until it was ashes.

But wait. If Annie had a novel or a screenplay waiting in the wings, why didn't she agree to meet me at the farmers market?

I got out of bed, turned on my laptop, and put "Annie Doherty" and "Ireland" into a search engine. I got a lot of hits, but none seemed to be my Annie.

I leaned over the dog diary to re-read my last entry and groaned. Unless you were actually inside my head, it *did* read like I was trying to hook up, and Annie's lack of response made it perfectly clear that I was not on her romantic radar.

Only one thing was certain: I had to stop all this Annie-speculation and renew my focus on Oliver. Like him or not, he was the brass ring. So it was time to ask her some questions and hold her answers up to the light.

I decided to craft my next note on the theory that Annie might be a writer who went to considerable trouble to get samples of her work on the kitchen counter of an agent.

10/29/15
Dog Diary
Thursday, 5:00 a.m.

Hi Annie,

Your stories are back in here, but during their short hiatus to my office I showed them to my boss. After reading them, Peter took off his glasses and said, "So you're telling me that this woman leaves you a new fairy tale every night?"

"Yes. Every night."

"Then you know what she is, don't you?"

"What do you mean?"

"This Irish woman, do you know what she is?"

I shook my head, "What are you talking about? What is she?"

"Wake up, Daniel. That dog walker of yours is a Scheherazade."

Annie, you didn't respond to my invitation, and in looking back I can see how easily it could be misconstrued. If I were a woman, alone and in a different country, I might not agree to meet a semi-stranger for coffee either, even if I had been entertaining him for days with fantastical stories.

So please, allow me to make myself less of a stranger.

I am known by a small but select group of females as a heartless jerk incapable of falling in love. Each in turn soon gave up on me, more with a sad shake of the head than with dishes flying. It has happened so often that I have to concede the ladies are right. Apparently I have skipped or tripped over some developmental step that makes me incapable of true intimacy. I've made my peace with that, and recently have been lucky enough to meet Victoria, a lady who seems to suffer the same affliction. (Does that make us soul mates, or soul-*less* mates?)

As you know, I was on the brink of losing my job when a young, snot-nosed genius appeared with a manuscript that is destined to be both a bestseller and a major motion picture. If I can edit his manuscript without alienating him, his book will also be the starting pistol for The Daniel Ashe Literary Agency. That remains a major *if*. He doesn't like me, I don't like him, and the process is taking the tuck right out of me.

Ah, but the dream!

A major part of my fantasy future involves a magnificent white stone building that sits on the beating heart of West Hollywood. It is the ideal location for my agency.

Yesterday morning there was a realtor's sign in front!

Only a week ago I would have driven by, but now, with the snot-nosed genius on board, I swerved into the parking lot and went inside. The receptionist directed me to the west wing, saying "I hope you like it!"

It is perfect. There is one big office, three smaller ones, a conference room, a small kitchen area, and a back door for easy access to a green space for Eddie. I walked around and tasted what my life would be like if I had the wherewithal to rent this space and start my own agency. My employees would pitch to me. The bulk of the earnings would be mine, and I would be free from Peter's mercurial temper. Between the rent, the deposit, and the start-up costs, all I would need to make it happen is two million, five hundred thousand dollars.

Wait. I don't have two million five.

A year from now, with my client's bestseller thrilling the

reading world and a movie deal in the works, I could easily borrow that kind of money. But by then this property will belong to someone else's dream.

Ah, timing. If only I had some cyber theft skills.

Anyway, I am not yet out of the woods. To get to that finish line my focus must be completely on the snot-nosed genius and his manuscript. So no vacations, no pickup basketball games, and thanks to Victoria, I can swear off any more feeble attempts at conventional romance.

I hope I have convinced you that I am not looking for a date. Even without Victoria in my life I wouldn't do anything to upset the Annie cart. You are too valuable to me as dog walker, artist, and storyteller.

But these questions about you and your stories are keeping me awake. And since you have repeatedly promised (and failed) to cure my insomnia, the least you could do is answer those questions. So please, meet me off the written page on Saturday morning.

By the way, Sparks originally belonged to an ex-girlfriend. Three months after we broke up she appeared at my door saying she was moving in with a man who was allergic to dogs, and that if I didn't take Sparks then and there, she had no recourse but to leave her at the pound. So I accepted the leash. I have had a thousand occasions since to resent that ultimatum, but now that I know how Cap'n Sparks conducts herself on the high seas, keeping Sparks has become the one thing from that relationship for which I am grateful. So thank you for that.

I hope that is enough information for us to continue down the road to friendship.

So, Saturday: coffee and scones?

Daniel

P.S. I don't know the term for the opposite of "pedophile," but for the record, I am not lusting after your grandmother. If I worded my last postscript to imply otherwise, I apologize for creeping you out.

It was impossible to give Oliver my all that day—in part because of Annie, in part because I kept coming up with inventive ideas on how to murder Cameron the Zygote.

Around eleven o'clock I left the conference room to stretch my legs. As I walked down the hall I saw him in my office using my computer. I stormed in and growled, "What the hell are you doing?" The Chinese tattoo on his gulper went up and down as he clicked furiously. He jumped out of my chair. "Oh hi," he said, not meeting my eye, "My computer isn't working and I needed to check my email. I would have asked but you were with your client."

I glared at him as he scurried away. I immediately called our IT person and said, "Val, is Cameron having trouble with his computer?"

"Not that I know. Why are you asking?"

"Because the little shit was on my computer. Can you tell me what he was doing?"

She put me on hold for five minutes while she checked through the activity log file. "Okay hon, a file called 'The Blue Season' was sent as an attachment to Cameron's box."

"Thanks, Val."

I marched into Peter's office and told him what happened. He called Cameron in and demanded an explanation.

"I know it looks bad," he said, eyes pleading with Peter in an over-the-top performance, "but my intentions were good. I really want to become more of a team player, Peter, I do, and anyone can see that Daniel and Oliver aren't getting along. I could help! I'm a *lot* closer to his age, and I know I could relate to him better than Daniel." The little vermin turned to me, "I understand you're mad right now, but think about it. You *know* you're pissing off that kid. We'll be lucky if he doesn't storm out and find another agency. Now that I've seen the manuscript and know exactly what you're doing, I could take over for a day or two. Give you a break. Reel Oliver back in and commit to us a hundred percent."

"Are you fucking kidding me? I see you near my client and I'll put that stupid tattoo on the *back* of your neck."

Peter stood up. "Daniel, I'll take care of this. Go back to your author. Cameron, *you* sit down." I nodded at Peter, slit my eyes at Cameron, and walked out the door.

As soon as Oliver left for the day I pulled out his contract. There it was in reassuring black and white, Oliver's signature designating me as the agent for *The Blue Season*. I made several copies, slid one under Cameron's door, and put the others in an envelope to take home with me. Then I changed the password on my computer and turned off the automatic sign on.

I trusted that Peter had laid into Cameron, so my drive home was dedicated to the various ways Annie might have responded to my offer.

Heart thrumming, I entered my kitchen. The diary was open, there was no drawing.

10/29/15
Dog Diary
Thursday, 2:00 p.m.

Dear Daniel,

Reading your note was a great comfort to me. But first let me say that I do not believe you are incapable of falling in love. You are too self-effacing, too witty, and frankly, too handsome for such a tragedy to befall the women of America. As for your Victoria—you have truly found a rarity. A woman who cannot love? In all my living life I have never heard the like. She must be a formidable creature to behold.

Second, while you have never fantasized about my grandmother, it is only because you have never seen a young photo of her. Very Katherine Hepburn.

And finally, you seem quite distracted by your work, and hearing the why of it, well, as we say back home, "Tis only a stepmother that would blame you."

I certainly hope your new client gives your career the boost you'll be wanting. Please tell me more about him. What do you like about the book he has brought to you? What makes him snotty? Surely one so young should take advice from a professional!

That said, thank you kindly for your offer. While intrigued at the idea of a scone made in Los Angeles (really now?) I am working on a project that keeps me up late, and I rarely get out of bed before noon.

And—does it need to be said?—A girl might ask herself the why of meeting a man who has sworn off love.

Annie

P.S. By the by, you cannot lure an Irish lass from bed with the promise of a scone. It's the full Irish breakfast she'll be wanting. White sausage, black pudding, rashers, colcannon, or, English though it may be, maybe even some bubble and squeak!

———

This note was such a relief that I was tempted to shuck Boy Genius the next day and hang around until Annie showed up. We could walk the dogs together. She would answer my questions. She would… well, probably scream to find me lurking in a house she expected to be occupied only by dogs.

No. Terrifying her wasn't the way to go. Besides, with the Zygote panting at any chance to sabotage my career, this was no time to take a day off. Maybe I'd see Annie again, maybe I wouldn't, but I had to protect my relationship with Oliver. Until his manuscript was placed with a publishing house, I needed to focus every neuron on editing *The Blue Season.* No more obsessing about the Irish storyteller.

With that resolution solidly renewed, I went to bed.

An hour later I stopped kidding myself. Apparently I had zero control over the ever-expanding part of my brain that wondered about *her.* Annie Doherty: artist and fabulist. Who was this woman who imbued her stories with humor that was both dry and sweet, and always, *always,* with a wink to the reader? How she did it, and why she did it, was as mysterious to me as her astonishing eyes.

10/30/15
Dog Diary
Friday, 5:50 a.m.

Hi Annie,

Friday is here. I've had an awful week with my difficult client and deserve a break. Like an hour over coffee with a reasonable adult who just happens to have a delightful accent. So if you find yourself awake around eleven o'clock, please take me up on my offer to treat you to a scone made in L.A.

Hope to run into you.

Daniel

P.S. Thinking you might be convinced to come out tomorrow morning if I found a restaurant that served a full Irish breakfast, I scanned local menus. I couldn't find any matching dishes, but figured that had to be just a difference in the way we use language. What you call "Colcannon" could well be our "Western Egg Sandwich." So I went to Wikipedia.

Bubble and Squeak: Let's see ... not Champagne and pork roast as the name would imply, but a relic from World War II when leftovers from the week were chopped up, combined with potatoes and fried in lard. Hmm. Considering all the electrical blackouts during the war years, in exactly what vile state of decomposition were those leftovers? Wikipedia says the "squeak" comes from the sound it makes while cooking. No doubt from the dying screams of billions of bacteria.

Colcannon combines that delectable vegetable, cabbage, with mashed potatoes. Mmm, a flavor that must be just short of palatable!

White Sausage. "A mix of leftover pork, oatmeal, and suet." I believe this is the recipe we use in America for our birdfeeders.

Annie, up to this point, everything in your beloved Irish menu was entirely dependent on combining vegetable refuse with potatoes or meat by-products.

(Note to the British Isles: World War II is o-v-e-r.)

That brings us to *Black Pudding*.

From the name I expected it to be either the darkest of chocolate delights, or the treat that Tiny Tim blathered about: "Oh the pudding, the pudding!" But no. It is "congealed blood encased in intestine."

Good lord, Annie. That has to be what Vlad the Impaler served his guests.

Ms. Doherty, were I to sit down to any one of those dishes I would spend the rest of the day vurping. (*Daniel Dictionary: vurp. v. When one burps up a small chunk of vomit, not far enough to spit it out, has to choke it back down, then tries unsuccessfully to obliterate the ghastly sensation with vigorous brushing and gargling.*)

Pass the corn flakes, please!

P.P.S. Question: Historically, what exactly led to Ireland's inverse relationship of identifying the most unpalatable foods with the most adorable names?

VIII
Kiss My Arse

Annie's drawing that night was of the boxer with three legs wearing what appeared to be a bib made of jewels.

10/30/15
Dog Diary
Friday, 2:40 p.m.

Dear Daniel,

How happy I was to see Elsa back at the dog park today. After the dogs enjoyed a frolic, they sat down beside me, and Elsa told me the rest of her story as Allura.

The Mantel

Emil believed he owned me, but I had kept a secret from him. Even in our happy, early days, even as I lay sated in his arms, something stopped me from telling him I was a rich woman.

The men I took behind that velvet curtain had given me money, yes; but if one tried to do more than I permitted, if he was rude or smug or rough, my slender fingers deftly relieved his pockets of all they held before I called for my guard to haul him away.

I had learned the stealthy art from the gypsy girl, Marchetta, a dark beauty who impressed upon me often that a smart woman never falls in love. "Men are only a means to an end," she said, "and that end is riches!"

For Marchetta and I to keep large amounts of money in our wagons only invited predators, beatings, or worse, and in those days a woman was not allowed to open a bank account unless she had a husband or a father along to put his name on it as well. So each time our caravan neared Prague, Marchetta and I took all the watches and money we had accumulated to Master Jeweler Zdenek.

Marchetta would study every bauble in his shop before choosing her new necklace or bracelet or earrings. But I had a different purpose. On our first visit, I had asked Zdenek if he could make me a jeweled garment that would drape over my chest like chain mail - one that would become the top part of my performance costume. Zdenek smiled puckishly and patted my hand. "I know exactly what to do!" he said with his finger in the air. "Take off your dress please, so I can measure you."

Marchetta helped me with my buttons, pulled off my chemise, and I stood there naked to the waist as Zdenek's clever hands pulled the tape across my bosom this way and that. But if the master jeweler was surprised to see my little third arm, he said not a word.

Ten days later, just as the men were taking down our tents, Zdenek's son came to my wagon and handed me a package. When I opened the velvet box I let out a cry.

The piece was spectacular. Shaped like a small apron, the flexible mantle was composed of mere glass stones, yet it appeared to be made of rubies and garnets.

Quickly I locked the door of my wagon, took off my blouse, and tried it on. I could hardly believe my eyes when I saw my reflection in the mirror. Never had I looked more seductive. The stones draped and exaggerated every rounded curve and valley.

Because they were connected by silver links, small triangles naughtily exposed the skin beneath. I lifted my arms and swayed. I twirled. Every movement was more suggestive than the last.

From Melk to St. Petersburg, I wore that provocative garment for each performance. When I moved, the necklace moved, and the men who came to my performances stood mesmerized, waiting for the next moment when even more might be glimpsed.

Wearing it emboldened me. When I took the richest-looking man from the crowd behind the velvet curtain, I simply held out my hand until he put three times the amount of money in it than I made before I owned the necklace. Why not? I knew he would pay anything in his pocket to kiss my neck and fill his hands.

Between our arrivals to his shop, Zdenek sought and put aside every large garnet and ruby he found. Once Marchetta had chosen her new adornment, the three of us would bend over the mantle and choose which of the glass stones Zdenek would release from their prongs to be replaced with authentic jewels.

By the time I was twenty-three, the piece was worth a staggering fortune, and Marchetta was jealous. She kept my secret, but she had not done nearly so well. Worse, her lovers and her family stole from her often, and she bristled every time she saw me in my costume. Our friendship cooled. Still, I was happy. Each morning I told Todor my newest fairy tale, and he would tease me and make me smile.

One day after meeting by Croi's cage, I noticed Todor tip his head and look at me in such a way that made me think, "He loves me!"

From that moment on, each time our travels took us by an exceptionally pretty town, I wondered if the people there would accept a girl with three arms, a man with three fingers, and a lion to live among them.

But then, God help me, I met Emil.

What stopped me from telling my new husband about my wealth? I believed I loved Emil. Of the hundreds of men I'd taken behind that velvet curtain, it was only his hands and mouth and body that brought me pleasure. Yes, I had married hastily, but I was not a complete fool. A warning voice deep inside said, "Take your time now, Allura. There is no rush. Keep your jewels a happy surprise to tell him in a month or two."

But then I heard how scornfully Emil spoke of artists that pandered to the rich. And that was exactly what I had done. I feared if my husband knew that the stones in the necklace were not made of glass—that I had used my artistry to acquire such wealth—it would condemn me in his eyes.

Ah, but soon enough I learned that he was even greedier. His lofty ideals weren't real. Why else would he paint me in the nude—his own wife in a shameless pose—if not to tantalize wealthy men into a frenzied bidding war?

When I was too forthcoming about my wish to return to the circus, when Emil confiscated my travel papers and beat me, I fell out of love. It was only my secret wealth that gave me hope of escape. And I admit it, it pleasured me to flaunt those rubies and garnets before his eyes. I wore the mantle every time he forced me to dance. I smiled when he slid it off my breasts. I reveled in his ignorance. Once he dropped it to the stone floor. "Don't worry," he said, looking at it where it lay. "None of the glass broke."

Ha!

After I saw Emil's body at the morgue and had pulled my traveling papers from his pocket, I went back to our rooms and put the mantle on once again. The weight of it was like a tonic. I felt stronger than I had in two years. It stayed next to my skin as I wrapped up Emil's scandalous painting, put on my traveling cape, and headed to Prague.

I got there one week before the circus was to arrive. I went directly to Zdenek and watched as he popped out one large ruby and reset the space with cut red glass. With the money he gave me, I rented a suite of rooms, had three new dresses tailored so as to make my third arm undetectable, and on the morning the circus arrived, I had my hair fixed in the latest style.

All the while I wondered, how would Todor react to see again the woman who had left him with barely a fare-thee-well? I stared at my reflection. I had suffered with Emil, and was afraid Todor would notice that I was thinner and needed a touch of rouge to restore the pink to my cheeks. But of all the men I had ever known, Todor was the one who cared more about who I was than what I looked like. Somehow I needed to prove to him that I still had the bold imagination he loved.

I bought a ticket, entered the circus tent, and sat among the citizens of Prague. I watched as old friends did aerial acts. I laughed at the clowns. I gasped when Helo the bear growled. Finally Todor and Croi took the ring. How assured he was! I saw he was older too, but the new brooding look about his eyes made him even more handsome. I took deep breaths and pressed my hands to my knees. I had to stay as calm as possible.

As always, when his act was nearing its end, he took requests from the audience. "Make him wave!" someone shouted. Todor put his hand on the lion's head and a moment later, Croi lifted a giant paw and the crowd cheered. "Make him wrap his tail around your leg!" "Make him pretend to be asleep!" On it went for a few minutes, and then I stood up and walked into the ring.

It was a brash act, and one that so shocked the crowd that they hushed to such a silence that I could hear my own heart beating in my ears.

"Great Todor," I shouted, and saw a look on his face that was at once both happy and sad, "May I kiss the lion?"

Todor put a hand to his chin as if to ponder such a dangerous request. Then he gestured me to approach Croi.

I took one slow step at a time. When I was but a foot away from the lion's massive head, I paused, and someone shouted, "Madame! Get out of there!" I put a hand to my bosom as if my courage was failing. But then I took that last step, stopped, and knelt in the sawdust, my skirts lapping over his fearsome paws.

Croi let out the low, deep, growl of a lion—a sound felt in the marrow of any human that hears it. Women and children cried out in fear. Men shouted. I clasped my hands together as if in supplication, then opened my arms, exposing my vulnerable throat and heart to the powerful beast. Croi growled again, longer and deeper than before. Hundreds in the crowd screamed in terror for me.

I put one hand on each side of his face. I whispered, "I love you, dear lion." Croi put his head down as if in prayer, and I leaned forward and kissed between his brows.

The crowd leapt to their feet and cheered.

Todor helped me up. We bowed, and the three of us walked out together through the performer's flap.

Once away from the eyes of the crowd, Todor grasped my shoulders and said, "Is it really you?"

Tears filled my eyes. I put my arms around his neck. He lifted me in the air, holding me as if it was the happiest moment in his life. I felt in that embrace his goodness, his kind spirit. I felt like my life was about to begin again.

Then, abruptly, he set me down and released me. Confused by the sudden change, I followed his gaze. Marchetta had appeared behind me.

"You're back," she said, looking from me to Todor.

"I am. My husband died, and I decided to come back to the circus."

"So sorry," she said. "But also so glad to have you here, dear friend. Especially now. Todor, did you tell her our happy news?"

I turned to Todor, but he kept his eyes on the ground and shook his head.

"Todor and I are to be married in two days at St. Vitus cathedral. You must come!"

"Married?" I looked to Todor, and when he didn't raise his eyes I knew it was true. "How ... when did ..."

Marchetta stepped up and put her arm around Todor's waist. "I can't wait to tell you all about it," she said, "but first promise you will come to the ceremony."

"Of-of course," I stammered.

"Excellent." she said. "Your hair, I must say, is a revelation. So modern. I would love to have mine styled just so for the wedding. Was it done here in Prague?"

I struggled to make sense of what she said, and it took me several moments to answer. "Uh, yes, it was. Just this morning."

"Oh please, would you take me there tomorrow?"

"Of course," I said. Paper was found, and I wrote down the address of my apartment before walking stiffly out of the tent.

At 10:00 a.m. the next day Marchetta appeared at my door.

"I can't believe your timing," she said and sat on the bed. "Gone two years, and you show up now, looking like a countess. Go to hell, Allura!"

I paced in front of her.

"Sit down," she spat, "or pack. I want you gone."

"Marchetta, do you love him?"

"Love? Don't be an idiot. You fell in love with some painter and how did that turn out? Todor fell in love with you, and became a ghost who spent months barely speaking to anyone but that damn lion. Love is ridiculous. Didn't I teach you anything?"

"So you admit that Todor loves me."

"Go. He's mine."

"But if you don't love him, why do you care?"

"He and his lion will protect me. He's so famous now that Petar gave him the green wagon. And I've done better, too, since you left. At first, everywhere we went the men in the audience shouted 'Where's Allura? Bring her out!' You were this legend they kept clamoring for. Some duke in Vienna even sent Petar a note offering a thousand silver thalers just for your address. Ridiculous! I may not have a third arm, but there is nothing magical about that, no matter what anyone thinks." She fell backward on the bed. "I have lived in your shadow too long."

"I am sorry, Marchetta. But I believe Todor and I belong together. What am I supposed to do? Back away when you don't even love him?"

"Well he doesn't love you anymore," she said, looking up at me with hooded eyes. "You broke his heart. I soothed him. One night I slipped out of my bed and found him walking in the dark with the lion. I took his hands and I put them under my night-gown. I said, 'Forget her,' and for a while he did. Still, I saw he longed for you. He even tried to avoid me. So I sent him a note and told him I was pregnant. It didn't take him long to show up and ask me to marry him."

I sank to the floor.

"Oh don't be so dramatic, Allura."

"Are you pregnant or aren't you?"

"Of course not. I will never have a baby, but I will have Todor tomorrow, unless ..."

I swung my head and stared at her. "Unless what?"

She ignored me, rolled off the bed and walked over to the wrapped painting. "Is this it?" she asked, "The painting your husband did of you?"

I stood up and faced her. "What do you know of this?"

"Petar heard from his rich friends that men all over Europe are speculating about a nude painting of a woman with three arms. They say it's the most erotic painting in all of Europe. Of course Petar knew that was you. Why do you think that duke wanted your address? He wanted to see it. Everyone wants to see it. You will make a fortune, damn you. The rich just get richer."

Marchetta walked slowly around the room.

"Which brings me to the necklace. I went to Zdenek yesterday to pick up our wedding rings, and he said you had been there a week ago. When I asked about your necklace, he changed the subject; and it was obvious he regretted telling me he had seen you. So, I need to know, do you still have it?"

"Why?"

"Perhaps we can strike a bargain. That is, if you didn't sell it off to live like a queen."

"There is nothing you have worth a single stone of that necklace."

"Except Todor."

I stared at her, speechless.

"You hand me that necklace, and I disappear."

"But he'll go after you. He thinks you're carrying his child."

"I'll tell him I miscarried."

"No!" I said, my mind suddenly as clear and focused as the bluest sky. "You will only get that necklace if you tell him the truth. I don't want him pining for a child that never was. I want him to know how you lied to him. I want him to know that you don't love him."

"And then the necklace is mine?"

I leaned forward and searched her greedy face. Even if Todor would never be mine, at least I could save him from her treachery.

"Yes, Marchetta. Then the necklace is yours."

She ran to the dresser and began pulling out drawers. "Of

course," she said, "I could just take the necklace from you and still keep Todor."

"You could. I know you are stronger than I am. But it's in Zdenek's safe. If you want it, you and I will find Todor right now. I will stay hidden, but where I can hear you, as you tell him all your filthy secrets."

"But not about the necklace."

Much as I would have liked Todor to hear the extent of her evil nature, if he knew about this bargain he wouldn't stand for it. And if Marchetta didn't take the necklace, she wouldn't leave the circus.

"Not about the necklace. He will never know."

We each kept our part of the bargain. I hid behind scaffolding while Marchetta told Todor the wedding was off, that there had never been a baby, and that she had never loved him.

"Todor, I know you don't love me, so it is better for both of us if I leave. I have come into some money, and I plan to live in Spain."

He didn't argue, and she walked away.

An hour later we met at Zdenek's. Marchetta had packed her satchel and showed me her travel papers. "Don't worry, Allura, I'm leaving. He's a good man, you know. I like him. But I will like being a rich woman ever so much more."

Zdenek opened his safe and I reached in and pulled out the velvet box and handed it to Marchetta.

"You are a stupid girl," she said. "Or maybe I am the stupid one!"

I smiled and said, "We are only being true to our natures."

I left Zdenek's shop for the last time.

The next morning, wearing a simple daytime smock like I used to, I stood by Croi's cage until Todor appeared. His eyes on me were full of love.

I said, "I have a new story for you."

Annie

P.S. Tomorrow at the farmer's market—"It's a long shot," as you'd say in this pistol-packing country. If I'm not there by eleven fifteen, please don't wait around a minute longer. Not even a one.

P.P.S. Mr. Ashe, at least we bestow on our dodgy foods the redeeming feature of a pleasant name. Americans eat hot dogs, pigs in a blanket, and garbage plates; so you, sir, can kiss my arse!

———————

I decided not to call Leandra. I knew she'd like this story, but to understand the Marchetta character I would first have to explain about Victoria being as immune to falling in love as I was; and at the moment, that was a condition that embarrassed me for the both of us.

IX

Eye-a-Land

I have never peeled a cucumber, diced a tomato, or stuffed a pepper. My only business at the farmer's market is to buy empanadas from a lady named Esperanza. They are delicious, expensive, and worth the parking nightmare.

The week before I hired Annie, I was waiting in Esperanza's line for my savory fix when the woman ahead of me turned and lifted a small scone out of her bag. "Have you ever tasted one of these?" I shook my head and she handed it to me.

One bite and I was transported! Not the floury, tasteless puck I expected, but buttery, crumbly, and sweet. My benefactress pointed to the scone vendor, and I went home with a bag full of the triangular delights.

Now I couldn't wait to prove to Annie that American ingenuity had perfected the recipe.

Go U.S.A!

I got to the market early. I had failed to give Annie a landmark at which to meet, so I was compelled for the first time ever to venture away the periphery of prepared food and into the earthy heart where genuine farmers sold their goods.

It was like stepping onto the streets of yore.

There were vegetables still attached to their hairy roots, and people whose need for raw ingredients was so great that they filled giant canvas sacks and dragged wheeled wagons.

There was Annie!

I jumped over a box of avocados to catch up, but no, it was a teenager with dyed hair. I wandered. I scrolled to her name in my phone's contact list, but decided a call would make me sound desperate.

Then I spotted her at a stand. I sprinted around tables of organic peppers and artisan cheeses and was still in full throttle when I realized it wasn't Annie, but a redheaded vendor. I slowed to an amble and stopped at her table. She was busy with customers, so I feigned an interest in artichokes while I studied her. Her hair was wavy and tied back in a ponytail, though tendrils had escaped at her temples. Her eyes were a tawny auburn, her cheeks and lips a luminous pink, and she was covered with freckles, some even on her eyelids. She looked so vibrant and alive it was as though she had sprung from the earth as organically as her tomatoes.

I failed to walk away in time and she turned to me, pointed to the artichoke in my hand and said, "How many?"

How many indeed? I smiled and complimented her on her produce. She told me everything was picked in the early hours. As I handed her items from the table I asked where her farm was and how long she'd been coming to this market. She decided I needed a bag with handles.

I was conversing, out loud and fluently, *with a redhead!* The give and take was so intoxicating that I ended up with enough produce to host a party for vegans.

But the real Annie, the one of fanciful drawings and fables and arresting green eyes, was nowhere to be seen. After another forty minutes dragging around my new bag with handles, I gave up and headed home.

Damn.

I had been so sure she would show that I had even outlined a sequence for our conversation. After teasing her about scones and black pudding and Irish pessimism, I would have told her that Peter Flood had read her stories, and that we both agreed that a Cap'n Sparks children's series had cartoon and trademark potential. With the right marketing, Cap'n Sparks could appear on backpacks and lunch pails. Her crooked tail would become a lesson that imperfections don't hold you back. I would have offered to help her storyboard the project. I would have promised to provide feedback on her early drafts. I would have ....

Only she hadn't shown up.

If I was her only friend in town, why hadn't she come to meet me? I had confided more to Annie about my job problems, about Victoria, and about my dream of starting my own agency than I had to my own sister. We had a real connection. And dammit, if she was going to continue to sit in my kitchen and write me into her stories, I think I deserved to know why.

Victoria, on the other hand, arrived on time Saturday night. She was gorgeous in a crisp, white shirt and red slacks. After acknowledging the dogs with a quick pat on each head, she turned her attention to me.

We feasted on salad, empanadas, and a dessert of scones and peaches. We talked about our families, danced around our political leanings, and laughed about some of our quirkier clients. When we took our dishes to the kitchen sink, she leaned against the counter and suggested over the rim of her wine glass that I show her the rest of the house.

The moment we walked in my bedroom she closed the door.

Our coupling was a shade more adventurous this time, and I think we both understood that with practice we were going to get very good at pleasing each other.

After Victoria left I took the dogs for a long walk and

obsessed some more about Annie not meeting me. I fell asleep around 2:00 a.m. only to wake an hour later, unsettled by a dream. I closed my eyes to retrieve the last few frames, and found myself once again in the garden on Mount Olympus.

It looked exactly the same as it did in my dream all those years ago.

I heard a noise and turned around. Coming toward me was Meggie, the first of the bog girls to agree to Echo's terms. She was arm-in-arm with two other redheads. The one on her right was the vendor from the farmer's market, the one on her left was *Annie*. I gripped the edge of the mattress and sat up.

I tried to shake it off. *It's not possible*, I reasoned. Neither Annie nor the vendor could have been in the original fantasy.

But what if they were?

That thought was so disturbing it had to be pounded out of my head. I threw on shorts and went for a jog in the dark.

11/2/15
Dog Diary
Monday, 7:00 a.m.

Tsk tsk, Ms. Doherty!

Saying "kiss my arse" is not only unladylike and no way to talk to your employer, we don't even have "arses" in America. We have bottoms, rear ends, and butts. We have tuckuses and hineys. There's the backside, the fanny, and the keister. Buns, booty, and the gluteus maximus. But no "arses." Not a one.

I forgot the other day to thank you for the earthquake warning and for introducing me to the Irish worldview. With all the Guinness and whisky consumed on your island, one would think that the inhabitants would be in a better mood.

(Oh right ... I forgot. They know the next meal could be a congealed blood sausage.)

You asked about my client. He is lean, with hair gelled into a hundred coiled worms, and he uses a half-voice, half-whisper to lend himself mystique. That he wrote such an amazing novel I can only attribute to a higher force giving him one gift and one gift only. Oh, I suppose he's handsome in a wannabe-eccentric sort of way. But I don't get the impression he is successful with girls—though once the book is published there will be literary groupies from sea to shining sea clamoring to jump in his bed. Getting there is the ugly part. This boy fights me on every edit. The manuscript is fantastic, yes, but with numerous oddities that need cleaning up. And while most authors are grateful to have untidy phrases pointed out and fixed, he is not one of them.

Thanks for asking and for listening. I am happy you think of me as your friend. I, in turn, am amazed how at quickly you have become my confidant.

As for Saturday, I will admit disappointment. I hoped a minor tremor would have launched you out of bed, and as you landed on your feet you'd say, *Life is short, so why not meet this Daniel character? He seems a decent sort, but if he turns boorish, I will simply spit out the joke of a scone he forced on me and walk away.*

With that possibility firmly in mind, I walked around the market for a good hour, taking note that while awash in blondes and brunettes, Los Angeles is sorely lacking in the genuine redhead department.

Another consequence of your not showing up was that I bought more produce than any one person can reasonably eat. As that is clearly your fault, I insist you take the bag on the counter off my hands. Under the zucchini and peaches and artichokes you will find a white eggplant. I don't know what one does with such a thing, but it was so different, so otherworldly, that it made me think of you sitting at my table and writing me fairy tales.

Now, are you wondering what you missed by snoozing the morning away?

I have news.

My boss would like you to write and illustrate a Cap'n Spark's storybook. He thinks with her crooked tail not holding her back, she will do for kids with body issues what Dora the Explorer did for ethnic differences.

For the record, Peter never considers a property until it is finished, so this is unprecedented. If you are at all intrigued by this idea, I'd be happy to help you chart the waters. And while I want you to seriously think on that offer—and believe me it is a good one—there is now a more pressing matter at hand.

I just got off the phone with Peter and he has a dog-related job for you. He is going to London for a month to set up a new office for our affiliates. His wife desperately wants to go with him, but cannot bring herself to put her dog in a kennel. Except it's more than leaving the dog. They want someone living in their house while they are away. Someone competent, who truly loves dogs, of course, but who will also take care of the hundred tropical plants in the conservatory, boss the cleaning staff around, and make sure that wily squatters don't set up a meth lab in their million-dollar kitchen. Someone smart. Someone they can trust. Someone they will shower with greenbacks.

I gave Peter your number, along with a recommendation that compared your love of animals to that of Francis of Assisi—and in that comparison, "Fran-Man," as the critters knew him, came in a very weak second.

Sometime today Peter's wife will be calling you. Her name is Clarissa.

I met their dog once, two years ago at a Christmas party. He's a big dog on comically short legs. His name is George.

If you were to ask my opinion, I'd say take this job and charge them outrageously as they can afford it. It's not him, it's Clarissa. She inherited an obscene amount of money from an auntie in Texas, and she is devoted to getting the best of everything. The higher your bill, the more valuable your services will appear. Their house is palatial, and I have no doubt they will leave you with all the creature comforts.

Annie, I hope it's okay that I gave them your number.

Daniel

P.S. I would love to hear why you lived in Russia.

P.P.S. If I crossed a line when I asked you to meet me for coffee, I am sorry. But I won't apologize for thinking you are the most fascinating person I know nothing about.

———————————

At work three hours later, during one of my much-needed breaks away from Oliver, Peter waved me into his office.

"Clarissa was gushing on the phone. She met your Irish dog walker and hired her on the spot. Says if you were a smart boy you'd marry her. I told her about the dog stories she leaves, and she can't wait to start getting some about George."

Annie's drawing that night was of George, standing in front of Peter's house and holding a sign that said, "Welcome Annie!"

11/2/15
Dog Diary
Monday, 3:05 p.m.

My Dear Friend,

Charming a lass with plump round peaches and long firm zucchini is one thing, but when you compare her to an eggplant, you have indeed crossed a line. But thank you for the produce.

Clarissa Flood called me before I read your note.

"Hi! Are ya Annie from Eye-a-land who takes carra Daniel's dogs?"

I squinted into my memory banks. I knew that accent ... could it be ... was I talking to none other than *Elly May Clampett?*

Yes, I answered, I am Annie from Ireland.

She told me her name, our common link to you, and begged me to come to her house and meet her as quickly as possible. "Annie, we jist gotta meet right nawh, as soon as you kin git hea, Ah can't wait, Ah jist caan't!" I was going to put her off until after I'd walked Sparks and Eddie, but she said, "It dunn't matter one itsy bit how much y'all charge."

In my twenty-nine years I never heard the like. Such a statement could only be made by a member of your famous "one percent." As a student of American culture it was my duty to see this lifestyle for myself.

As I drove to the moneyed hills, I sang *Old Jed's a millionaire. The kinfolk said, 'Jed move away from there!' They said Californie is the place ya oughtta be, so they packed up the truck and they moved to Bev-er-ly.*

And there I was!

I parked in front of a mansion that had only slightly fewer pillars around the portico than the Acropolis. Straight away the tall, red double doors opened, and out stepped a stunning stranger in billowing white pants and glittering silver slippers.

She met me in her driveway and bent down to hug me with such force as to nearly lift me from the earth. Pressing her cheek to my cheek, she said, "Annie from Eye-a-land, ya'll are my savyour!" She pulled back, her hands firmly around my upper arms, and gave me a shake as if to gauge my mettle. Then she threw back her head to laugh. "Y'all are perfect. Perfect! Follow me!"

She tottered off from room to room and I felt like Alice tagging behind the white rabbit.

Clarissa is my first Texan. She is so tall! So blond! So American! Her teeth blinded me! Pardon my exclamation points, but she is the most exclamation-point-worthy person I have ever met. I followed her guileless glow from room to room. She taught me how to work the copper cappuccino machine, the sauna, and the remote control for the "window treatments." (Like consumptives and asthmatics, American windows are apparently in need of therapeutic intervention). A crew will come in and clean the house every Friday. There is a pool man and a gardener; and now there is me, temporary mistress of the manse.

I will be sleeping in their enormous bed because George likes it there, and it is too difficult to move his custom-made ramp. I also have an expense account with some kind of restaurant that thrives solely on delivering amazing meals to rich people. I told Clarissa she was too kind, but I enjoy working in a kitchen.

"Oh honey, I neva cook," she said as she leaned against the eight-burner Wolf stove. "And don't y'all think about cooking, eitheh." Her nails tapped a tune on the handle of one of the dual ovens. "Who has time? Order whatever y'wahnt. They bring it tah the back dowah in about twenny minutes. Make sure y'all try their lobster fettuccini."

Then I saw a cloud pass over her face. "Ah got to tell y'all about that damn lizaahd."

She signaled me to follow her. We walked into a plain room full of shelves and bins. She stopped short and pointed a French-tipped nail at a good-sized glass aquarium. "That there evil creatcha is Leonahhd," she said, her tone dripping with contempt. "This is as close as ah git. His food is right over there, and Peter will leave directions. Don't let him get too close to yah hand, as he bites. I'm really looking forward to him passin' on. Ah don't suppose y'all could forget about feedin' him?"

I don't think she was joking.

George and Leonard aside, I will have to keep my eye on a pesky problem with the climate control for the wine cellar, and if it falters I have to "pull in the troops."

(American military lingo—so handy for every occasion!)

I will skim the pool, look after the sizable rainforest they have going on in the conservatory, and keep track of the cleaners who are "lazy" and will try to take advantage of me being a stranger—ditto the gardeners. The pool man is a flirt and I should know he's married with many children.

"Though there ah some," she said with a nod to the neighbor, "who don't care 'bout such thangs!"

Then there is George. Oh my! A truly handsome Welsh corgi, with a strip of white up the top of his muzzle that spreads open on his forehead into exactly the shape of the dome of the Taj Mahal. Surely it is a sign that this fellow has amazing insight and wisdom.

He will be one to learn from.

I start this Friday. Clarissa has already given me the keys to the kingdom, along with the code for the security system. She is thrilled, as am I. She is leaving me a laptop to use to send her reports. She is certain it will pick up her Wi-Fi even if I'm in the gazebo by the jasmine bushes. I have free roam of the house, though she said she stays out of Peter's upstairs office.

"Honey, that computer is not to be messed with."

Sensing it was time to close the deal, Clarissa grabbed my arm and hugged it. "Annie deah, I don't know how much to pay y'all." She then offered me a preposterous, completely outlandish amount of money. Too stunned to find my voice straight away, she jumped in and doubled her offer.

I put my hand up in a 'Stop' gesture. "No, No, Clarissa, far too much!"

"No such thang," she said, and quickly wrote out a check for the entire amount.

As I drove away, I was so fearful it would fly out the window that I pulled it out of my pocket and sat on it.

Now, here is a question for you. Twice during our meeting, Clarissa declared with complete authority that I could be trusted because I was from "Eye-a-land!"

How common a sentiment is this in America?

Where I come from, you are not allowed to walk down the street with a new friend until your mother confers with your grandmother about which branch of what family tree they are from. This includes any scandal by any ancestor over the last hundred years. But here I was hired by both you and Clarissa inside of three minutes. She is going to leave me alone in a mansion full of priceless art and furniture and wine, bank statements, financial reports, and important numbers and passwords. It defies logic. So let me know. If trusting an Irish-born person is a prejudice in America, then I should capitalize on it.

"Greedy children?" my advert would start. "I am available to open your safety deposit box, be the executrix for your will, or carry your cash or jewels across town. You can trust me, gosh and begorrah, because I am from Ireland!"

What do you think?

Anyway, thank you for the recommendation. Living in that palace will make me feel like I won the sweepstakes.

Annie.

P.S. To answer your question, I went to Russia to paint, and ended up getting married. We had two very difficult years together, and then my husband was killed in a traffic accident.

I was enjoying Annie's letter, but then her postscript was like a splash of ice water in my face. Married and widowed? And was "difficult" a euphemism for abusive?

The next morning I used *my* postscript to pry for more information.

11/3/15
Dog Diary
Tuesday, 5:30 a.m.

Hi Annie,

No, thank *you*. Clarissa loved you, and that means my stock at work just shot through the roof. Two proposals I made yesterday were given serious consideration.

Wow. It really is who you know.

You asked how Americans feel about Irish people. I will say that in my experience prejudices are very hard to define or justify. In college, I had a professor who said I needed to enrich my writing by digging into the anguish I suffered growing up.

I said, "Anguish?"

She said, "Of course. You are a mix of three races, which means you belong to none of them. You must have suffered immeasurable angst. Use it!"

I nodded and backed away.

Curse my angst-free childhood! When we moved about as a family, the attention we drew was thanks to Leandra. She was such a knockout that strangers seeing her frequently tripped over their own feet. We heard so often that she was living proof that race mixing led to perfection, I believed we were indeed the standard bearers of the future.

Then, in one off-hand comment, an adjunct professor made me realize how that particular vanity doomed me to a life of writing mediocrity.

Back to your question. I'd say a woman from Ireland does have a certain trust factor built in. It could be the charming accent. It could be that we think yours is a country with a high moral code. Or it could just be you. This is a city built on artifice. Eight-year-olds dye their hair. Men in fishnet stockings and nipple rings hand you coupons on the street. And try as we like, we can't miss the huge cadre of attention-seeking women who came to L.A. ten or twenty or thirty years ago but didn't make it in the movies. They are so easily identified by their taut, tanned hides on surgically altered bodies, that I couldn't help but name them.

Plips are the ladies with thick puppet lips.

Pliptits are Plips with huge silicone breasts.

Plipettos are Plips or Pliptits who totter on stilettos, whether they are walking their dogs at seven in the morning or meeting their comrades and rivals at noon for the kind of drinks that would put me under the table.

The point is that you, Annie from Eye-A-Land, don't even

wear makeup. You're the most authentic-looking human in town. No wonder Clarissa handed over her security code!

As for me? I think I know a good person when I meet one. Daniel.

P.S. I was surprised to learn you were married. Now I'm picturing you in a cold-water Russian flat, eating borscht, writing stories, and wearing gloves with the fingers cut out. How close am I?

X
The Winter Palace

Instead of losing my cool with Oliver, or Cameron the Zygote, or the rude cashier at the Vallarta Supermarket, I began to react as Todor would—with a knowing smile and a shrug. When Peter went into full-bully mode, I channeled brave Blend, stood my ground, and he quickly backed down. And instead of tweaking bad news to keep my clients' feathers unruffled, I was as bare-bones honest as either of my alter egos. Some sputtered at first, but they always thanked me.

My characters were leaching into my psyche, and the results were impressive. People smiled, women flirted, Peter listened more and barked less. Just road testing a higher civility made me realize how duking it out in L.A. for seventeen years had swept me off my natural course. The more it worked, the more I trusted Annie's judgment. If she saw threads of these courageous, honest, and affectionate men in me, then I was buying in.

The crazy part, and I knew it was absurd, was believing that I was making Todor and Blend proud of me.

So if Annie wasn't really a dog walker, if she used that as a ruse to get her stories in front of an agent, well congratulations to her; it worked. Corresponding with her had become the best part of my day. Each time I figured out one of her clues I felt I was earning my way into our very exclusive club. And now that she had agreed to take care of the mansion, I had reason to hope that she would stay in L.A. long enough for me to convince her to work on a children's book. When *The Blue Season* was launched I would make the time to help her.

Annie was my friend. I wanted her to stay in my life.

On Tuesday, at the stroke of noon, a feast was delivered to the conference room at Floodgate. There were sandwich wraps, broccoli salad, pita chips, hummus, and blonde brownies. Right behind the delivery man was Victoria.

"I hope you don't mind," she said, dazzling Oliver, Peter, Cameron, the intern and myself. "I thought you men might enjoy a treat today."

I introduced her around, and we sat down to eat. Our conversation initially centered on the food, but Peter asked enough questions about Victoria' firm to give the impression that he might throw some business her way. Victoria then turned her glow on Oliver. "I hear you are a literary genius. I'm so honored to meet you now, before you become world famous."

The kid *smiled*. Until that moment I didn't know his facial muscles were even capable of making that happen.

After our surprise lunch, I walked Victoria to the outer door of her office.

"You're too much," I said. "Thank you again. I've never been treated so well."

"Get used to it," she said, "because this," she pointed from herself to me, "*works*. I like you, Daniel. You and I make a lot of sense together. We're not going to get all crazy in love. We respect each other. I know this sounds way too soon, but we would have a very sane marriage. Two people who want the same thing, and who have each other's back."

"I ..."

"You don't have to say anything. I just want you to know that I am looking to get married again, and I'd like you to consider the pros and cons of a life with me. If you decide you aren't interested, there will be no hard feelings. But you will have to let me know one way or the other. So give it some thought."

With that, she kissed me softly then walked through her door.

That night the diary was open to a drawing of Eddie and Sparks. Above their heads was an imagination cloud with George inside.

11/3/15
Dog Diary
Tuesday, 2:00 p.m.

Dear Daniel,

You asked about Russia. When I was there it wasn't the writing of stories I was doing, it was the telling. And here is a bit of my own.

I have an identical twin. Jennie and I were nine years old when our parents died in a car accident. Grandma Rose might have been able to put up with one of us, but as a pair we proved too lively, and she sent us to boarding school just outside Dublin. When we graduated we went on to Stella Maris College for Women—a very private school in Kilkenny where my aunt was a professor. Jennie and I had a history of hijinks, and my grandmother insisted we needed to go where someone she trusted could keep an eye on us.

I'll wager you've never heard of Stella Maris. It's a small

school, less than four hundred students, and rather a secret outside certain circles. But imagine, if you will, a women's college *itself* wearing a corset so tight that taking a free breath is all any of the students can think on. That's how strict it is. Then add a lot of statues of saints in the chapel and library, their prayer hands beseeching the heavens for everyone's continued virginity.

We had a curfew, a dress code, and an honor system that included turning in any girl who wasn't following the rules. But what really sets Stella Maris apart is that most of the students come from other countries. Saudi parents, Russian parents, American, Chinese, Greek—you name it—seek out Stella Maris as the place to keep their daughters safe; either from a world gone politically or morally wrong, or from their own enemies. Three sisters from Mexico each had their own bodyguard!

Our unofficial school song said it all:
I go to Stella Maris so pity me,
There's not a man in this damn nunnery,
And at ten o'clock they lock the doors,
I don't know what the hell I ever came here for.
I'm going to pack my bags and homeward bound.
I'm going to turn this damn school upside down.
I'm going to smoke and drink and pet and neck,
What the heck.
The hell with the priests and nuns!

Jennie studied languages, and I studied art. She was far more serious and studious than I, and we drifted apart. I made three grand American friends, and the four of us were of a mind and devoted to fun and mischief. We developed a talent for outrageous pranks that embarrassed the stodgy administration in every way possible.

After graduation, Jennie moved to Paris and got a job with the DGSE, and I took a position as an art teacher at a school in Peebles, Scotland. It was while we lived at this distance that we found our way back to a loving, sisterly relationship.

Three years later we came into our inheritance.

My parents had owned an insurance company and had excellent policies on themselves. When they died the money went into a trust fund managed by my grandmother, and that woman is a genius with investments. Even after paying for our school and our trips abroad to holiday with our friends, she managed to preserve the original sum. When Jennie and I turned twenty-five, the balance transferred directly to us.

We knew it was coming, and we put a much discussed plan into action. I quit my position, Jennie left her bare flat in Montmartre, and we moved into a beautiful two-bedroom apartment in the 6th arrondissement. While Jennie continued to work long hours and was frequently on assignments out of the country, I spent my time devoted to the café life of Paris.

When I wasn't with my friends, I was at galleries making bad copies of the great masters. For me, it was all about living the life. My friends from Stella Maris would cycle through, and we tied pretty scarves around our necks and enjoyed romances with exactly the kind of men our families warned us against.

Eight months later I said goodbye to Jennie, packed up, and bounced around between the Czech Republic and Germany, from to Italy to London, and back to Italy. My college roommate from America flew over, and together we sketched and painted our way up that boot, having brief romances with men who were either very poor and handsome or very rich and old. After she left I headed to the last stop of my grand art tour: the Hermitage galleries of The Winter Palace in St. Petersburg.

One day at the gallery, sketching as usual, I felt a man standing too close behind me. I turned to give him a "bugger-off" look, but was stopped cold by his stormy beauty.

His eyes circled my own. He said something in Russian. I shook my head and whispered, "I don't understand your language." He took hold of my hand.

I didn't take it back. I couldn't! While it was only our hands touching, it felt exactly as if we had started to make love right in the middle of the gallery.

He said, "I have waited for you, and now you are here."

He drew me behind a pillar and tipped my head up to the light. He studied my eyes. "*Bozhe moi*," he whispered. "I am saved!" Then he kissed me.

We married four days later.

"Marry in haste, repent at leisure," Grandma Rose said when I called to tell her.

"Epic mistake," Jennie said. Both were right. I would soon hate my life there.

Forgive my rambling.

Before I sign off, I want to thank you. I feel stronger now than I have in a long time. Our correspondence has helped me in ways you cannot yet guess.

Gratefully,

Annie

P.S. Oh, but you are a devil Mr. Ashe. I will never be able to look at one of those tanned ladies again without evaluating what category of "Plip" she belongs in.

P.P.S. Sparks and Eddie have heard about George and are anxious to meet him. Every dog knows that the Corgi is the ancient drover breed the Celts brought to Wales, and like the band of humans they came with, those hearty canines learned to communicate with the wind and the trees. Just imagine the wisdom from which we will all soon benefit!

What had that Russian bastard done to Annie? Any scenario I imagined ended with me meeting him on a basketball court and nailing him in the face with my elbow—and yes, I get that punching someone out doesn't sound like the noble person I was aiming to be, but defending women and children from brutes *is* the moral imperative. Ask Blend. I think I know him well enough to say that given the chance he would have happily disemboweled Black Bart for abusing Nin.

Annie had opened a door with her first sentence but had failed to walk through it. So when I wrote back the next morning I prodded for more.

11/4/15
Dog Diary
Wednesday, 4:00 a.m.

Hi Annie,

You said you were telling stories, but you didn't say to whom. I just had a vision of you holding a sign on the street that read: "Storyteller! 100 rubles!"

Please clue me in so I don't come up with even more outlandish ideas.

I went online and found some photos of Stella Maris College for Women. Holy Wuthering Heights! Before you and your friends graduated and seduced every able-bodied man in our NATO Alliance countries, you inhabited what appears to be a movie set of an idealized village built on the moors. One can only imagine (and trust me, I did) the number of virgins who got the hands-under-the-cable-knit-sweater treatment from the village boys in the dark corners of those ancient stone buildings.

Speaking of virgins, I took note that Stella Maris is run by the Sisters of The Immaculate Conception. Is it too literal an interpretation to think this order is dedicated to the intact you-know-what?

My next virtual tour was of the 6th arrondissement.

Good God in the morning! Just how much money did you two inherit? Clearly enough for young redheads and their legions of lovers to cavort in the most expensive and artistic section of Paris.

Damn. I've lived such a boring life.

Finally, and I swear I'm not a stalker, just an insomniac with dark hours to kill, I Googled DGSE.

Hold on. What exactly did Jennie do for France's tighter, smarter and more secretive version of the CIA? You said she studied languages; so for the prying eyes at the NSA I'll say for the record that I'm certain she only interprets messages from behind a desk. Certainly I would never imply that such an agency would see the advantages of using an identical twin team to slip into soirées—you, a decoy, flirt-seducing the evil prey, while Jennie slides into an upstairs office where she finds his plans for world domination. In a tiny recorder that slips over her tooth, she whispers its details using the uncrackable twin language you two developed in the crib.

Uh oh. Through your earpiece you hear, "Abort! Abort! Abort!" You manage to disengage from the evil prey's hairy embrace and tiptoe to the door—your hand reaching for the knob—when his henchmen storm in, throw Jennie to the floor, and hold up the recorder they slapped out of her mouth.

When the evil prey hears the odd language, he squints and says, "You two aren't going anywhere."

Okay. Sorry. That got dark and dangerous real fast. I'll just dwell a moment on one irresistible visual: twins in trench coats.

I hope Sparks, Eddie and George get along. Does this mean my dogs will go to visit him at the mansion on the hill? I was in that house for a Christmas party two years ago and spent the evening looking at priceless paintings, onyx fireplaces, and a kitchen worth three times my entire townhouse. Accompanying me to that party was Sparks' original owner. On the ride home she spoke of nothing but the size of the pantry. I thought: *pantry?* What about the wine cellar, or the conservatory, or the Renoir in the dining room? Now that I know Clarissa doesn't even cook, I wonder what the heck she has in there.

Daniel

It was another night with plenty to ruminate on. What had happened to Annie during her marriage? How many lovers had she left in all those countries? What did her twin sister really do for the DGSE? If Annie wasn't a dog walker, and the fact that she had inherited a decent fortune made it highly unlikely she needed the hundred and fifty bucks I paid her each week, then when would she ask me to read her screenplay?

Then there was the astonishing news that Victoria Millman wanted to marry me. *Me.* A forty-two-year-old, love-disabled insomniac who had been found seriously wanting by a score of less accomplished women. And she was everything I lusted for in life. With her beside me I'd crack out of my middle-of-the-road rut and soar. I'd open my own agency. We'd buy a great house. Travel. I'd be in a sophisticated relationship with a woman who didn't care that I wasn't in love with her. No, much better than that. She *preferred* me that way.

I would be an utter fool to let this opportunity slip away. I looked down at my left hand and imagined it with a gold band–proof to the world that I wasn't some sad, middle-aged bachelor eating pizza every night off a tray table.

Marrying Victoria could be the turning point in my life. No. Not could be. *Would be.*

I decided to do it. And soon. The day *The Blue Season* found the right publisher I would get down on one knee. And I would treat Victoria as well as Todor and Blend treated Allura and Nin. Just minus the soppy love part.

My happy resolution felt solid. Felt right. Until an Irish brogue in my head whispered *She must be a formidable creature to behold.*

Formidable? Like Mount Everest? Like Cruella de Vil? Like that other woman who couldn't love, the morally corrupt Marchetta?

I tried to chalk it up to what I knew about Annie. She was a romantic whose characters found true love in circuses and on the high seas. But Victoria and I were realists who didn't believe in fairy tales.

A woman who cannot love? In all my living life I never heard the like.

Dammit Annie. Were you telling me that I've been blinded by Victoria's dazzling surface?

The next night I came home to a drawing of George driving a convertible, the ends of his jaunty scarf flying in the wind, and the longest letter from Annie so far. I took out a beer and settled in.

11/4/15
Dog Diary
Wednesday, 2:00 p.m.

Dear Daniel,

Ah, opening a pantry door is like Carter peeking into Tut's tomb. Everywhere you look there are wonders and echoes of a life well-lived. *Step in*, the pantry beckons. Put your hands on chocolates from Belgium, truffle oil from France, sun-dried tomatoes from a roadside stand in Santorini. This is where you find the spices used only at Christmas. Where you keep the little burners for melted butter, capers large and small, dishes with tiny feet, sea salt, stocks for soups, bags of nuts, baskets of onions and potatoes and garlic, tins of tuna and chicken and ham. There's a Panini press and a mandolin, jars of jam and pesto made last summer, and next to the rice and the herb-infused vinegars is a row of shopworn cookbooks, each with pages blistered by drops of batter or sauce. When one has a well-stocked pantry, anything is possible. You want cookies or cocoa or biscuits or stew? Wander in. You want to remember a special moment? Reach for the red paste from that little shop in San Francisco, or the pâté from Marseille, or the saffron from Spain. A pantry centers the soul.

Clarissa asked me to drive "the Z" while she is gone, to "keep it in condition." The name made me think it was a tank of some kind, but no, it is a sleek, white thing that makes one think of deep kisses on a bed of money. George loves to take rides, and with your permission I will bring him to your place most every weekday so I can take all three to the park. I sense that sweet boy would benefit from the company of other dogs.

As to your question: The person I told stories to was Alik,

my husband. He had this idea that indigenous people have certain skills bred right into them, like racehorses or bloodhounds. Weaknesses, too, and if I poured myself a glass he would sneer that I was succumbing to the Irish fondness for drink.

But it was that same Irish-ness that made him believe I had somewhere inside me the gift for making up stories. He'd point to a man on the bus and say, "What about him, what does he really want, and why can't he have it?" I tried to beg off, but Alik would have none of it. He'd sit there, arms folded, like an audience that has waited too long for the play to begin. Wanting to please my new husband, I made use of my artist's eye. If someone resembled an animal or an emotion or even the weather, I'd use that impression to decide what he or she wanted out of life. From there it was a short leap to come up with the conflict that would stop or delay the heart's desire.

As you might have guessed by now, Alik was a writer. He'd been working on a book for five years and had reached an impasse. The day we first met he had come to the art gallery hoping that the genius of master painters would inspire him.

Instead he found me.

When I heard how blocked he was I said—very off the top of my head—"The answer is twenty chapters earlier, on the first page. Start off in a different city with a mysterious character who would disappear by page three."

"Go on," he said.

"Then, go back to twentieth chapter, bring that city and that character back again to solve your problem."

Alik looked at me like I'd just handed him a pot of gold. He kissed me goodbye and ran back to his book to make it happen. He returned the next afternoon and convinced me to marry him.

The way Alik prodded me to concoct stories was his way of tuning me up so I could do the same for his characters. One morning, about a month after our wedding, I was at the market watching the deft knife skills of a fish seller. She was at least sixty years old, still lovely, but I saw an old sorrow on her once-perfect face. When I got home I asked Alik if he was ready for my next story. He crossed his arms and nodded. I said, "There was a beautiful young fish seller who caught the eye of the arrogant chief of police. She rebuffed his advances, for her true love was the sweet fisherman who stuttered with everyone but her. The chief of police was not to be thwarted. He waited for his rival on the dark street, beat him to death, and threw his body into the Volga. The fish seller learned what happened to her lover from a frightened neighbor. With no hope of legal recourse, she lured the chief of police to her bed, and at the moment of his greatest pleasure, she drove a knife into his heart. That night she filleted the meat from his bones, mixed it with fish guts, and in the morning she fed him to the gulls."

To me it was just another in the endless stream of quick stories I'd been making up for Alik, perhaps more gruesome but otherwise no better or worse than the others. But when I had finished, he walked over and handed me the first hundred pages of his book. "You are ready," he said.

His story was good. I thought there was little I could do to make it better, but when I looked up to say so, I saw in his eyes the raw hope of a man who had been treading water too long. So I started speaking. I don't know where it came from, but I heard myself describe a maniacal plan that put his main character in what seemed a hopeless death trap.

When I was done Alik pushed himself off his chair, knelt in front of me, and put his head in my lap. He was weeping.

For the next eight weeks he ignored me while feverishly writing my plot twist into his manuscript.

I'd never felt so alone. Without the constant passion that defined our relationship, I looked at my marriage with new eyes. My grandmother and Jennie were right. I'd made a mistake. This dark, humorless Russian had yanked me into his life for no reason other than to be his muse.

I'd had enough. I was suffering, alone with an obsessed man in a strange country. One morning I took his hand and said I was unhappy and wanted a divorce so I could go back to my own life. He tipped his head and looked at me as if I'd woken him from an intense dream. He pulled his hand away, gathered up pages of his handwritten manuscript, and placed them in front of me. "Read this, Anna."

There it was, my idea, spun into gold.

My hand trembled. In my lap was undeniable proof that Alik's artistry was more important than my happiness, more important than our marriage. I looked up at my disheveled and wretched husband and he said, "It's time, Anna. Do it again."

So I did.

How many settings did I dream up in that old bathtub? How many new characters came to life while I was on the bus? But no matter how excited I was with a new plot for his story, I had to wait until he asked for help. If I broke his focus, Alik would scream in anguish. Once he pushed me out the door and I sat in the hall for hours in my thin nightgown, cold and miserable.

He suffered, and so did I. Knowing his gift could only bloom if he was sheltered and placated, I adjusted to his every mood. When he sought my help we shared a day or two of true partnership. Otherwise he was curt with me. Sometimes he was vile. One night, a year and a half after our wedding, we drank a bottle of wine and he pulled me onto his lap. "Do you want to make me happy?" he asked. I said I did. "Then call your sister and have her visit us. I want the two of you in my bed."

I warned him to stop talking, to let go of me. He did neither.

The next morning I went to the embassy and asked the consular general for help. She told me that a divorce in Russia is cheap and easy if both parties are Russian and there is mutual consent. But unless Alik agreed to the divorce, the postponements could take months or years. I brought the paperwork home, and was in the bedroom trying to make sense of the directions when Alik walked in. I said, "We're done. Get yourself another muse. We're getting a divorce."

He grabbed me by the arms and pinned me to the wall, hissing in my face that I was selfish and stupid. I said, "I'm glad you think so. That means you won't miss me, because I'm going whether you sign the papers or not."

Alik pulled me to the kitchen table. He went to the sink and came back with a glass of water for each of us. "Sit Anna," he said. I did as he asked only because I believed I was only hours away from never having him order me around again.

His voice was quiet. "You know I would have been finished with this book by now if you hadn't talked me into the major revision. It is adding months to the re-write."

I had to laugh. "Alik, we both know that if it weren't for me your book would be just another endless, dreary Russian novel that no one in the West would read."

I meant to wound him, and I did. Alik was obsessed with becoming famous in the United States. He had written his book in English, wrestling with every sentence a hundred times over so it would be in the authentic tongue of the audience he was after.

He glared at me. Then a cruel smile came over his face

and he left the kitchen. When he returned he had my passport in his hand. With his eyes steady on mine, he slid it slowly into his pocket.

It felt as if the progress of my life had come to a stop.

"I will give this back when the book is done," he said. "You were right in your critique, Anna. The changes I'm making in the rewrite are critical. The book will be a masterpiece. So even if you don't love me anymore, you owe it to the book to stay and help me finish. We can do it in six months." He closed his eyes. "And when it is done you can go. But I think you will find that once I am free of this book, I will be a different person. A better husband. I will be rich. You will love me again. We will live in Paris with your sister, the three of us together. You will be happier there."

The idea of Alik anywhere near Jennie sent ice to my heart. I said, "I will stay and help you on two conditions."

He laughed and tapped his pocket. "You will stay regardless. But what will inspire you to help me?"

I met his gaze. "First, I will help you as much or as little as you like, if you agree on the life of your brother Sergi that on the first of May you will hand back my passport. Second, if I still want a divorce on that date, you will sign these papers."

He scratched his cheek. "That is only four months, I told you I need six."

"If you want my help, take the deal."

He glared at me for several moments, then nodded.

I put the divorce documents back in the envelope, wrote "May First" on the front and taped it to the side of the dresser so he would see it every day. When I turned around he was standing very close.

"Take off your clothes," he said.

"Leave me alone, Alik."

He grabbed. I fought.

It did not go well for me.

Alik meant to weaken me. Instead he sharpened my hate to a point that would never dull.

I went to the embassy the next day to apply for a new passport. The clerk leaned close, and with her eyes on my bruised neck she said, "It takes up to four months to get a new passport, *lapochka*. Are you sure yours is truly lost? I would have to report that to Interpol, and anyone who tried to use it would be arrested. Even if it's *you*."

Four months. But what if I could get my hands on the original in a week? In a day?

I told her I'd take another look for it. The clerk touched her own throat and said, "I hope you find that passport, and soon!"

I felt the heat of shame on my face.

I left the courthouse and headed to the bank, whispering a thank you to Jennie. Every time Alik and I talked ourselves out of an expense, every time I had come close to telling him about my inheritance, I heard Jennie's "epic mistake" comment in my head and stopped myself. I reasoned that if I had made a terrible mistake, at least I wouldn't have to give up half my fortune in a divorce. Now at least I had one advantage: Alik believed I was a poor artist living on a meager savings account.

I made arrangements to wire in enough money to cover both the divorce and a first class ticket home. I bought a fine leather satchel and filled it with my best drawings and a change of clothes, and kept it in a locker at the airport. I could walk out of the apartment with only the clothes on my back if need be. I could escape the moment I got my passport back.

Alik tripled his efforts to finish the book. He lived on bags of peanuts and endless cups of tea. He slept an hour here and there, sometimes right at his desk. His skin broke out. He rarely bathed. I often heard him weep.

Many a night he woke me, begging for my help. He'd make me toast. He'd tell me he owed his life to me. We'd work on a scene together for hours, and he'd stroke my hair and swear he didn't deserve me. Then later that same day, if I so much as turned on a faucet, he would scream that I was sent from hell to sabotage him with my distractions.

One day in March, as I waited for a bus, I noticed how the people around me were reflected in a shop window. Transparent, we were like ghosts who didn't know we weren't flesh anymore. I put my hand up to gauge where I was in relation to the crowd, and it froze in the air. The woman with her arm up was the saddest ghost of all.

I turned and walked as quickly as I could to the park. I leaned my head against a tree and asked myself what had become of the lively girl from Stella Maris, the happy artist from Paris, the creative cook from Florence? Alik had smothered her. To get her back I would do whatever I had to.

There were six weeks left before Alik would hand back my passport. I checked and rechecked my money. I booked my flight. I gave little gifts to the few friends I'd made.

Then it was five weeks. Then four.

With the deadline approaching I began to panic. What if Alik didn't keep up his end of our agreement? He had trained me to look inside people to read their heart's desire, and I saw his clearly. He believed I had transformed him from a good writer into a great one. I didn't see how he would chance to let me go.

It would all be so easy if he would just die.

Tainted peanuts ... a heart attack ... a stroke.

I would slip my passport out of his pocket, play the sad

widow, then board a plane and sip champagne as I watch Russia disappear from the window.

On April thirtieth Alik walked into our bedroom and announced he was done. He pulled the divorce papers off the dresser, tore them in two, and tumbled onto the bed and slept.

I walked the neighborhoods for hours, steeling myself for the ugliness to come. When I saw him destroy the divorce papers I knew his mind had twisted our agreement from what it was—him giving me back my passport and agreeing to the divorce—to what he wanted: if he finished in four months I would stay with him.

When I walked in the door, Alik was smiling. He had showered and dressed. He took me in his arms, told me he loved me and couldn't have written the book without me. "Our life with Jennie in Paris will be everything we ever wanted!"

I turned my face.

"I'm happy for you," I said. "I know the book will be a success and you will be rich and famous. But I'm bowing out. It's over between us. I already have a plane ticket. In five days I'm going home."

I felt his body stiffen. He whispered in my ear, "No, Anna. You love me."

"I stayed until you finished the rewrite. Now I want a divorce. You made a promise and you will keep it."

Alik let out a sound between a cry and a roar as he threw me against the wall. My head hit the metal hinge of the door, and I sunk to the floor.

"I put myself through the agonies of the damned for you," he shouted, "I did it all for you!"

My hand was covered in blood from touching my head. I held it out and said, "This is how you love me?"

"I swear it to God, Anna. I will kill you before I let you go."

"And these are the words of a loving husband! Here's a better idea, Alik. Just kill yourself!"

He stormed out the door.

I crawled to the bathroom. Holding a cold, wet towel to my scalp I searched through the clothes Alik had left on the floor. No passport.

Alik's threat to kill me hung in the air as I pulled my backpack from under the bed. Like a fool I had kept my part of the bargain, and what good had it done me? I would have to hide out in a rented flat in Strelna or Metallostroy and hire a lawyer to get my passport and secure a divorce.

I tried to move quickly, but felt as if I were immersed in a waist-high lake of gel. I couldn't remember which drawer had my underthings. I headed to the kitchen when I meant to go to the bath, lost in my own apartment. I let out a sob of terror. My brain couldn't be trusted just when I needed to be at my best. Would I even be safe on the street? What if I collapsed? What if Alik came home before I could get out? My eye landed on the milk bottle we used for loose change. I emptied the coins into a drawer. If Alik came through the door I would … *what?* I had never hit anyone in my living life. What if I was too weak to knock him out? What if adrenaline made me swing it so hard as to kill him?

I rinsed the blood from my hair and toweled it dry as best I could. Fifty minutes had passed since Alik had left and it was long past time for me to go. I had my coat on when there was a knock on the door.

Two policemen. I knew enough Russian to make out "husband" and "accident." They took me to the hospital. The doctor patted my shoulder and told me Alik had stepped in front of a bus. He was dead.

She led me to the body. As I looked down at my husband

the doctor handed me a plastic bag that contained his wedding ring, his wallet, and my passport.

I had wished him dead, and now he was.

I had told him to kill himself, and maybe he had.

Four days later, moments before I left our apartment for the last time, I took the milk bottle off the dresser and put it in the trash.

Annie

I stood up, leashed the dogs, and took them for a long walk.

I knew two things: One, I hated Alik with every fiber of my being, and two, Leandra was right. Annie was both Nin and Allura.

11/5/15
Dog Diary
Thursday, 5:00 a.m.

Dear Annie,

If wishing a person dead actually worked I'd be the only one left in my office. Freeways would be empty. The world would be without telemarketers, bosses, and politicians. The Plips, Pliptits and Plipettos would cancel each other out.

It doesn't work like that.

You were very brave. You dealt with an impossible situation with great honor, and you have nothing to feel guilty about. I only wish I had an equally riveting personal history to offer in exchange, but while you were in Baltic museums having transcendental sex with handsome strangers, I was sticking to an eight-mile radius of work to home, with an occasional basketball game thrown in. You were learning to flambé in Florence, and I was ordering a pizza to be delivered because it was too much trouble to go out and get one. Yet somehow, even after all you've been through, you still believe in love. And me? Even when perfection is in my arms, there is no flicker in my heart.

Ah, but murderous thoughts? Yup, that's right up my alley. Believe me, Annie, they mean nothing. Not a day goes by that millions of women don't think, "When my husband is dead I will …."

You know I have my share of well-honed theories regarding the supernatural abilities of redheaded women. But even in my wildest imaginings on the subject, those powers fall short of getting rid of difficult husbands just by wishing it so. You are not responsible for Alik's death. You breathed life into his novel and into him, and in return he abused you.

He is not the victim.

I have to leave for work, but I want you to know how glad I am that you are keeping Sparks and Eddie on your list. I was afraid I would lose you for a month. Now I can look forward to reading about the adventures of all three dogs.

Daniel

P.S. Thank you for explaining the pantry mystique to me. My meal preparation is limited to peeling back the film before I microwave my dinner.

———————

I knew I had shortchanged her. She had revealed more to me in her last note than in all the previous ones put together, and what did I offer in trade? *Don't feel guilty for wishing your would-be-killer dead.*

Working with Oliver was so gruesome for both of us that morning that by noon we tersely agreed to call it a week and start back fresh on Monday. I watched him head straight for Cameron's office and thought, *fuck it*. Those two could braid each other's hair if they wanted, just as long as I was the agent on the contract.

I sat down with chapter eight of *The Blue Season* open in front of me, but it was a different mystery taking over my thoughts.

Once Nin and Allura broke free of the abusive men in their lives, they sought out *my* characters for romantic purposes. But did it follow that Annie had such an interest in me? We enjoyed writing to each other. We even flirted a little, but the only time she had actually laid eyes on me I was a twitching lunatic who shoved her into a pane of beveled glass.

God help me. I was the *second* man to knock her head into a door.

So no. The romantic aspect Annie used in her stories didn't mirror her true feelings for me. They had to be the kind of red herring smart writers use to throw the reader off.

When I got home I would have to pull out the stories and dig deeper.

I looked down to read a few sentences of *The Blue Season*, but before I made my next note in the margin, realization struck.

"Annie was foreshadowing," I whispered.

Nin gave Blend priceless pearls to use to buy a ship. Allura gave Todor the painting that would finance their future. And one day soon, Annie would give me Alik's manuscript.

That night her drawing was a simple cup of coffee next to a laptop.

11/5/15
Dog Diary
Thursday, 2:15 p.m.

Dear Daniel,

Thank you for putting up with my wounded conscience.

I will move to the Flood mansion tonight. Clarissa says that George becomes inconsolable when he sees suitcases come out, so my first job is to take him for a long walk so his parents can pack their bags and hide them in the garage. Then it's up to me to divert him in the morning when the airport limo comes to pick them up.

I won't be putting the dog reports directly into the diary this month, but rather emailing them to both you and Clarissa. Know that I will spend as much time as always on walks and in the park with Sparks and Eddie, but at George's house I can tap away on their stories poolside, sipping iced tea in a gazebo surrounded by jasmine bushes.

Not that your kitchen isn't lovely.

Annie

P.S. The white eggplant you gave me has been transformed into a parmesan dish that is now in your refrigerator. Preheat your oven to 350 degrees and bake for forty minutes. I am glad you have film-peeling experience, as you will need to put it to use before placing the pan on the rack.

––––––––––––

I felt terrible. Sooner or later Annie would realize she

should have just sent me her late husband's manuscript from her village in Ireland. I would have said yay or nay—end of story. Instead she traveled across an ocean and a continent, posed as a dog walker, wrote me stories, became my confidante, and even made me dinner. And it all worked against her. Now I was the last agent on planet Earth who should be reading that manuscript. How objective could I be about a bastard who choked my friend, threw her against the wall, and made a show of putting her passport in his pocket before he forced himself on her?

The only thing I liked about Alik was the fact that he was dead.

XI
Cured?

I met Victoria and her two sisters at La Paella for drinks and tapas. After the first pitcher of sangria the three women took on a teenage vibe, whispering in ears, squealing at my jokes, and checking other tables to make sure they were attracting attention. After the second pitcher, family legends were shared that cast "Vics" as a sister who was as bossy as she was mean.

"If I wanted to borrow her coat for church I had to agree to make her bed and clean out the litter box for a month!"

"And remember the swing?" said the other. "We spent an entire Saturday putting together a swing for Vics, climbed that tree over and over, got rope burns from the knots, and she wouldn't put her book down to even come out to *look* at it!"

I smiled, nodded, and chalked it up to jealousy, as neither sister had Victoria's looks, brains or success.

Then, as if on cue, all three women turned their attention on me.

"Where was your mom born?" "How did she meet your dad?" "Who do you take after?" "Do you have a picture of your parents?"

These ladies were on a mission. I was an ethnic pot of stew, and they wanted to know the key ingredients. They weren't quite drunk enough to come right out and ask my racial origins, and I thoroughly enjoyed playing innocent of their true intentions while thwarting them at every turn. "My mom was from San Francisco, my dad from Cincinnati," I said. "They met in Phoenix where they both taught high school. I don't have a picture of them with me, but," I pulled out my phone, "here is one of my sister."

Their bubbling chatter became hushed amazement, and I thought: *That's right, girls. This is what can happen when you venture beyond the blonde.*

As we parted on the street I gave Victoria a quick kiss and promised to meet her for lunch on Monday.

Sunday morning, as I ate the last peach from the farmer's market, I again gave myself kudos for conversing with the red-headed vendor as fluently as I would with any other friendly stranger. Even my hand held steady as it accepted change from her fingers. *Major* leap forward. Especially since the vegetables, the open air, and the straw under my feet made the atmosphere so particularly medieval that I half-expected the Sheriff of Nottingham to show up.

Well done, I thought, then, *wait a minute!*

I suspended my efforts to clean the last of the flesh off the furrowed surface of my peach pit.

I was fine with that vendor because I knew she couldn't bewitch me. But does that mean I'm cured? Or does it mean that another redhead has already filled that bill?

XII

Dear George

11/9/15
Dog Diary
Monday, 6:30 a.m.

Hi Annie,

The extent of your magic is not limited to your stories. The eggplant dish was easily the most delicious meal I have ever eaten inside my house. Possibly anywhere. You have opened my eyes to a vegetable I have sanctimoniously avoided for forty-two years.

Hope you had a good first weekend at the mansion. I will be interested to hear how Sparks and Eddie get along with George. The email address I open without fail is: danielashe@ floodgatemedia.com

Daniel

Monday, 11/9/15
From: adoherty77@yahoo.com
To: Clarissa and Daniel
Subject: Dog Diary, 4:00 p.m.
Dear Clarissa and Daniel,

While George wept to see his parents go, he bravely ate a good breakfast, accepted many hugs and kisses, and had several walks around the neighborhood. Sunday we took a ride to the beach where he was much admired, and today we went to Daniel's house, met Sparks and Eddie, and the four of us walked to the dog park.

George was an instant sensation. He sat near my legs as one by one every dog came over for an introduction. I overheard a Great Dane ask George what he thought about the dog park. George looked around and said, "A lovely note in the song of the universe." This answer was whispered to all the other dogs, and they thought him very wise.

"I have a problem with my person!" blurted BiBi the Maltese. "Can you help me, George?"

"Harrumph!" said Winston the bulldog. "First he will tell me where to find my lost tail."

A ruckus started. Every dog wanted George to solve their problems. I whispered in his ear that it would be up to him to think of a way to help them all.

On the ride home George came up with a plan we both considered brilliant. He will write an advice column!

We immediately set up a blog. As I posted the invitation to animals to submit their problems, I asked George, "What about humans? Can you take letters from them as well?"

"I can," he said.

Requests for sage advice have already trickled in. If you go to www.corgiadvisor.com you will see photos of George and Leonard and read the first letters.

I think giving him this job has taken his mind off missing you a wee bit.

Annie

I clicked on the link. Up came a picture of the back of George's head, and between his great pricked ears was a "Dear George" letter on a computer screen. In the right corner of the blog was a thumbnail photo of "Leonard the Lizard." Below was a brief invitation to the animal and human kingdom, followed by these letters.

Dear George,

In my past life I was an Irish writer, famous for my clever plays, infamous for my outrageous lifestyle. I was as well-known for my lovers as for my wit; but I paid for my sins with jail time, poor health, and a ruined reputation. I can deal with being a house cat this time around; it is my surroundings that are unbearable. I was once renowned for my aesthetic sensibilities, and yet here I am, shut in with a hideous décor my humans describe as "country." Well, this ill-painted trash does look like it belongs in a barn. Was I really reincarnated, or is this hell?

    Ernest

Dear Ernest,

"Housecat" is three tiers above "playwright," so you are advancing nicely! Your job now is to show humans how to live and enjoy the moment. So sit on a lap and purr. It is your chance to teach the one thing that you are better equipped for than anyone else I know: *The Importance of Being.* Ernest.

Dear George,

I was born into a puppy mill. Mom was too exhausted to teach us much, and I've been making some stupid mistakes since my humans brought me home. Help!

    Larry

Dear Larry,

Establish a place for yourself on your human's bed. No matter what they say, they really want you there. I know this because I sleep between my parents, and I hear them brag all the time that I am the most effective birth control they have ever used.

Dear George,

When my dog is in the house and sees a dog walking outside, she barks and barks, but the dog outside never barks back. When my dog is the one on a walk, we hear barking from the dogs inside the houses we pass, but my girl never barks back. Why?

Susie

Dear Susie,

When we have a human on a leash, we are, quite simply, too cool to bark.

Dear George,

How do I get some respect around here? They walk me twice a day, feed me, and pet me a few moments when they get home, but that's it. I focus on them one hundred percent, and want more than a one percent return. What can I do? They used to fawn all over me before I grew up.

Arnie

Dear Arnie,

Refuse to poop.

"Arnie didn't poop!" your mom will say after the walk, and an hour later your dad will take you for another walk, come home with the same news, and your mom will get on the floor and rub your tummy and feed you chicken. Then your dad will throw a tennis ball for half an hour in the hope that exercise will solve the problem. When they get tired, go ahead and put your muzzle on their knees and look mournful, and you'll get a total body rubdown. When you finally do poop there will be great rejoicing and tug of war games and Snausages.

Tuesday, 11/10/15
From: clarissaandpeter@gmail.com
To: Annie and Daniel
Subject: George

Annie, you are a hoot! How did you know that George sleeps right between us? He does!

We had an easy flight, and our apartment here is charming. Peter is just reading your blog and thinks you're deep in the Bordeaux. Ha! Hope all is well there.

Love,

Clarissa.

Some sleuth I am. Annie had pegged George to become an advice guru the moment she saw the spire shape of the Taj Mahal on his head. She tried to clue me in with talk about corgis and their insight into all living things, and still I didn't see that his story line would be The Wise One.

Tuesday, 11/10/15
From: danielashe@floodgatemedia.com
To: Annie
Subject: The Importance of...

Dear Annie,

How fortunate for me that Clarissa uses the 'reply to all' option to respond to you. I'm not sure she got the Oscar Wilde reference, but I nearly fell off my chair. She is right about one thing. You *are* a "hoot."

Looking forward to reading more from the Ann Landers of the dog world.

Daniel

Tuesday, 11/10/15
From: adoherty77@yahoo.com
To: Daniel and Clarissa
Subject: Dog Diary, Tuesday, 8:00 p.m.

Dear Daniel and Clarissa,

Clarissa, I plucked up my nerve and ordered my first meal from the delivery restaurant. Seafood bisque and a Thai chicken salad. The man who came to the door refused a tip, saying that you had an agreement and it was all included. Very generous. Thank you! Everything was delicious.

Elsewise, all here is well. George is splendid, and I am very much in love with him.

Annie

P.S. Am attaching a couple of letters to George, but there are dozens more to see on corgiadvisor.com

Dear George,

I'm new in this house, but my mom makes such a big deal over me that Dad is getting jealous. Every morning she will hold me and kiss me and say, "You are my sweetheart. Mommy loves her little baby boy, yes she does. You are the handsomest boy in the whole world and you are Mommy's best baby." Then she turns me over and kisses my belly. She sometimes puts my whole paw in her mouth and says she could eat me I'm so gorgeous. Of course, I like the attention, but I can see Dad is feeling left

out big time. He always says, "Why don't you do that to me?"
She snorts and shakes her finger at him. But gosh, why doesn't
Mom say and do the same things to him?
   Cooper

Dear Cooper,
   Your mom knows that if she kisses daddy's belly neither
one of them will get to work on time.

Dear George,
   I am a human and have always wondered about the names
dogs use for each other. My dog's name is Elroy, but since read-
ing your column I realize that there's a lot of communicating
going on between dogs, and I bet other dogs call him something
besides Elroy. Right?
   Mike

Dear Mike,
   Absolutely! Most of us get our nicknames from a signature
move or smell. For instance, I have a friend name Bo whose
human immediately snatches up his droppings. Bo turns
around to admire what he's done, and looks completely lost
when he doesn't know where to find it. We call him Little Bo
Poop. My friend Sparks is known as Trips Humans on the
Stairs. My buddy Eddie is known among us as Double Duty.
   As you know, your boy Elroy keeps lifting his leg even when
zippo comes out. That's why we call him Faux Pee.
   Our nicknames change with our circumstances. A few
weeks after my litter was born, everyone called my mom Teats
a' Sagging. Now it's back to Pretty Girl.

By the way, her name for me is Worth the Effort. But you know how moms are.

Dear George,

Once or twice a week my humans kick me off their bed. I know what they're doing, so why can't I just stick around and wait it out?

Ed

Dear Ed,

Be proactive! Don't wait to get kicked off the bed. As soon as your humans sidle up to each other, move to the far corner like I do. No hurt feelings. When they are done, hop on their bellies to demand some attention. Yes, it knocks the air out of them, but it makes the point that you are not to be ignored. Mom will stroke you for several minutes.

(Dad will already be sleeping.)

Wednesday, 11/11/15
From: danielashe@floodgatemedia.com
To: Annie
Subject: My day
Dear Annie,

I find myself logging on to my computer for the sole purpose of checking up on the latest from George. In order to keep the original dog diary complete, I print out your email and website postings, punch holes, and click them into the binder. So glad you are helping George find his true potential.

Work without Peter at the helm should mean I get to slack off, but in reality I am spending endless hours across the table from the young man I told you about. I do not like him as a person, and it's obvious he feels the same of me. We are now more than halfway through editing his manuscript, and I keep my eye on the prize. If everything goes according to plan, his book will be a sensation.

So why, when I think of it hitting the market, does my chest feel like it's full of thin glass bottles rattling against each other? Is it because I'm excited? Or am I afraid that I will be shattered if something goes wrong?

I know I am pinning too many of my hopes on this character. I don't trust him, he has no loyalty to me, and now that my dream is within my grasp, I'm half-convinced that something will come along to make it disappear. It doesn't help that another agent at Floodgate, a weasel by the name of Cameron, wants to steal my client away. Yesterday, when my author didn't show up, I took a walk down the hall and saw him sitting in Cameron's office. I burst in the door, and through bared fake-smiling teeth, said, "Hey, it's time to get started. Thanks, Cameron for keeping him company."

If my writer decided to jump to Cameron, Peter would fire me for two reasons: 1) I was unable to meet the author's expectations, and 2) he'd fear I would find a way to take revenge on Cameron at the expense of the company.

Remember my take on murderous thoughts?

Sorry to ramble and rant.

Daniel

P.S. Now that you have enlightened me to the Irish sense of doom, I have to wonder if my current worries are a result of contagion. Is your Irish-ness rubbing off on the furniture, and then onto me?

XIII
Portal

Victoria and I became lunch partners. I watched her rake croutons off salads, and she watched me scarf down thick sandwiches and fries. One day, as she eyed the steak hoagie in my hand, she told me she did her cardio in the morning and worked out with weights every night when she got home. I said, "If we end up together, are you going to whip me into better shape?"

She tipped her head. "It would be my pleasure."

"Uh oh."

"Well, you do spend too many hours sitting down every day. A little running, some upper body work, cutting out fast carbs, and you'd feel a lot better. We could have a lot of fun exercising together."

"Carbs? Like no more beer?"

"Well, no one would begrudge you a beer on a Saturday night!"

I smiled weakly and heard an Irish accent in my head say *She must be a formidable creature to behold!*

When I got home, above Annie's short note was a drawing of Sparks, George, and Blend leaping into a black, oval hole.

11/12/15
Dog Diary
Thursday, 3:30 p.m.

Dear Daniel,

I have been thinking of your last letter. I am very happy that you are confiding in me. I hope your author doesn't betray you. That Cameron you work with is a snake in the grass. I have a very bad feeling about him.

By the time you read this I will have reported on the dog walk on email.

Annie

P.S. I'm not leaving any "Irish-ness" on the furniture, you wanker, though you should be so lucky.

Friday, 11/13/15
From: adoherty77@yahoo.com.
To: Daniel and Clarissa
Subject: A new partnership

When George and I entered Daniel's house, Sparks was lying on her side and panting. She told me she had just tumbled home after taking an unknown portal.

"Unknown portal?" I asked.

"I was on my way to my ship when I noticed a perfectly oblong, black hole across from my usual corridor. It looked very much like the mouth of the Rangonian sea monster that once tried to suck up my ship, so naturally I stepped into it."

"Sparks, I don't know if you are brave or just foolish!" I said. She stayed silent until I tapped my foot and asked, "So, where did this portal take you?"

She lifted her head to look up at me. "I found myself in the future. There I was, as best as I could tell, two human years from now—still of fine figure by the way—but everything else had changed." She fell silent and closed her eyes.

"Go on then, what did you see?"

"I saw you getting married," she said and slit her eyes to watch my reaction. "You were in an ancient limestone building."

"That would be the monastery back home!"

"And there were three wise old women who helped you dress."

"My grandmother Rose and her sisters."

"There was a portly young man in brown robes waiting for you to walk down the aisle."

"That would be Brother Thumb Sucker, my childhood friend. He would perform the ceremony." I bit my lip and leaned forward, "What did the groom look like?"

"Humans!" Sparks snorted. "Who cares what he looked like? He smelled like he would love you forever. What more could you want?"

"Well," I said, "did he … *smell* … like a smart and gentle person with a good sense of humor?"

"That he did."

"What else did you see?"

"I saw Daniel. He had three books on the bestseller list and a movie deal. He will be a huge success."

"That's grand!" I said, but she turned her head away and moaned.

"Sparks, what's the matter?"

She got to her feet, and with a silent wave of her muzzle directed me to follow her to a separate room in order to speak to me in private.

"You know I've become very fond of George," she said, and kept her face averted in the unmistakable way of a female in love. "And when I looked for him in the future, I saw that he would no longer be coming to the park with us." She took a deep breath and sighed a sigh as long as a dachshund.

"Sparks, it's true that when I stop living at George's house I won't be bringing him over here anymore."

A cry caught in her throat. I had to come up with an idea, and fast. "Listen, what about your parallel worlds to the future and to the sea—can't you invite George to go with you on adventures?"

She pondered this for a few moments. "I tried to interest Eddie into taking a voyage once, but he said his legs were too long for the deck of a ship. That wouldn't be a problem for George, now would it?"

"No. He's only two inches taller than you are, and heavy as a stone. Let's go to the park and you can talk it over with him. If he agrees and finds he likes it, it doesn't matter where he is in the world, he can always travel with you with just the wanting of it."

Sparks leapt against my legs for a hug, we went to the park, and she and George huddled together and made plans.

XIV
The Lord

Sunday, 11/15/15
From: clarissaandpeter@gmail.com
To: Annie and Daniel
Subject: Merry Olde England

Dear Annie,

I am so proud of George! I always knew how smart he was, and now he has a way of proving it to the world. Once I'm home, I am going to throw you a party. You are such a blessing in my life. I want you to meet all my friends, but especially my brother Drew. He has been crazy for redheads his whole life.

I am alone today, but tomorrow we're going to leave London and drive to Bath.

Daniel, Peter says to give him a call. He wants to know how it's going with the book you're editing.

Clarissa

Wednesday, 11/18/15
From: adoherty77@yahoo.com
To: Clarissa and Daniel
Subject: Dog Diary, 6:00 p.m.
Hello!

Clarissa, I hope you enjoyed Bath. Lovely town, terrible tasting water.

Everything here is grand. Tomorrow I will make sure the cleaners work hard all day.

Sparks and Eddie and George are best friends now who compare notes on what they learn from the others at the dog park. They often amaze me with all the past life connections they uncover. After George and I got home I asked him if any of the dogs remembered me from the past. He paused a moment and said, "Why be concerned with that, Annie girl?"

"I was just wondering."

He sat down and said, "Eddie and Sparks and I have talked a good deal on this subject of late, and we agree that it is best for humans to concentrate on being human. It is so hard to get that right. If you fail, you will come back as a wild animal and be forced to live by tooth and claw." He looked to the sky, "Ah, but if you can get it right, you could come back as someone's beloved dog. There is no higher clarity, no more noble a life, because the love in a dog's heart is the purest of all."

There was nothing for me to say. I kissed his forehead and put my arms around him for a good long while.

Clarissa, how fortunate you are to live with that one.

Annie

———————

George's website seemed to double in readership by the hour. Dozens of new tongue-in-cheek letters appeared daily. George answered math questions, historical questions, and even dealt with marital relations:

Dear George,

My human is quite the actress in the bedroom if you get my drift. Being a parrot, I naturally learned to imitate her verbal performances to a T. She and her husband always got a kick out of my imitations at the breakfast table, until last week when I shrieked, "Oh Pedro, Pedro, Pedro!"

Her husband's name is Auggie.

Now I live in the laundry room. Help!

Calvin

Dear Calvin,

Humans pretend to mate for life. As you have sadly learned, they get very upset when that boat gets rocked. The good news is you have a life expectancy that will outlive the marriage. Try to stay sane in the laundry room, and I predict that by spring, you will be perched attractively, front and center, at their "We're Divorcing" garage sale.

Dear George,

My human dad, who is a large male, defers to even the smallest female! I don't have a human mom yet, but he is looking. When he invites prospective mates over he walks behind them from room to room, he doesn't sit until they sit, and he serves them food before he takes any for himself. He has no alpha male qualities! I'm so ashamed I'm thinking of running away. He hasn't landed a mate yet, but when he does, will she be my pack leader?

Toby

Dear Toby

Yes, and a special word of caution. Don't nip her. We believe this is the reason so many of us have our bollocks removed.

He came up with solutions to inter-species discord.

Dear George,

I used to be a very happy dog, but then my parents brought home a kitten. I admit I was jealous and wasn't very nice to her. I would position myself so she couldn't get by me to get to our parents. I ate her food. I snarled at her if she got near my bed or my toys.

Well, now that kitten is a cat and she hates me. She sits on the armrests of the sofa and if I trot by she swipes my head with her vicious nails. Sometimes she hurls herself from the top of the refrigerator onto my back with all her claws digging into me. I never know when it's going to happen, and it's creeping me out. She is evil and I'd like to get rid of her. Got any ideas?

Scratched

Dear Scratched,

Cats are killing machines. She would love to cut one eye out of your head and leave the other in so you could watch her bat around the first. You do *not* want to fight her.

While alleged to have nine lives, permanent disappearances have been reported as a consequence of their one fatal flaw: *Curiosity.* Bide your time. Sooner or later someone is going to leave an outside door ajar, and when that happens, nudge it wide open and tell her you saw a dead fish on your walk three streets over. If that doesn't work, chase her out and into the next town if possible. She could be gone for days, or even forever if you're lucky.

Unfortunately there is something called an "indoor-outdoor" cat. If she is one of those, I'm afraid you're screwed.

He even gave out advice on grammar.

Dear George,

My parents used to say words like "park" and "walk" and "car" in casual conversation, and naturally I responded by barking and jumping at them and running circles by the door. Then I noticed they started s-p-e-l-l-i-n-g those same wonderful words as if they had forgotten how to put the sounds together. Soon as I heard that rat-a-tat cadence I went wild! Inexplicably they stopped in favor of sign language—like wagging two fingers upside-down for a walk, or putting their hands at ten and two like they were steering a car. Even easier to understand! A couple of days ago they gave that up and now they pull out their little pocket devices and tap on them to let me know it's time for me to rev up for an outing. They are adorable! My question is: Why do they keep changing the signals that it's time for all of us to leave the house together?

Franklin

Dear Franklin,

I believe it's to encourage brain growth. My parents are trying to sharpen my comprehensive skills in a similar fashion. Their newest technique is to hum to get each other's attention, then make their eyebrows go up and down while their eyes slide to the door. You're right. Humans are very entertaining! I can't wait to see what they come up with next. Whatever it is, I'll be there at the door to insist they take me along.

But the letter that sparked an online war was this one:

Dear George,

Recently my parents "found the lord," whatever that means, and things have gotten a lot duller around here. What's going on?

Dear Frankie,

While you and I know we have as big a piece of The All inside us as every other creature, most humans believe there is some ethereal "father" in charge who elevates their species above all the rest. Our top canine scientists have concluded the reason for this delusion is the oversized human brain. It allows in so many distractions, cares, and woes as to deafen it to the voice of The All.

There are some who can take the massive stimulation. Others feel too burdened, and they transfer their cares and responsibilities to this celestial father in the sky.

Notice how your parents bow their heads in supplication. This is because they believe this all-powerful dad needs to be thanked for every bite of food. They ask him for favors. Beg his forgiveness.

I know, Frankie, it's a lot to wrap your mind around, so let me give you a relatable scenario.

Think back to our time in obedience school. Do something right and you earn a treat; do something wrong and you have your leash yanked. Remember how dead boring the "long sit" was? No running or jumping, no barking or joy? Well, having "the lord" in charge is their version of the long sit. The expectation is that such good behavior means that one day—when they die—they will finally get their reward.

You read that right. They think that by denying the flesh the glorious gifts it could fully enjoy in life, they will somehow get an even better deal when they are less than a wisp of smoke.

What can you do to help?

Rest your body on your human's body. Look with all your

love into their eyes. If they are not tapping on their phones or watching their televisions, they just might understand and savor for a moment that *this is it*. Eternal love. Here and now.

Friday, 11/20/15
From: danielashe@floodgatemedia.com
To: Annie
Subject: Now I get it

Good grief Annie. George isn't the Druid, you are! Did you leave Ireland on your own volition, or did the clergy toss you off the Cliffs of Moher?

Since the night of my bog girl dream I half-suspected that—thanks to the ancient magic in their veins—redheads were impervious to human evolution and moral conventions.

This letter of yours doesn't convince me otherwise.

Daniel The Wanker

Friday, 11/20/15
From: adoherty77@yahoo.com
To: The Wanker
Subject: Your suspicions about redheads?

All true.

Annie

Friday, 11/20/15
From: danielashe@floodgatemedia.com
To: Annie
Subject: I knew it!

Listen, are you lonely rattling around in the mansion? Perhaps I could come over, or you could come here, and we could walk the dogs together for a change?

Daniel

Friday, 11/20/15
From: adoherty77@yahoo.com
To: Daniel
Subject: Friday and all alone

Dear Daniel,

There are three bathtubs and five showers in this house. Were they all mine I would invite homeless folk in for a good clean up and serve them beans on toast. (Another delicious breakfast staple, why does no one eat it here?)

But this is not my home, and I'm glad of it. I close the bedroom door tight, wrap my arms around George, and pretend I'm sleeping in a two-room cottage instead of a twenty-room mansion. I looked forward to the cleaning people bustling about, but they went about their business without a hint that they were willing to chat.

(Now I know why the lady next door gives the pool bloke the nod!)

So, yes, I'd be delighted for some company. Seeing as tomorrow is Saturday, perhaps you'd like to come over for a swim?

Annie

Friday, 11/20/15
From: danielashe@floodgatemedia.com
To: Annie
Subject: With bells on!

I will be there at 1:00 p.m.

Daniel

P.S. No one eats beans on toast here because, well … yuck.

XV
Creek Something-or-Other

Friday night I took Victoria to an Indian restaurant where we clinked our glasses of mango *lassi* and toasted, "To us." She was very interested in how things were going with Oliver, and outlined for me the steps I needed to take to put together a successful business plan for The Daniel Ashe Literary Agency. I was sold. "You're hired!" I told her.

Before the meal was over she made two attempts to talk about marriage, which I deflected from force of habit.

At her door I declined her invitation to spend the night, citing an early morning appointment with a prospective client (technically true if I could convince Annie to write a Cap'n Sparks storybook). When I heard the words leave my mouth I shocked even myself, and Victoria gave me a you've-got-to-be-kidding look. I took her in my arms and gave her a lingering kiss. Then I said, "Meet me Sunday morning for a run and I'll take you for breakfast anywhere you like."

At 6:00 a.m. I walked the dogs in the soft, quiet air that is unique to Saturdays, sensing an unusual satisfaction with all things. Painful as it was to work with Oliver, *The Blue Season* was close to being fully edited and would soon be sent to the publishing gods with my name attached as agent. How long would it take for that first call? What kind of delirium would follow as the bidding war began? Or was I deluding myself, and the book was not the breakthrough I thought it was? No, no. The book had it all: a fresh use of language to excite the literati and a story that put thrill seekers on a bullet for the ride of their lives.

So it was no wonder I felt good, but the reason I felt *great* was because I was finally going to see Annie. I don't know where I got the nerve to invite myself over, as persistence in the face of previous rejection was a new one for me, but I was glad it worked.

As I stripped down for my shower I discussed my options with the dogs. "So guys, what will I say to Annie? Should I be a good guy and ask to see the manuscript her dickwad husband wrote? Or will I leave him out of the conversation entirely and just enjoy the day?"

They remained silent on the subject, and I decided to stop over-thinking. I would just go to the mansion and let our conversation take a natural course.

I put on a pair of black slacks, a pale blue linen shirt, and then stuffed a towel and swim trunks into my gym bag. I walked the dogs again. When it was finally time to leave I felt I was forgetting something. Striding through my townhouse did nothing to jog my memory, so I grabbed the gym bag and drove to the hills.

Flowers! I slapped the steering wheel. Why didn't I think to buy a box of chocolates or a cake, something to hand to Annie when she opened the door? Now there was no time left. Cursing myself for being a social moron, I pulled in front of the mansion and started walking toward the giant red doors.

A woman stepped out and shouted over George's very loud bark; "Hallo! Come in."

I stood still. *Is that Annie?*

She was waving me in and I forced myself forward, wondering if my memory was playing tricks. Her hair was swept up with a pearly clip. She was wearing a lavender sundress that showed off admirable proportions that I hadn't guessed at before, and I pride myself on having superb mental x-ray vision. As I got closer I saw her light tan was really thousands of tiny freckles covering her arms and legs.

She smiled, put both hands around my forearm, and I almost lost my balance. I'd been giving redheads such a wide berth for twenty years, that having her touch me in such a familiar way startled me by how wonderful it felt.

"Good t' see y' here. Come in," she said.

This was the moment I should have handed her something. Instead I just stared, still in shock from the touch, but more so from how different she looked. This Annie wasn't an elf at all. Again, I noticed she wore no makeup, only now I understood why. Annie had pink cheeks, rose colored lips, and dark auburn brows and lashes that framed her astonishing green eyes. Her palette was so luminous it would have been a sin against nature to cover it with anything from a tube.

"Thanks for having me over," I said.

"Follow me."

She headed through the round marble foyer and down a long hall. There might have been museum quality art on either side of me, but nothing could drag my eyes away from her movements in that dress. I was absurdly happy to have this lovely, barefoot Irish woman all to myself for the afternoon. It seemed I'd been waiting for this for years.

One step into the kitchen and I stopped short. There was a man sitting at the counter.

"Daniel, this is Drew, Clarissa's brother."

My smile dissolved. I stepped forward and shook his hand.

Money. From the artful haircut to his hand-stitched Italian shoes, this guy was covered in it. Equally irritating was the fact that he was absurdly handsome, in that obvious blonde and dimpled chin sort of way.

"Well," I said, forcing the smile back, "I didn't know Annie had company today."

"I just got into town," he said, his voice so professionally trained that I half-expected him to turn camera left and say, "Now for the weather."

He looked at Annie. "Imagine my surprise to find this pretty little redhead in the kitchen instead of my Amazon sister! I am not disappointed, quite the contrary," he winked at her. "I just wish Clarissa had told me she was going to London, though from what Annie says it was quite last minute. I knew Peter was going, and I thought I'd surprise Sis with a visit for a week or so."

"Ah," I said, despising him for the wink, "Well it's nice to meet you. Where did you drive in from?"

"Monterey. I'll be here for a few days on some business, then I'm heading to Mexico to take a look at some granite for a remodel I'm doing on my kitchen. If it's as beautiful as the photos, I'll seal the deal and head back home."

Again I felt my smile fade. "Oh, are you staying here?"

Annie was placing glasses of lemonade in front of us. "Drew will stay in his usual room," she said. "We just talked t' Clarissa on speaker and she said, 'Annie, you can tell him t' shoo,' and I said *I* could vacate and go back home and Drew could look after George."

Drew nodded, "And my sister said, 'Are you kidding? My brother is a *man*. I need you, Annie from Ireland, to take care of my baby dog and my house!'"

They smiled at each other and it felt like a cold steel ball landed in my gut.

Drew drank down his lemonade and put the glass in the

sink. "Daniel, it was great to meet you. I have some errands to run this afternoon. Annie, sorry I have to leave, but I should be back around seven or seven-thirty. Do you want to have dinner together?" He looked to me. "Will you still be here?"

"Probably not."

"Daniel is going to be here for at least the afternoon. Perhaps I can convince him t' stay for dinner."

Drew picked up his car keys, "Then maybe I'll see you both later. Have fun. The pool looks very inviting. You lucked out with such a warm day for November." He walked out the kitchen door and turned to wave before stepping into his Porsche.

"So … that was unexpected," I said.

Annie took her time moving her eyes away from the driveway. "Aye. I feel like I should be leavin' but Clarissa made me promise t' "hold down the fort," which I'm thinkin' comes from your General Custer making a few soldiers stay behind when he went off t' slaughter the poor Indians."

"That's about right," I said, feeling my smile return.

"But then Drew said something t' Clarissa that I never heard before. He said, 'If you want, I can 'get the hell out a' Dodge.'"

I nodded. "Ah, that one is very Wild West. There was a major gunfight going to take place in Kansas in a town called Dodge. Everyone knew it was going to be a bloodbath, so even today, when someone thinks they ought to get away pronto, they say they are going to 'get the hell out of Dodge.'"

Annie walked over to her tote bag and pulled out a steno pad. "I write all your military and cowboy sayings down," she said and ran her finger over a column. "Here, listen to these three: 'Bite the bullet,' 'Armed t' the teeth,' and 'Don't shoot off your mouth.'" She looked up at me. "Now why do y' think

Americans are obsessed with having weapons between their lips?"

I tapped my forehead. "You know, I never thought of it that way. Maybe dentists started those sayings to get more business." I stood next to her to look at the list, bending low enough to pick up a faint scent of spring flowers. I saw entries like "Get along little doggie," and "Take the bull by the horns." I said, "You could add 'Get off your high horse.'"

"No sir, that one belongs t' Ireland. We say it anytime someone acts like a royal Brit."

Annie looked up and our eyes met. There it was: that wedge of brown in her iris. And this time I realized it wasn't a flaw. It was a *beauty mark.*

"People use idioms everywhere," she said, "but this is different. Here it's as if all these sophisticated L.A. types pick a minute here and there to put on a folksy act, like there's a director shouting 'Action!' and everyone steps into character. 'Easy peasy,' they say, and, 'Now you're cooking with gas,' and, 'let's chew the fat.' The problem is I keep visualizing idioms *literally.* Yesterday I was standing in line at the grocery and one woman said to another that she bought a car that was 'brand spanking new' and she had to 'pay through the nose.' So I'm seeing her in my mind's eye, spanking the trunk of a car while coins were falling out a' her nostrils. Don't laugh! With my head going elsewhere, I end up missing whatever is said next, so I come off as being inattentive and rude."

"Oh, I'm sure no one thinks you're rude."

"All the same. Here, take your lemonade. We have snacks waitin' on the table in the gazebo. Any chance that you know how to play cribbage then?"

"I do not."

"Would you like t' learn?"

"I have been waiting all my life."

"You're a liar, Mr. Ashe. A liar and a wanker *and*," she flashed an amused smile as she turned for the door, "a man who thinks I stepped out a' the fourteenth century. Is that about right?"

She had nailed me perfectly.

As Annie explained the rules of cribbage I felt like an amphibian during its first moments on land, filling its virgin lungs with air. After all those years of darting, dodging and sidestepping, I was now sitting inches from a redhead and *hoping* she'd touch me again.

Annie dealt a hand of cards.

Uh oh. What did she just say? Something about "fifteens." "Double runs." And what did the board with all the holes mean?

"I'm an idiot," I said, pointing to the cards. "All I know how to play is poker. Which is a great idea. Have you ever heard the term, 'strip poker?'"

Annie opened her mouth in mock shock. "My Grandma told me to steer clear a' lads like you, and now here y'are, and I'm stuck with ya for the whole afternoon!"

Our eyes locked. We were flirting again, only this time there were no keyboards or miles between us. I had to either make up some excuse and slide back into my pond—or dare to inhale the alien air of redheads.

She said, "We'll play a hand and you'll catch on. The only thing I forgot t' tell you is that if all the cards in your hand are the same suit, you get four extra points."

We played our cards and I missed out on every pegging opportunity.

"Annie, I don't think it's fair that you are forcing me to play a game that requires advanced math skills, while you clearly mean to distract me with that medieval accent of yours, which frankly I think you're faking."

She laughed, snorting a little.

"Oh for God's sake, now you're conjuring up baby pig sounds. No wonder I keep making mistakes."

She laughed harder, snorting again, this time much louder.

"Huh! Did I say ...*baby* pig?"

She reared back and pointed at me. "Yer a wicked pearson y'are," she said. "Truly wicked. And take a look at your hand. You've a triple run! Y' caught up t' me so quit your bellyachin'."

In the next hand the flipped card, which she called "the starter," was a club. After the play, Annie said that since all the cards in her hand were hearts, she got to take an additional five points. My crib turned out to have all diamonds, but when I tried to take my additional points, Annie stopped me.

"No, Daniel, in the case a' the *crib* those four cards have t' be the same suit as the starter."

I scrunched up my face. "What?" I put my forearms flat on the table and shook my head. "Annie, it's shameless the way you're making up rules just to win." She tried to protest but I held up my hand, "No, no, no. You come to our country and you use your red hair magic to move into a mansion, then you lure me into some ancient Druid game I've never heard of and make up rules that work for you but not for me." She gave a shriek and snorted again, and we both went wide-eyed and started laughing like stoners, our hilarity escalating each time we caught eyes.

When we finally wrested control, she wiped her nose with a napkin and said, "Mother Mary but you're a fiendish man. I was trying t' look all cool and L.A. and now I'm teary."

"On you it looks fantastic," I said, which was true. Her skin glowed a deeper pink and her green eyes sparkled. After taking several calming breaths she said, "Shall we swim? I've already got my suit on." And with that she stood up and pulled her dress off over her head.

Annie had the body of a healthy college girl. No sinewy gym-rat muscle, no anorexic bones poking out, just smooth, curving female flesh in a chocolate brown suit that fit her like a stocking. It was several moments before I realized she was waiting for me to go change into my trunks. I closed my eyes and waved one hand back and forth in front of my face. "For future reference, you need to give a guy a little more warning before you whip off your dress. I can hardly breathe."

"Go on with ya!" she laughed, pulling the clip out of her hair. Then she jumped in the pool and hopped up to wave me in. Seeing her wet and bouncing was really too much. I pointed to the house to indicate I was going to change.

As I walked through the kitchen I whistled one long note. *Annie was stunning.*

A quick look at myself in the bathroom mirror had me cursing my recent sedentary lifestyle. I sucked in my gut, walked out the door, and wasted no time diving over her head. I swam the length and returned to her.

"What a grand swimmer y'are! I'm dead afraid a' leaving the shallow end."

"Well if you want to do a length, I'll swim right next to you and give you a hand if you need it."

"Right."

She bit her lip and began to paddle toward the other end. As soon as she crossed into deeper water I kept right next to her.

"You're doing fine, relax a little, keep your body out behind you, you're halfway there."

"Jaysus, I'm doin' it!"

When she reached the wall she grabbed it, and even though she was tired from the struggle, she looked thrilled. I treaded water next to her and said, "Six weeks of training Annie, and you'll be ready to represent Ireland in the Olympics."

"Bollocks."

"Seriously, how is it you live on an island and don't know how to swim?"

"In Ireland a person can get plenty wet just walkin' outside," she said gasping. "Now make sure I make it back t' the other end."

Seeing she needed more time to recover, I said, "No, wait," but Annie had already pushed off. A moment later she disappeared under the water.

I grabbed her elbow, pulled her up, and turned her around. With my arm diagonal over her torso, I used my body to keep hers right at the surface. A few strokes later we were in the shallow end and I set her down. "Are you okay?" I asked.

"Ready t' die of embarrassment," she said. I was about to turn away when she tugged on my arm. I bent down and she kissed my cheek. "You're not really a wanker, y' know."

"Uh, yeah, I am."

"Y'are?"

"I must be, because I want you to sink under again so I'll get another kiss."

She laughed and curled her index finger for me to bend down. I presented her with my cheek, but Annie put a hand on either side of my face, turned it forward, and put her lips to mine.

Liquid light shot through my veins.

How many moments it lasted I cannot say. I was suspended, body and soul, until she pulled away. She lifted her lids slowly and looked into my eyes, brushing her lips with her fingers. It was the most beautiful gesture I had ever seen.

"I think we best be drying off," she said and turned away.

We sat side by side on the edge of the pool with our feet in the water. Every moment that ticked by added distance between us and that kiss, and I needed to say something soon or it would be insurmountable.

"Annie," I began, looking down at the improbable number of freckles on her thigh, "Up until a minute ago I was a virgin redhead kisser. All I can say is ..." I put my hands on top of my head and popped them away like my brain exploded. "Holy God!"

She laughed, her eye crinkle so heartbreaking I had to turn away as I continued. "So far you've turned me into a lion tamer, a sailor, brought a major client to me, now *that kiss*. Fair to say I've been right all along about the magic of redheads."

She knocked her shoulder into my arm, and I exaggerated the effect by toppling to the tiles. "Good lord, you're half my size and twice my strength!"

She made little fists and held them up like the Notre Dame leprechaun and we both laughed.

"But seriously, Annie, did you actually grow up surrounded by sheep and crumbling castles?"

"I did!" Then she said the name of her village. It sounded so foreign, and she said it so quickly, that I only caught the first of the four syllables, which sounded like *crick* or *creek*.

"It's an hour or so south a' Dublin, and home to one of the oldest monasteries in Ireland. You already know Jennie and I were orphaned when we were nine, and that we came into money when we turned twenty-five. But I promise you, I would a' given it all up in a heartbeat for one more hour with my parents." She swirled her feet in the water. "At Stella Maris

I lived with the same three Americans right until graduation." She shook her head and smiled.

"Great memories?"

She looked at the sky. "I told you we were pranksters that never got caught. And the more the school buzzed about our last prank, the more inventive we became with the next. We were so good that we started t' believe we were invincible." She looked back down at the water. "Things spun out a' control one night, and in our haste t' get away, I left something behind. Even t' this day I'm worried it will connect me to that night." She shrugged. "Anyway, since I've been writin' the dog stories, I had myself a thought that I could write a memoir about Stella Maris. Does that sound vain and ridiculous?"

"No. I'm already very intrigued. Just promise to let me see it before you send it to any other agent."

Annie nodded. "Then I will start tomorrow. So don't be askin' me to tell you any more about Stella Maris. I want you t' read it all with fresh eyes." She patted my arm. "Enough about me then. Did you grow up here in California?"

"No. Phoenix, Arizona."

"Goodness, what was that like?"

"Very, very hot. But good. My parents taught high school. My maternal grandmother was Japanese and from San Francisco. She not only bore a child out of wedlock, but that baby, my mother, was whiter and rounder of eye than expected. Grandmother Miho did well for herself. She and my mother both got college degrees the same year. My mom took a teaching position in a Phoenix high school, and that's where she met my dad, a chemistry teacher. He was also bi-racial. Caucasian and African American. They got married, a year later I was born, and ten months after that my sister Leandra came along."

"I hear in America, babies born that close together are called 'Irish Twins.'"

"No one has ever called me Irish *anything*," I said and we both laughed. "Wait, I've got a picture of Leandra on my phone." I got up and brought my cell over and showed Annie a couple of photos.

"Jaysus, she's really beautiful."

"She is. And she speaks perfect Japanese. She lived in Tokyo for nine years as a newscaster. Married a rich American over there, and they had a son. They got divorced a few years ago. Now she lives right here in the valley. Her boy will be off to college next year."

"Do y' speak Japanese then?"

"I can barely order sushi. Leandra got all the language genes. Anyway, we lost mom to cancer five years ago, and dad to a heart attack a few months later. I think he just missed her too much to take care of himself."

"Sad. Both of us orphans." She patted my knee. "Let's speak a' happier things."

Here was the opening I'd been waiting for. "Well, I have a question, Why did you leave me that first story?"

She kicked up some water with her toes. "I was drawin' you a picture a' the dogs, but a minute into it I had a hiccup and the line went wrong. Straight away I saw that if I added a lot more lines I could turn Eddie into a handsome lion. So I did. Then a story came to mind to explain the why of it, and as stories always do, it ended up making sense of itself. In that case, it answered your question as to why you always need to take an extra bag for Eddie on walks."

"My sister said you wrote it to mess with me. For being such a putz about redheads."

"Ah, then she's not only beautiful, she's smart. It *was* great fun to poke away at your phobia, so if you'd asked me back then, I would a' said the same."

"*Would* have said?'"

"That was the truth of it in my mind until you told me that Peter called me a Scheherazade." She leaned back on her elbows. "That was like a clap a' thunder. Did you ever find yourself actin' this way or that without really understanding the why of it, then one day it all made sense?"

"You're talking about when something like instinct takes over?"

"No. A bigger reason. Like your subconscious is aware a' what's coming and preparing you. Like when I was at Stella Maris. My friends and I pulled off these elaborate pranks, and all that time we thought it was just t' have fun. But for us to succeed we first had to learn new skills, like how to work the telephone switchboard, or copy keys, disengage alarms, and find our way through the tunnels in the dark. Then one night we needed to know absolutely every one a' those skills or we would have been ..." she widened her eyes, "in *serious* trouble."

"Jeez. I can't wait to read that memoir."

"Well, my point is, after you told me what Peter said, it got me thinking about the legend of Scheherazade."

I scratched my head. "Ah, the Persian Queen. Okay, let's see. In *The Arabian Nights* the king killed his first wife when he caught her cheating with another man. He was determined never to fall in love again, so every day he married a different virgin, spent the night with her, and had her beheaded in the morning. This went on until one of his brides was Scheherazade. She got in his bed, he deflowered her, and then her sister knocked on the door and begged the king to let her in so Scheherazade could tell her one last story before she lost her head the next morning. The king never slept anyway, so he said go ahead, and Scheherazade talked through the night. But the sun rose just before the climactic ending of her story, so she stopped. The king had to get on with his day, and gave her a reprieve on the beheading so she could come back to his bed that night and finish the story. Which she did, but immediately started a new story. This went on for a thousand and one nights. One of her tales was about Aladdin and the lamp."

"Aye, but did you know she didn't *have* t' marry the king? Her father was his advisor, and well-born women didn't have t' queue up to be one a' the brides. But she volunteered in order to stop the bloodshed. She knew that all the young women before her had tried t' use their beauty or their wits t' make the king fall in love with them, but they lost their heads the next morning all the same. Scheherazade had an advantage over all the others. She knew the king had closed his heart."

Uh oh. Annie was on the verge of comparing the sleepless, cold-blooded king to the love-immune insomniac sitting next to her. It was time to finish this subject and move on. I said, "So instead she told him stories, knowing he would keep her alive so he could learn how it all panned out. Good strategy."

"And it took him a thousand and one nights to finally realize he was in love with her and commute her death sentence. Three years." Annie fluttered the water with her feet.

"Maybe he was a hard nut to crack."

"Oh please. I could a' done it in a fraction a' the time."

"How so?"

"Her stories revolved around a merchant traveler, but if it were me in his bed, I'd make sure he could see *himself* in every adventure. I'd say, 'Dear King, there once was a great prince who would a' lost his claim t' the crown unless he could capture a golden chest, one that could only be opened by his father.' Then in my story I'd have the prince outwit and vanquish the supernatural creatures protecting the box, nearly dying himself each time but discovering in the process that what was inside that chest would either destroy his country in an all-consuming fire, or bring them the peace they needed to survive. By the fifth night or so I'd have the prince in my story back to his father's royal tent. I'd describe the old king's gnarled fingers hesitating on the lid of the box, and then I'd stop and not tell the end. My husband would be mad at first. But before he could behead me, I'd convince him that his soul had entered the prince in my story, and if I were killed, I'd be taking it with me."

"Jeez, he'd be terrified."

"Exactly. And he deserved a little comeuppance after killing all those innocent girls. I'd promise t' tell him the end the story in one year, letting him know that if he treated me with great love and respect it would be a good ending. Otherwise," her index finger slashed across her throat in a kill gesture.

I shook my head. "Annie Doherty, you have just convinced me that you *are* the real Scheherazade."

She pulled her feet out of the water, put them on my back, and shoved me into the pool.

On my drive home the smile only left my face when I pictured Annie and Drew, two glowing and perfect examples of their respective genders, clinking wine glasses over dinner.

"Delicious," she might say.

"Yes you are," he would whisper as he ran his fingers up her arm.

I only realized how hard I was gripping the steering wheel when my hands started to ache.

After walking the dogs, I looked up the Scheherazade legend. I read several boring critiques on it, and was almost dozing when I happened on an expert whose words snapped me awake: *The new queen understood her stories alone wouldn't save her. She would never be safe unless the king transformed into a man who could open himself to love. So Scheherazade devised stories that would guide him into becoming such a man.*

I clicked off, thinking *Dear God.*

XVI
Indelible Ink

Sunday morning Victoria and I did a five-mile run in Griffith Park, toweled off, and went to Settler's Diner for breakfast. I was bringing the fork to my mouth when she said, "So, Daniel, have you been thinking over the idea of us getting married?"

I made a conscious effort to not look like a deer caught in the headlights.

"Please understand that I wouldn't bring this up if we were kids in love. But our connection is different. And I don't want to waste time on someone who isn't ready for what I'm proposing."

I noticed my fingers were pinched white from clutching my fork. I put it down and wiped my lips with my napkin.

"Um, actually, I have thought about it. I see it makes good sense. I do. But even without the 'in-love' part, don't we need more time to see if we're compatible? Married people take vacations together. They eat together. They have children together."

While her forehead remained as smooth as the top of a custard pie, her lips curved downward.

"Children? Daniel, you're forty-two and I'm thirty-seven. I just made partner and you'll be opening your own agency soon. Children don't make sense for us. And as for eating, you order what you like and I order what I like. Easy. I don't get a camping vibe from you, and any other type of vacation is fine with me." She took a deep breath. "Look, I'm not going to drag you to the altar. As I said before, I'm ready. If you're not, just let me know."

This woman didn't kid around. A life with Victoria would be clear and clean. Goal oriented. Good for me. Very good for me. So what was holding me back?

That kiss.

I had relived it a thousand times. But Annie wasn't mine. She was a gypsy who could disappear to Machu Picchu or Kiev or back home to Creek-Something-or-Other. I'd be a fool to let Victoria get away. I almost grabbed her hands. I almost said, "Set the date beautiful, I'm in!"

But I didn't.

Instead I did the math. Annie was here at least until Peter and Clarissa returned in sixteen days.

"Victoria, I am so in the middle of editing this book that I can't focus on anything else. Remember, your mindset is way ahead of mine on this. I need a little time to catch up. Would you give me three more weeks? Let me concentrate on getting this manuscript in shape, then we will either shake hands and part ways, or we will go ring shopping."

She studied me for several seconds then said, "Okay, Daniel. Three weeks."

Monday, 11/23/15
From: Adoherty77@yahoo.com
To: Clarissa and Daniel
Subject: Monday
Hello!

All is well here. Sometimes Drew is around, and sometimes he's off on American adventures. I imagine him surfing or skydiving or such, though he denies all.

George is healthy and happy and he loves Sparks and Eddie so much that he starts to pant and bark in utter joy when we approach their house. He is also more outgoing at the dog park.

You have probably noticed the picture of Leonard the Lizard in the corner of George's web page. I put it there just for fun, it never occurred to me that some foolish creature would ask him for advice. Clarissa, after you read what happened you may wish to ask Peter to counsel Leonard when he gets home!

Annie

Intrigued, I went directly to the corgi web site. The first of the day's letters were to George.

Dear George,

How is this for awful? I am half malamute, half pointer, and guess what my human calls me? "Moot Point!"

James

Dear James,

Humans aren't known for their sensitivity. One of my friends is a skinny Irish setter, but you don't hear me calling him a 'Mick Light.'

Dear George,

I was a pound puppy. My parents love me, but lately I wonder if they are embarrassed by my lack of a pedigree. The Newfoundland at the east end of our fence says his ancestors were carefully bred to help fishermen pull nets from the sea and haul wood from the forest. The Maltese on the west side says she was bred to be a therapy dog and everywhere she goes she gets num-nums. What gives?

Shorty

Dear Shorty,

Nature loves diversity. Being a mutt gives you the genetic edge, my friend. Sure, those thoroughbreds might have in-bred, near-mystic talents, but you'll be healthy and running up mountains long after the Newfie's hip dysplasia and the Maltese's obesity have made them shut-ins.

On a sidebar, Shorty my friend, chicks dig exotic-looking guys. So any way you cut it, you are one lucky wanker!

I high-fived the air. I'd made it into a George letter!

The next was the letter to Leonard that Annie referenced in her email.

Dear Leonard,

George is busy answering letters, but you look really smart, so I decided to send my question to you.

I'm a dog that you might have seen walking in your own neighborhood.

By day, my dad is a very successful businessman. He employs lots of people, he sits on community boards, and he has been married to my mom for many years and they have four grown human children. The problem is, dad likes to dress like a lady when he walks me!

Mom is an invalid and stays upstairs. Every night after dinner, dad tells her he is going to drive me to the park. He comes downstairs and puts on lady clothes, makeup and a wig. Then we motor off to different neighborhoods and stroll.

Yesterday dad paired a floral sweater set with a flirty kick-pleated skirt and strappy sandals. No sooner did we step out of the car then we ran right into a man who used to work for dad. Someone he had fired. This man did a double take. He knew dad looked familiar but couldn't place him.

That was too close!

How can I help my dad to stop dressing like a lady before someone recognizes him and the word gets out? It would destroy his standing in the community, and our happy home life would be ruined!

Name withheld upon request

Dear Dog,

Leonard does not withhold names upon request. You are Buddy, a basset hound living with Edward and Jean McMillen of 75 E. Lockhurst Dr., Alpine, California.

Monday, 11/23/15
From: danielashe@floodgatemedia.com
To: Annie
Subject: almost drowned

Jeez, I was drinking coffee while I read the Leonard answer. I'm still coughing!

Thank you for Saturday. Everything was wonderful—the snacks, the music, the conversation were all first rate. You are a terrible swimmer, but you get *very* high marks for the bathing suit. Then if we factor in your eyes ….

Also, thank you for teaching me how to play cribbage, or should I say your made-up version of the game. I have got to look up those rules.

Okay, I was about to sign off, but I might as well tell you that there is one gesture of yours from Saturday that I can't get out of my mind. We were out of the pool and mostly dried off, just talking, when you casually fingered back mounds of red curls. Then, without benefit of a mirror or that hair clip, you got all of it up in some kind of round twist at the back of your head—*and there it stayed.*

Red hair magic!

(The evidence mounts.)

Your friend and admirer,

Daniel

Tuesday, 11/24/15
From: Clarissaandpeter@gmail.com
To: Annie and Daniel
Subject: Advice please

Hi Annie!

We love England. I am shopping like crazy. Peter has a few days off and says we should go to Ireland! We need your expertise. What should we see and do?

We think it's great that George is getting famous. We went to his web site and it's very funny what folks are saying about him and good old Leonard. We also appreciate that you are not using their last name, as some of the advice is pretty racy. That one about the Lord I would not want my mom to see!

I hope my brother isn't a bother. I sent him an email right before I left telling him I was going to London, which obviously he didn't get around to reading. I'm so sorry he barged in on you. What did he think when you answered the door?

Well, I'm heading to Harrods for a new clutch, and then to Fortnum and Mason for lunch. I am addicted to their Welsh rarebit crumpets.

Love,

Clarissa

Wednesday, 11/25/15
From: adoherty77@yahoo.com
To: Clarissa and Daniel
Subject: Wednesday

Dear Clarissa and Daniel,

Clarissa, after the excitement of London, I say skip Dublin and get yourselves into Ireland's countryside. Drive south. Stop at village pubs for a pint; ask the barkeep if it's true there are no snakes on the island, and if anyone at the bar has family in the States. Believe me, you will get an earful and it will be grand. Visit the sweater knitters and the little textile mills. Wind around the Ring of Kerry. Stay at B&Bs and go for the full Irish breakfast. If Daniel chimes in with any comments about this, ignore him.

You can walk up hills and take photos of the sheep and the streams and the cliffs. For lunch, get a curried chicken sandwich with chips and order one slice of banoffee to share for dessert. It is so sweet your teeth will hurt, but you will finish every bite. Get lost and ask for directions, and don't laugh if someone tells you to take a right when you see the old dog lying on a blue porch. That old dog will be there!

I'm getting homesick. You will have a lovely time.

Drew didn't knock on the door. He used the keypad on the garage to get in, so I was already dialing the police when he told me he was your brother. He looks so much like you that I knew it was true.

He is no bother. He swims before breakfast, and later today he is going to teach me how to dive. He's out and about a lot, and when he's here he works in your upstairs office. We sometimes eat breakfast or dinner together.

Annie

I felt nauseous. Teach her to dive? More like he found a good excuse to have his hands all over her body.

To get my mind off Drew molesting Annie, I went to the Corgi Advisor website. There were about twenty new letters. Leonard the lizard got another request for advice.

Dear Leonard,

I'm your typical restaurant rat. I stay hidden until the humans have gone home, then I scavenge for any food left out. It's my job and I do it well. What I'd like to know is why my kind is so despised. How is it that dogs and cats and birds get to live in the light of day and eat expensive food and have trips to the vet, and all I get from humans is revulsion?

Unloved

Dear Unloved,

It's all about poop.

Humans are obsessed with it. They build great indoor temples for their own needs, they follow their dogs around with plastic bags, and they provide cats with special boxes that get cleaned out every day.

No one tells *me* where to take a dump and I'll tell you why. If it wasn't for the millions of years' worth of reptile crap all over the world there would only be sand and swamp out there. We're responsible for the soil that started to grow food so other land creatures could evolve. But do we get any accolades for pooping all you mammals into existence?

No. We do not.

Back to your problem. You "go" all over the place, the humans see those little currants you leave near their precious food and they set horrible traps to kill you. My advice is to go where they never look. That way you may gorge to your heart's content without fear of retribution.

Oh jeez. Hold on. George just weighed in on the subject. According to The Golden One it's *not* about the poop. "Dogs and cats and birds are gorgeous," he says, then—looking right at me—he adds "but rats and some *other* creatures only look good in sewers."

He's lucky I can't get out of this glass box.

But my favorite letter in this bunch gave me a glimpse into Annie's life.

Dear George,

My mom has started dating a guy so old he has more hair coming out of his ears than I do, and I'm a papillon! At first I was happy for her. It is important that humans have some pack time with their own, I always say. But this old dude has behaviors that need correcting. He pushes me off the furniture, and not in a nice way, either. If I bark, he yells at me. He calls me "yappy" and "little sh-t." Once, when mom wasn't looking, he kicked me across the room. He talks about how much nicer cats are, and that if she got rid of me he'd buy her a pair of kittens. Lately he has been trying to convince her to let him move in with us. She isn't saying yes, but she isn't saying no either. This guy has got to go! What can I do?

Jill

Dear Jill,

Rose, the grandmother of my dog sitter, is eighty-one in people years, quite lovely, and has a nice stack of stocks and bonds and bank accounts. Rose has two widowed sisters who are also well fixed. Every now and then some old fellow flirts with one of these grannies. Sure, they're flattered by it, but then Rose says, "Remember sisters, all an old man wants is either a nurse or a purse." They nod their heads and get back to their bridge game. That's the wake-up call *your* mother needs to hear.

Wednesday, 11/25/15
From: danielashe@floodgatemedia.com
To: Annie
Subject: The old sod beckons!
Hi Annie,

Your description of Ireland makes me want to dig out my passport and book the next flight. I picture you there: shopping, waving to your friends, laughing and singing in the pubs. Actually, I don't want to go to Ireland unless you are there to show me around. As green as your eyes are here, I bet they illuminate in your native home.

As long as we are on an Irish theme, you might as well know that when I read your stories and letters I try to add in your accent. I do the same for Clarissa's letters as well. Which reminds me, why do you think Drew doesn't have a Southern accent? I imagine a snooty New England boarding school was involved.

(Whack!)

Thank you sir may I have another?

(Whack!)

There is a free outdoor concert on Saturday in the park. The Philharmonic puts one on every year. I thought I'd take Sparks and Eddie, and wondered if you and George would like to join us. It starts at four o'clock. We could take a picnic supper, a blanket, and a bottle of wine.

Daniel

Thursday, 11/26/15
From: adoherty77@yahoo.com
To: Daniel
Subject: South of the Border

Dear Daniel,

Thank you for the invitation. Unfortunately I promised Drew that I would go to Rosarito with him on Saturday. There's a special block of granite down there that he's considering for his kitchen remodel, and says he needs another opinion. We're leaving very early as it takes about two and a half hours each way. I'm excited! I have never been to Mexico. I will ask a neighbor to come over to walk and feed George about noon. Sorry to miss the concert.

Annie

Thursday, 11/26/15
From: danielashe@floodgatemedia.com
To: Annie
Subject: Stay put!

Annie, find a pen with indelible ink and write my name and phone number around your belly button so the Mexican authorities can contact me when they find your body.

Yes, I hope I just scared you, because thinking of you crossing into Mexico with a man you met a few days ago makes me feel like an elephant is standing on my chest.

Really, don't do it. This isn't Ireland, and sure as hell *Mexico* isn't Ireland. Remember those girls at Stella Maris who had their own bodyguards? Mexican drug lord daughters. And if it came to a showdown, what would Drew be more concerned with—protecting you or his thousand-dollar haircut? Stay put. Invite me over right now so Drew is reminded that you have a tall, grumpy friend who cares about you. Go ahead. Make my phone ring!

    Daniel

Thursday, 11/26/15
From: adoherty77@yahoo.com
To: Daniel
Subject: A favor

Darling Man,

    You are adorable. Thank you for caring. I am confident that Drew has better things to do than murder me in Mexico. He is really a dear person, as open and guileless as his sister. We're crossing over, will only be there a few hours, we'll eat a picnic lunch, and then it's back across the border. I'm thinking we'll be home by six.

    An imposition to be sure, but is there any chance you could come by and walk and feed George? Drew just told me that Peter has some kind of feud going on with the neighbors, and suggested I ask you instead. Anytime around noon?

    Annie

Friday, 11/27/15
From: danielashe@floodgatemedia.com
To: Annie
Subject: Groan

Yes, I will walk George. I will also spend the day worried that Drew is bartering you for a kilo of heroin.

Indelible ink. My phone number. Your navel.

Turn off the security system and leave me a key under that hibiscus planter by the back door. I'll give George a run and feed him. Put his dish in the fridge.

A very worried,

Daniel

———————

I spent a few quality hours in bed that night picturing Annie innocently putting together a picnic basket in the kitchen while Drew stood in the doorway planning his seduction strategy. Then off they'd go, talking and laughing and singing to the radio. Once over the border they would pass concrete, tin and adobe houses until they got to Rosarito. Drew would yawn and pull into a hotel: *Come in with me, Annie. I just need to lie down for an hour and then I'll be alright.*

Bastard.

I've been to Rosarito. I've seen the shops where granite and marble are cut with circular blades dripping gallons of water; but don't tell me there are types of stone down there that aren't available at any upscale kitchen-remodeling center in the States. Was it that much cheaper? What about border taxes and the cost of transporting something that heavy to Monterey, and why would Mr. Bags of Money penny-pinch anyway?

The only bright spot in my day was at work, watching Cameron pace around his office like a lost rat. Apparently the little twit needed to suckle off Peter's ... I'll say *praise,* to keep his bluster up. With his mentor too far away to protect him, he knew enough to keep away from me. But clearly the Zygote was in panic mode. He hated that I had landed the biggest fish of the year, and he'd been kicking our intern out of his office so he could console himself in private. Something up his nose no doubt. Personally, I enjoyed seeing him sweat.

It was a bit after twelve on Saturday when I pulled into Peter and Clarissa's driveway. I walked to the back of the house, tipped over the hibiscus, took the key, and heard George bark as I worked the door open. I knelt to calm him as he circled frantically around me.

"Okay buddy, I'm here. Your girlfriend took off with some pretty boy, but I'm true blue and you can count on me. Here, let's snap on your leash and take a walk."

George sat until his leash clicked, then tried to pull me into the dining room.

"Wrong way. C'mon, let's go for a walk." As I opened the door I heard a creaking sound over my head. I stopped and listened a moment, then walked back through the kitchen, stood at the bottom stair and yelled, "Hello! Anyone there?"

Nothing. I had a moment of hope that Annie had reconsidered the trip and either forgot to tell me, or—better still—had planned to surprise me. But no one answered and I decided it was just a random house sound.

I pulled George back down the hallway and through the kitchen. As we stepped outside I heard what sounded like one of the big, red doors at the front of the house clicking shut. I jogged around the shrubs to the entrance. There was no one on foot, no car traffic, just the back of a man on a bike. To my left I saw the next-door neighbor walking around the Range Rover in his driveway. We nodded to each other. Obviously it must have been his front door that I heard.

After our walk we came in the back and George nearly

pulled me off my feet in his effort to be free. When I unhooked his leash he took off and raced up the stairs.

Again, I was uneasy. I didn't know if George was a high-strung dog and this was just his nature, or if some unauthorized person had been up there. I hesitated. I didn't like the idea of going upstairs in Peter's house, but knew I wouldn't rest easy unless I investigated.

Halfway up I stopped and listened, but all I heard was George. At the top of the stairs I looked left and right. There was only one door open. It was Peter's office. George was snuffling under the desk and I walked over to look.

"Seriously George, there is nothing there. No rat, no toy, no food."

I sat down in the plush leather chair and took in what real money can buy. To my left was an antique bookcase with mother-of-pearl inlay. Every lamp in the room was a spectacular work of art, and the desk I was sitting at looked like it once belonged to a French duke. Thankfully, nothing seemed out of place. I leaned forward, my hand resting on the computer mouse, and studied a pair of photos to the left of the monitor. One was of Peter and Clarissa holding George between them, she smiling, he looking considerably less grim than usual, and the other was of Drew and Clarissa waving from a sailboat. When I stood up the chair did make a creaky sound, but would I have heard it downstairs?

I left the office and decided I'd better do a quick check of the other bedrooms. The first was painted dove gray and had a double tray ceiling over a large four poster bed. There was a leather suitcase leaning against the wall, and the bathroom counter had toiletries in black bottles with silver script. This had to be where Drew was sleeping.

I looked in three smaller bedrooms before I got to the

double doors at the end of the hall. I pushed them open and stood there, shaking my head. The room was massive in scale, and finely designed with cove lighting, stunning Japanese folding screens, a stacked stone fireplace, a sitting area, and beveled French doors that opened to an ornately scrolled wrought iron deck—the perfect spot for an L.A. power couple to sip morning coffee and think, *yeah baby!*

The door to the bathroom was open and I stepped inside. It was bigger than my living room.

The tile was pale green onyx, there was an ivory stone tub on a black granite platform, and Annie's terrycloth bathrobe was hanging on a hook next to the rain shower. Her toiletries were on the counter between two square stone sinks. I stepped closer and took inventory: sunscreen, lip-balm, deodorant, toothpaste, moisturizer, hair clips, and an electrical appliance that looked like flat barbecue tongs. I picked up her wide-tooth comb and imagined her in front of this mirror, grooming for the day.

My tour of the upstairs complete, I decided George had a vivid imagination. If a thief had been here he would have disturbed *something*. But there wasn't so much as a drawer ajar.

XVII
Boyfriend Status

Sunday, 11/29/15
From: adoherty77@yahoo.com
To: Clarissa and Daniel
Subject: And he cooks!

Hello!

Drew and I went across the border yesterday to examine giant slabs of granite, quartzite, and marble. Nothing was to his liking, and after a walk on the beach and some trinket shopping, we came home. He says he has a few more things to do in L.A. before he heads back to Monterey.

Daniel, thank you for taking George on his afternoon walk.

Drew and I got back here about five-thirty and we three strolled around the streets playing "Name That Tune." He's a fine singer and would be very popular in the pubs back home.

Clarissa, tonight your brother is going to make me dinner. He wants me out of the house from five to seven so I will get the full impact: scent, sight, and flavor, all at once. He is charmingly excited about it, and trying to be secretive, but I saw a package of raw shrimp in the refrigerator.

Annie

———————————

Oh brother.

Drew sings! He cooks! He walks on beaches!

Or was that on water?

Her subject line alone curled my lip into Elvis territory. Just when was the millionaire Bachelor/Iron Chef/American Idol going to pack up and leave?

Monday, 11/30/15
From: adoherty77@yahoo.com
To: Daniel
Subject: My boyfriend?

Dear Daniel,

I am so grateful to you for taking care of George. You might be a terrible cribbage player, but you are a dear and trusted friend.

How frequently my mind goes back to our afternoon together. I think on how you saved me, how you teased me, and how we laughed like loons. I haven't lost it like that in years.

Now, dear man, I have another favor to ask.

Last night, after Drew and I walked George around the neighborhood, we were making ourselves bowls of ice cream, just talking and laughing, when he took me in his arms and kissed me.

I didn't kiss back. He whispered in my ear, "Is something wrong? Are you and Daniel an item?"

I pushed away and said, "We are."

He picked up my left hand. "Well, I don't see a ring here," he said and kissed my fourth finger. "Perhaps he's not as serious about you as I am."

I told him we were quite new, but that my heart was set on you. He was trying to be a gentleman about it, but clearly the questions he asked were to find out if we'd been intimate. I forced a change of subject.

Daniel, I am so sorry for this. It's such an awkward situation for me, with him sleeping down the hall. On the odd chance that you and he cross paths, I hope you back up my story. I'm very worried that Peter knows about your Victoria, and if he does, and Clarissa does as well, then my ruse is up. Please let me know straight away. I don't know how much Drew confides in his sister.

Oh what a tangled web we weave.

Annie

P.S. You haven't mentioned your young author for a while. I hope it's because he's become more amenable to your suggestions. Did you ever tell me his name?

Monday, 11/30/15
danielashe@floodgatemedia.com
To: Annie
Subject: I accept!

Hi Annie,

Peter did meet Victoria, but he is not one to gossip. Worst case scenario, you will soon get an urgent call from Clarissa telling you that I am a cad.

Also, Annie, I want you to know that there are no ties binding Victoria and myself, save our mutual inability to fall in love. It's an odd situation, even to me.

In the meantime, I am honored to be claimed as your boyfriend. Elaborate for Drew on that theme all you like. The following would sound especially good with your accent: "'Tis true what they say about tri-racial men y' know," (pause to flutter eyelashes and sigh.) "No one's more amazin' than a *Cau-bla-sian!*"

To gel our couple status in his mind, I'd like to take you to

Bardi's this Saturday night. Their homemade pasta will take your taste buds back to Florence.

Thanks for asking about my young client. His name is Oliver Nikitin, though I have come up with many a sobriquet for him, the most current being Pissant. I think he might have a genuine personality disorder, so I'm trying to be less judgmental.

Off to work.

Daniel

P.S. Lock your bedroom door and slide the back of a chair under the knob.

P.P.S. And keep a baseball bat handy.

―――――――――

Drew. Now there was someone I'd like to see sign up for colonizing Mars.

I didn't sleep worth a damn that night, worried on the one hand that Annie might decide blond, handsome and rich wasn't such a bad idea after all, and on the other wondering if I should tell her that George acted like there had been an intruder in Peter's home office. In the end I decided *why upset her?* Nothing had been disturbed, and once Drew left she would be alone in that cavernous house.

On Tuesday, Oliver showed up a full hour late. We took our usual chairs, and as I pointed out the next edit I was proposing, he waved me off and said, "I'm done with this shit. I don't care anymore. Whatever you think needs fixing just go ahead and fix, for Christ sake."

I stared at him but he pointedly kept his head turned away. Finally I said, "Oliver, there are only thirty pages left. I need you to at least read along with me. If you're serious we can get this done today."

"Then what happens?"

"I'll go over the book again myself, make sure it's everything it should be, and then I'll send it to my boss in London. He'll read it. He may recommend some other edits, and when he's done, the two of us will discuss which publishers to send it to. We'll make some phone calls to the right people, and then off it goes. It's a very good book, Oliver. We're optimistic that we'll get an offer on it soon."

"So we get an offer," he said, absently twirling a wormy lock of hair. "Then what happens?"

"Then we negotiate a deal. The people at the publishing house may make their own recommendations for more edits, but sooner or later the book goes in stores and online, it gets reviewed, everyone loves it, and we all get rich." I raised my brows, expecting the mention of money to garner some enthusiasm.

"Do I travel around and sign copies of the book?"

"Yes. And while that may sound like a lot of fun, after five days on the road you won't remember if you're in Cleveland or St. Louis."

"I think I'll like that."

"You'll also do radio and TV interviews."

"Yeah? What kinds of questions will they ask me?"

"Well, they'll want to know what inspired you." I looked up at the ceiling and rolled out a finger for each point. "They'll ask how someone so young has such a breadth of experience. They'll ask when you lived in, or visited, all the countries in your book, and if your characters are based on real people. They'll want to know about your writing technique, which authors you read, and how you compare yourself to Nabokov and Grisham or Irving and Koontz—whomever *they've* read, which they only do to prove to their audience how smart they are. They'll definitely ask how much of the book is true. You should also be ready to provide some specifics on what inspired you for different aspects of the story, including how you did your historical research, and who the people were that helped you along the way: mentors, professors, writing workshops that you've attended, and, of course, your agent."

I figured that last part would make him roll his eyes, but when I looked over at him he was motionless and pale.

"Hey, don't worry. You're the one who wrote the book. Just answer their questions and have some anecdotes handy, then pack up and hit the next city to do it all over again."

"What the hell are anecdotes?"

I squinted at him, "You know, little personal stories that are usually insightful or funny."

"Oh. Yeah."

He looked down at the floor for several seconds then held up his coffee mug and left.

Something was off. I skimmed half a page of the last chapter when it hit me. Oliver had just spoken using his real voice.

He didn't return for fifteen minutes. Then thirty. I walked up and down the hall a few times, looked out the window, checked the bathroom, and that's when I realized he wasn't coming back. I called his cell and left a message. I called his home and got Mrs. Nikitin. She said she would have him get back to me as soon as he walked in the door. The end of the day came with no call.

Oliver's reaction gnawed at me. Fact was, I had never asked him how he came to write the book. Granted, he wasn't easy to converse with, but the truth was I had treated him differently from the start. I was too worried about my job, too excited to get this book under contract, and in my rush, I had failed to ask Oliver the questions I always ask my other authors.

And—damn it—I was jealous.

Oliver was the same age I was when I wrote my lackluster screenplay. His writing was superior in every way. I could have forgiven him his talent if he had been more socially engaging, or a little bit humble. I would have conversed with him, taken him to lunch, and found out how he knew so much about Europe of the eighteen sixties. I would have learned how many drafts he'd done, who his mentors were, all the usual conversational subjects between authors and agents. But Oliver was a whispering diva, and the truth was, I loathed him.

Even though a lot of weird stuff had gone down that day, when I got in bed I somehow managed to relax my muscles and begin the drift to sleep. It didn't last. Two questions still vied for my attention:

1. Would Drew break down Annie's resistance?

2. How was it possible that a literary genius didn't know what an anecdote was?

XVIII
Kiss Me Again

Tuesday, 12/1/15
From: Clarissaandpeter@gmail.com
To: Annie and Daniel
Subject: Matchmaker!

Hi Annie,

My brother has cruised on his looks and sweet nature all his life, and my family didn't help—we doted on him every step of the way. A lot of gals have fallen into Drew's lap, and he's made mistakes. But now I think he's found exactly what he needs.

(Hint, hint!)

Drew's first wife was anorexic and needed to see a psychiatrist every single day. She was too busy taking care of herself to look after him. His second wife was a professor, and when she realized he wasn't interested in reading books or discussing politics, she gave up on him.

He's always dating, but just isn't getting serious about anyone. Now my brother is almost forty, and I'm thinking that what he really needs is someone who doesn't have emotional problems (like wife #1) and isn't serious all the time (wife #2). Someone fun, but all the same, grounded.

Annie, I just talked to him on the phone, and he said things about you like "naturally beautiful" and "I don't even care what she's saying, I can get lost in her accent."

That man is smitten!!

If you like him, I hope you give him some encouragement. Yes, he's a bit immature, but kind of like an adorable, playful puppy—and you know that if a puppy gets the right training he can turn into an amazing adult. Like our George!

Think about it. I've never heard him sound this enthusiastic about anyone. Ever!

Got to go, but will write later about our amazing trip to Ireland.

Love,

Clarissa

I looked up from my computer screen. It felt like there was a hard knuckle in my ribs.

Or was it in my lung?

No, wait. It was ... it was ...

It was in my *heart.*

Wednesday, 12/2/15
From: danielashe@floodgatemedia.com
To: Annie
Subject: Nauseating

Dear Annie,

As Clarissa is still using the 'reply to all' button, I got to see how she is trying to pimp you out to her little brother. Rehabilitate and bring light to his life—the tragic Nordic god with bags of money, too handsome to find true love.

Give me a break.

Annie, there's always a reason why a man over the age

of thirty-five is single. Simply put, there is something wrong with us.

Take me. I'm alone because the women I dated eventually understood that I wasn't going to fall in love, and they moved on.

Take me. I'm alone because I sought out women who were what I wanted to be: focused and type-A, hard driving and successful. I hoped their polish would rub off on me and we'd become this L.A. super couple blazing to the pinnacle of our careers.

Take me. I kept making the same mistake and didn't fall in love because it turns out that what I went after was the last thing I needed.

It took an unforeseen stimulus coming into my life to jolt me into figuring that one out.

Don't take Drew. He prefers your accent to the content of your thoughts.

Don't take Drew. He's never had to work at anything, never had to struggle, and you and I know that is the only way we grow up. Drew has let his fortune disable him. It's such a common occurrence that F. Scott Fitzgerald made note of it when he said: "The rich are not like you and I." Considering Fitzgerald was only half Irish, and you're a hundred percent, I expect you to have twice his insight.

Now poor Drew is stumbling into middle age, and here is Clarissa, a loving sister who hopes you will re-cast him from fresh clay.

I'm saying there is mold on that clay.

Don't take Drew.

Take me.

Daniel

I hit send and waited. For the next ninety minutes I felt like I was trapped under a capsized boat and treading water, my life sustained by only a small pocket of air.

And it was running out.

Wednesday, 12/2/15
From: adoherty77@yahoo.com
To: Daniel
Subject: America vs. Ireland

Darling Daniel,

Granted, I married once in haste, but put that aside for the moment as I explain how romance historically works in Ireland.

As teenage girls we give shy glances to a lad, and he either acts like a wanker or he gives shy glances back. This generally goes on for a month or two. Then we engineer a chance meeting at the grocery and ask him to walk us home. We hand him our bag of oranges. He is terrified and we do all the talking. This goes on for some weeks.

Exasperated, we tell him we want to see a certain film. We wait, and if he continues to look at his feet, we ask if he wants to go with us.

Three or four films later we manage to get him to kiss us. Yanking him in by the shirt may be required.

If he introduces us to his ma and she invites us to dinner, we attend family functions for a year or two before we get engaged. But if he fears breaking his ma's heart, we never meet her. Some girls will secretly date the momma's boy until exasperation sets in and it's time to look for a lad who isn't so firmly attached. Moving to America or Australia may be necessary.

So imagine me, in the space of three minutes, reading first Clarissa's letter and then yours. It had me walking around the kitchen, having imaginary conversations with the two of you.

Daniel, I should never have kissed you in the pool. It was brazen behavior on my part, though truth be told, there is a case to be made that the fault is really yours. While I am just a lass from a tiny village in Ireland, you are a dashing American who makes clever fun of me, and saved me from drowning!

Anyway, my time in this country is coming to an end, and it would be wrong to kiss you again.

Annie

P.S. In any case, I accept your invitation to dinner.

––––––––––––––

So that was that. It was time to start pulling away. We'd have our dinner on Saturday night, maybe write each other a few more letters, then Annie would be off for parts unknown, and I'd slip back into the mold I made for myself.

She's leaving me, I thought, and suddenly it hurt to swallow.

Thursday , 12/3/15
From: clarissaandpeter@gmail.com
To: Annie and Daniel
Subject: Ireland!
Hi Annie,

Your advice was perfect. We loved Ireland. We just drove around (and around and around those roundabouts) and took pictures and went to a distillery, and naturally I had to go to Waterford Crystal. I bought a lot of gorgeous glass. We ate and drank and "chatted up" the people in pubs, and I found beautiful throws and blankets at a little textile mill. So be on the lookout for many boxes to arrive. I'm set for Christmas presents for all my friends!

How are you and Drew getting along? Maybe you can convince him to stay a few more days ;-)

We had several questions we wanted to ask you, but the only one I remember right now is this: Why do sheep from the same flock have different colored spots of paint on the sides of their bodies?

Love,

Clarissa

Thursday, 12/3/15
From: adoherty77@yahoo.com
To: Clarissa and Daniel
Subject: color-coded sheep

Dear Clarissa and Daniel,

Clarissa—I'm so glad you loved Ireland.

The sheep that are pregnant have painted spots in one color, and the ones that aren't in another color, and those poor ladies are destined soon for the plate.

I think Drew is planning to leave in a few days. It was lovely to have him around. He plans to visit Ireland just after I go home next month, so it is certain we will meet again soon.

Annie

―――――――――

That last sentence packed a lot of bad news. Annie was heading home, and Golden Boy was following.

I tried to override my gut reaction with logic. I'd known for a while she wasn't going to stay, and except for one afternoon and one kiss, ours was a friendship via the written word. That didn't have to stop.

"Dammit!"

I slammed the lid down on my laptop, banged out the back door, and walked the length of my neglected yard half a dozen times.

Annie had feelings for me. It was in her stories. It was in her kiss. But she was poised to disappear from my life, unless ....

Now it was up to me. I could let her go without a word, or I could tell her on Saturday night how much I wanted her to stay.

Saturday felt like months away. At least I could lay some groundwork. I went back inside, clicked on corgiadvisor.com and started to type:

Dear George,

Please help. My girl is leaving the country and she's being pursued by a man who is better looking and a lot richer than I am. What can I do?

Daniel

While I waited for a response, I trolled through the latest letters looking for any to Leonard.

Dear Leonard,

Do you have feelings?

I'm in middle school and my science teacher told us today that reptiles are all "old brain" and are concerned only with eating and mating and fighting. He says you don't have any executive brain function, by which he means you cannot reason, or feel happy or sad. I'm looking at your picture and think that's sad. Is it true? Are you missing out on love and joy and such?

Marcus

Dear Marcus,

Let me dig deep: ah yes, here's a feeling—a strong desire to sink my teeth into a wimpy kid who makes stupid assumptions.

It's human prejudice that keeps us in glass cages. Your species uses phrases like "Murdered in cold blood." And "Cold-blooded bastard," as if having cold blood is innately evil. Believe me, we are better off without all those messy feelings. Let me out of my cage and I'll show you the simple, focused purity of reptilian success.

Live and take no prisoners.

Real life example: Cat got my tail? No problem, I'll just grow a new one.

Time for dinner? Invite some friends over and *eat the bloody cat.* She deserves it after the tail incident.

Dear Leonard,

If I took a razor blade and cut my finger so the neighbor's dog could smell my blood, would that make him more likely to obey me?

Joel

Dear Joel,

I don't know, but it sounds reasonable. If you decide to try it let me know what happens.

NOTE FROM LEONARD THE LIZARD

Readers,

Yesterday some fool of an eleven-year-old asked me a question about physiology, and I told him that I didn't know how a dog would react to blood spurting from his hand. After he stole a razor blade from his grandfather, the twit sliced his finger open and tried to get the neighbor's dog to heel. That dog must have thought the boy said "meal," because what happened next made the babysitter throw up half a quart of Diet Pepsi all over her Juicy jeans. Look, I'm not George. I claim no super powers of problem solving. If you write me I'll write you back, simple as that. Don't blame me for what happens if you listen to me; and for Pete's sake, don't any of you try slapping attempted manslaughter charges on me just to make a quick buck the way Joel's parents are doing.

And then George's answer to my letter arrived.

Dear Daniel,
    If she loves you, there is nothing to worry about.
    George

Thursday, 12/3/15
From: danielashe@floodgatemedia.com
To: Annie
Subject: Leonard takes the day
Dear Annie,

First: I'm thrilled that Leonard is giving you license to channel the dark side of your humor.

Second: Annie, it doesn't look like Drew is going to give up on you. Naturally, I get where he's coming from. You are a beguiling goddess, while we are bumbling men of a certain age with nothing but failed relationships in our wake. Neither of us is worthy of you, but I promise, only one of us can even begin to appreciate your ingenious mind.

Therefore, and I mean this, it would be seriously wrong for you *not* to kiss me again.

Daniel

P.S. Looking forward to seeing you Saturday night.

Friday, 12/4/15
From: clarissaandpeter@gmail.com
To: Annie and Daniel
Subject: the damn lizard

Hi Annie,

Leonard is a sicko! I read that letter and called Peter over and said, "Look at the trouble your damn lizard is getting into!" Ha! Anyway, we are floored by George and Leonard's success.

Peter says he wants to talk to you when we get home. I think it's about your Cap'n Sparks stories. Which reminds me: I know George and Sparks were planning on synchronizing their naps so they could go on adventures together. Were they successful?

Peter also told me this morning that we are coming home a week early. I asked why, but he was out the door. Anyway, we'll be getting in around dawn this Sunday morning. I'm packing right now. Please plan on sleeping in the guest room Saturday night. We might just decide to crawl into our bed with George for an hour or two. Then, how about the four of us going to lunch? I can't wait to see how amazing you and Drew look together!

I am worn out from shopping. Who knew that could even happen? Plus I really miss my baby.

See you very soon.

Love,

Clarissa

Friday, 12/4/15
From: adoherty77@yahoo.com
To: Daniel
Subject: Ahead of schedule

Dear Daniel,

My landlady is seventy years old and stands outside grilling dinner every night wearing a tiny yellow bikini. I bought sandals from a man who stayed on his knees and sang show tunes at me. The gardener has eight steel rings in his nose. So even though you harbor deluded theories about redheaded women, you are still the sanest person I've met in Los Angeles. Please relinquish your goddess fantasy. Unlike me, Aphrodite never slapped her alarm clock and muttered "Bugger" as the first word of her day.

I am very glad to hear that Clarissa and Peter are coming home early. I am ready to leave my stewardship of this mansion. Being here has been a dream, but the experience has taught me that the good life is not the one handed to you by someone else.

Handsome man, I look forward to seeing you tomorrow night and going out for a taste of Florence. Sometime between the antipasto and the risotto, I will tell you the reason I came to L.A.

Annie

It looked like Annie had waited long enough for me to ask to read Alik's manuscript. I should have obliged her already. Now I'd have to admit over our meal that my opinion of Alik is so deep-seated and negative, that the only fair thing would be for me to give his book to another agent who could be more objective.

I was even more relieved than Annie about Peter returning early. *The Blue Season* wasn't just any book, and I didn't relish the idea of sending it off on its own to London. It's always better to sit in the same room to hash out the particulars.

With Peter soon to arrive, the crunch was on. I needed to make two pristine copies of the edited manuscript, draft a synopsis of the book, come up with a list of likely publishers, and call some author friends who might agree to read the galleys and give us blurbs for the back cover. Come Monday morning, I'd be in a foot race to beat out Cameron for Peter's attention.

Happily, Oliver never returned. When I called his home his mother told me he was still too ill to leave the house, but that he had faith in my edits, and to move ahead.

So I did. I went back and made all the previous edits that Oliver had nixed. I was in the zone, feeling like I was conducting a symphony—smoothing this, hurrying that—making every page clearer and more resounding. I did what I should have been allowed to do from the beginning, and it felt wonderful.

Every few hours I put aside my fevered edits of *The Blue Season* for a few minutes to scan for another Leonard letter. Finally...

Dear Leonard,

My brother Ed is a sixty-four-year-old Vietnam vet with post-traumatic stress disorder. Years ago the VA docs declared him to be one hundred percent service connected, so he brings in big bucks and doesn't have to work. He spends his days in the nude "entertaining" himself while watching adult channels. Unfortunately, he keeps his drapes wide open. The neighbors are up in arms, and the UPS lady told me he better not order anything breakable, because from now on she is going to toss his packages from the door of her truck.

Two weeks ago Ed mangled his right hand while moving an old fan from the path of his pet hamster, Gook. The bandages prevent his usual form of self-entertainment, and now he's be-coming irrational. Any suggestions? I'm worried about him.

Brother's Keeper

Dear Brother's Keeper,

The lady who types for me has a grandmother named "Rose." Rose was a volunteer Grey Lady at London Hospital after the war, and recalls that in her day no sacrifice was too great for one of our fighting boys. Even now she wears a Royal Army medal on her bosom, placed there lovingly by Field Marshal James Caswell in recognition for all the times she went that extra, *personal* mile, to help out a bandaged hero.

I take it America's VA does not provide this service. But if I read your letter correctly, your brother only mangled his right hand. One of Rose's favorite sayings is, "Sex is like a game of Bridge. As long as you have *one* good hand, you don't need a partner!"

Saturday, 12/5/15
From: danielashe@floodgatemedia.com
To: Annie
Subject: Your own grandmother?

Dear Annie,

Immoral.

Depraved.

Hilarious.

Now I know why Grandma Rose sent you to the most repressive college on the planet.

Here's what I don't understand. How is it possible that you inhale ordinary air into your extraordinary bosom, then exhale into life a pirate dachshund, a three-armed Croatian belly dancer, and a hamster named Gook? Good God. The sheer audacity of that name gave me a very painful hiccup.

Listen, in a few hours I'll be done editing the book I've been working on since about the time I met you. It is incredibly freeing. We have much to celebrate on our date. Can I pick you up tonight at seven?

Daniel

Saturday, 12/5/15
From: adoherty77@yahoo.com
To: Daniel
Subject: dinner

Seven it is.

Drew just left, missing his sister by one day!
I'll be waiting for you in a new dress.
Annie

Saturday, 12/5/15
From: adoherty77@yahoo.com
To: Clarissa and Daniel
Subject: See you soon

Dear Clarissa and Daniel,

Drew has gone home. It was wonderful to have his company. When he gets to Ireland next month I will show him around for a few days.

Clarissa, George has said he will wake up and run into your arms no matter how early you get in. Your bed has fresh linens. Sleep off your jet lag if you wish, and I will feed and walk George and we'll read the paper together until you get up. I look forward to hearing about your trip.

This afternoon, once inside the dog park, Sparks and

George laid siege to quite the upper crust baby carriage. They circled and barked and I rushed over to apologize to the not-so-young mother. She scowled and reached into the buggy, pulling out a pair of Chihuahuas. Both little creatures were wearing tiny boots on their feet. With a sick feeling in the pit of me, I saw there was no baby in that carriage at all! Had she left her infant alone at home? Afraid for her mind, I crouched in front of her and said, "Where is your baby, mum?"

She leaned away from me, picking up each dog to kiss on the forehead. "These *are* my babies!"

I stood up.

So there was no desperate baby to save, but surely the wee dogs must be quite damaged, forced as they were to be wearing orthotics on their feet and having to ride in a carriage. I said, "I'm so sorry your dogs are lame."

"You're not from around here are you?" she sniffed. "These dogs have delicate paws, and I'm not about to let them get all rough and calloused." And with that she pulled a boot off one dog and put the paw to her lips.

Clearly she was daft.

I said goodbye and backed away. George and Sparks followed me, and when we were a good distance from the carriage George said, "I know what you're thinking."

"Do you now?"

"You're thinking that American dogs are spoiled and babied, but in this case you could not be more wrong. Those two dogs need some coddling on this side, because no one in the parallel sea world works harder or in more dangerous conditions than they do."

"Don't be ridiculous. What could those wee things do?"

"For you information, they are Lee and Andra, the crack

rescue team of an ice breaker ship. They have made many famous rescues."

"Go on with ya," I snorted, certain George was having a bit a fun with me. "How is that possible?"

"Did you not see their boots? Where others would freeze their paws off, those two are well protected. They can stand for hours on the coldest tundra, and they are light enough to walk on the thinnest ice."

"So who have they rescued?"

George looked over at Sparks. "Me," she whispered. "They saved my reputation not so long ago, and George and I were just thanking them again."

I sat down on the grass and motioned them closer. "You'd best be the one telling me what happened," I said, looking right at George. "Your mother asked to hear of any adventure you've had with Cap'n Sparks, and our time is running short."

"My mother? Goodness, yes, please take out your notebook.

Glic

by

George Flood

Sparks and I time our naps and bedtimes now so we may share adventures at sea. While I can't explain it, somehow we are able to spend weeks aboard the ship in just the few hours that our bodies are dozing here.

Sparks had a new contract to fulfill with King Craic, the tall, almond-eyed ruler of the large and prosperous country that has the shape of a butterfly. The king directed his men to load The Minerva *with gold bars, rich fabrics, glass vessels, fine perfume,* and an elephant named Glic. Our mission was to deliver these gifts of goodwill to King Malarki and his daughter, Alainn.

King Craic told us that he met Alainn when she and her father had come to his wedding ten years earlier.

"He surprised us when he arrived," Craic said, "Kings rarely leave their own countries to attend the weddings of other kings. However, Malarki needed an excuse to escape his wife. She had just learned a thing or two about his dalliance with a certain young pastry chef; so with my conveniently timed wedding invitation in hand, he packed up his eight-year-old daughter and left the queen in peace so that she might cool down. He and Alainn arrived at my palace a week before the wedding and were put up in a lovely suite of rooms.

"Being the groom I spent my time as I pleased, which included early morning visits to my stable of beloved elephants. This is where I first ran into Alainn. The young princess was enchanted by the gray giants, and she bothered the trainers with endless questions. But how could I be anything but charmed by a lovely child who shared my passion for pachyderms? On that first morning I let her feed them out of hand. Alainn held out a bunch of hay and said, 'Once upon a time this elephant was a magic mango tree, and anyone who ate her fruit was given their heart's desire.' Then we fed another and she said, 'This one was once a girl who could mimic the sound of any bird. And then this old fellow ...'

"I laughed. 'Little princess, how do you know these things?'

"Alainn looked very serious. 'Why, they told me of course.'"

It was then that Craic asked Alainn if she had a favorite. The child ran to a young female and hugged her leg. "This one. She was once a princess, just like me. She could draw pictures that looked as real as life, but when she grew up her father wanted her to marry a man she didn't love. She snuck into the woods where she met a hobgoblin, who, in exchange for a flattering drawing of himself, turned her into this elephant. And now she is very happy."

Craic had never met such a child! He knelt in front of Alainn and said, "You have the gift of stories, little one, and for that you deserve to ride this magical girl. Let me ask your father for permission. Stay right here."

Craic returned very soon, and the trainers helped him and Alainn get atop the beautiful elephant. Craic kept his long, tawny arm around the girl's waist, and together they rode to one of the many festivals being held in honor of the marriage. During that trip Alainn petted and kissed the elephant and emitted countless squeals of the most infectious laughter Craic had ever heard.

The next morning, when Craic entered the stables, the young princess was there waiting with hope in her eyes. He asked if she would like another ride, and Alainn ran to the same elephant. The trainers helped the pair up, and again the little girl delighted Craic with her laughter and a new story about the princess elephant. They rode together for the next three days. Each morning Craic asked, "Do you have yet another story for me?"

"Oh yes!" Alainn cried, and told the king her newest tale full of magic and love.

On the morning of his wedding, Craic walked out of his rooms and almost stepped on a large chalk drawing in the middle of the stone floor. He stopped and stared. He rang for his servants and ordered them to pull back the curtains and place eight oil lamps around the edges of the picture. Each additional illumination enhanced a stunning effect. The drawing was of an elephant, rendered not only in height and length, but seemingly in depth! Atop the elephant was Craic with his arm around Alainn.

The king had never seen anything like it.

Craic could not break away from all the ceremonies that

filled the next ten hours, and it was deep into the evening before he searched the banquet hall for Alainn and her father. They were not to be found. He ran up to their suite of rooms where he met a solitary maid sweeping the floor.

"King Malarki and his daughter, have you seen them?" he asked.

"Yes, majesty. They left to catch the tide for home," she said. "The child was already asleep in her father's arms, poor thing."

Craic glanced around the room, his eyes lighting on a pile of linens by the door. He walked over and picked one up. "What are these stains, these reds and blues and such?"

"Majesty," she said, "the child had chalk all over her arms and knees and feet this morning. It took two of us to clean her off and get her ready for the wedding. We asked her what she had been up to, and she said she had spent the night making you a present. Did you get a drawing from the child, your highness?"

Craic nodded. "Yes. And it was the best present I ever had."

A decade had since passed. King Craic was now a widower. It had been a loveless marriage, as so many royal unions are. Still he had respected his wife and remained faithful to her.

But as the days wore on he found himself spending more time in the company of his elephants, and this reminded him of that happy little storyteller who rode with him so long ago. One morning he summoned his ambassador and gave him a mission: He was to embark immediately for Malarki's court. The pretext of the visit was to keep up good relations; but the ambassador carried with him a very specific set of orders. If he ascertained that Alainn was not yet betrothed, he would take King Malarki aside and tell him that Craic was still a young man at thirty-one, and would like to make Alainn his queen.

Soon after he arrived at Malarki's court, the ambassador learned that Alainn was free of obligation and he made the proposal. Her father pretended to mull it over, but the ambassador could see that Malarki could barely contain himself. The Butterfly Nation opened its doors to all races and religions, and that diversity of skills and talents led to its legendary wealth. Craic himself was neither this nor that, but all together, and a perfect representative of his country. And what a country it was! Malarki had seen for himself the opulence of the palace, and the immaculate upkeep of even the lowliest farm. For Malarki to have his daughter singled out was an enormous honor, and one that would put esteem back in the eyes of his queen, who had been hounding him for a year to find Alainn a husband while the girl was still young and beautiful.

The ambassador cleared his throat and said, "Your majesty, the only stipulation King Craic has made is that your daughter—herself—desires the match."

The ambassador soon returned home with the news that the princess had grown into a most comely young woman. Then he looked down and said, "Sire, I was not given leave to speak directly to the princess. They have some rule there about her talking to men outside the family; but be assured that King Malarki was well advised of the condition. When he met with me the next day, it was to say that he and the queen had agreed to the match. When I inquired as to Alainn's happiness regarding the union, he waved his hand and assured me that his daughter would be most pleased to soon find herself the queen of our peaceful country."

King Craic thanked him, and bid him leave.

Skepticism dampened his joy. Why was there no letter from Alainn revealing she was ready to become his joyful bride? All the ambassador brought back was the word of her father—a man named, of all things, Malarki.

It did not bode well.

Craic was a man who had married a woman he did not love and who did not love him, and it taught him one thing for certain. It was better to live lonely as one than lonely as two.

Soon after, Sparks and I set sail with the hold full of gifts and the elephant Glic walking free around the deck.

Just as we were rounding the southernmost tip of the cape we ran into a treacherous storm that tossed The Minerva *around like a toy. Poor Glic! We had to tether her with irons and chains, but even so she was exhausted from the effort it took to stay on her feet. I was down below when I heard the floorboards snapping. I ran up to the deck and heard the men shout, "Elephant overboard!"*

We watched her struggle to swim in the roiling and bitter cold water. We had left port with a ramp especially designed for her, and we lowered it into the water, but by then she was far too weak to find purchase and drag herself on board. Our sailors devised a makeshift raft from a dozen life preservers, and two of them jumped in that freezing water and threaded her feet through the webbing of the straps.

Hours went by. Even though her weight was supported, the poor girl was cold and completely worn out. I knew if she fell asleep her trunk would slip below the water and she would drown. We were about to give up hope when Sparks saw Lee and Andra's ship on the horizon. We flew our distress flag. They were upon us in minutes and saw our predicament.

As their men set up a giant winch, Lee and Andra slipped on their boots and dove into the water. Their men threw them a large canvas cloth that had heavy clips at each corner. Lee attached one end to the winch with her teeth, while Andra took the other end in her mouth and dove under Glic's belly, then appeared on the far side of the elephant and attached the other two clips to the winch. Both dogs climbed on Glic's back and signaled their men to raise her out of the water.

What a sight! There was Glic, thirty feet in the air, dripping seawater with the tiny booted dogs on her back.

Sparks brought The Minerva right under the elephant. Carefully she was lowered to the repaired deck, and then a great cheer went up! We invited Lee and Andra to Sparks' cabin for some Snausages, while the crew used blankets to massage and warm the exhausted elephant.

We gave the Chihuahuas our hearty thanks. They yipped and said that as rescues go, this was an easy one. "She was mighty big, but clever enough to hold still," said Andra. "You would be surprised how often we have to chase victims down to save their lives!"

Three days later we arrived at Malarki's kingdom and anchored a good bit off shore. Sparks and I went in the first dingy to safeguard the bars of gold until they reached the king. We were escorted into Malarki's throne room and introduced ourselves, though anyone could see he could barely take his eyes off the gold. Moments later Alainn strode in, but stood apart from her father. For a human she was quite good-looking, having a long, shining mane and fine white teeth. But truth be told, she seemed anything but a happy bride-to-be.

As the dinghies made trips back and forth to relieve The Minerva of her burdens, and the gifts piled up in the room, we couldn't help but feel the tension between father and daughter rising as well. Malarki and Alainn didn't speak or look at each other. By the time the fine fabrics and glass vessels showed up, the young woman was near tears. I made so bold as to ask the princess if she would accompany us to shore, explaining there was one special gift that was for her alone and could not be delivered to the palace. She agreed at once, clearly relieved to get away from her father.

The Minerva *crew knew that as soon as they saw the fabrics reach the shore they were to lower the ramp and help Glic into the water. Their timing was faultless. As we stood with Alainn on the beach, all that could be seen at first was the dinghy that accompanied the swimming giant. I kept my eyes on Alainn's face as she stared glumly at the slowly approaching boat. As it got closer, a quizzical look overcame her. Then, as Glic's bobbing head and curled-up trunk came into view, Alainn, mindless of her silks, moved like a sleepwalker into the sea. The water was up to her bosom when she leaned forward, her hands cupped around her eyes. Soon she let out a cry. She turned to me and shouted, "Good dog, is that Glic?"*

Sparks and I were stunned. I said, "How do you know her name?"

Alainn cried, "She let me ride her a long time ago. She was my favorite elephant. I can't believe King Craic remembers this!"

"Princess," I said, "the king so loved the stories you told him, that you have never been far from his thoughts!"

Tears dripped from Alainn's eyes into the sea. As Glic emerged from the water Alainn wrapped her arms around the elephant's leg, laughing and crying at once. Glic remembered her as well, and let out a thunderous trumpet. The trainer helped Alainn up on Glic's back, and we all walked up to the palace together—Alainn laughing with delight, much like I imagine she did when she was a girl of eight.

The next morning we set sail again, this time with both the princess and Glic on board. On our pleasant trip back, Alainn confessed to us that she had recently fallen in love with a squire named Gorach.

Gorach wasn't handsome or smart, but when you are a

princess you are protected from men around the clock, so the pickings are slim. Alainn decided Gorach's low forehead meant he was determined, and his mouth breathing was understandable considering the amount of hair that crowded his nostrils. Yes, his codpiece seemed rather small for an adult, but Alainn was still vague on what exactly was behind this fashion ornament of men anyway. Besides her father and her very old tutors, Gorach was the only man she had contact with, and she imagined good things of him out of necessity.

On her eighteenth birthday Alainn decided she wanted to kiss Gorach. She believed that, like her, he had never shared a kiss, and that together they would experience pure love's first touch of lip to lip. She stepped around the corner of the armaments room where he was employed to polish the swords, and there he was all right, working his way through the bodice lacings of Nathair, the very same pastry chef that Malarki had dallied with ten years earlier.

Poor Alainn was devastated. She decided she could never love again—that a heart once broken could not be repaired—and whatever other nonsense young humans believe when first love is crushed. The very next day she headed to the throne room to tell her father she wanted to go to a nunnery, but before the words were formed, he told her that she would soon be married to the great King Craic.

"I was still smarting from being deceived by Gorach when you saw me," Alainn said, "and that is why I was so tearful. But everything changed when I saw Glic swimming toward me. I have long remembered how dashing Craic was, and how kind he was to me. Then, when I saw Glic in the water, and heard you say that Craic remembered every story I told him, I felt the light of true love wash into my heart! Gorach is no more than

an ant to me. All I want is to marry Craic and be his good and true partner in life."

When The Minerva landed, the ambassador met us on shore and escorted us to the inner chambers of the palace. He said to Alainn, "King Craic wishes you to go through these doors, princess. He will meet you in that room." He bowed, indicating she was to proceed without him.

Alainn bit her lip. As she opened the door she turned to us and whispered, "Cap'n Sparks, George, oh please come with me."

We walked beside her. As soon as we crossed the threshold we saw twenty oil lamps in a perfect circle on the floor, forming a frame around the drawing of Glic.

Alainn approached it slowly, her eyes wide, her hands crossed over her bosom. She walked around the drawing twice, saying over and over, "I cannot believe this!"

We heard a door open and looked up to see King Craic step into the room. He bowed and said, "Princess, welcome to your new home."

I could sense the question in his eyes—had this young woman traveled there only in duty to her father?

Alainn forgot all her royal training and rushed into Craic's arms. He picked her up and swung her in a full circle, once, twice, three times, the both of them laughing with total abandon. Ah, but it was a lovely sound!

When he set her down she took his hand and pulled him to the drawing.

"My darling Craic, how did you preserve this? It is merely chalk, and subject to disappear a little more with every breeze!"

"I had a team of artists come in," he said. "They carefully applied many coats of clear lacquer. Still, anyone seen to step on this drawing is banished from the palace."

The happy couple walked hand in hand to the stable and

took a ride on Glic's back. This time the beautiful princess turned around, put her hand gently on Craic's face, and then their lips parted slightly to share pure love's first kiss.

Saturday, 12/5/15
From: clarissaandpeter@gmail.com
To: Annie and Daniel
Subject: Grateful

Darling Annie,

I am in tears. What a wonderful gift you have given me.

Love always,

Clarissa

XIX
The Sweetest Story

When Annie opened the tall, red door of the Flood mansion, the light behind glowed around her figure like a silver frame. Her dress was sleeveless and black, the fabric close to her body. This wasn't the medieval sprite who came to my door two months ago, or the flirty knock-out in a skintight bathing suit. This Annie was polished perfection. Most transforming, her hair was *straight*. It coursed without a ripple from her side part to several inches past her collarbone. She stood aside and I entered the round, marble foyer.

"You look very handsome, Mr. Ashe."

"Hello, miss." I said, pointedly looking over her head and around the room. "I've come to pick up Ms. Annie Doherty. Would you let her know I've arrived?"

"Wanker," she said, knocking into me with her shoulder. She picked a shawl up off the foyer table and bent over to pet George goodbye, her hair sliding over her bare shoulder in such a sensual way that only a lifetime of conforming to conventional norms stopped me from sweeping her into my arms. When we stepped outside she hooked her hand around my elbow, and I felt the Earth give up half its grip on me.

At Bardi's, the maître d seated us in a booth. His eyes lingering on Annie, he took the napkin from her glass and put it on her lap before walking away. I cleared my throat and pointed to the napkin still in my glass. "I see us non-gorgeous patrons have to fend for ourselves."

"Don't make me blush."

"Annie Doherty, I'm lucky I can even talk. You are the most beautiful woman in town."

"Bollocks."

"Okay. Clearly not the *classiest.*"

Annie laughed with a little snort, which got me going, and mercifully the waiter appeared before we made fools of ourselves. She ordered a glass of Prosecco, and I told him to bring us the bottle. As soon as we clinked glasses she said, "I want t' tell you more about the book that Alik wrote."

I nodded, thinking *might as well get the abusive, dead husband out of the way before the food arrives.* "Go ahead."

"Alik's plan was t' come to Los Angeles and live with his brother Sergi until his book was published. He had great faith in Sergi's negotiating skills, and trusted him t' get the best deal. But from the start I saw a problem with the length a' the book. I told Alik that maybe Russian readers might rush out t' buy a fifteen-hundred page novel, but the majority of English-speaking readers won't."

"You were right," I said. "Michener got away with it, but a new novelist? No. An average read in the industry is three to five hundred pages."

"Each time I brought it up he said he'd fix it later, then insist I help him with the next scene."

"You were the engine for his book."

"More like his muse."

"No, Annie. Muses only inspire. You gave Alik the conflicts and plot twists he needed to get it done. And truthfully, that's the only reason I want to read it. Where is the book now?"

"It's in the hands of his agent."

"Oh," I said, and put down my glass. "I thought you were about to ask me to read it and give you my professional opinion. Is it going to be published?"

Annie tipped her head, her finger gently circling the rim of her glass. "The agent is right here in L.A. and has just today finished editing the book. In fact, he thinks it will be ready t' go to a publishing house as soon as next week." She slowly lifted her eyes to look me dead on. The air between us stilled. It took me several moments to speak.

"Wait. Annie ...." I chuckled at the absurdity of what I was about to say. "You're not telling me that Alik wrote *The Blue Season*?"

She held my gaze several seconds before nodding.

My brain stopped working as abruptly as if a steel bolt had been wedged in the gears.

"I'm sorry, Daniel. Things got really bollixed up."

"But Oliver ... Who is he?"

"Alik's nephew." She closed her eyes a moment and took a deep breath. "After Alik died I went back t' Ireland and took his hand-written manuscript with me. Every day I typed up ten or so pages and saved them on a flash drive. It took me months t' finish." She paused, waiting for a response.

"Annie, I'm speechless, so you might as well keep explaining this to me."

"Fair enough. Before I left Ireland I'd made an agreement with Sergi. I would find an agent for the book, and he would deal with any a' the day-to-day decisions. We were going t' split the royalties."

She paused, and I nodded that I was keeping up.

"I started my search for an agent months ago. When I came across the Floodgate website and saw your picture, I couldn't get it out of my mind. I found myself thinking about you every day." She lowered her eyes.

"What happened to Sergi?"

Annie shook her head. "It was only when I was standin' right there at his front door that I learned he had died. I'm certain I looked at his widow the way you're lookin' at me right now. I had spent months with this plan, and I was shaken. She invited me in, and that's when I met Oliver."

"I can't believe you turned the book over to that character."

"A' course I didn't," Annie said, and rubbed the skin between her eyebrows with her ring finger. "I told his ma that with Sergi gone, I would just go ahead on my own. She asked if there were anything a'tal she could do, and I said I'd appreciate her directing me t' the nearest library; that I needed a computer for half an hour or so to send the agent my letter and the first chapter. She said that Oliver would be happy t' let me use his computer. He, a course, acted like that was a big imposition. I tried t' beg off, but his ma pushed him off the sofa.

"So I followed Oliver to his room. It was dark and smelly and I hated being there. He sat right down in the only chair, so I had t' stand behind him at the computer. I directed him to the Floodgate web site, and handed him the thumb drive. He clicked on your email address, and I had him open up and paste in my cover letter. That went well; but when he opened the manuscript itself and tried to cut and paste in the sample chapter, the paragraphs transferred over in single space. Your guidelines say samples have to be in double space, which is how I typed them in the first place. So I told him he had to delete and try again, which he did, but it wasn't any different; and the commands to change spacing didn't exist on his email. So he had to double-click at every line. After the first few pages, he turned around and said he didn't like people looking over his shoulder, and that he could finish it faster if I left. You know how he rolls his eyes."

"I do."

"So I said, 'Fine. Just be sure to let me know when you're done so I can check it before y' send it off. I'll be in the kitchen havin' tea with your ma.'

"Fifteen minutes later he walked in, handed me the memory stick, and said he had sent the sample off already. I said 'Oh dear! You didn't hear me say I needed t' check it before it went off?' He bugged his eyes out, said 'You're welcome,' and skulked back to his bedroom."

Annie looked down at her hands. "Daniel, I should a' stayed by the computer until he sent it off. I knew it even then. But he was so grumpy about me being there. It was his room, and he told me to leave, so I did.

"When I drove back to the hotel I believed my cover letter and the first chapter of *The Blue Season* were already in your mailbox."

It pained me to say the obvious out loud. "But Oliver didn't send it then. The little shit downloaded the entire book onto his hard drive."

"So there I was," Annie said, raising her eyes to mine, "thinking that with Sergi gone I'd better stay in L.A. until I heard from you. With some help from the desk clerk at my hotel, I found and rented the apartment from the bikini widow. After that I was at a loss with how to take up my time. Your agency site said it could take weeks to get a response."

Annie picked up her glass and took a sip. She looked like she needed to collect her thoughts for what was coming next.

"My landlady invited me for tea the day I moved in, and I was sittin' at her table, and next t' me was her phone book.

I started t' look through, jotting down addresses for art museums and the like, and since you were on my mind, I looked you up as well. I told my landlady the name a' your street, and she said she had a friend there, and it wasn't fifteen minutes away. So I drove by, and by God, there you were, going in the gates a' the dog park."

She smiled to herself. "You were even more handsome than your photo, and it was so dear to see such a tall man with a dachshund."

Annie glanced up and I nodded for her to continue, waiting for the boulder of all these revelations to roll into me.

"I pulled over to watch. All the dogs came over to you like they knew you were one t' play. You pulled three tennis balls out a' your pocket and started this game where you pretended t' throw a ball one way, but really threw it the other, and the dogs just loved it. You played with any that wanted in, but I could see y' were concerned about Eddie bein' too slow t' ever get a ball. So you held him back, you threw two balls really far, and all the other dogs went for them. Then you let go a' Eddie and threw the third ball a short distance just for him. He brought it back and you knelt down and hugged him, and he was so happy and proud that he wagged his whole body."

Annie's eyes softened. "That's when I said t' myself, *He'd be the one.*"

I blinked. "The one to agent the book?"

"No, Daniel. I'm saying' I thought you were the one ... for me. Back in Ireland, when I first saw your photograph, I thought: *Now there's a face I could look at for the rest a' my life.* Then when I saw you in person, and how you played with the dogs, how you challenged them in such a light-hearted and kind way, I was a bit over the moon. So I made up that advert with Sparks on the bottom, then drove back the next day and stuck it in your door. I could hardly believe it when you called me three hours later. I could barely look you in the face that night. You said something about how your neighbor would think I was your girlfriend, and I felt my cheeks burn off my face. You must a' noticed."

I didn't answer. I was adrift in her sea of disclosures, but there was a kink I needed to straighten out before I became lost.

"Sweetheart," I said, surprising and thrilling myself with the word, "believe me, I want to talk about us. I hope we get to learn everything about each other, but first, please explain why you didn't tell me your connection to *The Blue Season* as soon as you knew I had asked Oliver to bring it in."

"But how was I to know you contacted Oliver? The cover letter I wrote only had *my* phone number and email address. As far as I knew, *The Blue Season* was still in your queue."

"Right. Sorry. I feel like I'm caught in the mud. Annie, I called Oliver to bring in the completed manuscript as soon as I read the sample. We started working on it right away."

Annie nodded. "I know that *now*. But when y' first told me about working late with a difficult author, a' course I thought you were talkin' about another book. Over the weeks you referred to him as being surly, of having gelled-up hair, and that it was hard for you t' believe he had written such a masterpiece. Once or twice it crossed my mind that your author sounded like Oliver, but that seemed ridiculous and paranoid. It was four days ago, when you called him a 'pissant,' that I thought, okay, I'm going to ask for his name so I can put this crazy idea t' bed."

She was twisting her napkin.

"I was standin' in the kitchen when I got your response. There it was, 'Oliver Nikitin.' I sank right t' the floor. I must a' sat there a good fifteen minutes, holding George and feeling like the earthquake hit."

A new thought slammed into me. "Oh boy. I've got to tell Peter that the contract Oliver signed with the agency is worthless. Right now we have no right to agent that book."

"Are you sure then? Even though he's Alik's only living blood relative?"

"He'd only have a possible claim if Alik had left Sergi the manuscript in his will."

"Alik didn't have a will."

"Then you own *The Blue Season,* one hundred percent. Believe me, I've had two scriptwriters die before their work got sold, and the spouse owns the rights. Not the kids, and certainly not some nephew."

Annie looked at the ceiling. "I'm so glad I didn't go back t' Ireland like I planned. If I hadn't been here, if we hadn't become friends, the book would a' been published with Oliver as the author. Makes me sick to think it."

"And I would have lost my job. As soon as you came forward with the truth, Peter would've drop-kicked me out of the agency. What did you do after you read my email and you finally knew what Oliver was up to?"

"I collected myself off the floor and drove over t' confront him. I asked his ma if she knew what Oliver had done, and she started t' cry almost before I had the words out, so it was obvious she did. I asked her to leave so I could talk with Oliver in private."

Annie pursed her lips a moment. "I asked him why he did it. He sat there, silent, looking away. I just waited him out, and finally he said, 'What do you care? You got t' go to college and travel the world and what have I got?'

"I said, 'Oliver, it is up t' every person to make their own way.'

"He sneered and said, 'Don't you see, that's what I was trying to do!'

"I threw up my hands and told him that he needed t' go to Floodgate the next day and apologize for the trouble he caused and to tell you t' edit the book any way you saw fit. I said that was the only way I was going to share any a' the royalties with his ma."

"That's it!" I said, slapping the table with my palm. "Oliver came in and said he decided to let me do the final edits on my own. He certainly didn't own up to what he'd done. Please tell me you don't still plan on sharing the royalties with those two."

"I don't. I gave him that chance t' own up and he didn't." Annie took a sip of her wine. "The day after I talked t' Oliver I kept my phone handy, waiting t' hear your voice being all surprised by what he told you. The hours went by with no call, so I knew he was still pretending t' be the author. And I was not going to confront him again. The way he glared at me, like he wanted me dead, reminded me a little too much of Alik."

Annie paused, shaking her head side to side. "Daniel, we might have a very big problem. As I see it, Oliver is holding all the cards. He sent the sample from his computer, and the next day he brought you the whole manuscript printed out. It had his name on it, and he signed the contract with your agency." She opened up her clutch and took out a two-inch flash memory stick. "This is all I have."

She set it on the tablecloth.

I squinted for a moment. "Oliver had that memory stick to himself for, what, half an hour? Have you checked to see if the manuscript is still on it?"

She winced. "I didn't think t' look until I got back from

confronting him." She picked it up and dropped it back in her purse. "It's empty. He deleted *The Blue Season*."

Her lips pressed together in pain.

"Don't worry. I've got the original on my hard drive at work. If it makes you feel any better, I'll forward it to you and you can download it back to your memory stick."

"But the date appears on the download. It would look like we were in it together to swindle the book from him."

"I didn't think of that. Well, all you need to do is call your grandmother and have her send the original handwritten version. No one could argue with that kind of proof. And tell her to send your marriage license and Alik's death certificate as well."

She shook her head. "My grandmother is half-blind, and that manuscript is no way all together. It's pieced all over three rooms. I'd have t' fly home and do it myself."

"If it comes to that I'll go with you. But I'm sure it won't be necessary. The day after you told Oliver to confess, I told him the kinds of questions he'd be asked when the book came out, and he literally ran from my office and hasn't been back since. He knew right then he was in way over his gelled-up head. I have no doubt he's hiding in his room, sucking his thumb."

I took out my cell phone. "I'm going to relieve your mind right now. I'll call and tell him I know everything, and that he needs to come in to Floodgate Monday morning to sign a form that agrees the previous contract is null and void. If he doesn't show I'll get my lawyer involved."

Annie shook her head. "If you're sure the book belongs t' me, I should be the one t' stand up for it." She took out her own phone, scrolled her contact list, and then held it to her ear.

"Hello Oliver, this is Annie. I'm sittin' here with Daniel Ashe, and I've just told him everything. He says the only way you are not in a world a' trouble is if you show up at the agency on Monday t' sign a document that says you have no connection to that book. Only then will Floodgate keep your identity theft from the authorities. Understand? Oliver?"

Annie looked wide-eyed and pulled the phone away from her ear.

"He said, 'Yeah bitch, I understand,' and clicked off."

"That little worm. Annie, I promise you we'll get this straightened out on Monday. Think no more about Oliver."

Soon we were both smiling again. Our food came and I had to marvel at this wonderful turn of events. I was rid of that loathsome kid, Annie was going to make a fortune, and we would be linked together in a new and lasting way.

When our plates were removed, Annie picked up her glass and swirled the liquid. I saw mischief in the set of her lips.

"Daniel, that day we first met it was easy t' see you couldn't wait t' get me out a' your house."

Before I could respond she put up her hand to stop me.

"You were scared a' this," she picked up a lock of her hair. "When I read your first note I thought, so much for my crush; this man says he will never be in the same room with me again."

"And not three weeks later I was begging you to meet me at the farmer's market."

"That you did!"

"Then why didn't you show up?"

She shook her head. "Because I believed you hadn't seen the sample of *The Blue Season* yet. I knew that once you finally opened it and saw my name, you'd call straight away, and until that happened, I didn't want t' muddy the waters any more than I already had." She tilted her head. "Ah, but I loved how y' kept asking me t' meet. Then I was destroyed when you said it wouldn't be a date. You said all your old girlfriends agreed that you couldn't fall in love, and that you had met Victoria, a woman who was just like you." She looked past my shoulder. "When I read that I sat down in a heap. I felt sorry for m'self for a bit, then I remembered that note a' yours, when you said Peter had called me a Scheherazade—and I thought if that were true, then *you* were just like ...." she smiled a little and shrugged.

"The king in *The Arabian Nights* who couldn't fall in love," I said to save her the trouble.

"Yes." She inhaled slowly. "And I understood that I'd been using my stories to draw you to me the only way I could. But if I had met you at the farmer's market, if I had answered all your questions, that would have been it. You would have stopped thinking about me."

"Look, it's true that I went there with questions about you. How could I not? You were leaving me clues about your past ... making me a character in your stories ... it was keeping me up at night."

She smiled. "It was only after I didn't show up that you wrote I was the most interesting person you knew nothing about. That gave me hope. The next thing I knew, you asked if you could come visit me at the mansion."

"I don't know what to say. I can't imagine why you thought I was worth all this effort."

"Darlin' man, I told you already. You're the one."

"Annie, I feel like I'm breathing a new kind of air. Don't you know that you are completely out of my league?"

She leaned forward and put her hand on mine. "Don't *you* know that as attracted as I was to your photo back in Ireland, that was not a speck t' how I feel now that I know how kind and funny and smart y' are? You're the one out a' my league. You've been nothing but honest, while I pretended to be a dog walker so I could poke my nose into every corner of your life. You should be getting a court order against me."

"I'll get right on it."

She leaned back and tapped the table. "One day at your house I found an address book full a' women's names and phone numbers."

"All clients."

"Sure they are. You know what else I found? Your Social Security number, the passwords to your bank account, VISA, Amazon, and PayPal—all of it right in that one book. And you let the likes a' me, a complete stranger, into your house. I could a' made off with everything you own."

"Then I would have tracked you down, and not because I was looking for my money. The only woman I'm interested in isn't in that address book. She's sitting across from me right now. She can't swim, she snorts when she laughs, she has a nefarious past I'm not sure I even want to know about, and she's been stalking me."

"All true."

"I'm just saying that while I still think you're in denial about your magical abilities, I know you're human. Just an enchanted one."

"Enchanted, am I?" she said with a laugh.

There's no doubt about it." I pointed to imaginary bullet points on the tablecloth: "When we first met you were dressed like a boy from the early nineteen hundreds. Then I saw you in that swimsuit looking like a Vargas girl, and now you could pass for a Manhattan socialite. That's magic. Just like having red hair, and skipping around the world, and writing stories at the speed of light. And now you have brought me a book that's going to change both our lives forever. On the human side, you're not perfect. You married a man you only knew for four days. You left Oliver alone with the life's work of your dead husband. And between what you did at Stella Maris, and the men you left in your wake around Europe, don't even get me started on your morals." Annie opened her mouth to protest but I cut her off. "There were some poor judgment calls in there. But real people make mistakes. Those names in my address book would attest to a few of my own." I reached for her hand. "But somehow you and I are sitting here together, and I have never been happier. You are adorable to me. And just for the record, while I might be slow on the uptake, if you had met me at the farmer's market, I think I would have realized soon enough that I was falling for you."

"Falling? You? Am I hearing this right?"

"I prowled that market like a panther. I practically knocked over tables to get close to a redheaded vendor thinking she was you. If I had seen the real you, I would have been the happiest man alive. Just the way I felt when we played cribbage. Just the way I feel right now."

Annie picked up my hand and kissed my knuckles.

"I don't suppose you have that bathing suit on under your dress," I whispered.

"What?"

"You in that bathing suit—that's the image I want on the back of my eyelids when I breathe my last."

She was quiet.

"Beautiful girl, I want to be with you tonight."

She widened her eyes. "Bold as brass y'are! You're asking me t' be a wanton woman then?"

I nodded.

She whispered, "You're not the least bit a shy Irish lad, now are ya?"

I smiled, my eyes intent on her lips.

We entered the Flood mansion through the back. Annie turned off the security system and propped the door open with a cast iron squirrel statue. "So George can come and go," she said. "Else he barks."

She led me to the pool. "Do y' know what I like best about this climate?" she asked as she slipped off her heels. Before I could answer she unzipped her dress and let it fall in a puddle at her feet. Her bra and panties were ice blue lace, and her skin picked up dancing shimmers from the lights under the water. She moved slowly, climbing down the ladder and stepping back into the water, her eyes never leaving my face. I peeled off my own clothes and dove in, surfacing right in front of her. She put her hands on my shoulders and we came together for a kiss.

Her wild flesh!

It was everything our first kiss was, and more. When it ended she put her mouth near my ear and said, "Do y' know how beautiful y' are to me?"

I shook my head.

"Then take me to a proper bed, Mr. Ashe, and I will show you."

We climbed out. I wrapped her in a towel and carried her through the open door and up the stairs. When I set her down on the sheets she circled her arms around her head.

I recognized it as the pose in the painting of the girl with three arms.

"Allura." I crawled toward her. "Nin," I whispered as I traced her body with my fingertips. "Alainn."

She pulled me to her and kissed me.

The world disappeared. I heard nothing, saw nothing but this woman. My lips were on her neck, her shoulder, her breast. I had been thirsting for her and I would not, could not stop. Every sound she made, every movement, inflamed me. There was no trial and error. No first time jitters. I was making love to the artist, the prankster, the storyteller—and it was the truest moment in my life.

I said it.

"I am in love with you."

And then I drank her in.

Later, with Annie's head on my shoulder and her finger drawing swirls on my chest, she told me the sweetest story I'd ever heard:

"There once was a lass from a tiny village in Ireland who saw a photograph of a handsome man in America, and thought *Someday I will make love to him, and it will change me forever.*"

XX
Part Two

Being in love, whatever that meant, whatever vulnerabilities that opened, was so beyond my control that I would have given over to sleep once I got home Saturday night, but my mind churned on Annie's revelation over dinner that it was her late husband who wrote *The Blue Season.* That changed the trajectory of my life as abruptly as a soldier turns 180 degrees when he hears, "About Face!"

How soon after he was alone with the manuscript did Oliver decide to download it to his hard drive and erase it from Annie's memory stick? A minute? Two? And what made him do it? I'd had the loathsome task of working with Oliver for a month and still couldn't fathom how his mind works. Nor did I want to.

Victoria also made many a guest appearance to my agitated mind, and I knew on Monday, sometime between going over the edited version of *The Blue Season* with Peter, getting a signed statement from Oliver, and having Annie come in to go over the new contract for the book, I had to slip into Victoria's office to tell her that marriage wasn't in the cards for us.

By four in the morning I'd given up on sleep, made myself coffee, and planned our incredible future. Now it was Annie who would be my partner to bring *The Blue Season* to the world. She would make a fortune, I was rid of the odious Oliver, and soon I would leave Peter and start my own agency.

Sunday I waited until noon to call Annie. She didn't pick up, and I imagined she was lunching with Peter and Clarissa or driving home. I sent her a text an hour later. I called her at four, again at five, again at seven, each time leaving a voice message.

Much as I tried to convince myself she had inadvertently turned off her ringer, not hearing back left me with a raging case of insecurity. For the first time in my life I had told a woman that I loved her, and then the next day she didn't take my calls?

One sleepless night I can handle. Two—forget it. But not hearing back from Annie was only half the reason I remained wide-eyed. I spent hours rehearsing how to tell Peter the news that Oliver Nikitin was not the author of *The Blue Season,* and that was a conversation that needed to be handled like a vial of nitroglycerin.

Under the best of circumstances Peter's temper could be swift and misdirected. Unfortunately in this case, as the agent who brought Oliver to Floodgate, the bullseye for this colossal fuck-up was definitely on my back. I've seen Peter go from zero to Code Red because we lost a mediocre contract. How would he react to hearing we didn't have a legitimate claim for *The Blue Season*, a property he expected would bring every movie mogul hat-in-hand to the Floodgate door?

By dawn I decided my best bet was not to lead in with the explanation of how Oliver had duped us. Let Peter hear first that the rightful owner of the manuscript was coming in to sign on with us, and that she wanted me as the agent and no other. "We dodged a bullet!" I'd say, and "Thank God we found out now," and "If I hadn't discovered that Oliver stole the manuscript ...."

While I hoped it would be enough to keep the lid on his Vesuvian temper, I was anything but confident. Peter would understand in a flash that if *The Blue Season* had hit the market with the wrong author, we'd have been sued and ridiculed right out of business. And like most people with short fuses, it doesn't take much for his to light up.

The next morning I came in to work early to print off two fresh copies of *The Blue Season* and get them on the conference table along with red pens, four bottles of Peter's favorite vitamin water, a bowl of apples, and a stack of bagels. When I was done, it was the picture-perfect setup for Peter and me to sit down together and go over our final edit of the manuscript.

But I took no comfort.

I went back to my own office, kept the door open, paced, and listened. Peter had been in London for the better part of a month, and if there was going to be a foot race between Cameron the Zygote and myself for his attention, I was determined to win. Unfortunately I knew it would only be the first challenge of the morning, and I was jittery from not having slept in two days.

At nine o'clock I heard Peter's voice and dashed into the hall. Cameron attempted to scoot by me, but when he saw what I saw—Peter with a pair of police officers—he disappeared in a flash. *Ah,* I thought. *The Zygote was about to be arrested!* As entertaining as that would be any other day of the year, right then it meant that Peter would be agitated before I could even get a word out, and that was the last thing I needed.

When he was thirty feet away, Peter pointed at me and said, "That's him. That's Daniel Ashe."

The cop strode forward, turned me around by the

shoulders, and cuffed my wrists behind my back. His female partner said, "Daniel Ashe, you are under arrest for grand larceny and identity theft. You have the right to remain silent. If you ...."

What the hell? "What's going on here?"

Peter sneered, "What's going *on* is you stealing two and a half million dollars from Clarissa using my own computer, you son of a bitch. They pulled your prints off my desk. You and that redhead are both going to prison."

I opened my mouth, ready to demand an explanation, when all the loose oddities from my visit to the Flood mansion the week before now fell together like pieces of a puzzle.

"Peter," I said, "listen to me! Someone *was* in your house last Saturday. I came over to walk George and heard a chair squeak overhead. I thought it was my imagination, but then I heard the front door close. I ran around your house but only saw a man on a bike and thought I was mistaken."

Peter's eyes were slits. "I hired you before you had a lick of experience and this is how you pay me back?"

"For God's sake, Peter, I didn't do it. Whoever *did* got away too fast. I went upstairs to see if anything was disturbed, and that's when I left prints in the office."

"Tell it to your lawyer."

As the officer pulled me down the hall I called over my shoulder, "Where's Annie?"

"In jail where she belongs. The same cop holding you dragged her out of bed yesterday morning. Annie's the one who fingered you."

———

I called Denis, my attorney. We'd been roommates in college, where, thanks to the difference in our heights, we were too often referred to as "Bert and Ernie." Denis had come to L.A. a year before I did, landed a position as an associate in a big law firm, and allowed me to sleep on a pull-out in his living room until I'd earned enough to move into my own apartment.

As I waited in my cell for him to arrive, I thought about this one particular night, many moons ago, in a sport bar. I was with three media lawyers watching a game when the breaking news came on that a jury had acquitted a young woman on trial for killing her little girl. It made no sense. The evidence against her had been stacking up for months—had seemed irrefutable. Everyone around us booed and threw pretzels at the TV. One of the lawyers shouted over the din, "Proof positive that jury trials are the only way to go if you're guilty."

"Is there another option?" I asked.

Lawyer Two nodded. "Yeah. You can request a bench trial. No jury. But don't try it if you're culpable."

"Very true. Juries are for the guilty," said Lawyer Three and aimed his beer bottle at the screen. "And the results are right there, walking tits out with that shit-eating grin on her face."

"And if you're innocent?"

Lawyer One shook his head. "Then the smart move is to waive your right to a jury. Judges are stupid and senile," he looked to his comrades and they raised their bottles in agreement, "but they're still a lot more predictable than a jury. If you're innocent, you're more likely to walk free if it's up to a judge."

On this, One, Two, and Three agreed.

By the time Denis showed up at my cell I had relived that conversation so many times that the first words out of my mouth were, "I want a bench trial."

"Whoa, settle down," he said and sat next to me. "Let's hope it doesn't come to that." Then he told me what he knew.

"You're charged with transferring two and a half million dollars out of Clarissa Flood's brokerage account. They believe you entered the Flood property a week ago Saturday and used their personal computer, which is linked to the account, and transferred the money out at noon. The cops are scratching their heads over the amount taken as she had over eight million sitting there. They know the house sitter," he glanced at his notes for the name, then looked back up at me, "Annie Doherty, an Irish citizen who was arrested on charges of aiding and abetting, was in Mexico with Mrs. Flood's brother for the day, and that you came over to walk the dog for her. If you can verify you weren't in the house at noon that'll go a long way. Right now the cops aren't looking for anyone else because they found your prints on the desk and computer mouse. Come up with an explanation for that, proof that you weren't there at noon, and the grand jury won't indict you."

I winced. "I *was* there at noon. I came in to walk the dog. He was agitated and I thought it was because he didn't know me very well. I heard a little squeak overhead and called up the stairs. I thought maybe Annie had changed her mind about going to Mexico. When there was no answer, and no other sound, I figured it was nothing. I leashed up the dog and we were just stepping over the back threshold when I heard the front door close. So I jogged around the conservatory and saw a man on a bike wobbling a bit, like he was just getting started, but no other traffic. The next door neighbor was in his driveway, so I figured what I'd heard was his front door closing. He noticed me looking at him, so I waved. Then I took the dog for his walk."

Denis let out a long exhalation. "I won't pussyfoot," he said. "This is bad. It looks like someone set you up."

Good man, Denis. Not a moment of doubt that I was innocent.

"But who would set me up? And why?"

"That's what we have to find out." Denis patted my knee. "Who would have it in for you?"

I shrugged. "Well, I'm sure there's a lot of writers who don't like me. I've turned down thousands of scripts. But I can't imagine anyone taking it this far."

"Think on it some more. Someone jealous of you. Someone obsessed with getting even on some score. That has to be a very short list."

I threw up my hands. "No clue."

Denis looked up at the ceiling. "I'm sorry to say this, but with an eyewitness placing you at the scene, and your prints on that computer mouse, unless the guy on that bike walks in here and gives himself up, the grand jury will indict you."

I fell back against the wall.

Denis took out a yellow pad and a pen and asked, "So what's the security like at the Flood mansion?"

I didn't answer. I knew he said something, but I was in such a funk it took me a while to process it. He prodded, "Daniel?"

"Sorry. Um, you need a key, and once inside you have about a minute to input the security code on a pad by the door or the agency alerts the police."

"So how did you get in to walk the dog?"

"I had a key. When Annie asked me if I could do it, I wrote back saying I would, and told her to turn off the security system and leave me a key under the hibiscus planter by the back door."

Denis put the pen down. "Wrote? All this on email?"

I nodded.

"This is not good news. First, you instructed her to turn off the security system on a record that can be read in court, and second, hackers in this town love to read the email of rich people, and you gave them a blueprint on how to get into an unsecured mansion."

"Annie's not rich."

"But she was using the Flood Wi-Fi."

"And Clarissa's laptop."

Denis groaned.

I pushed away from the wall. "Is Annie out on bail yet?"

"No. They brought her here yesterday morning, and a few hours later someone from Immigration and Customs Enforcement took her to a holding center in Santa Ana."

"Forget me for now. Get her bail squared away first."

"It's more complicated than that. There are only a handful of ways a person can be released from immigration detention after being arrested on criminal charges, and she's not eligible for any of them until a clear money trail is found to eliminate any possibility of money laundering. Without that, she is subject to mandatory detention without bail."

I ran my fingers through my hair. "This is crazy. How could she be charged with anything if she wasn't even in the house when it happened?"

"They think she conspired with you."

I sat back on the cot and shook my head. The world was spinning out of control.

"Daniel, who is this woman? What is your relationship with her?"

"It's ..." I looked around for the right word. "Intimate. Close. She was my friend and now we're in love."

"When did you meet her?"

"Two months ago."

He tipped his head. "That's fast. Do you see each other every day?"

"Actually, I've only seen her three times."

"Three times? So you ... what? Talk to her on the phone every day?"

"No. She was my dog walker. She left me notes and stories, and I wrote back. We learned about each other that way."

Denis nodded. "I see. Okay. Before she moved into the Flood house, where was she living?"

"In an apartment about fifteen minutes from my house. I don't have her address."

"You've never been there?"

"No."

Denis rolled his eyes. "Oh, boy. I'm sorry to tell you this buddy, but from my seat, she's the one who set you up."

"Not a chance."

Denis tipped his head back and looked at me, his eyes hooded. "Just hear me out. This dog walker has a key to your house. She could have spent hours going through your papers, your photographs, your address book." He stood up and walked in front of the bars, his head down, speaking to the floor as he reasoned it out. "Then when she moved into the Flood mansion she had all the time in the world to go through Clarissa's financial statements, found her most vulnerable account, and when you agreed to come over and walk the dog for her, she had her accomplice in place at the computer upstairs, waiting for the moment you came in the back door to transfer the money out."

"Jesus. Where are you getting all this?"

"But could I be right?"

"No! You couldn't be more wrong. Annie is a good person."

258

"And you're not blinded by love?" He turned, his eyes steady on mine.

"I'm not."

"Tell me how she came into your life. Tell me everything you know about her," he said and sat next to me.

So I did. I started with how I hired her, even admitting to him my phobia about redheads and how I acted like a jittery fool when she came over to pick up a key. I told him about the fantastical stories she left on the secret lives of my dogs, how they always included me as a romantic hero, and that I had recommended Annie to the Floods to dog sit for them while they were in London. I described our afternoon of cards and swimming at the Flood estate, and finished with a brief recap of our date Saturday night.

Denis stayed quiet while I spoke, his gaze past my shoulder. When I was done he said, "So, during your pool date a few weeks ago, she told you that all through college she and her friends pulled off sophisticated pranks. Then she admitted over dinner Saturday night that she wasn't a professional dog walker, that she tricked you in order to get to know you, and in all these dog stories she cast you as characters that fell in love with her characters because she had a crush on you and wanted to draw you to her."

I shook my head. "I can see how that must sound to you."

"It sounds like this woman doesn't do anything straightforward. She amuses herself by gaming people. So how can you be so sure that she didn't groom *you*? Set you up to take the fall?"

"Because I know her. She wouldn't do anything to harm me."

Denis blew air out from puffed cheeks. "Whatever. I can tell you this, the agents at ICE will be in no hurry to let her go unless the charges against both of you are dropped. Even if a judge decides she's innocent, she's been consorting with you, a suspected felon. They could deport her on a dime. And if you're convicted, she could be permanently barred from the United States."

I put my head in my hands. I wanted Annie out of that holding center, and if deportation was the only quick solution, I was all for it. "Okay, what if they drop the charges against her and she gets deported before I get cleared of all this nonsense. Can she come right back?"

"Not unless she appeals to the State Department. They could agree, or they could let her paperwork sit in a corner for five years."

"Jesus."

"The important thing for us is that she stay in California until this is settled. Hopefully the charges against both of you will be dropped, but if they aren't, we'll need her to testify for you at your trial."

Denis asked more questions, took more notes, and as he packed up to leave he said, "You know, I'd understand if you'd like someone with more trial experience."

"No thanks. I can't afford a *good* lawyer," I said, and he smiled wanly. "Believe me, you will be great. After all, I had a solid reason for being at Peter's house, and I don't have the money. But please, try to do everything you can to help Annie."

"I will. Though ICE is famously unhelpful to outside lawyers."

Denis stayed for my arraignment, and Leandra showed up to post my bail. She drove me back to the parking lot at Floodgate Media so I could get my car, and on the way I told her everything. When I was done I asked, "Do you think Annie could have anything to do with all this?"

"Of course not."

When she dropped me off she asked if I'd come over for dinner.

"Thanks, but no. I want to be alone tonight."

On my drive home I thought about the subtle eye shift Denis made when he said we needed Annie to stay in California so she could testify on my behalf. In that tiny movement I saw he wasn't being completely truthful. Regardless of what I said, Denis believed Annie set me up, and he didn't want her to slip out of the country and leave me to take the blame. I worried his prejudice meant he wasn't going to break his neck to help her.

I would go to the ICE detention center Santa Ana first thing in the morning.

XXI
The Big Gun

As soon as I was home I called Peter to let him know that Oliver Nikitin was not the author of *The Blue Season*.

He hung up on me.

I sat down and sent him an email and it bounced back undelivered with an inset screen saying I'd been banned from the Floodgate server. I called Cameron's cell. He heard me out and laughed. "Nice try asshole. Two hours after you were arrested, Oliver came in and signed a new contract with *me* as his agent. Hope you have a great time in prison."

I called Denis.

"Can Annie sue Floodgate if they go forward with Oliver as the author of *The Blue Season*?"

"She can and she should. As long as she has proof her late husband is the real author. You said her grandmother can't send us the handwritten version?"

"No. Annie said she'd have to go to Ireland to piece it all back together herself. I was going to go with her."

"How long does it take for a book to get published?"

"Depends. Publishers make editing suggestions of their own, and sometimes they hold a book back so it doesn't compete with another they're bringing out. Could be six months, could be a year or more."

"Okay. I'll draft a letter to Peter Flood. Maybe it'll worry him enough to hold back on sending the manuscript to publishers until we get this cleared up."

"Thanks."

"Listen, Daniel, as far as the computer theft, keep in mind that the burden of proof lies with them, not us."

"And they have my fingerprints and an eyewitness."

"Well, we'll ask for a bench trial and hope we get a judge who believes us."

After we hung up I closed my eyes and saw Annie in my mind's eye in each of her incarnations: the waif in oversized clothes I hired to walk my dogs, the bombshell in a strapless bathing suit, the smartly dressed sophisticate who dropped her little black dress by the blue light of the pool.

Now she was wearing a jumpsuit. What must she be thinking and feeling?

As for me, I imagined what I'd be doing that moment if she hadn't crossed an ocean and a continent to turn my life around. I certainly wouldn't be facing a possible prison sentence. I'd still be working at Floodgate Media, competing with Cameron the Zygote to impress Peter, and would probably be engaged to Victoria.

Victoria.

My eyes snapped open. She'd left me two text messages and now it was almost five o'clock. I picked up my phone and called her.

"Oh God, Daniel, I heard you got arrested this morning. What happened?"

"It's a big mistake. Listen, can I come over tonight? There's something we should talk about."

"Hold on, let me close my door. Okay, I'm not one to wait for heavy news. Tell me now. Do you need a lawyer? What can I do to help?"

I took a deep breath. "Victoria, I don't know how to say this, but I've fallen in love with someone else. I'm sorry."

There was a pause on the line. She cleared her throat and said, "Say that again."

So I did.

"You … a man who assured me you were incapable of falling in love, who slept with me not ten days ago, you're telling me that between then and now you've fallen in love?"

"I'm sorry, but yes."

"We talked about getting *married*."

I closed my eyes and apologized again.

"You bastard. I was ready to start a life with you. Help you get your own literary agency off the ground. We would have been great together."

"I don't know what else to say."

I heard her intake of breath. "Do you mind telling me why you were arrested?"

"Grand larceny. Peter Flood's wife has money missing from one of her accounts and they found my fingerprints on the computer mouse that was used. I'm hoping they find who really did it in a day or two."

"And I hope you go to prison," she said and hung up.

———————————

Ten o'clock Tuesday morning I was at the front desk of the Santa Ana immigration office where I was informed that as the other suspect in her case, I was the one person not allowed to visit, write or even speak to Annie on the phone.

I went back to my car and called Denis. "There's not anything I can do about that," he said. "Listen, I've found out some new information. Can you meet me at the coffee shop across from my office at twelve-thirty?"

I was already at a table waiting when he came in. He looked harried and sweaty. He told the waitress to bring him a beer before he even sat down. She walked away and he said, "Drew Ouster. Clarissa's brother. You said you met him?"

"Yes. He was in the kitchen a couple of weeks ago when Annie invited me over to the Flood estate to swim."

"And he and Annie were in Mexico together the next Saturday when you came over to walk the dog."

"Yes."

His beer came and he took three deep gulps. "Well hang on to your hat," he said. "Drew Ouster is paying Barry Farnsworth to represent Annie."

I must have looked as confused as I felt. Denis said, "Barry Farnsworth is one of the biggest legal guns in California. Prime time." He took another gulp. "Besides being *very* bad news for us, I'm left wondering why Drew Ouster would pay a fortune to free the woman charged with aiding and abetting the felony robbery of his own sister."

I rubbed the side of my head. "Because he's in love with her."

"*What?* He's in love with her too?"

I nodded.

He shook his head. "This must put a rift between him and his sister."

"She's probably all for it. Clarissa is crazy about Annie. She wrote a letter trying to convince her to marry Drew."

Denis looked up at the ceiling and muttered something under his breath. I'd never seen him this agitated.

"Are you okay?"

"To be honest, no. We are in deep shit. In order to clear Annie Doherty of the charges against her, Barry Fucking Farnsworth is going to start a backstage campaign with the city prosecutor to pin it all on you. Before he's done, everyone in that office will think you are some kind of Svengali who mesmerized his unsuspecting client into turning off the security system and handing you the key."

"Isn't that just a version of what you were going to do to Annie?"

He shot me a look. "Look, unless we can find that money, and that's a big 'if,' our only shot is to make the judge firmly understand that the only reason you were in that house was at Annie Doherty's request. If that casts doubt on her intentions, so be it."

I shook my head. "What good would it do me to set Annie up? If she went to prison my life wouldn't be worth a plug nickel."

Denis lifted his glasses and rubbed his eyes.

"Out with it," I said.

"Okay. In seemingly no time flat, both you and Drew Ouster fell in love with this woman, and his sister, the victim in this theft mind you, is 'crazy' about her and wants her as a sister-in-law. I hope she really is on our side Daniel, because if she is that charismatic when she goes on the stand, she could sway the judge one way or the other."

"She *is* on our side."

He picked up his beer and finished it off. "She'd better be."

XXII

Jennie

A few days after my arrest we learned that mine were the only prints found on the desk and computer mouse. I thought it worked in my favor. "Obviously the real thief cleaned his prints off the desk," I said to Denis. "If he hadn't the police would have found Drew Ouster's prints there as well. We know from Annie's letters that he used that office."

"Or it means that the cleaning crew that came on Friday did a bang-up job."

Damn.

A week went by with still no leads as to where the money from the emptied Cayman account went. Then, at five o'clock on Sunday afternoon there was a knock on my door. I saw Annie on my stoop through the glass. I yanked the door open, picked her up and tried to kiss her.

"Stop, stop! I'm Jennie Hicks! Annie's twin!"

I set her down and stumbled back.

"Goodness," she said smoothing her dress. "I'm sorry about this. And I can't stay. Drew Ouster is expecting t' meet me for dinner and I've a drive ahead a' me." She took a step away. "I shouldn't a' come."

"No, no, please don't go. Come in. Please."

She looked up at me. "But for a minute and no longer."

She stepped in and I directed her to a chair. I sat across

from her, unable to stop myself from staring. "I'm sorry," I said, "It's just that I've never seen identical twins this ..."

"Identical?"

"Yes."

"Look, I don't mean to upset you, but I felt we needed t' meet."

"I'm very glad you're here."

She tapped her fingers on the arm of the chair, and said, "I came for two reasons. And I'll get right to the point. Annie says you're innocent. Drew and Mr. Farnsworth that you're guilty, and even if you're not, they're determined t' convince the judge that you are. When I asked them if they shouldn't be looking at other possibilities, they tell me your defense team will try t' put the blame all on Annie."

I rubbed my head. "I don't have a team. I have an old friend defending me, and I told him that Annie is completely innocent."

"Good."

"But ..."

"But what?"

"I think my lawyer will take whatever advantage he can of the fact that the only way the theft was committed was because Annie turned off the security system."

Jennie Hicks closed her eyes for a moment. "Then thank God for it."

I was confused. "Thank God for what?"

"She's like t' be deported by next Sunday or Monday."

"What!"

She nodded. "Mr. Farnsworth has been working hand in glove with Jeffrey Holder, the district attorney for the city of Los Angeles who is handling the felony case against you. Come Saturday morning the two a' them are going to take

Annie's deposition. Mr. Farnsworth plans to—and this is his word—'navigate' what she says, and if he succeeds, Jeffrey Holder will drop the charges against her. Annie will be free, but her status will change from a suspect who needs to remain in custody in the United States, to an alien who consorted with a suspected felon. Once that happens, Mr. Farnsworth will get her something called a 'voluntary departure bond' and she'll be on the next plane t' Ireland."

Annie would be free. I had to feel happy about that, but it also meant she wouldn't be here to testify in my defense.

Jennie Hicks stood up. I stood as well. "Wait," I said. "You said there were two reasons you wanted to meet me."

"It's not important."

"No, please."

"Alright," she said, crossing her arms in front of her body. "It so happens that my sister has epically bad taste in men. All of them bastards. And yet, bad as they were, none of them ever got her arrested. So yes, I came here to see you with my own eyes."

"Jennie, I swear to you, I am as innocent as Annie."

"If you say so."

She turned and walked to the door. We stepped outside on the stoop and I said, "Will you please tell Annie that I love her and miss her?"

She shook her head. "I'm not even going t' tell her we met. She's had a hard time of it. Very hard. Annie's not the kind a' person who should ever be locked up, and I want her t' be free and away from here."

"And away from me."

"Yes. I'm sorry, but she needs to put this behind her."

I thought those would be her last words, but as she faced

the driveway she said, "My sister is extraordinary. One of a kind. Do y' know that?"

"I do know," I said, my voice breaking. "Annie is the love of my life."

Jennie turned, looked at me for several seconds, gave me a sad smile, then left.

I collapsed on the sofa. Jennie Hicks wanted me out of the picture. And she was heading to meet Drew Ouster, a man who was also in love with Annie, and who was bankrolling a famous lawyer in order to see me locked up in prison.

XXIII
Searching for Annie

One week after my encounter with Jennie, Denis sent me a text to say that Annie had been acquitted of all charges and put on a red-eye flight to Ireland.

I called her cell. After one abrupt ring a recording told me the number was no longer in service. I half-expected that. Annie had been using one of those temporary, prepaid phones while in the States.

I sat right down wrote her an email.

Darling Girl, I am so relieved you are free and we are no longer barred from communicating. Call, or send me your new phone number. I can't wait to hear your voice.
Love, Daniel

I hit send. I checked my email a few minutes later to see the transmission failed, with the message, "Address not found."

I swore loud and long enough to make the dogs skulk away. I looked up the number of the ICE holding center in Santa Ana. When the receptionist heard what I wanted, she connected me to a supervisor who said, "We don't give out addresses."

"But you don't understand. She's my girlfriend."

"Then you should know where she lives," he said and hung up.

The expression *I was beside myself* could not have described my situation more perfectly. One half of me had to prepare for my day in court while the other half was obsessed with finding Annie. I checked my email every few minutes. I kept expanding different Google maps of Ireland for towns and villages south of Dublin that began with a "C" or a "K." Their names—*Kilkenny, Cloghan, Kildare, Carlow, Cashel, Kinsale, Kildare, Croom*—rolled over my tongue like a chant, but none of them were four syllables long or sounded anything like "Creek" or "Crick."

I searched "Rose Doherty in Ireland" and found her in Derry; also in Donegal, in Lurganbrack, Glenvar, and dozens of other towns that didn't begin with "Creek" or "Crick."

I searched "Jennie Hicks in London" and wasn't surprised to come up empty-handed. Having worked for France's secret service, I suspected Annie's twin knew a thing or two about keeping a low profile.

After three days of dead ends, a thought woke me in the night, and I headed straight to my laptop and the corgiadvisor.com blog.

There had not been a single posting since Annie was arrested. Still, I took a shot:

Dear George,
   Golly, I have been so worried about you and the lady who types your letters. Please tell her I don't have her new phone number or email. Ask her to call me. I love her and I miss her.
   Daniel

Five days went by. Sometimes when I checked there'd be a new comment from a reader who either missed George or was curious about my relationship with his scribe. Finally "George" replied.

Dear Daniel,

I am safe and happy with my mom and dad, though my time as the corgi advisor has come to an end. The human who read my letters and typed my replies, the one you know and asked after, has left the country.

I hope you join me in wishing her well, for she has begun a daunting task.

Know that she is very concerned about the challenge you are facing. She worries on it every day. But in order to do what is best for the both of you, she needs seclusion. Please respect that. For now, and for some time to come, she cannot be disturbed. Even by you.

She said one more thing: "Tell Daniel to read the dog stories. If he looks between the lines he will understand what I have set out to do."

George

I would have started to comb through the dog diary to see what was "between the lines," but it had been subpoenaed into evidence for my trial. So I leashed up the dogs, took them to the park, and as they enjoyed sniffing the trees, one dark thought after another gripped my mind.

Did Drew and Barry Farnsworth convince Annie that I really was the thief? Had she gone into seclusion to re-evaluate her taste in men? It's impossible not to see the similarities: First a husband who stole her passport and kept her a prisoner, then after a single night with me she was arrested and kept under lock and key.

No wonder she needs time off.

When we got home I read the letter from "George" again and wondered *Is Drew barred from seeing Annie as well?*

XXIV
Abs and Babette

My trial lasted two days.

My judge was the Honorable Babette Lebold, a Pliptit who sported an undeniable look of lust for the buff and tanned prosecutor for the city of Los Angeles, Jeffrey Holder.

I smiled weakly at Denis, my short, balding and bulbous defender, and tried not to worry.

Jeffrey "Abs" Holder explained the city's version of the case before calling Peter to the stand. When my old boss didn't even glance my way, I felt a sudden surge of hope. Peter was never one to back down. If he still thought I was guilty, I believed he would have glared daggers at me.

His summary was succinct. Every Thursday morning for the last fifteen years he checked on his and Clarissa's accounts, and that was when he discovered that one of hers had been breached five days earlier. He called the fund manager and they quickly traced the transfer to the Flood's home computer.

In order not to upset his wife, he told her they were going to return home a week earlier than planned and suggested that if she wanted to shop for anything else in London she'd better do it that day. As soon as Clarissa left he pulled up her emails.

"And why did you do that, Mr. Flood?"

"Naturally I suspected Annie Doherty. She was a virtual stranger in our house, hired on Daniel Ashe's recommendation. But I knew that Clarissa's brother, Drew, who was also staying in our home for a few days, had taken Ms. Doherty on a day trip to Mexico. I wanted to know when they had been out of town before I jumped to any conclusion."

"And what did you find?"

"It was on the email stream between my wife and Ms. Doherty that I learned Drew and Ms. Doherty were in Mexico the day of the theft, and that Daniel Ashe offered to come over at noon on the pretext of taking care of our dog."

"I object, Your Honor," Denis said, standing up. "Inference on the word 'pretext.'"

"Sustained," the judge said. "Keep to the facts, Mr. Flood."

Abs turned back to Peter. "Once you understood that Ms. Doherty and Mr. Ouster were a hundred and fifty miles away at the time of the theft, and that Mr. Ashe had access to your house to walk your dog, what did you do next?"

"I called the police and told them about the theft. I told them about Annie Doherty and my brother-in-law staying in my house, but being out of town that day. And I told them Daniel Ashe had come over at some point to walk the dog."

"And did you find out later when he came over?"

"Yes. The police interviewed my neighbor who saw Mr. Ashe outside on my front lawn at noon."

Peter was dismissed. When he walked by and still didn't look my way, I again got the sensation that despite his testimony, he had stopped believing I was the thief.

Peter's neighbor was next, and quickly pointed me out as the man he saw at the Flood residence at noon that day.

A detective was called to the stand who said the prints pulled off the mouse and desk in the Flood office matched mine. "Bingo!" he said.

Denis questioned him as to why he thought my prints were on file in the first place. When the detective said, "I'm sure I don't know," Denis said, "Five years ago, Mr. Ashe volunteered to give up his Saturday mornings to teach basketball to developmentally disabled children, and the state mandates that anyone who works with this population be fingerprinted."

He made it sound like I might still be doing it, which was hardly the case. At the time I was dating a woman whose little brother was on a team that was preparing for the Special Olympics, and for one month each player had a "shadow" volunteer on the court who talked them through their plays. Still, I felt like Denis scored a point or two in making me out to be a good guy.

That glow didn't last long. Drew Ouster took the stand, and *he* made no bones about glaring at me. It was also the first time in two hours that the Honorable Babette Lebold peeled her eyes away from Abs.

It was eighty degrees outside and Drew was wearing a cable knit Irish sweater. As soon as he took the stand he locked eyes with me and fingered the collar. His message was clear. He'd been to see Annie in Ireland.

Drew testified that I was "visibly irritated" to find him in the kitchen the day we met. He said that after I had offered to take care of the dog, he asked Annie how I would get in, and she told him that I had given her explicit instructions to turn off the security system, as well as where I wanted her to leave me a key.

Denis stood up. "I object, Your Honor. This implication that Mr. Ashe originated the idea of looking after the dog is prejudicial and patently false. In the dog diary, submitted into evidence, Annie Doherty states, and I quote, 'Is there any chance you could come by and walk and feed George? Drew just told me that Peter has some kind of feud going on with the neighbors, and suggested I ask you instead. Anytime around noon?'"

"Okay, Counsel. Sustained."

Drew turned to latch eyes with Babette. "Your Honor, *I'm* not the one who directed Annie to turn off the security system. What no one here has told you is that as soon as Mr. Ashe realized that Annie was falling for him, he callously used those feelings to take advantage of her sweet and innocent nature."

Denis objected.

As if on cue, Abs pulled a manila envelope off the prosecution table, took out two documents, handed one to Babette and one to Denis. "Your Honor, placed in evidence is this sworn statement of Annie Doherty, taken while she was in holding at the immigration center in Santa Ana. Please allow me to read from the affidavit."

Babette nodded.

"Question: Ms. Doherty, do you have a personal relationship with Mr. Ashe? Answer: Yes. Question: Are you in love with Mr. Ashe? Answer: I am."

My girl!

Abs turned to Babette, "Your Honor, Ms. Doherty is just what Mr. Ouster said: an innocent woman from a small village in Ireland who was deceived and manipulated by Mr. Ashe. That was so evident to the State of California that the accessory charge against her was summarily dropped. The next day the unfortunate young woman was deported, thanks only to her association with a suspected felon." He pointed at me.

Denis stood up. "Your Honor, while it is *very* convenient for the prosecution not to have Ms. Doherty here today, her absence is a serious detriment to the defense of my client. The district attorney was only too happy to see that she was deported so she could *not* testify in the defense of Mr. Ashe."

Babette picked up the pages and said, "I have read Ms. Doherty's deposition, which is her legal testimony for this case. I find it well-constructed and suitably complete. Sit down, Counsel."

Abs called Victoria to the stand.

She looked demure in a pale pink dress, and held a handkerchief in her hand.

"Ms. Millman, please state for the record your relationship with Mr. Ashe."

"We were a couple. We were talking about getting married."

"The theft in question of two million, five hundred thousand dollars took place on April twelfth. When was the last time you and Mr. Ashe discussed getting married?"

"April thirteenth"

"And what was the gist of that conversation?"

"Daniel said that once he was done editing the book he'd been working on, we would shop for a ring."

"Did you know Mr. Ashe had been to the Flood residence the day before?"

"No."

"Did you know that Mr. Ashe was also in a romantic relationship with Ms. Doherty?"

"I did not," Victoria said, twisting the hankie in her hands, and with a fast turn of the head, Babette shot me a look as if I'd left *her* at the altar.

When I took the stand, Denis jumped right in with some damage control, and I answered in a level voice:

"Yes, I have been to the Flood residence on two prior occasions."

"Yes, I did work for Peter Flood."

"I did know he was in London, and I did ask Annie Doherty to disengage the security system the day I left my fingerprints in the office. But as you heard, she *asked* me take care of the dog, and when I got there, that dog was clearly upset by something upstairs. While I was leashing him up I heard a squeak overhead; but when I called up the stairs and no one answered, I decided it was just a curious house sound. As I was walking through the back door with the dog, I heard what sounded like the front door closing. I ran around the house to see who it was. There was no one on foot, no car traffic, just a man on a bike, who I now believe is the thief."

Abs objected, and Babette advised me to keep my opinions to myself.

"That's also when I noticed the neighbor in his driveway. Naturally, at the time, I thought the sound I heard was *his* front door closing.

"After the walk, the dog bolted up the stairs, barking wildly, and I felt it was my duty to investigate. He ran directly into the office, and was furiously sniffing under the desk, so I sat in the chair to look around to see if anything was disturbed. That's when I left my prints on the desk and on the computer mouse."

"Mr. Ashe, did you steal two million, five hundred thousand dollars from an account held by Clarissa Flood?"

"I did not."

"Thank you."

Abs took over.

"Mr. Ashe, did you ever tell Ms. Doherty about your suspicions that someone might have been in the house that day?"

"No. There was no sign that anything had been disturbed and I didn't want to upset her."

"Of course not, especially since the only person in the house at the time of the theft was you."

Denis objected, Babette sustained, and Abs stepped back

to his table and reached under some papers to pull out the dog walker diary. He held it in the air.

"Your Honor, the defense has already included this three ring binder and its contents into evidence as regards to the agreement for Mr. Ashe to take care of the dog. The prosecution would like to refer to another page that will shed some light on this case."

Denis stood up. "I object, Your Honor."

"Overruled, Counsel. You're the one who submitted this diary into evidence."

Denis sat down, Abs flipped to a marked page, and I heard my own words ring out.

A major part of my fantasy future involves a magnificent white stone building that sits on the beating heart of West Hollywood. It is the ideal location for my agency.

Yesterday morning there was a realtor's sign in front!

Only a week ago I would have driven by, but now, with the snot-nosed genius on board, I swerved into the parking lot and went inside. The receptionist directed me to the west wing, saying "I hope you like it!"

It is perfect. There is one big office, three smaller ones, a conference room, a small kitchen area, and a back door for easy access to a green space for Eddie. I walked around and tasted what my life would be like if I had the wherewithal to rent this space and start my own agency. My employees would pitch to me. The bulk of the earnings would be mine, and I would be free from Peter's mercurial temper. Between the rent, the deposit, and the start-up costs, all I would need to make it happen is two million, five hundred thousand dollars.

Wait. I don't have two million five.

Abs paused here and swept his arms in an expansive gesture. "Your Honor, Mr. Ashe didn't say two million, four hundred thousand, three million, six hundred thousand, or any other number. He said 'two million five.' The exact amount stolen from Clarissa Flood from an account that had over eight million."

Abs picked up the diary and continued to read.

A year from now, with my client's bestseller thrilling the reading world, and a movie deal in the works, I could probably borrow that kind of money. But by then this property will belong to someone else's dream. Ah, timing! If only I had some cyber theft skills.

Abs placed the diary in front of Babette as he repeated the last line slowly, shaking his head and squaring his shoulders, giving us all the full impact of his gym workouts.

Denis stood up. "Your Honor, let me repeat for the sake of the prosecution, Daniel Ashe has no criminal background, he had been asked by Ms. Doherty to come to the Flood residence that day, and the L.A.P.D. has looked high and low and has not found a single link between my client and that money."

Abs snorted dismissively, lifting one finger. "Except for his fingerprints on the computer mouse."

He lifted a second finger. "Except for an eyewitness who saw him there at the time the transfer was made."

He lifted a third finger. "Except that the amount stolen was exactly the amount Mr. Ashe needed to start his own agency." He wiggled those three fingers then turned to the judge. "And Your Honor, *really*, don't we all know by now that a cyber-hacker can make money disappear without a trace?"

She nodded and leaned forward and said, "My financial identity has been stolen *twice.*"

Abs put on a sympathy face, Babette smiled gratefully, and I knew I was screwed.

The next morning I watched her Plip lips form the word

"Guilty." I was sentenced to serve five to seven at the Los Angeles County Penitentiary.

The moral of my story is this: Media lawyers don't know jack shit about trial law. Get a jury no matter what.

XXV

The Dong and The Badger

The *Los Angeles* County Penitentiary is known as "The LAC." For inmates this is less an acronym than a description of all the omissions that bore open holes into your chest. Lack of women, lack of foods you want to eat, lack of driving your car, or having a phone in your pocket, or taking a crap in private, or walking outside at will—every freedom gone.

On day one I hobbled in, shackled at the wrist and ankle, as one steel door after another clanged shut behind me— the soul-numbing equivalent of hearing dirt shoveled onto your casket. Our chains were removed, the intake guard said something, and the eight other new inmates started to take off their jumpsuits. Confused, I pointed to my own and he said, "*Now,* inmate. Take off everything."

My mind, my soul, whatever it is that I really am, disengaged from my flesh to hover several feet over my head. From this new vantage point I became an artless puppeteer, fumbling to work the arms and legs of the body below. Once naked, I watched myself submit to having every facial orifice lit up before bending over while the guard snapped on a pair of latex gloves.

I thought *You poor bastard.*

Moments later, still naked, I tried to swallow around what felt like a broken walnut shell in the center of my throat, and I knew two things: I had rejoined my body, and it really sucked to be me.

Day after day, all I had to rely on was myself. In *The Shawshank Redemption*, which played on the rec room TV three times my first week, Tim Robbins lucked out with the Morgan Freeman character to mentor him through the hazards of his new life. But I was alone. At least once a minute I had to remind myself to inhale.

During my second week, a powerfully built inmate with a maze tattoo on his bald head stuck out his foot and tripped me on the stairs. I went sprawling, banging my shoulder and head on the metal landing. His barking laugh added humiliation to my pain. A few hours later, he sauntered towards me in the mess hall, grabbed my arm and whispered, "Don't worry sweetheart, Daddy will kiss your boo boos and make them all better."

He walked on. I asked the inmate behind me, "Do you know that guy?"

"Yeah. Steer clear. We call him The Dong."

That night, *The Shawshank Redemption* was playing yet again in the rec room, and I settled in to lose myself in the story; but this time when Tim got cornered in the shower by the Sisters, I stood up and headed back to my cell.

It was almost three weeks in before I laughed for the first time, and it surprised me. A kid at our mess table was exaggerating his own sexual daring, and when his bullshit was identified as bullshit, hilarity followed. "Okay," he shrugged, "maybe it wasn't Beyoncé I got to dry hump in that coatroom, but it sure looked like her!"

At least he had the grace to laugh at himself. It's the alpha dogs that have no sense of humor, at least when it comes to anyone laughing at them. I ridicule no one. My goal is to leave prison with all the parts I came in with.

Day twenty-six I was in the shower when a forearm put me in a choke hold. This was a scenario that had haunted my sleepless hours, and I was quick to react. I stomped on the instep behind me, elbowed the body, and as the arm around my throat loosened I clutched it with both hands, wrenched myself free, and turned to my attacker.

The Dong.

We were face to face and a yard apart when I saw it: a foot long, uncircumcised, and blotched pink and gray, like skin that had been badly burned long ago. He grabbed and pointed it at me. "All for you, beautiful. On your knees."

"What's *really* going to happen here," I said, my voice slow and menacing, "is me ripping the stupid maze off your skull and shitting in the hole."

I leapt and spun in the air—a move perfected on basketball courts since junior high—and came down with my elbow to the side of his head. He reeled in a half-circle, and I sprang forward and socked him just below the eye. He turned and swung at me, missing by several inches, and before he could regain his balance I put my foot squarely on his backside and sent him into the tiles with everything I had. He took the brunt of the impact to his face and belly, and the double smack made for a very satisfying sound. He looked up from the floor, unfocused and defeated.

"We're done," I said, and left before he could gather his senses.

As I nursed my knuckles, I felt less elated by my performance than worried about the fallout. If I had learned anything from *Shawshank, Cool Hand Luke,* and *Escape from Alcatraz,* it was that regardless of fault, anyone involved in a prison fight got thrown into isolation.

Thirty minutes later a guard appeared and said, "Warden wants you."

As we walked through a labyrinth of corridors, I went over in my mind what strategy I would use to keep my sanity while in the hole. I knew the dialogue of *The Godfather I* and *II* by heart, so that would keep my brain focused for a few days. I could go over every scene in *A Perfect Storm, Caddyshack, Annie Hall* and *Airplane!* In fact there were so many movies in my head I could play out, that when the guards finally opened the door they'd be asking themselves *Do I smell popcorn?*

After several steel doors closed behind us, the floor changed from concrete to carpet. We were deep in an area of offices when the guard knocked on the only door with a glass insert. A buzzer went off, letting us in. The young man behind the desk indicated I was to continue alone into the warden's office.

The warden, Matt Badger, was in his fifties, compactly built, and had an attitude of dealing with problems quickly and moving on.

"Sit down, Mr. Ashe. May I call you Daniel? Good. I have a proposal for you that I think you'll like."

"Yes, sir."

"You were a screenplay agent. You have a master's degree in fine arts."

I nodded.

"Well, in their infinite wisdom, the legislators of the State of California have eliminated the salaried instructors for the Arts in Corrections program, a program *I* started. I had six years of statistics to prove that the men enrolled in those classes were less troublesome and had less recidivism." He raised his brows. "Can you guess where I'm going with this?"

"No, sir."

He stood up and walked around his desk, stopping in front of me. "I want you to teach creative writing. You've got the right degree and the kind of real-world experience these guys respect. If you agree to teach a few classes, I'll provide the space and supplies." He half-sat on the edge of his desk. "It'll make your time here go faster."

No isolation.

I must have smiled because he nodded as if I'd agreed. So I shook my head and said, "Mr. Badger, I'm sorry to say I can't take you up on your offer. I'm not a teacher. I don't know anything about developing a curriculum, and even if I did, there's no way I could control a room full of convicts."

"Sure you could. The men sign up to be in the class. They're grown-ups."

"Actually sir, they are robbers and rapists and murderers."

"Who are not in class to rob or rape or murder *you*. These classes attract a fair number who are in for non-violent crimes: fraud, drugs, even using a computer to steal."

With that statement he went from a smile to a smirk.

"Look, Mr. Badger, I'm trying to stay under the radar. Do my time and go home. I get the whole computer reference, and the fact is, I would actually need internet access to prepare. I'd have to read up on criminal psychology, group dynamics—I can't even think what else. I couldn't go in there cold. If you don't want me near a computer, then that eliminates my chance to teach."

"I see what you're getting at, and I respect that you want to be fully prepared. It confirms in my mind that you're the right man for this. I'll just have IT put up a few firewalls, but otherwise, research all you want. How long do you need to prepare?"

This guy was too much. I suspected a lifetime of overeager participation in classes and seminars, his hand shooting up with yet another exuberant comment while everyone else moaned.

I had to disappoint him. The LAC was a stagnant algae pond whose surface I intended to skim like a water bug. I couldn't let this Eagle Scout yank me under. Excuses weren't working. I stood up, prepared to say a simple no thank you, but before I could get the words out Matt Badger said, "I don't like being disappointed. You understand me?"

His tone was different: no longer friendly, no longer man-to-man.

"I do sir, but—"

His eyes were cold. "And I have a stake in this. It's important to me. You believe that, don't you?

"Yes."

"So important, Daniel, that not only will I post a guard outside your class, I'll make it clear that they are to take good care of you *all the time.* You would be too valuable to my program to be out of commission for any reason."

His gaze on me was unblinking, and I understood. Matt Badger knew what had happened in the shower. My next thought chilled my heart.

Did he … would he actually … engineer something like that?

"Yes, sir!" I heard myself say, the powdered eggs from breakfast liquefying in my gut. "I would be honored to teach some classes. Set it up."

I needed to get out of there, but Matt Badger had more to say. "There's a perk to the job. You get to have lunch with me twice a month. I'll need to know how things are going."

I'll say this much, the warden gave me good press.

A poster of a quill pen appeared outside the mess hall above a jubilant font announcing, "Learn Writing that Sells." The class description said the teacher was a seasoned L.A. agent who had brokered hundreds of movie and television scripts and who would share the secrets of "writing that sells!"

Secrets? Like *abracadabra*? Like skipping over the need to read extensively, or understand the elements of storytelling, or work endless hours alone on your craft, and then, lucky you! Welcome to months or years of rejection!

I started to panic. The LAC was full of men who had a proven lack of impulse control, and that was not a group you want to disappoint.

Thirty-one inmates signed up. I met with them on a Monday night, handed out gel pens and notebooks, and told them their first assignment was to write a one-page essay that described the best meal of their lives.

Major shit storm.

In my defense, I truly believed I had come up with an ideal way to evaluate language skill levels. A great meal evokes the kind of sense memories that can make poets out of paupers and popes alike. But the thirty-one men told their friends about the assignment, and by dinner everyone was one-upping each other about their mother's pork chops, a steak joint in Houston, a burrito place in the Mission district, or the home-made pasta in Little Italy. It turned into a week of shouting matches and trays of prison food sliding down the walls. The infirmary treated black eyes and broken ribs.

The guard who unlocked my cell door said, "Warden wants you, and is he ever pissed!"

Matt Badger didn't waste a moment. "What the hell were you thinking?"

"I'm sorry, sir."

"You're *sorry*?" He stuck his jaw out in barely contained rage. "You've created a virus of discontent, Daniel, a *virus*." He walked around his office, waving his arms, "The kitchen servers are afraid for their lives. You don't call attention to the difference between the best meal a man has ever eaten and what's on his prison tray. Jesus H. Christ! I should put you on the serving line. You deserve it."

"I understand if you want to call the whole thing off. I was just trying to get writing samples so I could divide the men into proper classes. Here," I said and held up the thirty-one essays. "Based on this first effort, I can tell you that there are eight who write at about the fifth grade level or below, fifteen who function near the high school level, and seven who write at the college level or better. This guy, Jack Tempert," I held up an essay, "has actual talent."

Matt Badger glowered at me for a long moment then held out his hand. "Let me see that." He read Jack's essay and handed it back to me.

"I'm not calling it off. You are going to do this." He took a deep breath and pursed his lips. "Divide the men into three classes. Just be careful from now on. You're supposed to divert these guys, not incite them. Got it?"

XXVI
Redemption

I gave all three classes the same assignment: write a one-act play involving four characters or less. The men were given a Class D clearance, which allowed them to sign out either a typewriter or an old-fashioned word processor. I went over the basics of script formatting and wished them luck.

It was during my next lunch with Matt Badger that I threw out the idea that we could put on the plays. "We did this in my playwriting class in grad school and it pushed everybody's creativity to the max. These men are writing one-act plays, very short. Each would be half an hour, give or take. We could do three or four a night."

"What kind of costs are involved?"

"Zero. No need for set design or costumes. Just actors on that stage in the chapel reading the parts in front of an audience."

He agreed. I posted a sign-up sheet for volunteers, and soon sections of the LAC felt like the Actors Studio, with men of all ages and sizes walking to and fro practicing their lines. Some of my students insisted on directing their own plays, some wanted to act, and several preferred to be in the audience. The chapel stage was booked constantly for rehearsals. Tickets to the performances were free but limited, and when we learned that every play was sold out, it added to the general stress and excitement.

Over a three-week period we put on two to four "flash" plays a night, Thursday through Sunday. Matt Badger attended all of them.

Putting on the plays was a lucky impulse. The thrill it gave the men to see their work performed turned out to be an enormous morale builder. At our next lunch I told the warden I couldn't get over having so many willing participants.

"It's L.A.," he said, waving his fork. "Everyone wants to be a scriptwriter, a director, or an actor."

The next assignment I gave was for each man to write an essay about his life. It could be inclusive or just a slice in time, but it had to be true.

Most made themselves into tragic heroes. Two men handed in essays that gave me a bone-chilling look into the mind of the sociopath. But in that pile there were five raw jewels.

Five!

In each of them, I saw the moment when the very act of writing shifted the author's perception of himself, and how in finding the truest words in his arsenal, each man had come to a new and more honest conclusion.

I couldn't have been more proud.

The story by Jack Tempert was, again, in a class by itself. His talent glowed like a lighthouse in a storm.

I brought those essays to my next lunch with Matt Badger and told him I had an idea.

"Some of these men are absorbing instruction like sponges, and they are only going to get better. So I was thinking, why not collect the best stories and put together an anthology? There might be a niche market for that kind of book."

Matt Badger put down his fork. "It would have to be their own work and their own words," he said. "And we can't sugarcoat their stories, but we also can't let anything vile get through. It would be a tightrope."

After pondering a few moments longer, he leaned back in his chair. "Yes. Definitely. I want you to go with it. Just make sure you don't end up with a lot of self-serving treatises on why they should get a new trial."

"Agreed."

"I take it you know a publisher who would consider such a book?"

"I think so. If you'd like I could call her and see what she thinks of the idea."

He pointed to his phone and I made the call. Once my friend at the publishing house got over the fact I was in prison ("Are you fucking with me, Daniel?") she said she trusted my judgment and would read anything I sent her. "I can't promise we'll publish it, but I am very intrigued."

From then on I took great care with each assignment, wanting to steer but not confine the inmates' creativity. The best work I kept in a blue corrugated box under my cot. My plan was to whittle the stack down to twenty stories, fifteen essays, ten poems, and three plays. When done, I planned to submit the completed collection under the title *Internally Free*.

Matt Badger made plans of his own. During our next lunch he told me he'd already talked to several other wardens, and after this first anthology found an audience, subsequent editions would be made up of stories from the winners of a statewide competition.

"Daniel, I expect it will go national. Someday there will be *Internally Free: Silver Anniversary Edition*. It all starts here, with us. But this first book has to be a success. It has to come out big. My reputation is at stake here."

I put my hands up in a *whoa* gesture. "Hold on. We have

one gifted writer at the LAC. *One.* Even with the best efforts from the others, *Internally Free* won't make a ripple outside a very limited audience. Hundreds of brilliant books hit the market every year; and beyond that, most readers dodge anthologies because they remind them of freshman English class. The editor I called works for a small indie publisher, and all she said was that she'd look at it. No promises. Believe me, we do not have a Hemingway in every cell!"

Matt Badger squinted at me. "This is my baby, Daniel, and I expect you to deliver it. End of story."

XXVII

The Daniel Ashe Literary Agency

Jack Tempert gave us plenty to talk about. Early on he handed in an intensely rendered tale of love and revenge about a prisoner who had been feeding a bird in the courtyard for a year. One day the prisoner watched as his bird hopped toward crumbs thrown by another inmate, who then sprung forward to crush the animal for sport. The rest of the story had the bird lover taking retribution, all the while appearing to be a model prisoner.

The story was not only satisfying and true to the desire for justice, the writing itself was so advanced that Matt Badger gave me permission to work with Jack one-on-one to help him develop his talent. The next story he handed in was a heartbreaker, written from the point of view of a twelve-year-old boy whose father was serving a life sentence. With a bit of polishing we sent it to *The Atlantic Monthly*, and they agreed to publish it.

But I couldn't get his bird story out of my mind. I sat down with Jack and told him about a college girl who engineered sophisticated pranks, learning valuable new skills along the way that ended up saving her hide. "Jack, you could turn this story into a novel. Have your bird lover switch from one prison job to another, along the way making friends, gaining access, and developing new talents that will help him take his revenge. You've got everything you need right here. Interview guys that work electrical, laundry, kitchen. You'd add a host of other characters, additional story lines and subplots."

He was reluctant at first, but once we storyboarded it and brainstormed a back story for each ally and foe, it fleshed itself out and he became as disciplined as any pro. Every few days he'd show me what he'd written, I'd give him my feedback, and we'd talk about what could happen next.

It took just four months for Jack to finish his book. I picked an artistic font for my masthead, went online to send the first chapter off to several publishing houses, and The Daniel Ashe Literary Agency was born.

Starting an agency might seem a bold move when the only seat in your office is a lidless toilet, but I had nothing to lose. Jack's book was accepted, and *The Stationary Man* will hit bookshelves in six months.

I enjoyed teaching, which I didn't expect, and I was good at it, which was a complete shock. Matt Badger's sign-up poster was right: I was a seasoned pro with secrets, after all.

XXVIII
Doubts

Though my days were focused, nothing could stop me from thinking about Annie when the lights went out.

Five to seven years. That's a lot of nights for an insomniac to mull things over, and it didn't take long for some of those thoughts to take me places I didn't want to go.

First, I had to at least consider the possibility that I had ended up at the LAC thanks to a lack of judgment. While entertaining any negative thoughts about Annie felt like a betrayal, the very act of teaching the basic rules of storytelling pushed my nose into it.

Rule One: Every story has a protagonist.

Rule Two: Every protagonist takes a life-changing journey.

Rule Three: That journey is imperiled by antagonistic forces.

Rule Four: Along the journey, the protagonist will be aided by allies, such as mentors and lovers, and thwarted by antagonists, such as tricksters and shape-shifters.

Corollary to Rules Three and Four: The best antagonists, the ones that sell books and give moviegoers the creeps, will hide their intentions by masquerading as a mentor, friend, or lover.

So, from a story-building point of view, which archetype was Annie?

First she became my friend, then my lover. In either case that made her an ally.

But by her own admission she was a prankster, which qualified her for the trickster category.

By depicting me in her stories as characters with honorable qualities, she helped me discover those facets in my own personality, and that made her my mentor.

And finally, the fact that she looked different each time I saw her, put her in shape-shifter territory.

In a literary sense, Annie covered a *lot* of ground.

In September of 2016, after six months at the LAC, and dozens of phone calls to Denis asking when the dog diary would be released from the evidence room, he finally had good news.

"You're spoiling the surprise," he said. "I handed it off to your sister yesterday. She's going to bring it with her when she visits you on Saturday."

I was speechless for a moment.

"So you're happy about that?"

"Of course," I said.

But was I? At first I wanted to study the dog diary for clues to the "daunting task" Annie was going through during her seclusion. But now I had another reason.

While I loved Annie and wanted to trust that everything she told me was true, if she had duped me, if she was indeed my clever antagonist, I believed she would have found it irresistible to embed traces of her true intentions in one of her stories.

Three days later Leandra handed the diary to me.

"Good thing I came early," she said. "The guards had to paw through this. They especially liked the nude drawing of Nin the Selkie."

"That should never have happened. I got permission from the warden himself."

It took me several moments to notice the look on her face. "Something's up. What is it?"

"I didn't know if I should bring this or not," she said as she pulled a hardcover book from her bag and handed it to me.

The cover had white letters on an indigo background that read:

The Blue Season

by

Oliver Nikitin

It felt like dry ice burning my fingertips. I opened the back flap. There was a photo of the young genius looking soulful, but I could see immense self-satisfaction just below the surface. I flipped through the first and last pages but found no acknowledgments. That made sense. Oliver had no mentors to thank because he didn't write the book.

Yet there was his name on the cover.

After I said goodbye to my sister I headed back to my cell, sat on my bunk with the dog diary on my lap, and considered the wisdom of not opening it. Inside was every hand-written story and letter, along with printouts of all our email exchanges. If the only thing that kept me going at the LAC was the belief that Annie was my true friend and the love of my life, what would happen to me if I discovered something that challenged that? Wasn't it better just to trust that what happened between us was real? I was thriving in prison. I was a teacher. I'd started my own agency. Why throw myself into turmoil?

I tapped on the cover of the dog diary for a long minute, then opened it.

Seeing her first drawing of me as Todor made my eyes well up. How simple and wonderful my life had been not so long ago. I turned the page. Her handwriting was so familiar, so personally hers that I could almost feel the heat of her body.

The unfairness of my incarceration slammed into me fresh, and I vomited into the toilet.

I rested my head against the cool wall. When I felt strong enough, I sat back on my cot, opened the diary and scanned the pages, taking care not to get drawn into any story this first time through. This worked until my eyes stopped on the sentence, "She is going to leave me alone in a mansion full of priceless art and furniture and wine, where there are bank statements and financial reports and important numbers and passwords."

I closed the diary, dropped it in the blue corrugated box and laid down. I remembered how Annie scolded me for leaving out my address book, saying she'd found enough passwords in it to make off with everything I had.

The next morning I picked up a pen and wrote:

A) Fact: Annie inherited a decent fortune several years ago. She had a Swiss bank account her own husband didn't know about. She is used to having money, and she knows how to hide it.

B) Possible: Annie might have burned through her inheritance "livin' the life" and hosting her friends in Paris and Florence. If she looked through Clarissa's personal papers like she had mine, she could have found an irresistible way to replenish that Swiss account.

C) I'm totally fucked: If Annie stole exactly two and a half million dollars, it was because I told her, in writing, it was the amount I needed to start my own agency and she knew it would help seal my fate.

I looked down at my words. This was dangerous territory. You don't open a door like that without warping it, and warped doors never shut properly again.

So I went darker.

What about *The Blue Season?*

I hadn't doubted Annie's story for a second. A brilliant Russian seemed a far more likely author for that book than some lackluster kid from south central L.A. My dislike of Oliver made it only too easy to disregard the fact that he was the only one with actual evidence that the book was his, and what was that compared to the crisp visual images that Annie's story supplied? At Bardi's, Annie insisted she be the one to call Oliver. But did she? Or had she been talking to silence, making threats to no one? What about the empty flash drive in her purse? Was it a prop to support her story? If so, she had worked it so brilliantly as to lead me to ask her if she had checked it to see if the manuscript had been deleted.

I stood up and walked to and fro. Annie wasn't an evil genius. She couldn't be. I was so furious with myself for even entertaining the thought that I dumped everything back into the box and kicked it under my cot. Then I sat down, closed my eyes, and tried to blanch it all from my mind.

XXIX
It Speaks

I know four in the morning.

I know how it quiets everything, promises nothing, and holds the world so still that even the flowers of May clamp back their perfume. If there were a Ph.D. for four in the morning I would have earned it by now. So when—at my signature hour—the blue box under my cot hissed, "Hey, Nitwit!" I knew it wasn't a dream.

I lifted my head, waiting for a guard to continue the conversation with himself, or an inmate to mumble something more in his sleep—anything to prove my directional signals were off. But the only sound was the singular drone of a distant exit sign.

I settled back on my side, grabbed a fist-full of blanket, and pressed it to my exposed ear. I hadn't slept worth a damn since I got the diary, and now there were only two hours left before the ugly chorus of daylight noise kicked in. I tasted metal on my tongue and wondered if hearing voices was a symptom of having a toxic level of iron in the blood.

To calm myself down I tried to imagine inhaling through my right nostril and exhaling out the left, but gave up in ten seconds, certain that the Dalai Lama himself couldn't meditate away the wackiness of getting lip from corrugated cardboard.

Through the foam of my pillow the voice said, "Okay numb nuts, pay attention. This is important."

My eyes flew open. My hands became fists. With flight not an option I had to fight back this delusion before Beetlejuice and Jacob Marley sailed through the bars holding hands. And it's not particularly hard to boil up a pot of fury when you sleep seven inches from a steel toilet. I thought of my arrest, my trial, getting choked by a rapist and blackmailed by the warden. And yet, thanks to my own skill set, I was one of the most respected inmates at the LAC. I had earned some chops here, and sure as hell didn't have to put up with trash talk from dried wood pulp.

"Oh calm down and listen," it scolded. "This isn't the box talking, you dolt; it's your insomnia. What? You think you can go for decades without a decent night's sleep and *not* hear voices?"

I let my fists release. Talking insomnia might not be a sign of sterling mental health, but at least I knew it came from my own head, which on the crazy scale had to rank a thousand clicks lower than conversing with a paper product.

"I'm only going to tell you this once and then you're on your own. Are you ready?"

I thought *go on.*

"You've heard of 'six degrees of separation'?"

Of course.

"In prison there are only two."

I waited for more but that was it.

I swung shaky legs over the edge of the cot and sat up. I didn't need murky missives in the dead of night. If I was going to suffer a psychotic break, I think I deserved a straightforward message, not this cryptic bullshit.

While four in the morning has its minuses, I'll leave those to the other Ph.D. insomniacs. My thesis would prove how that hour is the skeleton key for the brain, when every lobe and gyrus is ready to remember in sad, perfect detail the bitter resignation etched on the face of your geometry teacher ... that one discolored tooth on the kid that lived next door when you were ten ... the smell of gin from the pores of a maiden aunt who died twenty years ago.

But along with the detritus there are fruitful new veins to mine full of ideas and possibilities that elude the daylight hours. So I closed my eyes and let my four a.m. brain roll out scene after scene of the movie *Six Degrees of Separation*.

Stockard Channing, as Louisa Kitteredge, was initially afraid of the young Will Smith when he showed up bleeding at her upscale Manhattan apartment. Soon he dazzled her with his stories and the exceptional meal he pulled together from the vegetables in her kitchen. By the end of the movie, Stockard realized that getting conned by Will was more than an amusing tale to share at cocktail parties. He woke her up to the shallow life she'd been living. In the final moments of the film she tells off her pretentious husband, turns on her heel, and hits the street a transformed woman.

I rubbed my chin and thought *dammit.*

If talking insomnia had the gall to insinuate that Annie had conned me—and that I was better off because of it—then talking insomnia could just fuck off.

I fell back to the pillow.

Moments later I rolled off my cot, my forearms sweeping the dark floor until I found my notebook and pen. I sat down and scribbled: *I have thirty-one criminal minds at my disposal. If there are only two degrees of separation in prison, one of those men knows who stole the 2.5 mil.*

I crawled back onto my cot and heard a gasp. This time I knew it wasn't a guard or an old man lost in the dark. It was me, seized by a moment of hope.

At first light I wrote out what I believed to be a comprehensive course of action, and any comprehensive course of action deserved a title. Mine was "The Nitwit Plan."

The Nitwit Plan

Step One: Read a section of the dog diary before lights out, then use the skeleton key of four a.m. to recall my life and thoughts when the entry was written. This will prime the pump for...

Step Two: Find my second degree of separation from among the men in my classes.

Step Three: Use that information to get the hell out of prison.

Step Four: Take the first plane to Ireland, find Annie, and bring back Alik Nikitin's handwritten manuscript to prove she owns The Blue Season.

It was Step Four that I feared.

I had come to prison consumed by one question: *Who framed me?*

But as the weeks and months stacked up, and still no word from Annie, I started to ask myself another: What if I go to Ireland and find that Annie doesn't have Alik's hand-written manuscript? What if, her back in a corner, she tells me she made up a connection to *The Blue Season* like she made up the stories she wrote down?

Jesus.

Prison I could take. Seven months were behind me already. But what if everything I knew about Annie was a lie?

That would destroy me.

XXX
Half a Manuscript

I began.

What I liked best about Step One of the Nitwit Plan was how much it felt like a conversation: Her, me, her, me.

Every evening I read an entry from the dog diary, went to bed with my notebook, and when I woke in the dark I wrote out exactly what was happening in my life and in my thoughts at the time of the entry. The next morning, I typed out and added those pages to the dog walker diary. After a few weeks of this, when the binder was too stuffed to close, I pulled out the stack of pages and placed them unbound on the cot.

Huh. I thought. *Looks like half a manuscript.*

I started to turn away, then swiveled back.

Am I … writing a book?

I put my hand over my mouth, feeling the smile beneath my fingers. Finally, after all these years, I had a tale to tell that was uniquely mine. But unless I knew for certain who stole Clarissa's money, and who authored *The Blue Season*, this was just a pile of paper.

I reached for my notebook and wrote: *Annie is Allura, Nin and Alainn, and all of them have no agenda other than to love me as Todor, Blend and Craic. So she loves me. She loves me with birth defects and amputations and with a crown on my head.*

God, I hope that's true.

I turned the page and wrote:

What if Annie hadn't shoved at the door of my life?

I'd still be a free man. I'd still be working at Floodgate Media and duking it out with Cameron the Zygote. I'd be in a loveless marriage with Victoria.

This was familiar territory. Now I had more to add:

I wouldn't be a teacher.

I wouldn't be gathering material for Internally Free.

I wouldn't be mentoring Jack Tempert.

I wouldn't have found the courage to start my own agency.

And I would have remained that very odd anomaly—an insomniac who was sleeping through life.

Some people need to have a few wrinkles on their face before they sit down to write a book. Others need to fall down a well.

Apparently I fit in both categories.

XXXI
Step Two

I had completed Step One of The Nitwit Plan. With the details of those seven weeks with Annie fresh in my mind, I was prepared to find my second degree of separation.

I told the men in each class that instead of building their own story from the ground up, they would be doing what many well-paid script and ghost writers do: jump into a story with established characters and write a new installment.

On the whiteboard I wrote *Annie, Oliver, Peter, Drew, Alik,* and *Clarissa.*

"Take careful notes. I'm going to supply you with a biography for each character on the board, and flesh out the details of the seven weeks prior to my arrest. Your assignment is to write a credible story to prove me innocent."

They laughed. They shouted out Red's famous line from *The Shawshank Redemption*: "Everyone's innocent in here!"

I laughed along, then held up my hands to restore order. "Guys, you can write yourselves innocent on your own time. But this assignment, the one you will be graded on, the one that might get you published, is for me."

In my ten o'clock class Popo, an older inmate who handed in sexualized stories about the ladies of his past, raised his hand and asked, "If the hacker had the account number and password, why did he have to use the home computer? Couldn't he just hack in from anywhere?"

In front of him, Jimmy Short-Timer—so named because he started most conversations with, "I'll be outta here soon and ..."—turned around in his seat and said, "Because this guy wasn't a hacker. He didn't have the account number. Look, you got real money, your home computer is linked to your financial institutions. Click, sign in with a single password, which I'm guaranteeing is written down on something within arm's reach, and that's it, baby. Zero sophistication. You try to login from any other computer, and not only do you need the account number, there's a three-step verification. One wrong answer locks you out."

I snapped the lid on my marker and pointed it at him. "Okay, Jimmy. So exactly where were *you* November twenty-eighth, two thousand fifteen?"

For the next two weeks I had to answer questions everywhere I went.

What does Clarissa look like?

How old is Peter?

How rich is Drew?

Does Annie write to you in prison?

Each time I answered that last one I found myself looking at the floor. "No," I said, and left it there. I didn't elaborate. I didn't make excuses. I wanted them to draw their own conclusions.

———

The stories came in, and I separated them into piles depending on which character the author revealed as the thief.

Five were written tongue-in-cheek to help me discover that it was, indeed, me. In one story I was the victim of a Turkish flu that robbed me of my recent memory. The other four had me suffering from an advanced case of denial. They all suggested I grow up and take my medicine.

Pile Me.

Pile Peter had three stories, all sharing a theme of Peter being blackmailed by a lover demanding money. In two cases that lover was another man. Having no real assets of his own, he could only tap into an account he shared with Clarissa. In these stories Peter kept close tabs on the email stream between the dog walker and his wife, and when he learned that Annie and Drew would be traveling to Mexico, it was easy to get a trusted friend into the house to make the transfer. Peter, being six thousand miles away, had the perfect alibi. Unfortunately, I incriminated myself by leaving fingerprints in the office. At that point Peter had to let me take the fall.

I found it hard to buy that Peter stole the money, but I had to admit it would explain why he couldn't meet my eye at the trial.

Pile Annie had *seventeen* stories.

Statistically, the criminal mind was dishing out very bad news about the woman I loved.

The most frequent premise in Pile Annie was that she was a chameleon who changed her accent, her name, and her history as she moved around the world. She got herself hired as a private assistant, a house cleaner, a nanny—always with the intent of doing a thorough search of assets so she could make off with the biggest payoff. Her genius was gaining trust, and the method she used on a literary agent was obvious: She left me stories.

Agents know movie stars, producers, and directors. Gaining my confidence was the first step, and in this she was so successful that after knowing her for only three weeks I had wholeheartedly recommended her to Peter and Clarissa.

In Popo's story, the twist was that Annie barely knew Alik. She met him at a coffee house in St. Petersburg, came home with him, and after a graphic sex scene (uh, *thanks* Popo) Alik fell asleep and Annie looked for something to steal. She came upon his manuscript. After reading a few pages she stuffed it in her backpack and left. When Alik awoke and found his only copy missing, he was so distraught that he committed suicide.

The film noir aspect in the Pile Annie stories was so strong it had the screenplay agent in me mentally pitching to HBO and Netflix. "So this gorgeous sociopath ruthlessly manipulates and disposes of men. Think *Body Heat, Black Widow* and *Basic Instinct*, but with a continent-hopping redhead."

Film potential aside, the Pile Annie stories truly unsettled me. None more so than Jack Tempert's, in part because his talent made it read like it was happening before my eyes, in part because his premise was that Alik Nikitin was *alive*.

Alik, full of bluster and bravado over his masterpiece, brought Annie and his novel to L.A. When he learned his young nephew had also just written a book, he offered to critique it to help the kid out. But as soon as Alik read the first chapter, he knew Oliver's book, *The Blue Season,* made his own novel look like child's play.

Alik unhinged. He drank. He punched holes in the wall and accused Annie of thwarting his talent. The night she found him at his laptop researching poisons she realized that her already volatile husband was now a dangerous madman.

Alik had a short list of agents, and he made it his business to learn everything he could about each of us. In the end, he picked me. I was the right age, single, and desperate for a big win at work. In short the perfect candidate to both dazzle with a potential bestseller, and to be seduced by his beautiful wife. He had Annie make up the dog walker flier, and he stuck it in my door.

The day after I hired Annie, Alik convinced Oliver to send me a query and the first chapter of his book.

Alik assumed that by the time Annie made her big reveal —that Oliver had stolen the manuscript written by her "dead" husband—I would believe her and cut Oliver out. The next day, Oliver's body would be found with a suicide note.

In Jack's story, Alik's plan included hiding out until the book was published. Then he'd show up to admit to the press that he suffered from a depression so extreme that he had faked his own death so his wife could move on with her life.

The snag in his design was my initial lack of romantic interest in Annie. I had, in fact, informed her in my first note that we must never be in the same room again.

For her part, Annie feared that if she couldn't reel me in, her deranged husband would murder Oliver before she could stop him. In desperation she drew pictures and left me stories that flattered me as a noble and romantic hero. She bought Oliver time by assuring Alik that I was flirting more and more in each of my notes. Soon, she swore, I would trust anything she told me.

It was when Annie moved into the mansion that Alik saw a new opportunity. While he still demanded that his wife convince me that her "late" husband was the true author of *The Blue Season,* now there was also the possibility that they could return to Russia with a chunk of Clarissa's fortune.

Annie went along. She believed if her husband had real money he wouldn't kill Oliver, and might even agree to a divorce. Then she would be free to pursue her new romantic interest.

Me.

But Alik had made decisions he didn't share with Annie. He didn't make the transfer at nine in the morning as they agreed, but waited until he heard me enter the house. Instead of taking all the money, he transferred out exactly two and a half million.

Alik knew the timing and amount would incriminate me.

In Jack's story, it was Alik that I saw on the bike that day. And as he had hoped, I went upstairs to investigate and left my fingerprints in the office.

When I was done reading I stood up and threw the pages against the wall.

Pile Drew had six stories.

In Jimmy Short-Timer's version, while Clarissa got her inheritance in a lump sum, the rich aunt had a lower opinion of Drew's ability to handle money and set him up with a trust fund. A confirmed gambler, Drew not only burned through his income every year, he owed a great deal of cash to a loan shark who was running out of patience. When Drew read Clarissa's email about going to London, he decided to sneak into the empty Flood mansion and take her Renoir off the dining room wall. He knew he could borrow enough against it to both pay off his gambling debt and stake himself at the tables. With the confidence of a true gambler, he believed he'd soon win enough to get the painting back with no one the wiser.

But when Drew opened the back door and found Annie in the kitchen, he had to come up with a new plan. He snooped around the upstairs office, found the password to a vulnerable account, and hired a young blackjack dealer from the casino to make the money transfer while he and Annie were in Mexico.

I liked Jimmy's plausible explanation of why a rich guy would steal money, and was about to give him an "A" when

I saw a hand-drawn arrow at the bottom. I turned the page around and saw two printed sentences.

You really are innocent. Cancel our class tomorrow and meet me alone.

That night when the lights went out, I tried and failed to imagine any scenario where Jimmy knew Drew. So his contact, my second degree of separation, had to be the young blackjack dealer.

When I created the Nitwit Plan my major worry from the outset was that the legendary abhorrence inmates have for snitching would stop anyone from coming forward to tell me what they knew. So I was grateful that Jimmy Short-Timer went this far. But if the young blackjack dealer in his story was a friend, a relative, or even just an acquaintance of an acquaintance, I knew Jimmy wasn't going to tell me his name. And without that, all I had was a story from a convicted felon. It wouldn't be enough to get my case re-opened.

At least I thought, *I know it was Drew.*

I wasn't that surprised. Drew had complete access to the Flood mansion. He'd been using that office for a week, and he'd already fallen for Annie. When she told him she'd ask the neighbor to walk George while they were in Mexico, Drew told her that Peter was feuding with the man and suggested she ask me instead.

That's all it took to put me in the mansion while the blackjack dealer upstairs made the transfer.

I fumed the night away, picturing Drew looking smug in that Irish sweater as he told the judge that I had manipulated Annie.

I looked forward to the day that I could return the favor.

The next afternoon I got to the classroom first, moved two of the student desks face to face, and paced until Jimmy showed up. We took our seats and I picked up his story. "Thank you for coming forward," I said, pressing my feet into the floor to keep my voice steady. I was a moment from asking him a question, and his answer would either keep me a prisoner or set me free.

"Will you tell me the name of the blackjack dealer?"

Jimmy's eyes shifted left and right and left again. Then he pointed to the story in my hand and shook his head. "Oh, I get it. No, no. You've got it all wrong."

"I ... You said to meet you here. Your story?"

"Yeah, fiction," he said and rubbed his chin. "For a grade. Look, I met the asshole who set you up. Shared a cell in the county lockup with him for about four hours. He got picked up for cocaine possession. Asked me what I was in for, and when I told him for robbery, he asked how much I made off with. I said, 'Nine grand in cash and jewelry,' and the jerk laughed like I was pathetic and small time. I said, 'Glad I'm amusing you. I suppose you've done better.'

"He smirked and said, 'You bet I have. I stole two and a half million dollars from my own father.'

"I said, "So you couldn't wait to inherit the dough?' and he said that would never happen, that he was a bastard who hadn't even met his father until he was nineteen, and by then the older man had married a rich woman from Texas who had an innocent nature. A Bible thumper. Said it would go down hard if she found out he had a grown son out of wedlock. But he agreed to help as long as it was done on the q.t. So he put his son through a couple years of college and got him a job."

I was excited. It was the right amount of money, and the wife sounded exactly like Clarissa. "Who was this guy? What was his name?"

Jimmy shook his head. "Oh man, I've been trying to

remember. This conversation was almost ten months ago, and I probably only heard his name once. Sorry."

I stood up and walked to the window. *So that's it,* I thought. *My only view of the outside world will still be through glass fronted by a grid of iron bars.*

"He was a white dude," Jimmy said behind me. "Had that vain cokehead attitude."

"Yeah," I said absently, thinking about which wall I would kick in as soon as Jimmy left.

"And he had this stupid tattoo. Some word in Chinese, right over his Adam's apple."

My body turned in slow motion.

"Was his name ... *Cameron?*"

Jimmy snapped his fingers and pointed at me. "That's it!"

I walked back and sat across from him again. "Did he say anything else?"

"Yeah. That dude could talk! When I asked him how he got hold of the money, he said he worked at his father's business, and once the old man was out of town, he waited till everyone left for the day, then went into his dad's office, turned on his computer, and that's when he found a keylogger icon."

"Which is what?"

"It's software that allows you to read anything typed on a company server. Documents, emails, even deleted drafts are all there to see. And what he was looking for was dirt on his rival at work. *You.* Said he wanted to take over some big client of yours that should have been his in the first place. When he read your emails and found out that you'd start your own business if you could get your hands on two and a half million dollars, he paid it no mind *until* you gave instructions to the house sitter to turn off the mansion's security system and leave you a key."

Jimmy leaned back. "Once he read that he lost no time. He faxed all the forms necessary to open an anonymous account in the Caymans. Then he had a bike rack attached to the back of his car so he could park blocks away and ride the bike over early in the morning and hide it in the bushes. He got in his father's house, looked around on the computer, and found a linked account. Then he waited. When he heard you come in he transferred out the money. Bragged to me that he killed three birds with one stone. He got the dough, he got you out of the picture, and he took over your big client."

"So," I said, reasoning it out as I spoke, "when I heard the chair squeak and called up the stairs, that must have rattled him enough to make him bolt out the front door when he heard me leave out the back."

"No doubt."

"So when I told your class the details that put me in prison ..."

"I knew right then I'd met the dude who pulled it off. Remember Popo asking why someone would need to use the home computer if they knew the passwords to an account?"

I tapped my fingers on the desk. "Yes. And you told him it was because the thief *didn't* know the passwords that he had to use a computer that was linked to the financial institution." I picked up his story. "So even though you knew what happened, you wrote this because ... you didn't want to be a snitch?"

"Exactly."

"What changed your mind?"

Jimmy reached over and took the story from my hand. "Well, it's like this. When my play was put on you gave it a standing ovation. You didn't do that for everyone, but you did it for me, and it was like ... the best moment of my life. So yeah, I made up the Drew story because I wasn't going to rat on anyone. But the whole time I felt like a shit. It was in our class, just before I handed this in, that I scribbled that message to you on the back, figuring *what the hell*. I didn't owe that annoying cokehead a damn thing. And besides, I won't be running into him in prison. As you know, I'll be outta here soon."

I had to laugh, and he joined in.

"Thanks to you," I said, "we'll *both* be outta here soon."

———————

Denis set to work. He had enough information for the police to look into Cameron's finances, and once they found he'd opened a Swiss account on the date the Cayman account was emptied, everything clicked into place.

Three weeks later I was cleared.

I was let out of the LAC on Monday, December fifth, 2016. One year to the day since I last saw Annie.

After Matt Badger shook my hand he handed me a summons. I was scheduled to appear in front of a grand jury on Friday at ten a.m. in the case against Cameron.

That gave me four days to get to Ireland and back.

It was time for Step Four of the Nitwit Plan.

XXXII
Lost Among Sheep

All those sleepless nights in prison, all my plans, and what I never saw coming was the affect women would have on the seam of my heart.

A sniff of perfume at the ticket counter and I mistook my insurance card for my VISA. Girls floated like angels on the escalators, their impossibly smooth faces and astonishing profiles had me white knuckling the handrail to stay upright.

And they were everywhere. Standing in front of me, giving me change, breathing in and out, and all so beautiful that it hurt to look at them straight on. But even a sidelong glance at something as innocent as the female ponytail put a lump in my throat. At the LAC, old cons tied their gray scraps of hair at the base of their skulls with a twist tie and called *that* a ponytail. It was solar systems away from the thick, vibrant ropes of color that swung like new music as the airport stunners strode by.

On standby it took three flights to get to JFK, and then a five-hour wait for an empty seat to Dublin. I didn't mind. The bustle of humanity riveted me, and after being tethered for nearly a year to a small patch of concrete and stone, I savored every takeoff into the clouds like a glutton with butter sauce on his tongue.

The plane landed Wednesday morning. I rented a Toyota at the Dublin Avis counter and headed to Grafton Street.

Leandra had taken in my dogs, took care of the sale of my townhouse, and visited me in prison nearly every week for a year. She had done so much for me that I made it my first order of business to buy her an authentic Irish lace tablecloth. As I made my way back to my rental car, I passed the bronze statue of Molly Malone, the cockle and mussel seller made famous in song. Molly is a looker; in no small part because the scalloped bodice of her dress reveals nearly every bit of her stupendous bosom. I was twenty steps past when I heard shrieks of laughter. I turned and saw a group of college-aged girls surrounding the statue, pushing out their own chests as far as possible for a picture.

I think Ms. Malone gets a lot of that.

I put the tablecloth in the trunk of the Toyota and headed south.

I had a map. I had GPS. What I didn't have was the full name of Annie's town. For seven hours I tried to navigate the sea green landscapes south of Dublin with one syllable to serve as both compass and rudder, and it wasn't enough. In every village I hopped out to ask, "Do you know a place named creek or crick-something-or-other?"

Eyes squinted and faces contorted as the locals tried to decipher how I might be mangling their language. Some shrugged. Others smiled and assured me that what I was *really* looking for was Creggenbaun, or Cloonacool or Carrickmacross. Soon there were so many storybook names in my head that I had to shake them off or doubt the one syllable that brought me here. "Creek," or something very like it, was what Annie had said by the pool that day.

Confounding me further were the roundabout signs. They looked like Stonehenge on its side with the supporting rocks splayed out from the circle as if in astonishment. Impaled on every rock-prong were two names for each location. On top was the Irish version - a Celtic hieroglyphic of improbable letter combinations and imaginative accent marks. Below that was the English translation, looking drab in a plain-Jane font. But these were only the main cities. It wasn't until I was inside the roundabout, circling in the wrong direction, on the wrong side of the road, and with cars coming at me in nauseating ways that I got a glimpse of the signs for the villages. They were the ones I needed time with. But hesitate in a busy Irish roundabout, and you, my friend, are *fooked*.

I never factored in getting lost. I was certain the car rental agent would hear me out, take a map from his pile, and circle "Crickmcfincle" or some such word, and in ninety minutes I'd be knocking on Annie's door. Instead, he became the first to furrow a brow, the first to offer up a Mother Goose name that wasn't even close.

At dusk I gave up my fruitless zigzag around the Emerald Isle to get some bearings over dinner. Mercifully, there is nothing easier to find in Ireland than a pub.

I stepped through the door. When the patrons stared my way a beat too long, I wondered just how far off the tourist circuit I had wandered. The interior was dark and rustic, and looked so much like the drawing of the Mead Hall in *Beowulf* from the Norton Anthology that I imagined raspy exhalations coming from the rafters.

Grendel?

On the bare chance the monster was up there, I wasn't going to rouse him from his millennium snooze with an order for a "Bud Light." No. Grog, or something like it, was the only way to stay under his radar.

"A Guinness, please."

I would have no regrets on my choice of drink. On the

contrary, once I got past the first bitter sip it somehow became as smooth and wonderful as honeyed nectar on my tongue. Every subsequent gulp felt as though I were flooding my body with a much needed elixir. As I drained the pint my sour mood likewise transformed. I no longer felt a stranger in a strange land. My shoulders relaxed. I remembered how wonderful it was to be free.

I studied the foam trail in my glass and had to wonder *is Guinness the Irish Prozac?* Considering that my acute disappointment at the top of the hour had just been replaced with something like cheerful resignation, I whispered, "'Tis!"

Better still, the healing powers appeared to be cumulative. The second pint showed me the folly of being too eager to make this trip. Even when the warden put that summons in my hand it still didn't stop me from heading to the airport. Reason and logic be damned. I was a man with a plan!

Seventeen hours to get to Ireland, four more lost on the road, and two pints of Guinness later, and I was finally ready to admit I was a fool on a fool's errand. The window in which I had to find Annie, to hear what she alone could tell me, was closing fast. The only smart thing to do was find a bed for the night, drive to Dublin in the morning, and get on a plane back to the States.

Even disappointing decisions can be a relief, and I signaled for a third pint, confident that one more dose of the foamy liquid would free me from any lingering doubts about my resolution to go home. I'd come back to Ireland when all the legal issues hanging over my head had been dealt with, and I wouldn't leave until I found Annie.

I ordered a corned beef sandwich, and as I ate I marveled at the journey that brought me to the Beowulf Pub. Not so long ago I was pitching scripts to junior moguls over lunches they never paid for, met writers and actors for games of basketball, and networked at parties where the canapés came with air and ass kisses. I was a small cog in the industry, but I had a laurel or two in my pocket, and the minor league took my calls as often as not. Still it wasn't enough. My last six months at Floodgate I was driving around with a sturdy carton in my trunk so I could empty out my office the moment Peter decided to replace me with a zygote.

And the only stable relationship in my life was with my sister.

Then along came Annie and *The Blue Season*. In a flash I was not only the golden boy of Floodgate Media, I had found a new friend who helped me realize what my life was meant to be.

Then I was arrested.

I looked down at the pint in my grip. The foam had curved from the rim to the bottom like a question mark. *Why go there?* It seemed to ask.

Why indeed?

And for once in my life I let a disturbing thought simply melt away.

The dart players behind me were swearing in extraordinary ways.

"Yer as ignorant as the back a' me bollix."

"Donkey shit upon ya!"

"There's nothing worse than a standin' prick!"

I'd never heard anything like it, and I would have turned to watch their game, but I couldn't take my eyes off the barmaid. She was truly ancient. The skin on her face was like tissue paper once scrunched then spread open to a thousand wrinkles. Tiny and stooped, in order to reach the handles of the beer taps she had to grasp the nearby ledge and step up on a stool. She had done this maneuver so many times over the years that her touch had worn the wood of that ledge down to a whitened slope. I had never seen anyone this frail or this old still working, and wondered if Ireland's version of Social Security had run dry. Was the island full of centenarians busing tables and breaking hips?

Without any prompting on my part, she told me that "the credit" was ruining the young ones; that they went out every night to buy their dinner with their plastic cards, with never a thought to the debt they were building instead of a family life. I missed a word or a phrase here and there thanks to the thickness of her brogue, but of this I was certain: she was the most adorable barkeep who ever poured a pint.

I heard myself say, "I'm Daniel. And what might your name be, darlin'?"

Never before have I called a stranger "darling" much less "darlin'," but she seemed to take no offense, and that made me like her all the more.

"I'm Nellie," she said.

I almost laughed. There couldn't have been a more perfect a name for this delightful lady. It was so ideal, that even though I was lost, even though I had suffered nothing but blind alleys, I said, "Nellie, I think I am in love with you."

"Go on with ya!" she said, and her smile added soft dimples to the wrinkles in her cheeks. "What are ya doin' here boyo?"

Boyo!

I glanced up to the rafters to see if Grendel found this as hilarious as I did. He remained mute on the subject, so I said, "Well, I'm looking for a woman."

"I'm seventy-three years married so look elsewhere," she said and the dimple went deeper.

"Ah," I said, "that's a shame fer me, sure it'is."

Slowly I put the pint down and glanced over my shoulder. Apparently the medicinal properties of Guinness came with the side effect of turning me into a local, and I feared if the genuine boyos heard my new accent they might decide I was mocking the old sod and make my back their new dartboard.

"This woman yer lookin' fer, where does she live?"

"Ah, Nellie," I said, careful to Americanize each word, "That is the problem. She told me the name of her village once, but that was a long time ago. All I remember is that the first syllable sounds like 'Creek' or 'Crick,' and there's a monastery there."

With that I pulled out my map and laid it on the bar.

"Before I left home I searched for towns in Ireland that began with a 'C' or a 'K,' but I couldn't find it. I thought that once I was actually here, anyone I met could tell me where it was. But no one has ever heard of it. I've been driving around for hours reading signs."

I covered the map with my hand, "Now I realize this trip was a mistake. The woman I'm looking for, I don't even know if she told me the truth. Maybe there is no such place."

"Ah, but there is," said Nellie with a wink.

I put down the pint. "You know it?"

"Aye."

She looked absolutely sure of herself, and I pushed the map toward her. "That's fantastic! Here, show me where it is."

Nellie shook her head. "Not so fast me boy. Before I show it t' ya I need t' ask a few questions."

"Questions?"

"Aye. What has this woman done t' ya that ya come all the way t' Ireland ta catch up t' her?"

I blinked a few times. In prison you don't ask a man his personal business. But was she really violating the laws of stranger interaction, or had I become a suspicious ex-con? I decided to shrug her off. "Well … it's really a long story."

Nellie swept her hand in an arc that took in the whole of the pub. "We *like* long stories."

She stood silent and waited a good twenty seconds for me to answer.

"Okay, well, in prison I started to write a book about her. I even brought it with me. Her name is Annie Doherty, and I can't finish the book until I know something that only she can tell me."

Nellie turned away, took three steps over to the beer taps, and with a practiced slide, she brought her footstool over and climbed up so we were face to face.

"Prison is it?" she said and shook her head sadly. "Daniel, me boy, I'm sorry, but ya got a lot more convincin' ahead before I show ya the town this lass comes from. I don't want t' be listenin' ta the news tomorra and hear ya went and kilt her!"

I reared back. "Kill her? Jeez Nellie, have you ever got the wrong idea."

"Then set me straight, boyo, because I'm not helping till I'm convinced a' your intentions."

I might have taken Nellie at her word—even admired the precautions she was using to protect Annie—but I was certain she had another motive. My livelihood once depended on being able to gauge how interested someone was in a story, and Nellie was hungry for mine. It was a feeling I understood well. But before I could figure out what to tell her, she said, "Ya say ya got the book? Then bring it in."

"Sure, I'll show it to you, but, uh, of course … you're not actually going to *read* it."

"Course I am. How else will I know if ya mean t' harm her? So get it. What are ya waitin' fer?"

"That's the problem," I said, swallowing hard and realizing too late that only a drunken idiot would have mentioned either prison or the manuscript to an Irish sprite so clearly determined to be entertained. "I can't wait. I've got a court appearance in California in two days. If I miss it, I'll get in trouble. I only mentioned the book so you'd see I was a literary type who wouldn't hurt a fly."

"Or yer a stalker and a murderer who is obsessed with the lass."

Jesus!

Nellie was unwavering, but I gave it one last shot. "Seriously, I'm almost out of time and it would take you all night to read it!"

"And it'll take ya maybe never t' find this town without me. So why don't I get ya a room fer the night, and ya can check back with me tomorra at ten in the mornin'. If I think yer not going t' hurt the lass, I'll show ya where she lives."

She had me. I nodded and pushed off my stool.

While I dug the manuscript out of my bag, Nellie made a phone call and secured a room for me at the bed and breakfast across the street. When I came back to the pub she was sitting at a table with a lamp, and I pulled the paper stack out of its padded envelope and set it in front of her. I went back to my drink and Nellie turned pages, getting up now and then to service the few customers that came in.

I watched her read. Sometimes she smiled, sometimes she looked my way and nodded a bit, and once she shook her finger at me and I tried to guess which thick-headed blunder she was chastising me for.

After my fourth Guinness I felt a wild itching in the middle of my chest. If two pints had given me a brogue, I worried four might be the number to make red Druid hair sprout between my nipples.

It was time to stop drinking.

I said goodnight and staggered across the street to my room. With my head on the pillow, I thought of all the people I had asked for help that day, and how not one of them could come up with the town that started with "Creek." Yet Nellie knew it instantly. Was it some kind of Irish Shangri-La, known only to the ancients? Would I have to climb a mountain to find it past the clouds?

At nine o'clock the next morning I took a seat in the breakfast room. A young woman set a plate of food in front of me that was crammed with eggs, a grilled tomato, fried potatoes, toast, beans, and oblong slices of a very dark sausage.

The Full Irish Breakfast!

I picked up my fork and pointed it at the meat. "Miss, what's this?"

"Black puddin', sir."

I put the fork back on the side of my plate.

Let other people believe in four leaf clovers or shooting stars. If my omen was a congealed blood sausage, I couldn't escape the thought that the only way I was going to find Annie was if I took a bite.

Thirty minutes later I was leaning against the door of the pub when Nellie rounded the corner, carrying the padded envelope in front of her like a cake. I took it off her hands, she unlocked the door, and once inside she turned to me. "Daniel, me boy, I still have one question fer ya," she said with her index finger high in the air.

"And what would that be, Nellie?"

"Do ya hold Annie Doherty responsible fer yer bad luck?"

I knew I had to tell her the truth. "Good and bad, yes."

She eyed me for a long second. "Yer an honest lad, I'll give ya that. Do ya promise not t' hurt the lass?"

"I so promise."

"Well, I've takin' yer measure and believe what yer sayin' so show me the map."

I put it on the table and she leaned forward, circling her finger before pointing to a string of letters that defied pronunciation.

Graiguenamanagh.

"Here 'tis," she said.

I stared at the word. Since eating that sausage I'd been vurping like a rock star, and what good had it done me? I sat down and took a defeated breath, already seeing myself heading out the door and back to the Dublin airport. I shook my head. "Nellie, that can't be right."

"'Tis!"

"How do you say it?"

"Craeg-na-ma-na. In Irish it means 'Village a' the Monks.' Lovely town. Not turty minutes away."

"Wait a minute … wait a minute!" I stumbled to my feet, "My God, that *is* it! All this time I was looking for a town that began with a 'C' or a 'K.'"

"Easy enough mistake for a Yank to make," she said with a wink, "and frankly yer accent is very confusin.' It took me a bit to put it together meself, so y' can't fault the young ones fer not knowin' what you were sayin.' But once I got accustomed to yer talk, and heard there was a monastery there, I thought, 'village … monks … why, the village of the monks! Graiguenamanagh."

I felt like jumping in the air. "Nellie, I am now completely in love with you."

"Again," she pointed to her thin wedding band, "married."

She dimpled for me. "Here, take yer book and go find yer Annie."

I left Nellie standing in the doorway. Before we parted she told me I'd be getting close to Graiguenamanagh when I saw the Abbey of Duiske.

"It'd be a shame were ya not t' go inside. 'Tis the oldest of its kind."

"I'll do that, I promise."

"And then the man y' want ta find is Michael, the owner a' the Waterside Guesthouse. He knows everyone in the village. He'll know where Annie is."

"Michael. Waterside Guesthouse. Got it."

Nellie nodded then tipped her head. "I'm glad ya went classy on describin' yer night with Annie. There's a lot a' trash in books nowadays. But I'll wager the thoughts a' that night kept ya warm in prison."

"Nellie! I lived like a monk in prison."

She wagged her finger at me. "I was up half the night readin' yer book. I want t' know if you and Annie end up together. I hate t' be kept hangin'.'"

"Dear lady, I promise if it gets published I will send you a copy."

I left the Beowulf pub with a hopeful heart.

XXXIII
The Monk and the Leprechaun

Knowing where I was going changed everything. I no longer saw the countryside as a chaotic maze, but as a visual orchestra of hills, sheep and cottages lined by miles of perfect stone fences. I was barely twenty minutes on the road when the pale yellow monastery of Duiske Abbey appeared. I pulled into the parking lot and turned off the car.

Realizing that Annie could be anywhere, that she could walk right in front of me, had me on the verge of hyperventilating. I needed to collect myself, and decided to keep my promise to Nellie and look inside the Abbey.

As I stepped through the vaulted door it felt like a feather brushed over the top of my head. This was the building where Sparks saw Annie marry the man who "smelled like" he would love her forever. If the trajectory of our relationship hadn't blown off course, that man would have been me.

Inside the nave were pamphlets about the history of the building. When I read it was constructed in 1204, I stepped back outside to take another look. In my world, buildings were "vintage" if they dated back to the 1960s. A monk was approaching and I said, "Excuse me, um, Brother; do I just keep going on this road to get to the main part of town?"

"That'd be right," he said and pointed the way.

"Thank you. I'm looking for a friend of mine who lives around here. Perhaps you know her. Annie Doherty?"

"Ah, Annie, you say?" He clasped his hands behind his back and put his head down. "No. Never heard a' the lass."

"Do you know a Rose Doherty, her grandmother?"

"No, no. Sorry."

"Anyone named Doherty?"

"Uh, no. Can't help you, but if y' cross over River Barrow Bridge and take a quick right, you'll see a four-story building, and that's the Waterside Guest House. Go inside and ask Michael where t' find your friend. He would know."

"Actually someone else told me to talk to Michael, so that's where I'll head."

I thanked him, walked halfway back to my rental car, then glanced over my shoulder to throw him a wave if he were looking my way. He wasn't.

I took another step, realizing I'd just seen something peculiar. I turned back. The monk was standing on the stoop of the monastery, facing away from me, his arms still behind him, one wrist over the other, and the first two fingers on each hand were crossed. Like a ten-year-old who had just told a fib.

I got in my car and started driving toward the bridge.

It seemed odd that he wouldn't know every surname in a village this small. Maybe I had the wrong town altogether? Had I been too optimistic when I heard how Nellie pronounced "Graiguenamanagh"? That would put me back to square one. Much as I wanted to find Annie, I'd had enough legal trouble for one lifetime. No matter what, in ninety minutes I would gun the rental car back to Dublin and take the first available seat on any plane to the U.S.

My drive into the village took me under a thick canopy of gnarled trees. On my right was the River Barrow, on the left were charming homes of stone and whitewashed clay, and ahead was a tall cobblestone bridge of seven arches, half-covered with untold thousands of small lavender and white flowers. I was just thinking the town looked more storybook than real when I had to brake to let a family of swans waddle across the road.

What next? I wondered. *Sneezy, Grumpy and Doc hi-ho-ing it around the next bend?*

Once across the beautiful bridge I turned right on a narrow road that took me by a slew of moored wooden boats. The tallest building on my left was a handsome four story with a brass sign bolted to the door that read "Waterside Guest House."

I parked and walked inside. To my left was an open restaurant with white stone walls, and straight ahead was a little man standing behind the front desk.

"Hello. Are you Michael?"

"M'self!" he said.

His ears stuck out, his cheeks were ruddy, and he had such mirth-filled eyes as to make me suspect that at least one grandparent was a leprechaun.

Thinking he'd be more likely to help a customer than someone who barged in with questions about his neighbors, I asked about room availability.

"I have a fine room fer ya."

"Before I decide if I'm staying, I need to make sure I'm in the right place. Have you lived here all your life?"

"Man and boy!"

"I'm from the States, and I'm looking up some friends as I travel."

"Are y'now? And just who might ya be lookin' fer?"

"Annie Doherty. She'd be about your age actually."

"Annie Doherty is it? Naw. No one in this town by that name anymore."

"You mean there was an Annie Doherty here once?"

"Sweet Jaysus, course there was! Then there wasn't. Then there was. People come and go my friend, that they do."

There was such an uncalled-for level of sass in his voice that I felt my hackles rise. I was out of time and had had it with this Irish sport. First there was Nellie demanding my story, then the monk with his fibbing crossed fingers, and now this character. I glowered down, giving Michael a moment to appreciate our size difference. "I have a court appearance in Los Angeles Friday morning and I don't even have a plane ticket yet," I said. "If I do make it but even smell like Ireland when I get there, I won't make a very good impression. So I am, shall we say, motivated to cut the bullshit and find my friend and then head home."

"Smell like Ireland? What the fookin' hell does that mean?"

I looked to the ceiling for help. "It means I won't come off as a reliable witness if I come running into the courthouse in rumpled clothes and bloodshot eyes from traveling for two days. I've got a lot at stake here."

Michael leaned over the counter and curled his finger in a "come here" way.

I shook my head *no*.

"Okay. Ya need ta take a deep breath or two. I'm worried about that temper I see brewin'. The ladies of Graiguenamanagh don't take t' violent men."

I slit my eyes and Michael appeared to rethink his bravado.

"Might be I can get a message t' the lady yer lookin' fer. Then let's let her decide if she wants t' be meetin' ya."

Whoa...

Both the monk and the leprechaun *knew* I was coming here to find Annie. Apparently while I was sleeping off the

Guinness, my ancient friend at the Beowulf Pub had been busy making phone calls.

I puffed the air out of my cheeks and said, "What did Nellie tell you, Michael?"

"Ah, now we're gettin' ta the crux a' the matter," he said with obvious delight. "While Nellie thinks yer an okay sort, all I know is yer a convict who came an awful long way t' find a friend a' mine. Well, she's waitin' fer ya. Sitting' on a stone fence she is, and she'll stay there fer one hour. She's a little worried that ya think she's responsible for yer going' t' prison, and that yer mad at her fer not keepin' in touch. So it's up t' me t' decide yer intentions, and if yer going t' find her or not."

Annie was waiting for me!

"I know she's not responsible for me going to prison."

"Ah, that's not what ya told Nellie. You said ya wouldn't a' gone ta prison a'tal if it hadn't a' been for Annie."

Jesus. The leprechaun was right up to the minute on me.

"What I meant was that if I hadn't met Annie I wouldn't have been in the wrong place at the wrong time. That's all. Look, why don't you trust Nellie? I passed her test."

"Nellie I do trust. You, not so much."

I needed another tactic to get by this guy.

"Look, one of the reasons I'm here is to get Annie's permission to use her stories for a book I'm putting together. It's the one your friend Nellie read last night."

I immediately sensed an attitude shift and pressed on. "As for not keeping in touch, Annie warned me ahead of time that she wasn't going to write. Do I wish she had changed her mind? Of course. But she had to do what she had to do, and I've accepted that."

Michael nodded. Finally he said, "Okay Mr. Los Angel*eees*.

Enough already. But if I find out y' hurt a single a hair on her head ...."

"I'd rather cut off both my arms."

"Good. So, what y' need t' do is go out that door, take a walk over the bridge, turn right, and follow the path. The river will be on yer right, and a stone fence on yer left. Once you're around the bend you'll see her. She's waitin'. Go!"

It took me a moment to believe him. Then I bolted out the door.

XXXIV
Heart of Ireland

In the sunlight I felt so weightless I thought a breeze might send me into the river. Once over the bridge I turned onto a well-worn footpath, and as excited as I was, the bucolic splendor did not escape me. On my left was the charming stone fence, and beyond it were the yards of some rather grand homes built two or three hundred years ago. On my right was the narrow river, and on the other bank was a bright green field bisected by another ancient fence of stone. On one side of that fence were black-faced sheep, their voices clear on the air, and on the other were two horses and two very young foals. Each time the young ones stepped away from their mothers to frolic, they were so overcome with the joy of life that they leapt in the air, all four slender hooves leaving the ground at once.

I knew the feeling. It was how I felt the night I realized I was in love.

Around the second bend I saw Annie sitting on the stone fence, wearing a heather-colored tunic over black leggings and hiking boots. Her hair was longer, falling in soft curls and ringlets down her back. When she saw me she stood up. Her expression was somber, like she was bracing herself for the conversation to come. When she didn't take a single step towards me, I felt my smile fade.

I stopped a few feet in front of her.

"Hello, Daniel."

"Annie."

"You got yourself free."

"Yes. Turned out it was Cameron who stole the money. I'm going to testify against him in front of a grand jury the day after tomorrow."

She nodded and stepped back to sit on the stone fence again. I waited, and finally, staring at my feet, she said, "So I have to ask: did y' come here in a rush because y' figured it out?"

"Figured what out?"

"The clues. The ones I left in the stories."

I shook my head. "No. I'm here ..." I looked over at the foals, and wished my life were as simple as theirs; that I could say, "I'm here because I love you," and leave it at that.

"Annie, after I got arrested and tried to tell Peter that *The Blue Season* really belonged to you, he wouldn't listen. And now it's been published with Oliver as the author."

She nodded. She knew. And yet there was no outrage, no cursing Oliver and our bad luck, and the dread that had started in my chest when she didn't hug me now spread like venom through my veins.

"It's climbing even faster than I thought it would," I said, watching her face. "Everyone wants to get an interview with Oliver, and the fact that he's refusing to promote the book is only helping sales. They're comparing the little weasel to J.D. Salinger. I get sick every time I think of it."

Annie took a deep breath and nodded, looking very much on the verge of a confession.

"But *you* should be the one getting royalties hand over fist," I prodded. "That book is not only going to hit the number one slot; it's going to stay there for a good, long time. There are probably movie offers on Peter's desk."

Her eyes remained fixed on the ground, and my hopes sunk there as well.

"A year ago," she said, "I felt like the planets and stars had lined up in a singular effort to bring me happiness. The man I loved discovered that he loved me as well, I was about t' sign a contract for *The Blue Season,* and was expecting t' hear that Peter wanted me t' write and illustrate a children's book that was all my own. After being orphaned, and my troubled marriage, I finally felt like a real shift had taken place." She closed her eyes, "Then, suddenly I was in a jail cell. My life had fallen apart. I thought, "served y' right for being so happy.""

I sat next to her and put my hand over hers. "Annie, you'll be happy again. If you let me take Alik's original manuscript with me, I'll use it to prove that Oliver stole the book from you."

She pulled her hand away, and I thought *Oh no.*

Desperate for a few more moments of innocence, I reached into my knapsack and took out the padded envelope.

"I brought this for you," I said and handed her the manuscript. "It's unfinished, but I want you to keep it and look it over."

"It's your book? The one Nellie read?"

"Actually, it's more yours than mine. I brought it with me to get your permission to use your stories."

"A' course you can use my stories," she said, and put the envelope on the stone fence beside her. Then she took a deep breath—the kind you need for courage—and said, "So is it true then? You didn't come here because y' figured out the clues?"

"No. I never did. What was that about?"

She covered her face with her hands for a moment. When she took them away I saw a relieved smile had taken over her features. "I was dead worried," she said, and looked me in the eye at last. "I believed y' gave up on me for not sending any letters. I mean, how could you not? So it was certain in my mind that you must a' figured out my clues. I feared that was the reason you came t' Ireland and no other."

She pushed off the fence, reached into her tote bag, and handed me two CD jewel cases.

"These are for you, then."

"What are they?"

"Turn them over."

I flipped them to see that one was labeled *The White Season*, the other *The Red Season*.

The air stilled between us.

"Annie ... what are these?"

"Do y' remember me saying that Alik forced me t' stay with him until he fixed that problem—the one I told him he had with his book?"

I nodded.

"He finally believed it was too long. He wanted t' give up because he thought cutting it down would destroy it. I said, 'Why not divide it up into two books?' At first he said that would be impossible. He started pacing around the apartment, pullin' on his earlobe, all the while saying very softly, 'no, yes, no,' and after two hours a' this, he sat down with his journals and made all kinds a' notes. The next morning, he told me very calmly that he was going t' make it into *three* books."

Annie tapped on the jewel cases.

"When I got deported I came back to live with Grandma Rose. I started typing up the other books straight away. That was the 'daunting task' I told you was ahead a' me. The reason I needed seclusion. I felt pressed to get them done so I could send them t' Peter so he'd see once and for all that Oliver couldn't have written *The Blue Season*."

I was looking at her, dumbfounded.

"I know what you're thinking," she said, which was impossible as I was too stunned to form anything close to a cohesive thought. "You're wonderin' why I didn't just send him the handwritten manuscript." She shook her head. "But I'd left Oliver alone with my flash drive and look how *that* turned out. I couldn't trust sending the original so it could get lost, or even destroyed by that awful Cameron. I would a' brought it to Peter personally, but I was barred from traveling t' the United States. What I *could* do was this," she said, pointing to the CD cases.

I was struggling to remain calm. "Are these books ... are they as good? Are they in the same voice? I don't know what to ask."

"They're even better than *The Blue Season*."

My mind was racing. "Do you know what this means?"

She poked her finger into my shoulder. "It means you've got some serious editing t' do, Mr. Ashe."

I sprang to my feet, picked her up and swung her around, the both of us laughing like children. I put her down and walked figure eights in front of her. "This is beyond incredible. With *The Blue Season* climbing up the bestseller list, and all the critics speculating why Oliver won't be interviewed, imagine what's going to happen when this story comes out!"

I put my hands on the top of my head and stared at the foals across the river. "It's a real-life drama. A brilliant manuscript is stolen by the nephew of its dead Russian author, the agent who knows the truth is sent to prison because his rival at work set him up so he could take over the contract, and the beautiful Irish widow is deported because of her relationship to the convicted agent. The book gets published as the work of the nephew ... the agent manages to get out of prison, comes to Ireland to find the widow, and she hands him two sequels that only she knew existed, and that prove without a doubt that the nephew stole the manuscript!"

I stopped and held out my arms. "This will hop off the arts and entertainment section and end up on the evening news. Your face will be on television. The public will go on a crazy book-buying spree over the scandal! Annie, you can't *buy* this kind of publicity. You'll be courted by every reporter in America. No, no, more than America." I looked at the sky, "You're Irish; Alik was Russian; the book takes place all over Europe. This story is *global!*"

There I was, in the calmest place I'd ever seen, and I'd never been more excited.

"Now that you're free, will I be allowed back in the States?" she asked.

The States. There was a clock ticking over my head.

"Dammit, I have to leave now or I won't have a prayer of getting back to L.A. in time. God, I wish you could come with me. But the moment I'm done with the grand jury I'll do whatever it takes to get your passport cleared. With my record cleaned up, it should just be a paperwork exercise."

I paused. I had to say something, but felt so shy about it that I looked down at my feet. "Listen, Annie, I know a lot has happened to us, but I want you to know that my feelings for you haven't changed. I can't expect you to still love me, but I hope that you still trust me."

She didn't answer right away and I glanced up. Her hands were crossed over her heart, and her eyes were brimming.

"I do," she said.

"You trust me?"

She reached forward and took hold of my hands. Her eyes searched mine. "Darlin' man, a' course I trust you. And I've loved you since the day I saw you play ball with Eddie in the park. That's not going t' change."

I brought her hands up to my lips. She said, "I know y' have t' go. Let's start walking to your car. There is much you need t' do in the States for the both of us."

When we got to where I'd parked the rental, Annie handed me her tote bag. "Take it with you," she said. It was surprisingly heavy. I looked inside and saw a laptop. "You can pop the disks in and start readin' the books on your flight."

"I'm tempted to accept, but I don't want you to be without a computer."

"I'm not. I can use the PC I bought my Grandma years ago. The minute I'm cleared for traveling back t' the States, I'll be on the next flight. I taped my new phone number and email address t' the laptop, just in case."

"I'll call and write you every day."

"Darlin' man. I love you."

And just like Irish girls have done to shy lads for generations, Annie grabbed a handful of my shirt and pulled me down for a kiss.

XXXV
Home Again, Home Again

I got to Boston on an Aer Lingus seat between two elderly widows who spent the first hour one-upping each other on the quality of their Irish bus tours. "Oh yes, yes, we did that as well, but we spent that night in a castle!"

I tuned them out and slid *The Red Season* into the laptop. In moments I was transported into the menacing world of intrigue of which Alik Nikitin was master. Annie was right: It was even better than *The Blue Season,* and now I could see her hand in every gripping turn of the story. The hotel fire, the abortionist abducting the young girl, the courtesan in Paris who hid her leprous lesion under opera length gloves—all of it and more was Annie reaching into the dark, then handing her ideas off to Alik so he could put the reader on the edge of a razor blade.

I looked around the cabin of the plane, acutely aware that I was only the second person alive to read this masterpiece. In a year's time, people traveling on this very plane would be reading the same book.

When our meal came I slipped the laptop back in the tote bag, accepted my overcooked lasagna, and released the knife, fork, and spoon from the pouch. When I saw the three utensils in my hand, I nearly leapt out of my seat. Finally, I understood! Allura's three arms, Elsa's three legs, Todor's three fingers, the three perfect emeralds, and most obvious of all, the three pearls that Nin presented to Blend so they could live together with never a worry—all of it was Annie telling me that there were three manuscripts waiting to change our lives.

My clever girl.

And thank God for my genuine reaction to learning there were two sequels. If I had figured out her clues, if she believed for a moment that the reason I "came t' Ireland and no other," was to pick up the two manuscripts, I don't know how long we would have stood by the River Barrow, each still worried that the other had fallen out of love.

I finished the eleventh chapter of *The Red Season* as the plane prepared to land. I slid the laptop into the tote and closed my eyes. As we taxied to our gate, I made a small leap forward in rectifying my feelings for Alik Nikitin.

Yes, he had held Annie prisoner in his dark world of art and misery in order to use her imagination like a vending machine. And she had suffered. But she had not only persevered, she had provided him with the raw material and the push to turn his one book into three masterpieces. Annie would soon make a fortune, and it wouldn't hurt my bottom line either. These books were about to jumpstart The Daniel Ashe Literary Agency like an atomic bomb.

And Alik Nikitin was dead.

No matter what, that was still my favorite thing about him.

I landed in Los Angeles at eight forty in the morning, rumpled, bleary-eyed, and sporting a thick stubble of beard. I jumped in a cab, finger combed my hair and chewed on mints until we stopped in front of the courthouse. Nine minutes to spare. I ran up the stairs to Courtroom G where Denis pointed to his watch and mouthed "What the hell?" I took a deep breath and smiled wide.

I'd made it.

The grand jury listened politely as I recounted the facts of my employment, what had happened at the mansion when I went to walk George, my arrest, the classes I taught, and the assignment I had given the men to prove me innocent. Several people leaned forward when I recounted the meeting I had with Jimmy. They asked me nine questions and that was it. I was free to go.

Jimmy was waiting in the hall with a guard when we walked out. I nodded and he nodded back. He doesn't know it yet, but I've decided his one-act play will make it into *Internally Free*.

Denis and I headed to an outdoor café. Over lunch he told me that Clarissa had called him to say that she was anxious to apologize to me. She confided that she and Peter were having a rough patch in their marriage, but were working through it.

Peter. I could still see him pointing at me and saying he couldn't be happier that I was going to prison. Now I wondered how long he had really believed that I was the one who stole the money. Maybe guilt or love blinded him at the start, but I was sure he had figured it all out by the time of my trial, and still he let me take the fall.

All to save Cameron. His zygote after all.

I told Denis that my first priority was getting Annie's passport cleared so she could come back to California.

"We have a lawyer at the firm who used to work for the State Department," he said. "I'll talk to her. She can probably get them to expedite the paperwork."

Then I showed him the jewel cases for *The Red Season*

and *The White Season.* He sat mute while I filled him in, then whistled with excitement. We decided to pick up blank disks and thumb drives on the way to his office so we could make copies. He would keep one set, I'd have my own to do the editing, and the originals would go in a safety deposit box. He told me to ask Annie to send copies of her marriage license and Alik's death certificate.

At Denis' office we wrote a heads-up letter to Peter. It explained how Alik Nikitin, in the months before his death, had divided his original, lengthy manuscript into three books, and that upon reading *The Red Season* and *The White Season* we could report that these manuscripts fully supported Alik Nikitin's authorship of *The Blue Season.* Copies of these manuscripts would arrive at Floodgate Media by certified mail within forty-eight hours. We trusted that he would see for himself these sequels were not only by the same author as *The Blue Season,* they even surpassed it in quality. (There was no legal or ethical reason for telling Peter that last tidbit, but I insisted.)

Finally, we told him that Annie Doherty would soon arrive with the original handwritten manuscripts for all three novels and that the law firm was engaging handwriting experts and the unbiased opinions of esteemed literary experts to verify that Alik Nikitin was the one true author of all three manuscripts.

Denis finished by saying this letter was fair notice that Annie Doherty would soon be looking to Floodgate Media to account for and restore all monies owed to the estate of her late husband, to which she was the sole heir.

Leandra seemed very glad to have my company.

The night of my return from Ireland, as we had pizza and beer on her deck, I sensed that unless I could convince her that I had survived my incarceration without significant damage to my psyche, she was going to continue to treat me like a rescued POW.

"Leandra," I said, "I look back, and seriously, most years of my life blend together in one mediocre lump. But I'll always remember last year. I became a teacher, and I loved it. I discovered Jack Tempert. I came up with the idea for *Internally Free,* and I started my own agency. Prison was a turning point. I discovered a lot about myself."

I saw her shoulders relax.

It was what Craic or Blend or Todor would have said to a beloved sister. There was no reason to tell her of the fear, the sadness, or how each time my cell door locked it felt like a moment of death.

That was the kind of prison time I wished for Cameron the Zygote. Maybe it's not how my noble characters would feel, but screw it. Let *them* turn the other cheek.

Epilogue

Denis' law firm dealt with Oliver and Peter. Annie declined to sue for damages, but was soon awarded her rights for all past and future royalties from *The Blue Season*. Oliver had already spent a chunk, and Peter stepped in to make up the difference. I hear he's working hard to restore his reputation with the movie moguls who were bidding on the rights. Frankly, I wish him well.

When the story of Oliver's theft of *The Blue Season* made headlines, the book jumped to the number one spot on *The New York Times* bestseller list. It stayed there for sixteen weeks.

Annie became a media darling. Her looks, her accent, and her ability to tell a story with wit and flair put her on the cream of talk shows. I preferred her radio interviews. When she was on TV there was usually a massive screen behind her with a photo of the brooding Alik Nikitin. The women in the audience clearly loved looking at him.

Me, not so much.

Three weeks ago, just before Annie and I left the States for Ireland, *The Red Season* came out and debuted at the number one spot. *The White Season* isn't slated for publication until next year, and the publisher tells me it's already breaking pre-order records.

The Season Trilogy has brought the Hollywood lions roaring to my door. When Annie and I get back to the States, we're going to rent the penthouse at the Ritz-Carlton Marina del Ray, take meetings, listen to pitches, meet the potential screenwriters, then wave them out the door so we can sit on the veranda, order up pints of Guinness, and let the ocean help us make a decision.

In the midst of all the early hubbub, I used my new leverage to pitch *Internally Free* and Jack Lambert's second book, *Twenty*. Both found receptive publishers. *Internally Free* is not only getting some good reviews, I hear it's being used in criminal justice classes. *Twenty* hit the pavement running. It's a smash with young adults, and it lit up the sales of his first book, *Stationary Man*. Jack gets out of prison in two months. A week before I left for Ireland, I visited him at the LAC and showed him a hand-written letter from a very famous young actor, begging to buy the movie rights to *Twenty*.

I've hired two agents and two interns to help me with the slew of scripts and manuscripts that fill the inboxes of The Daniel Ashe Literary Agency. Eddie is our agency mascot. My sister kept Sparks.

I still meet with Matt Badger, only now it's over dinner at the Water Grill. I'll return to the LAC next year to conduct another writing class.

As I stand at the altar of Duiske Abbey, Grandma Rose sits in the first pew with a sister on each side. All three are wearing corsages and beaming at me.

I love these ladies.

The day after I met them, I stood in Grandma Rose's kitchen while all four women peeled apples for pies. Annie said, "Daniel, tell us your theory about the supernatural powers of redheaded women."

"No, no."

"But you must! There are four redheads in this room, and it's not fair that I'm the only one t' know about *Bog Girls*."

They all were staring at me with knives in their hands, so I complied.

When I got to how the redheads sexually siphoned the powers from Zeus and Merlin, I laid it on thick: "The god and the wizard had bedded thousands of women, but never in their immortal lives had they known such wild and inventive partners. The redheads knew things, did things the men had never dreamt possible. Hours later, when Merlin felt there was nothing left, and Zeus lay exhausted for the first time in ten thousand years, the women began a dance so sensual, so boldly erotic, that the men's bodies responded in spite of their fatigue. Zeus looked down and cried, 'How can this be?'

"Meggie smiled and said, 'You gave us your powers, but we are using our own to thank you one more time.'"

All three of the grannies had stopped peeling.

"So ladies, from that day to this, no man can find a truer ecstasy than in the arms of a redheaded woman."

For five seconds you could hear a pin drop. Then Grandma Rose said, "Aye. Now tell us somethin' that we *don't* know."

We laughed ourselves silly.

It wasn't ten minutes later that Grandma Rose said, "I predict we'll be gettin' a beautiful day for the weddin'!"

Her sister chimed in, "I know Annie will be with child before the honeymoon is over."

The other sister nodded, "It'll be a lad first and then a lass. Mark my words!"

I shook my head. "Predicting the future, all three of you. You have just proved my bog fantasy was true. I pronounce you … The Oracles of Ireland!"

That set them off again, jiggling cheeks and bellies and covering their mouths while shaking their fingers at me.

They are delightful. I tease them every day, and I am now very used to the phrase: "Go on with ya, boyo!"

Next to them in the front pew is Annie's twin, Jennie. I picked her up at the airport yesterday, and on our way to Grandma Rose's, she asked what I thought of Annie's first draft of *Stella Maris College for Women*. When I told her I hadn't been allowed to read it yet, Jennie nodded and changed the subject, but there was something about the set of her lips that made me think she was relieved to hear it.

Across the aisle is my sister Leandra, next to her is Michael. He is wearing a cravat for the occasion and looking every inch like he's hiding a pot of gold in the forest.

Sitting on the other side of Michael is Nellie. She is smiling and winking at me, and even though I am not under the influence of Guinness, I still think she is the most adorable creature I have ever seen.

Standing next to me as I wait is Brother Thumb Sucker (as Annie calls him), the man who fibbed about not knowing anyone named Doherty. They've been chums since first grade. He is about to perform the ceremony.

All in all, it is a cheeky cast of characters who are here to cheer us on as we take our vows.

Now a harp, a flute, and a violin are playing a distinctly Irish version of the wedding march. My girl appears. She is walking toward me. And just as Sparks predicted, she is about to marry the man who will love her forever.

Acknowledgments

I was happily writing a book about an ingenious prankster in a Catholic women's college in Ireland, when a conversation with a professional pet sitter on the island of Santorini changed the course of my writing life.

"I like to write, too," she said. "I leave my clients little stories about the secret lives of their dogs."

In less than a blink I knew she had given me a gift.

As soon as I got home I set aside the book I was writing, put some years on my prankster, and brought her to America so she could woo a reluctant lover with her dog stories.

So thank you, Vanessa Soracci. Your words were like a high-octane cocktail for my imagination.

I am grateful to my sisters and earliest readers, Susan Badger (who hated Leonard the Lizard) and Caryn Kulenkamp (who liked him). Also to author Lydia Netzer who had plenty of bad news about the original number of the dog stories, but said, "You've got something here. Don't give up."

Thanks to my friend and artist Michele Barnard who was kind enough to draw pictures of my characters to inspire me.

I owe a debt to Susan Adrian, a woman I met on a dog walk in Palm Springs who incredibly offered to read and critique this manuscript after knowing me less than fifteen minutes. Susan, thank you for your profound insights and encouragements.

A special thanks to my dear friend Nick Chicola, and to his brother, Denis. The wicked humor of one and the sweet humor of the other blended in my characters as it has in my life.

In these days when anyone can self-publish with a few clicks, I decided early on that if I couldn't interest a real agent in my work, my books wouldn't leave home. Cristi Marchetti, you are my real agent. Bless your heart for taking me in.

Sometimes last is far from least, and that's certainly true here. While everyone at Jolly Fish Press and North Star Editions has been wonderful, I am especially grateful to my editor Kelsy Thompson. Thank you Kelsy for holding my hand through the process. Your editorial comments always pointed me in the direction of a better manuscript, and your kindness and respect gave me faith and made the process a delight.

About the Author

Kathryn Donahue is a writer who lives with her husband and Welsh corgi in Batavia, New York. *The Dog Walker's Diary* is her first novel.